Nicholas Rhea is the pen-name of Peter N. Walker, formerly an inspector with the North Yorkshire Police and the creator of the *Constable* series of books from which the Yorkshire TV series *Heartbeat* has been derived. Two omnibus editions of these books, *Heartbeat: Constable Across the Moors* and *Heartbeat: Constable Among the Heather* are also available from Headline. Peter N. Walker is married, with four children, and lives in North Yorkshire.

Heartbeat
Constable on Call

Nicholas Rhea

HEADLINE

First published in 1993
by HEADLINE BOOK PUBLISHING LTD

10 9 8 7 6 5 4 3

ISBN 0 7472 4371 9

Typeset by
Letterpart Limited, Reigate, Surrey

Printed and bound in Great Britain by
HarperCollins Manufacturing, Glasgow

HEADLINE BOOK PUBLISHING LTD
A member of the Hodder Headline PLC Group
Headline House
79 Great Titchfield Street
London W1P 7FN

Heartbeat
Constable on Call

CHAPTER ONE

It was just after eleven o'clock at night and the telephone was ringing. It rang incessantly, its shrill noise filling Aidensfield Police House with the sounds of urgency. It could not be ignored; it demanded a positive and instant response.

'You get it, Nick,' Kate shouted. 'I'm in the bathroom.'

'And I've just got into bed,' grunted Nick. 'It's your turn. I'm on duty at six in the morning, I want an early night!'

'No, it's your turn. I took the last one, remember? And hurry up, it might be important. Whoever it is isn't going to give up. You can't just let it ring!'

Muttering under his breath, PC Nick Rowan struggled out of bed, wrapped his dressing gown around his body and hurried downstairs to answer the call.

'Aidensfield Police.' He was slightly breathless as he lifted the handset.

'Nick?' It was Dr Ferrenby's voice. 'Nick, please . . . Nick, it's Alex . . .'

'Alex? What is it?'

'Nick . . . I . . .' and then Alex said no more. There

1

were crashing noises in the background accompanied by the sound of groaning, then the telephone rattled as it fell on to a hard surface.

'Alex?' Nick was shouting into the mouthpiece now. 'Alex, for God's sake . . . Alex? Are you there?'

But Dr Ferrenby did not respond. Nick tried to get him to reply but there was no sound in the awful silence of the surgery. Nick wasted no time.

'Kate?' He ran upstairs and hammered on the bathroom door. 'Kate, quick, get dressed. It's Alex, something's wrong.'

They hurriedly threw on some clothes, then ran around to Dr Ferrenby's house; the upstairs lights were blazing and so were those of the surgery which was on the ground floor. Nick could see the gaping hole in the surgery window which had been pushed wide open, but the front door was locked and so was the surgery entrance. Kate had her own key, however, and this quickly admitted them.

Without a word, they ran into the consulting room. Alex Ferrenby was lying on the floor with shattered glass all around him. The scene was one of devastation. Nick took it in at a glance. The window had been forced open and someone had climbed in to wreck the place. The drugs cabinet had been raided and there was splintered wood and broken glass all over the floor. It looked as if ruthless burglars had been at work, but of primary concern was the blood on Ferrenby's cheek.

It had run from a wound on his temple and was congealed upon his pale skin. This was no mere burglary; whoever had done this was ruthless and dangerous.

Criminals of this kind would not hesitate to commit murder in order to plunder the homes of others. But these men had been seeking drugs – and that made them even more dangerous.

'Good God!' Nick bent down to touch Alex. He was still breathing. With more than a hint of relief, Nick said, 'He's alive, Kate. You see to him. I'm going to check the rest of the house.'

As Dr Kate Rowan bent to the task of caring for her partner, Nick made a swift but thorough search of the interior and then the exterior of the house. He searched all the grounds, outbuildings and surrounds of the surgery, but there was no sign of the perpetrators; eventually, he was satisfied that they were not hiding anywhere on or near the premises.

'They've gone,' he sighed. 'How is he?'

'He'll survive,' said Kate. 'Come along, help me get him on to a couch, I want a proper look at him. He'll have a terrible headache in the morning, but he's as tough as old boots. I might need an ambulance, though – he's had a severe blow on the head. An X-ray will be needed, his skull might be cracked.'

After lifting Dr Ferrenby on to the consulting couch and reassuring himself that Kate could cope on her own, Nick said, 'I'll ring Ashfordly Police. I hope somebody's in the office, we'll need to circulate this crime to the lads on patrol. Whoever did it can't be far away and I'll need to call the CID out for this one.'

PC Alf Ventress answered the telephone. 'Ashfordly Police.'

'Alf?' Nick spoke calmly and with deliberation. 'Alf, it's Nick. Listen. Aidensfield surgery's been done over, drugs taken by the look of things. Dr Ferrenby's been attacked, beaten over the head with a blunt instrument. I reckon it was the crowbar they used to get in. They've given him a right bashing. Can you circulate this to all mobiles, ask them to stop and check any suspicious motor vehicles seen in the locality? Check them for drugs. Some of the stolen ones are in bottles and some are in packets. They'll be labelled with the surgery name. I've no details of suspects yet, but I'll give you more details when I've had a chance to talk to Alex Ferrenby.'

'You'll need the CID to come and fingerprint the place?' asked Ventress.

'Sure, can you see to that?'

'Leave it with me, Nick, I'll call out the whizz kids from CID. You look after things at that end.' He paused. 'It's nothing to do with Greengrass, is it?'

Nick was surprised. Alf Ventress didn't have quite the fixation with Greengrass that their sergeant had. 'Claude Jeremiah? No, this isn't his sort of crime.'

'I didn't mean he's a suspect, but he's just been in here to report his car stolen. A big flash American job by all accounts, a pink Cadillac. He hasn't had it long enough to get to know its registration number! I just wondered if anybody had heard or seen a car near the surgery at the material time.'

'A pink Cadillac? I didn't know he had a car like that! How long's he had it?'

'Not very long. He said he'd got it on trial, he's

thinking about buying it. He reckons he's going to come into some money and this American chap from Fylingdales wants to sell the monstrosity. So Greengrass has got it on appro for a day or two, so he says. Now it's been nicked!'

'I don't believe it! I bet he hasn't even paid a deposit on it. I wonder if he's insured? Anyway, all that can be checked later. I'll ask about sightings when I'm doing house-to-house enquiries,' promised Nick. 'A car like that shouldn't be hard to miss, should it? The thieves can't be all that bright if they've stolen something as recognisable as that. I know the car – I've seen it around the village from time to time, when the American had it. So it's been nicked from Claude, eh? Serves him right. I bet he never locked it up!'

'So we're looking for Claude Jeremiah's car on the one hand and some villains who've nicked a load of pills and potions on the other, eh? Two serious crimes in one night,' grumbled Alf.

'Three,' Nick corrected him gravely. 'There was also a violent attack on an ageing doctor. A case of grievous bodily harm to add to the others.'

'And I thought I was having a quiet shift! Right, Phil Bellamy's here, he'll circulate details now. You get back to Dr Ferrenby. I'll drive Sergeant Blaketon out to visit the scene of your crime straight away. See you soon.'

'So what's happened, Rowan?' Sergeant Blaketon stood before the window of the surgery while two CID officers in plain clothes examined the woodwork for fingerprints. 'Give me an up-to-date situation report and an outline of the crime.'

'Dr Ferrenby's gone to hospital for a check-up and X-ray. Kate thought it best. It was a very severe head wound and she felt there might be a risk of embolism,' said Nick. 'He was conscious when he left here and I did manage to ask him a few things before he was whisked off in the ambulance. He said he heard a noise and came downstairs to investigate; when he entered the surgery, he found two men raiding the cabinets.'

'Time, Rowan?'

'Elevenish.'

'Go on.'

'Well, Sarge, they'd broken in with a crowbar and had smashed open the drugs cabinet. They were packing haversacks with drugs when Ferrenby disturbed them. They went for him with the crowbar, walloped him over the head, then ran off.'

'Ran off? How? All the doors were locked.'

'Back out of the window, Sarge. They got away with some amphetamines and barbiturates in bottles, canisters and packs, as well as some other drugs. Some could be lethal if they're misused. We'd better warn the public.'

'Descriptions, Rowan?' barked Blaketon.

'Some look like sweets, Sergeant, like Smarties. All different colours.'

'I meant the villains, Rowan, not the bloody drugs! Have we a description of the villains?'

'Oh, I see. Yes. Well, there were two men, youngish, wearing dark-coloured parkas, gloves, scarves and black balaclavas. One was tall and thin, in his twenties, so Alex believed; the other was a bit stockier and possibly younger, but it was hard to see, they had the balaclavas over their faces.'

'It sounds like the team that's done other surgeries in this area,' said Blaketon. 'Loftus and Whitby areas have both had a bashing. They know what they're after, they know who carries drugs, where they're kept and how to get at them.'

As he spoke Kate opened the door quietly and stepped in.

'Can I start to tidy the surgery, Sergeant?'

'Not yet, Mrs Rowan, the CID need to examine it thoroughly before anything's touched. Right, PC Rowan, you wait here until the CID's finished their examination of the scene, then secure the surgery when they've gone, and retain the key.'

'Right, Sergeant.'

'And I want these men caught, Rowan, I want no undetected crime waves in Ashfordly Section. Understand?'

'Yes, Sergeant,' said Nick. He didn't need telling twice.

Nick's enquiries in Aidensfield, supplemented by those made by the CID within the Ashfordly district, soon led to a pair of youths who were selling stolen drugs in the amusement arcades of nearby coastal resorts.

Nick's own investigations showed that, just prior to

being raided, the other surgeries which had been attacked had received a visit from a couple of youngsters offering to clean windows. And when Nick had questioned Kate, she had remembered two youths who'd called at Aidensfield surgery a few days before the raid. They were offering to clean windows, and in fact, Dr Ferrenby had engaged them for that purpose; he'd paid them seven shillings and sixpence for the job. Clearly, they had been looking at the surgery with a view to raiding it and their window-cleaning had provided them with all the necessary information about the layout of the premises and the whereabouts of the drugs cupboard.

Nick had also discovered from the local coastal police officers that the men operated along the Yorkshire coast-line from Redcar down to Bridlington, selling the stolen drugs in cheap pubs and amusement arcades. Their customers included gullible young people and even schoolchildren.

From two teddy boys he learned that the supposed window-cleaners had a lock-up shed in the grounds of an old brickworks in Leather Lane, Ashfordly. It was there that they stored their ladders and other equipment and, Nick's informants stressed, they used the shed as a store and distribution centre for their stolen drugs. His tip-off was that they would be there now; it was clearly the time to investigate that lock-up.

On his way into Ashfordly, he noticed Phil Bellamy patrolling in the section car. Nick waved him to a halt.

'Phil,' he said urgently, 'I've got a tip-off. Those burglars are using a lock-up garage in Leather Lane. I have to go there now, I'll need you with me.'

'You'll need more than me, Nick!' Phil protested. 'You should have words with Blaketon to get more men, CID even. If it's a drugs raid, you'll need our experts with you. The Drugs Section will have to be there. And Blaketon's not at the office just now, he's gone over to Strensford for a conference. You can't go in alone, you know that.'

'There's no time to worry about getting permission, Phil, the villains are in there now, with some of the stolen drugs. I got the gen from a couple of teds. We've got to go in now, before they disappear to Scarborough or wher- ever. We can catch them red-handed, in possession of the stuff. It's the perfect evidence.'

'Blaketon won't like it, Nick!'

'He's not here, so it's my decision. Look, we can radio for assistance, but it'll take time to get the cavalry here and we can't afford to wait that long. If we don't go in now, we could lose them.'

'OK,' grinned Phil. 'You've persuaded me. Count me in. I'm all for a bit of fun!'

'Right, park that police car out of sight, radio for help, then join me inside the old brickworks. It's just round the corner. There's a row of lock-ups. I'm not sure which is theirs, so I'll have to check them all. We'll be able to hear them inside. I'll see you there, but watch out for villains!'

'I'll be right behind you.' Bellamy sounded confident as he radioed for assistance before driving the police car out of sight.

Nick walked towards the old brickworks with his heart pounding. He knew the rules about drugs raids but there were times you had to ignore them and this was one of those times. He knew that if he didn't catch these men now, they might escape for ever.

Nick managed to gain entry to the complex without anyone seeing him but as he crept forward to examine the various sheds and outhouses, he heard the approach of a vehicle. Stepping deftly behind a huge stack of disused bricks, he noticed an old van heading in his direction. It was being driven by a young man.

The driver hadn't noticed Nick and parked some distance from the lock-ups. He climbed out of his vehicle and looked about him for a few seconds. Then he began to walk towards the lock-ups, all the time glancing around. He was obviously very nervous. Then Phil Bellamy appeared behind him.

Desperately, Nick wanted to shout for Bellamy to keep out of the youth's line of vision, but it was too late; the lad saw Bellamy and began to run, shouting, 'Baz . . . police . . . keep down!'

'After him!' yelled Nick to Bellamy. 'You get him, I'll deal with the lock-up!'

Bellamy needed no further instructions and, being a fit amateur footballer, was soon gaining on the fleeing boy. Nick dashed to the lock-ups, peering through cracks in the old doors, alert to sounds of activity or the smell of paint or petrol. Then, through the crack in the faded woodwork of one door, he saw a light. Pressing his face to the gap, he could see two oil lamps burning on a bench. The bench was crowded with small containers and bottles, the ingredients of Ferrenby's drugs cupboard, by the look of it.

'This is it,' he whispered to himself. 'Now or never . . .'

He peered inside again; there were two skylights and he could distinguish some ladders against one wall and the outline of a huge car covered by a tarpaulin. There was no sign of life, however, except the flickering flames of those dim oil lamps and the unmistakable smell of petrol. But the fleeing youngster had called out to somebody called Baz. Baz must be hiding somewhere in this garage. Where could he hide in such a small place?

Glancing behind him, Nick saw that Bellamy had caught the youth and was busy handcuffing him; he'd be taken to the waiting car and handcuffed to the steering column. That would take some time. That youth had shouted a warning . . . If his pal, Baz, who was surely in here somewhere, had heard that call, he'd be preparing to escape. Through one of those skylights, perhaps? Or by attacking Nick? Whatever, Nick had to stop him. There was no time to waste and there was no alternative but to go in alone.

He knew that if someone was inside, he would try to escape through the door as Nick opened it and so he eased it open gingerly, pulling it only wide enough for him to squeeze inside. Closing it gently, he stood in the gloom, smelling petrol, noticing a pool on the floor. His eyes were becoming accustomed to the dim light and he could see all the drugs and pills on the workbench, all neatly arranged in identical piles for placing into containers for sale. Then he lifted a corner of the tarpaulin.

Underneath was Greengrass's pink Cadillac. At that moment, a man burst from behind the covered car, shouting, 'Bastard . . . you bastard . . .'

A furious bundle of violence, the man leapt at Nick across the bonnet, eyes blazing and swinging a vicious iron bar.

Nick ducked. The bar whizzed over his head, knocking his helmet off as the attacker landed on the floor. Nick struck out, trying to produce his truncheon from its pocket, but failing. Baz was wild; the iron bar was searing and whirling above his bare head and so Nick went in close, ducking and weaving and cursing, and managed to kick Baz in the stomach. Baz staggered backwards and stumbled to the floor, landing in a pool of petrol. Nick went for him and threw two punches, but Baz had staggered to his feet; he continued to swing the iron bar, his aim wild and careless, the impetus almost throwing him off balance. Nick took advantage of this. Grabbing a spar of timber from the floor, he whirled it at the shouting Baz; Baz stumbled backwards again, yelling and cursing. He came to rest with his back against the workbench and took an almighty swing at Nick. But he missed and lost his balance; his arm knocked over one of the oil lamps and within seconds his petrol-soaked clothing was ablaze, making a whooshing sound as the flames spread in an instant. Suddenly Baz was screaming with fear. He threw away the iron bar, trying vainly to beat out the flames which had now reached his long hair.

But the oil lamp, still alight, had rolled off the bench and was heading for the pool of petrol near Greengrass's car. Almost too late, Nick saw it and kicked it aside, towards some old newspapers bundled in a corner.

'Help!' Baz was screaming now. Nick took off his greatcoat and tried to smother the flames which were threatening to envelop the drug-dealer. It made little difference. He threw the screaming man to the floor, avoiding the petrol, and rolled him in the greatcoat, shouting at Baz to stay calm as he tried to extinguish the flames. But as fast as one was put out, another burst into life, and then the heap of papers began to burn. Thick smoke gathered in the garage, enveloping the pink Cadillac.

'Out, we need to get out!' Nick yelled at his prisoner. 'Out, Baz, out . . . this way . . .'

But Baz was screaming in agony and terror as his hair burned; Nick bundled him forward, patting out the flames with his bare hands, and finally threw his weight against the doors. They opened suddenly – and Bellamy was outside.

'What the . . .'

'Get the fire brigade and ambulance, Phil. Quick . . .'

And Bellamy ran back to his police car to call the emergency services.

In the hospital, Phil Bellamy was guarding Baz who was receiving treatment for his burns, while Nick waited to have his hands examined. They were heavily bandaged. A staff nurse called to him and directed him along a corridor. As he went towards a small ward, he saw Kate walking in his direction.

'Nick!' she cried. 'Why are you here? Oh, my God, what's happened to your hands?'

13

'I tried to put a fire out,' he grinned.

'Are they really bad?' There was concern in her voice.

'Not as bad as the chap I had to drag out of the flames,' he said. 'I'll be fine. Why are you here?'

'To collect Alex. He's going home now.'

'Good. Fully recovered, is he?'

'I think so. He had a bad knock, but his skull's made of tough stuff. It wasn't broken, fortunately; he was just badly bruised and suffering from concussion and shock.'

'That's a relief. Well, we've got the villains who did it and they'll get their punishment before the courts. So if you can wait a few minutes longer, you can take me home as well!'

And so that day, Kate Rowan took home the two men in her life, one a partner in Aidensfield's doctors' practice, and the other her husband, the village constable of Aidensfield. Thus she found herself with a dual nursing role, as well as her usual doctor's duties . . .

From that day, however, Alexander Ferrenby was never quite the same. In the weeks that followed, he seemed to be slower in his movements, prone to dizziness and slightly forgetful; Kate watched him with some concern, thinking not only of Alex but also of his patients. In his present state, he might do something unexpected; he could present a problem if he was dealing with a particularly difficult condition in one of his patients. She had a dreadful feeling it was only a matter of time.

'I'm so worried about him, Nick,' Kate said one evening as they were preparing for bed. 'He's not the same man, not since that knock on the head. It really does seem to have affected him.'

'He's made of strong stuff, he'll recover.'

'I suggested he take a long weekend off,' Kate said. 'He's got a brother in Hampshire, he's going to stay with him for a few days. He leaves tomorrow, he's going by train to avoid the long drive. I think the break and the change of scenery will do him good.'

'He does get a bit tired nowadays,' mused Nick. 'If you want my opinion, I think he should retire and leave the practice. He is getting on a bit, you know, he's reached the official retiring age. He can't go on for ever. It's time he handed the practice over to you. You could cope with it, either alone or with a new partner.'

'Yes, I could, and I'd love to have this practice for myself. But I don't think the problem is just old age, Nick. I think that attack has affected him very badly. I'm going to keep a close eye on him when he gets back, and I'll look after him very carefully. He does need my care and attention.'

'He's not the only one!' chuckled Nick, holding out his hands, some fingers of which were still bandaged. She kissed him as he tried to cuddle her.

'I'm pleased your hands are bandaged,' she laughed. 'It means you have to keep them to yourself!'

'Just you wait till I'm better!' he said. 'I've not forgotten what these hands are for!'

'I'm your doctor,' she reminded him. 'And I say when those bandages can come off!'

'I might have to arrest you for cruelty to a captive constable!' he retorted.

'And I might have to give you something to calm you down!' She grinned, kissing him. 'Come along, bed time.'

'I need help to get undressed,' and he held out his bandaged hands with a sorrowful expression on his face.

'You can always call a doctor,' she smiled.

CHAPTER TWO

'Anything to report, Rowan?'

Sergeant Blaketon looked at the dripping figure of PC Nick Rowan as he stood in the cluttered office of Ashfordly Police Station. The snow on his uniform was melting and forming neat puddles on the highly polished floor.

'Rowan, you're dripping filthy water on to my clean floor. Get rid of that wet gear, hang it up somewhere to dry and before you do anything else, find a mop and clean up that mess. You ought to be ashamed of yourself, entering a tidy office in that shocking condition.'

Nick was tight-lipped. 'Yes, Sergeant. I'll mop it up. But you do know it's blowing a blizzard out there? There's five-foot-deep snow drifts on those moors, I had a right struggle to get in here. There's two farms cut off already on the moors above Aidensfield and I've ridden most of the way with my feet down to stop myself falling off. Like skiing, it was.' He glared mutinously. 'Fancy ordering me to come into the office on my bloody motorcycle . . . I'm freezing and soaked to the skin with melted snow. My hands hurt . . . they're still sore after that fire . . .'

'Stop grumbling, Rowan. Wimps grumble, not country constables on important missions. I wouldn't have asked you to ride in unless it was important. You could always walk, you know. Walking never did anybody any harm.'

'So what is it, Sergeant? What's so important it couldn't be dealt with over the telephone?' Nick had removed his outer motorcycling clothes and was hanging them in the passage.

'Stevie Walsh.' There was a note of triumph in Blaketon's voice. 'The armed robber.'

'He got ten years, didn't he?' chipped in Alf Ventress. 'But we never did recover the money. That's the fellow, isn't it, Sergeant?'

'That's the one, Ventress. Your local knowledge is as sound as ever. Now listen, all of you, Walsh is being released from prison today. This is confidential information, straight from the Regional Crime Squad. They want to keep tabs on him.'

'Does it affect us, Sarge?' Nick was holding his hands close to the radiator in an effort to get his circulation moving.

'Affect us? Of course it affects us, Rowan! He's from your bloody village and there's every reason for thinking he hid the money on your patch. His wife still lives there, Farm Cottage on the outskirts of Aidensfield, along the road to Elsinby. Remote sort of spot, hellish at this time of year but beautiful in summer. Every time there's a snowstorm, that road is cut off by drifts. God knows why they chose to live out there. Anyway, her name's Ellen.

She was a decent woman but was daft enough to get herself tangled up with him.'

'Love's a strange thing, Sergeant,' smiled Nick.

'I want none of your romantic theorising, Rowan. She married a villain and that's it; it's her own fault, a sign of stupidity, not love. Now, the word is that he'll return to Aidensfield soon, probably to have it out with his wife . . .'

'Have it out with her?' asked Nick.

'She never went to see him while he was inside. She gave him up as a bad job, I think, then she met another man as these abandoned ladies sometimes do. That's love, Rowan, or lust. So if he gets his hands on her, I hate to think what might happen. I wouldn't like to be in her shoes. You might have another case of GBH or worse to deal with. And, Rowan, if the proceeds of his last crime are hidden on your patch, he'll be coming back for that as well, won't he?'

'Yes, Sergeant.'

'And we want to recover the money first, don't we? Twenty-five thousand pounds, in used notes. Hidden somewhere and just waiting for him. Now, we need to prevent him getting it, wherever it is; we need to make sure he never gets his thieving hands on it and that it is returned to its lawful owner.'

'After all this time, Sarge? Won't the insurers have paid out?'

'That is no concern of mine, Rowan. If the proceeds of a serious crime are concealed in Ashfordly Section, I want them found and restored to their lawful owner.'

'Won't the Regional Crime Squad be conducting their own observations, Sergeant?'

'They will, but they're stretched like us, not enough officers to do everything that needs to be done. But if that money is stashed on our patch, Rowan, then we should be the ones to find it, shouldn't we? It matters not that the insurers might have paid out. If we keep an eye on Walsh, he might lead us right to the money. What happens to it after we have delivered it to the rightful owners is no concern of mine, Constable. It is not a constabulary matter, it is a matter for the civil courts.'

'Very good, Sergeant. You want me to go out, in all this snow, to look for Walsh?'

'Being a constable is not only a fair-weather job, Rowan. If it snows, it snows, the job must go on. Right, well, that's it. Walsh's mug shot is in our beat report, have a look at it so that you know him when you see him.'

'He'll have changed a bit in ten years, Sergeant.'

'Leopards never change their spots, Rowan. Now, anything else of importance to report?'

'Yes, Sergeant. An item of lost property.'

'Lost property? What is it?'

'Greengrass's dog, Sergeant. A lurcher, colour, grey, has the appearance of a very old floorcloth and answers to the name of Alfred.'

'You're not serious, Rowan?'

'I am. Poor old Claude struggled through the snow to report it missing. He's frantic, he's out there now in these blizzards, looking everywhere for Alfred, walking miles shouting the dog's name. And he blamed me for letting that fire destroy his car, so I want to help if I can. At first I told him I thought his car had a few paint blisters but it was burnt to a shell . . .'

'You'll get a few blisters if you worry me about Greengrass's dog, Rowan! I've more things to think about than a wandering poacher's hound. I'll bet he hasn't got a licence for it anyway. Now, on the subject of Greengrass's car, that awful pink boat-type of thing, was it really his? Are we liable for its loss?'

'He was in possession of it legitimately, Sergeant; he'd paid a deposit and had got it insured. He had it on approval for a few days, until he came into some money.'

'Money? You're not saying Greengrass is going to actually come into some real money, are you, Rowan?'

'He maintains he is.' Nick nodded.

'I can't bear the thought of that!' Blaketon growled. 'Greengrass without money is a menace, the thorn in my flesh, the burden I must carry throughout my service, but Greengrass *with* money – it doesn't bear thinking about. There's no justice in life, Rowan, no justice at all. A man like that should not be allowed to have money. People like me should have money, people who work and take responsibility.'

'Policing is a vocation, Sergeant, not a means of making money.'

'Vocation? Is it my vocation to look after people like Greengrass, people with more money than me? If that man is coming into money, can we assume that that terrible gawdy automobile was evidence of his new status in the world?'

'It was going to be. He reckons it had style. He saw it offered for sale; it was something he'd set his heart on, apparently, and so he'd got it on appro. I checked with the owner, an American at Fylingdales, and it was true enough. He trusted Greengrass to look after it for a day or two.'

Blaketon snorted contemptuously. 'The man must have been an idiot, Rowan. Nobody should trust Greengrass, not even for a few seconds, let alone a few days. He must have learned that lesson by now, his car's a heap of scrap metal. So, is that all?'

'For the moment, Sergeant.'

'Right, well, wipe up that floor again – you've dripped some more – then get on your bike.'

'But it's blowing a blizzard out there, Sergeant.'

'A bit of snow is nothing to us country folk! Townies can't cope with snow, we know that. But you are a townie no more, so go, Rowan, go. You are a rural beat constable in North Yorkshire and you are on motorcycle patrol duty.'

'Yes, Sergeant.'

The moment Stevie Walsh had waited for had finally arrived. Standing outside the prison gates with his meagre belongings, he drew in a long, deep breath of cool air. The scent of prison was no more. Gone was the stench of hundreds of incarcerated men, the stale scents of the cells, the awful reek of boiled cabbage, floor polish and disinfectant, the crash of cell doors and the jangle of the screws' keys. Instead, there was fresh air, even if it was laced with a few snowflakes.

This was freedom and it smelled good. And somewhere out there, the money – twenty-five thousand pounds of it – was waiting. Ten years' imprisonment, reduced to a shade under seven for good behaviour, had been the cost of that money. He could now head for home and a life of wealth and happiness – and Ellen. He had often thought about her while he was inside but why hadn't she visited him?

She had not written either, not a word. And yet, there had been no divorce and he knew she was still at Farm Cottage; his friends inside had kept him informed. The lads had a wonderful network of information from the outside through friends and relations. And now he was free and able to pay her a visit. A surprise visit in fact. He'd made sure no one knew of his intended destination, he'd told the screws he was heading for Manchester to stay a week or two with an aged aunt – he knew the Crime Squad would be watching and waiting at Aunt Ethel's. They'd wait a long time, he grinned to himself.

He took another deep breath, licked his lips and began to walk towards the railway station. But first, he had a telephone call to make.

Some twenty minutes later, he entered a telephone kiosk and rang the familiar Aidensfield number. It rang for quite a time before Ellen picked up the handset, saying, 'Hello?'

He recognised the voice but said nothing.

'Hello? Who is it?'

Again, he made no reply.

After she had repeated the words several more times, he replaced the receiver and continued along his way. So she was still there, still at the cottage, *their* cottage. He had often imagined his homecoming.

He'd imagined a blazing log fire in the grate with a kettle singing on the hob, a lovely table with a delicate lace cloth covered with nice crockery, home-made cakes and sandwiches. Tea in a large teapot, milk straight from the farm, the scent of home-made bread. Slippers in the hearth. Home. And a loving wife. A faithful wife. But if what he had heard was true, then Ellen had not been faithful or true to him; a man had been seen around the cottage, doing odd jobs, decorating, chopping sticks, cleaning his own car outside her door, leaving her house regularly on a morning.

Perhaps it was just a friend, a local man who had taken pity on her?

Maybe it was wrong to think otherwise, maybe she did need help when she was alone. But she had not come to see him, there'd been no word from her. Not even a birthday card or a Christmas card. Nothing. Perhaps he shouldn't have been so hard on her, so violent . . . he'd given her some beatings, it was true. Poor bitch. He'd been sorry afterwards, though, and had said so. And yet she was still in the same cottage. It was finished between them, he knew. But he had to go home. He had to see her.

He reached the railway station, shivering in the intense cold of the day, and checked train times. He had a wait of half an hour and so he went for a coffee and a biscuit, proud at being able to pay out of his own pocket. They'd given him some cash to get him home. He handed over the money with a smile, savouring the smell of the coffee, then settled in a corner to enjoy his snack. Outside, the snow appeared to be heavier and it was settling. If it was laying here in the south of England, then what was it like on the North York Moors?

He could remember some winters when villages on the moors around Aidensfield had been cut off by drifts for weeks; bread and other provisions had had to be carried in by helicopter. Sheep had been buried on the moors for days, cars had been abandoned, electricity cables had come down in the snow and cut off lights and power. But in spite of that, he loved the area. After all, it was home.

Even a criminal had to have a home to come back to. He never thought of himself as a criminal, not really, but he'd needed to be independent, and to be independent you needed money, and lots of it. And so he'd robbed a delivery of cash to a bank. It was as simple as that. His plan had been to live a real life in his cottage with a loving wife and even a family; he'd run a small business, quite legitimately. All he needed was enough cash to get started. Once he'd got enough to keep him going a while, he could relax, he needn't blow his top any more. He could be like other people who had money. But things had not quite worked out. He'd been caught and the judge had sent him to prison for ten years, saying it would have been a reduced penalty if the money had been found.

Now he still had the money, even if he had lost the love of his wife. He finished his coffee and went to the ticket office.

25

'Aidensfield, please,' he said.

'There's deep snow up there in Yorkshire,' said the clerk. 'But trains are still running. It'll take a long time, though, it's a slow journey. It takes all day from here. Now, do you want a single or a return?'

'Single,' he said firmly.

For Dr Alex Ferrenby, the few days' holiday with his brother had been a genuine tonic. Kate had been right, he had needed a rest and a break from the demands of a busy surgery.

His brother and his wife had fussed over him. They'd taken him out for walks and meals, had shown him the New Forest, the southern coastline and some delightful villages. They'd gone to a theatre and to a splendid restaurant and there was no doubt that the rest and the change had been a tonic. Alex was returning to Aidensfield fully rested and able to continue with his GP duties. There was no snow in Hampshire but the news said heavy snow had fallen on the North York Moors. He hoped the trains would get through. It was a long journey back to Yorkshire and he made an early start, constantly worrying about the awful weather forecast. He hoped there were no delays along the route, for he knew he must change trains at Reading, Birmingham and Leeds before taking the last train from York to Aidensfield.

But his first train was delayed slightly, and when he arrived at Reading, he found himself having to gallop along the platforms in order to catch his connection. The guard was shouting for him to hurry because the train must depart on time if it was to make its own connections in the Midlands and North, and so poor Alex, overweight and not really fit enough to run, found himself struggling with his luggage and fighting for breath. As the guard blew his whistle, Alex opened the first available door and struggled inside. The whistle sounded again, a long, shrill blast, and the train started to move.

Fighting to keep his balance as the train gathered speed, Alex was thrown into an empty seat. He decided to stay there. It would be far easier to remain here than to struggle along the corridors and between the seats to find another place. Panting and perspiring, he lifted his suitcase on to the rack, and placed his overcoat beside it, having removed his copy of *The Times* from the pocket of the latter. Finally, as the train was rushing along the line, he settled down in his seat. Only then did he take a look at the man sitting opposite him. For a moment, he could not put a name to the face, but the man had recognised him.

'Dr Ferrenby, isn't it?' He was in his middle thirties, rather pale-faced but of a burly build.

'Yes, sorry for the inconvenience, I almost missed my connection, the incoming train was late.'

'I reckon we'll be late home tonight, Doctor,' the man smiled. 'The weather's taking a turn for the worse, terrible forecast, heavy snow in the Yorkshire Dales and North York Moors. You are going to Aidensfield, aren't you?'

'Yes, I've had a few days with my brother, very pleasant. Forgive me, I do know your face, but, well, my age you know, I'm getting forgetful these days. I can't

27

remember your name . . . you are a patient? Were a patient, perhaps?'

'I was, a long time ago. You saw me when I broke my arm, this arm, fell off a ladder doing some decorating. Walsh is the name, Doctor. Steven Walsh, everybody calls me Stevie.'

'Really, ah, yes. It's coming back now. Walsh . . . Ellen, that's right, she's my patient.'

'And she's my wife,' smiled Walsh. 'Lovely girl, best thing I ever did, marrying her.'

'Farm Cottage, yes, I do remember now. She's been coming to see me regularly . . .'

'She never came to see me, Doctor, not when I was away.'

'Oh, you've been away? Overseas?'

'Your memory is short, Doctor, isn't it? I've been a guest of Her Majesty, doing time for armed robbery . . . I'm just out, today, going home for the first time.'

'Oh, God, yes I do remember now. How time flies! And you're out, eh? With remission, I trust?'

He nodded. 'Good conduct. Yes, I'm out well before my ten years is up and I'm on my way to Aidensfield. Home, Doctor. Home's a lovely place, eh?'

But Alex Ferrenby was barely paying attention, he was so overcome with the realisation that he had almost broken a professional rule by referring to Ellen's pregnancy. She had been coming to him regularly for that reason, and as he looked at the ex-prisoner opposite, a man known in the past for his violent temper, he realised that the birth was due at any time. Before leaving for his holiday, he had reminded Kate of Mrs Walsh's condition.

But if this man had been in prison, then he could not be the child's father.

'You said Ellen has been coming to see you regularly, Doctor. Nothing serious, I hope?'

'Oh, good heavens, no. Nothing to worry about, women's matters, that's all. She's very healthy, Mr Walsh, very healthy indeed.'

'Looks after herself, eh?'

'Yes, very much so.' But Dr Ferrenby was perspiring all over again. Did Ellen know this man was on his way to see her? Surely he did not know of her current heavily pregnant condition?

'Oh, God,' Alex Ferrenby said to himself, 'please protect that woman . . .'

And he turned his attention to *The Times* crossword.

'I've got to go out,' Nick told Kate as he struggled out of his heavy motorcycle gear.

'Out? But you've just come in!' she protested. 'And you're soaked, your legs and clothes are caked with snow and you're frozen!'

He continued regardless. 'I'll change my boots and socks, and put some other trousers on. I'm dry under this topcoat. But I thought I'd get the job done now, before I finish for the day. There's no point getting settled in and then having to turn out again.' He bent down to pull off his boots. 'Look, it'll only take half an hour or so. And when I come back, I'll have a nice hot bath and curl up in front of the fire with you.'

'Promises, promises!' She kissed his cold cheek. 'All right. I'll have something hot and ready to eat the moment you get in.'

'The thought will give my wheels wings,' he grinned.

'What are the roads like?' she asked.

'I don't know, I can't see them, they're all covered in snow!'

'Nick!'

'They're not good, luv.' He was serious now. 'It's snowing very heavily, there's drifting too, especially on the higher ground. And it's pitch black out there. No moon, no stars. A real black moorland night! There's no wonder they used to call this area Blackamoor! But the plough's been through to Elsinby so I should be all right. I'm going that way.'

'What's so important that you have to go out in this weather?'

'I've got to see Ellen Walsh,' he said. 'I tried to ring her from the office, but the lines are down. Her husband's coming home, I've got to warn her.'

'Husband? But he's at home now, isn't he? He brought her into the surgery only yesterday. She's pregnant, it was her final prenatal check. Anyway, why do you have to warn her? What about?'

'That isn't her husband,' said Nick.

'Well, it's the man she's living with . . .'

'And you assumed they were married? Well, they're not, and her real husband is on his way to Aidensfield, we think. He's just done a long stretch for armed robbery and he's got a history of violence. So I've got to warn her – and the fellow she's living with. She is still married to Walsh, remember, and she is pregnant – but not by Walsh. You see the problem?'

'Oh, Nick, how awful, especially for her. Yes, you must tell her. But can't it wait? Her husband will never get through in these conditions, will he?'

'The trains are still running, Kate, it takes a hell of a snowstorm to stop them, and they've got rail-ploughs on these local lines. All he has to do is to catch a train and he can get all the way to Aidensfield. And he can walk from Aidensfield to Elsinby even if it is snowing and blowing.'

'All right, but you're not taking your motorbike out, surely?'

'No, I popped into Mostyn's garage; they say I can borrow their four-wheel drive. A Landrover should get through. But I must warn her, Kate, I can even fetch her back into the village to stay with friends if necessary.'

Kate nodded, her face full of concern. 'Yes, do that. She can always stay here the night. Take care,' and she kissed him.

Nick, his greatcoat collar turned up against the storm, battled through the snow towards the garage.

The Landrover, which was Mostyn's general purpose vehicle and used for attending breakdowns in remote places, was ready and waiting. The garage had filled it with petrol and the engine had been warmed ready. Nick thanked Malcolm Mostyn for his help and said he should be back well within the hour. He let Malcolm know where he was heading, just in case things did go wrong but Malcolm told him to keep the vehicle until morning. In the unlikely event of the garage needing it, they could always come and collect it.

As he was leaving Aidensfield, with the wipers barely able to remove the thick snow from the windscreen, he saw the familiar figure of Claude Jeremiah Greengrass trudging through the storm. He eased to a halt, the lights showing the depth of the snow and the drifts which were forming in the strengthening wind.

'Claude!' Nick shouted as he lowered the window.

'Oh, it's you, Mr Rowan.' Claude came to the side of the vehicle. 'I didn't realise you'd gone to all the trouble of hiring a Landrover to look for my Alfred.'

'You've not found him, then?'

'No, not a sign, not a whimper, not a footprint in the snow, Mr Rowan. But if your lads are all out looking for him, then it makes me a happy man.'

'We'll do our best, Claude.' Nick hadn't the heart to tell him of Blaketon's dismissive reaction. 'You'll let me know if he turns up? Now, can I give you a lift anywhere?'

'No, you search the countryside out Elsinby way and I'll head for Maddleskirk and Crampton.'

'And don't you get lost, Claude. I don't want to have to turn out and search for you as well, you know. Looking for your Alfred is enough for one night.'

'Right you are, Mr Rowan, I'll be careful.' He shook his head sadly from side to side. 'By, I am worried about him, out in all this weather, all on his own . . .'

'Keep looking, Claude,' and Nick closed the window, engaged his gear and resumed his journey, leaving behind the khaki-coated figure of Claude Jeremiah. He saw his

bulky shape move into the centre of the road, to walk in
the tracks left by the Landrover. What a night to be
hunting for a lost dog . . . Claude must truly love old
Alfred, thought Nick.

The Landrover coped with the thick snow and within
twenty minutes Nick was easing along the lonely lane
which led to Ellen Walsh's cottage. Small drifts were
forming where the snow was driven through gateways in
the drystone walls but the vehicle ploughed its way
through them. Eventually, the lights of the cottage came
into view and Nick drove carefully into the yard, drawing
to a halt so that he had room to manoeuvre to begin his
homeward journey. He beeped the horn and after a
moment or two, a figure appeared in the doorway.

Nick doused the vehicle lights, climbed out and made
his way through the snow to the door. He saw that the
man was Roy Marshall, a cattle-food salesman he'd met
from time to time.

'Evening, Mr Marshall, it's PC Rowan.'

'I wondered who was calling at this time of night. Left
the bike at home, eh?'

'You bet! But I'm here to see Ellen, is she around?'

'Yes?' There was a quizzical tone to his voice. 'You'd
better come in.'

The cottage was cosy inside. A blazing fire filled the
room with its glow and there were clip rugs on the floor. A
table occupied a corner of the living room and Nick saw
tea cups and a milk bottle. Ellen Walsh struggled out of
her fireside chair to greet him; she looked extremely
pregnant.

'Don't get up,' Nick said. 'Please, stay there,' and the woman sank back into her chair with a smile of relief on her pale face. Her hair was rather untidy and her clothes looked cheap, but in her younger days, she must have been a very attractive woman.

'Will you have a cup of tea, Mr Rowan?' She pointed to the table. 'Roy, give Mr Rowan a cup. Milk and sugar?'

'Milk, no sugar,' smiled Nick, pulling out a kitchen chair. This kind of welcome was traditional on these moors, even for a visiting policeman, and so he settled on to the chair and continued. 'You must be wondering why I've come out on a night like this.'

'It's usually bad news when a policeman knocks on the door,' said Marshall.

'Well, first thing is your telephone's out of order, the lines must have come down in the snowstorm.' He paused. 'But it's about Stevie.' Nick accepted a cup from Marshall, avoiding meeting his gaze.

'It's all right,' said Marshall quickly. 'I know who he is and all about him, Ellen's told me.'

'He's being released today,' Nick went on. 'We think he might try to return to Aidensfield. The trains are still running so he could make it.'

'Aidensfield? You mean he might come here?' Ellen sounded terrified. 'But why, why come here? I've had nothing to do with him since he was put away. I want nothing to do with him, not now, not ever again. I'm hoping to get a divorce, he's been absent for seven years now.'

'He is your husband and this was his home, Mrs Walsh,'

Nick pointed out. 'Where else can he go?'

She began to shiver and Marshall went over to comfort her. 'I can deal with him,' he said with some bravado.

'You don't know what he's like, Roy, he really is brutal, vicious. We'd not be safe, any of us, not with me having your baby.'

'Look, I can handle it.' Marshall tried to sound confident but Nick could detect the tremor in his voice.

'All I can say is that it might be a good idea to leave this house, at least for the time being. With the phone not working you'd have a hard job raising help.'

'There's a kiosk down the road, Mr Rowan, it's often working when ours goes off. Overhead cables, ours, you see. But I'll lock up, we'll be fine. I'd hear him if he turned up here, believe me. He'd never get into the house, we'd see him off, even on a night like this. He doesn't frighten me.'

'He frightens me,' whimpered Ellen Walsh, holding her arms across her bulging stomach. 'I don't want him to harm the baby . . .'

'Look,' said Nick, 'I've got a Landrover outside. I can run you down to the village, or to a friend's house, until all this has blown over. You could even stay at my place, just until it's safe.'

'Nobody's going to force us out of our home, Mr Rowan,' said Roy Marshall. 'Not even Stevie Walsh. Especially not Stevie Walsh. Thanks for coming out to warn us, it is appreciated, but we can fight our own battles.'

'OK, if that's the way you want it. Well, I must be off.

Don't forget, call us if you need to, that kiosk's not far away.'

'Thanks, but once you've gone, I'll bolt and bar these doors, Mr Rowan. It'll be like Fort Knox in here.'

And so Nick returned to his Landrover, brushed away the snow from the windscreen and began his homeward journey.

CHAPTER THREE

Nick returned to the police house and parked the Landrover in his drive. With his head down against the driving blizzard, he battled his way to the door and entered, carrying in a flurry of flakes which patterned the floor. He stamped his feet and shook his coat to remove the surplus snow he'd collected even on the short journey from the Landrover, and hung his coat in the hall. His helmet he placed on the floor to dry.

'It's me,' he shouted through to Kate. 'I'm back.'

'How was she?' called Kate.

'Very pregnant,' he said, taking off his wet boots. 'That chap she's with is called Marshall, Roy Marshall. He's a decent chap, he'll look after her.'

'Well, come in and sit down. I've got a nice Lancashire hotpot ready, it'll warm you through. There's a log on the fire, your slippers are in the hearth and there's a glass of whisky poured ready. You'll not be driving anywhere tonight!'

'Thanks, luv. Just what I need,' and Nick padded through to the living room, rubbing his cold hands and

37

savouring the smell that wafted from the kitchen. He went across to the blazing fire to warm himself.

Suddenly there was a loud knocking at his office door.

'Oh, no!' he groaned. 'What now?'

'I'll go', Kate said. 'It might be for me.'

'No, I'm still half in uniform so I reckon I'm half on duty,' and so he went to answer the door. But even before he arrived, the knocking was repeated, louder and more urgent this time.

'All right, all right, I'm coming,' said Nick, opening the door.

'About time too!' and a snow-covered Claude Jeremiah Greengrass stood there with the flakes whirling about him like pieces of white confetti.

'Sorry for the delay, Claude, I was through the other end of the house. What can I do for you?'

'I saw the Landrover was back. I wondered if you'd found Alfred, now that you've given up and come home.'

'I've come home for my supper, Claude, but sorry, I didn't find Alfred. I went all the way to Elsinby, up to the heights and back again. I never saw a sign of him, not even a footprint in the snow.'

'Who is it?' Kate came through and saw Claude. 'Oh, Mr Greengrass . . . come in, don't stand out there. Nick, you should bring him in, it's not fit for a dog to be out there tonight.'

'But my dog's out there, Mrs Rowan, Alfred that is. The whole North Riding police force is out there looking for him, according to Constable Rowan, with never a sign of him. I'm right worried, really I am. I let him out this morning and haven't seen hide nor hair of him since.'

Claude stomped into the office of the police house, shaking himself like a huge hound and flicking wet snow all over the floor.

'We'll keep looking, Claude,' Nick assured him.

'Have you been out all day, Claude?' asked Kate. 'In this weather?'

'When your best friend needs help, Mrs Rowan, you never think of the weather. I've been out everywhere, hunting high and low, checking all his favourite places, digging into snowdrifts, looking into barns and out-buildings – and not a sign, not a whimper.'

'Poor old Alfred,' said Kate. 'And have you eaten?'

Claude sniffed the air; the magnificent aroma from Kate's kitchen was making his mouth water.

'Now you mention it, no, I haven't eaten. I've been so busy seeking Alfred, food wasn't important, but by gum, I could enjoy a plate of good old-fashioned Yorkshire stew.'

'Lancashire hotpot, actually, but look, Claude, take those wet things off and come through to the living room. Me and Nick are having our suppers on our knees, beside the fire. You're welcome to join us, there's plenty.'

For the first time that day a smile crossed Claude's face. 'By jove, Mrs Rowan, it's at times like this you appreciate the police force, isn't it? Getting their priorities right, out looking for a lost dog in these conditions. By gum, Mr Rowan, I really am grateful for the efforts you and the other constables are making.'

'It's all part of the service, Claude,' winced Nick as

Claude handed over his smelly old coat.

Nick, remaining in the kitchen to hang the wet things on a hook, missed the wry smile on Kate's face as she led their chattering guest into the living room.

'So, Mr Greengrass, Nick has been out looking for Alfred all this evening, has he?'

'He has, Mrs Rowan, a real nice feller is your husband, salt of the earth. I'll not forget this, you know. If ever he needs help and advice, I'll be there, with Alfred when we find him. Are we going out again, Mr Rowan?' he called into the kitchen. 'You and me? On night patrol, to look for him? There's plenty of spots we haven't searched.'

'Look, sit down and relax for a few minutes. I'll fetch some knives and forks,' Kate smiled.

'What did you invite him in for?' hissed Nick as Kate came into the kitchen.

'He looked worn out, Nick, he's been out all day looking for Alfred. He really thinks the world of that dog. Look, if he'd continued to search all night, I would have had another patient. And,' she teased, 'fancy you spending all day looking for Alfred? I had no idea you'd been doing that! Now, I do call that service. So be nice to him! Or I'll tell him you and your mates never gave his dog a second thought!'

'Fancy a whisky, Claude?' shouted Nick from the kitchen.

'I thought you'd never ask,' was the cheerful reply.

And so Kate and Nick settled down to supper with their guest. All the time, Greengrass talked about Alfred, about his likes and dislikes, his skills and his less welcome behaviour. He tucked into his supper with gusto and Kate gave him a second helping which disappeared like magic down his throat.

'You'll be going out again, Mr Rowan?' Greengrass asked earnestly when he'd finished his meal. 'Me and you make a good team, you know, we can work together well. You search the north and I'll go south, I'll check all the pubs if you can do the moors and woods.'

'Right,' said Nick. 'Rendezvous in the Aidensfield Arms in half an hour?'

'Right you are, Mr Rowan, I'll pop in and see George now, he's keeping an eye open for Alfred, you know. He likes the fire in there, does Alfred, on a cold night. You know that fire's never been out since Queen Victoria was a lass? Well, our Alfred respects a bit of history like that and loves to curl up in front of it. He might be there now, eh?'

'Yes, he might.'

'Well, I'll be off. Goodnight and thanks for the supper.' And Claude collected his belongings, put on his old coat and vanished into the storm.

'You did a wonderful piece of police public relations there,' smiled Nick. 'Well done.'

'The poor man, he really was upset, I do hope he finds Alfred.'

'He will, Alfred will come home when the time's right. Now, how about a restful night by the fire.'

'When you've done the washing up!' She smiled sweetly.

And at that point, all the lights went out.

★ ★ ★

They went out at Farm Cottage too. The tiny house was suddenly plunged into darkness as the heavy wet snow brought down the cables which crossed the moors. From the kitchen window, Roy Marshall could look across the dale and he saw that Elsinby was also in darkness; indeed the entire valley was without electricity.

'I'll get the candles,' he said. Igniting a cigarette lighter, he rummaged in the kitchen cabinet and found a box of candles. Every moorland home kept a stock of candles and oil lamps for such occasions and soon the little cottage was glowing in the dim light of half a dozen flickering flames. The fire, blazing with logs, also cast its light into the room.

Roy inspected the fuse box just to be sure that the problem was indeed the result of a power cut, not a blown fuse. Sure enough, the fuses were all in good order. There was nothing he could do to rectify the fault.

'We'll just have to sit it out,' he said calmly to Ellen. 'They'll soon have the power back on. The electricity board is used to this sort of thing. I've locked all the doors and windows, so we're safe enough here.'

'Roy?' Her voice was faint and pleading. 'Roy, I think it's coming.' And she held her stomach as the pain made her groan.

'Oh, God, not now! It can't!'

'It is, I know it is. I can feel it . . . Roy, it's coming, the baby's coming . . . I need help, get the doctor . . . quickly.'

'Doctor? But the telephone . . .'

'The kiosk, try the kiosk . . . please hurry . . .'

'I've rung the electricity board to report the failure,' Nick told Kate. 'The power's off in all the villages, a line's down somewhere on the moors. They're going out to see to it. They'll have one hell of a job in this weather, so there's nothing more to do but wait. I'd better go for a walk around the village.' Nick couldn't help but feel restless. 'With all the power off, some of the old folks might be worried. I'll pass the word round that the electricity board's having a look at it, so at least they'll know something's being done.'

Kate raised her eyebrows sardonically. 'My, you are conscientious. And you'll keep an eye open for Alfred, no doubt?'

'I might pop into the Aidensfield Arms just to make sure he's not curled up in front of George's fire.'

'You're not driving?' she asked with some concern.

'No, I'll walk, I'll leave the Landrover where it is.'

'Be careful, and don't be long,' and she kissed him.

'If I'm more than an hour, send a St Bernard to look for me.'

'I could always send Alfred the Lurcher!'

'If he's come home. He'll be lying somewhere having a whale of a time, will that one. He's not stupid enough to stay outside in this weather, mark my words. Nor is Claude Jeremiah!'

'And then you'll come back and spend the rest of the evening by the fireside?'

'Scout's honour!' he said, kissing her.

Nick began his lonely patrol of Aidensfield, checking the homes of pensioners and people living alone. He told them about the power line which had collapsed and asked them to tell their friends and neighbours. He organised help for people without candles or oil lamps, and brought scuttles of coal and piles of logs in for those less able than himself. Then he went into the Aidensfield Arms. The famous everlasting Aidensfield fire was blazing brightly with pine logs that spat and crackled in the blaze, as the regulars all sat around with their pints. Candles were burning on the bar and the smoke-room tables.

'Everything under control, George?' asked Nick when he spotted the landlord in the gloom.

'Good job all my pumps aren't electric,' said George. 'At least I can still pump beer from the cellar. It's off everywhere, eh?'

'A power cable's collapsed with the weight of snow, they're on their way to fix it,' said Nick. 'Pass the word around. Now, have you seen Claude?'

'He was in earlier, looking for Alfred. He had a quick drink then went out again. He's in a bit of a state about that dog.'

'You've not seen Alfred today?'

George shook his head. 'No, not a sign of him. Mind, he knows his way here so if he does come back to the village, he might pop in. If he does, I'll keep him till Claude returns.'

'Cheers, George,' and Nick left to go home. But as he walked up the drive, he saw that the Landrover had gone. He could see the tracks in the snow, already filling in with

a new layer of fresh white flakes. He went into his office
where a candle provided the sole source of light.

'Kate? You there?'

There was no reply. He went over to the telephone to
check that it was still working. As he listened with relief to
the dialling tone, he saw the note wedged under the
candlestick on his desk. In the flickering light, he read,
'Gone to attend to Ellen Walsh, birth imminent. Back
sometime, have taken the Landrover. Kate. XXX.'

Nick smiled. What a night for a new child to come into
the world! No power, no heat, no light and a village
knee-deep in snow! And a dangerous man heading that
way too . . . He sighed and began to take off his Welling-
ton boots.

Then the telephone rang.

'Aidensfield Police,' he said, somewhat wearily.

'It's the railway station,' panted a man's voice, sounding
distressed. 'There's been a derailment, a passenger train
from Eltering, coaches off the line, here in the station.
There's people hurt, we need help, Mr Rowan, desperate
help, there's only me here . . .'

'I'm on my way,' said Nick, slipping his feet back
into his Wellingtons. Before leaving, though, he rang
Ashfordly Police Station to alert Sergeant Blaketon;
Ashfordly would automatically contact the necessary
emergency services.

Alf Ventress answered the phone.

'It's Nick from Aidensfield, Alf,' he began.

'Don't tell me, you've found Greengrass's dog!' Alf
sounded cheerful. 'Or Aidensfield's cut off by snowdrifts

45

and you won't be able to see Sergeant Blaketon for six weeks!'

'Cut the cackle, Alf, this is serious. There's been a derailment at Aidensfield Station, it's the incoming passenger train from Eltering, coaches off the line and people hurt. I'm on my way now, I'll radio in with a sit. rep. as soon as I've got some firm details.'

'Oh, bloody hell, and I thought this snow was going to give us a quiet night, no traffic accidents, no burglaries or mayhem . . .'

'I'm taking the motorbike, it's got a radio on board; I'll be there in two minutes and will give a report as soon as I've assessed the situation. All right? You'll tell Sergeant Blaketon and then alert Division?'

'Blaketon's having a night off, he's gone to a dinner-dance in town.'

'He'll have to be told, Alf. You'll have to drag him away from his palais glide or whatever he's doing.'

'Leave it to me, Nick. I'll make sure everybody who should know does know. Kate will be attending, will she?'

'No, she's gone to a woman who's about to give birth, out in the wilds, so we'll need another doctor. British Rail might have one listed who they call out for this kind of thing. Ferrenby's not here either, he's gone to see some relations down south, but he's due back today.'

'On that train, mebbe?' said Ventress.

Nick frowned. 'Don't say that! Right, I'm off, Alf. I'll be in touch.'

Dressing once again in his wet clothing, Nick kicked his

Francis Barnett into action and sallied forth from the garage. Keeping his feet to the ground, he guided the slithering machine through the deep, even snow, ploughing a triple furrow along the road towards Aidensfield Station.

On the way, he spotted Claude Jeremiah trudging in the same direction and slowed down alongside him.

'Off again, Mr Rowan, eh? Has he been spotted somewhere?'

'Claude, a train's come off the lines in the station, we'll need as much help as we can.'

'He didn't jam his brakes on to avoid colliding with my Alfred, did he?' Claude asked anxiously. 'I've told him about crossing the line when there's a train coming.'

'Claude, for God's sake just get yourself down to the railway station and see if you can help.'

'Aye, right, Mr Rowan. Mebbe Alfred's jumped on to a train and gone down to London or somewhere. I often said I'd put him in Battersea Dogs' Home if he didn't behave himself. Mebbe he's gone to see it for himself?'

'You could always ask if he's in the left luggage office,' and Nick accelerated away. 'See you there.'

As he guided his motorcycle slowly down the steep hill towards the station, Nick's first impression was one of utter chaos. There were lights everywhere, the coaches having their own supplies; there was the steady hiss of steam and the sounds of people in distress; figures wandering about in a daze; shouts for help mingled with groans and cries of fear. He parked his machine near the

47

fence and walked on to the platform, taking a torch from his pannier.

He could see one coach partially on its side, its trolleys having separated from its body, each lying awkwardly across the rails with the wheels off the tracks. Several of the coach windows were smashed and snow was swirling inside to settle on the pale faces of the terrified passengers. Some doors were hanging open and a seat had been thrown out, to land on the embankment. The engine was standing by, still on the rails, and in the gloom he could see another coach which had also jumped the rails. It was upright, fortunately, but its wheels were also off the metals and they had sunk into the cinder track beneath.

Nick moved swiftly among the devastation, visually assessing the situation before clambering aboard to determine whether or not there were fatalities or serious injuries.

Then the signalman was running towards him.

'Mr Rowan, thank God . . .'

'All right, Jim, calm down. Any fatalities?'

'Fatalities? Oh, God, I hope not . . . this carriage, people hurt . . . look, it wasn't my fault, the points jammed, froze or something, I couldn't stop the train . . .'

Nick held out a calming hand. 'Nobody's blaming you. We've got to attend to these people, we've got to find out who's hurt, who needs help. Now, help me up to the step, I want to have a look inside.'

Many of the passengers in the upright coach were still in their seats, too dazed to move, and Nick bade them stay;

the coach was not likely to topple over and it was warm and dry inside.

He moved along the corridor, peering at people, asking questions, making jokes, reassuring them that help was on the way. Then he saw Alex Ferrenby. He was sitting upright in his seat, eyes staring directly ahead of him as if he was asleep or in a trance.

'Alex?' Nick touched his old friend, but there was no response. 'Alex? It's me, Nick.'

He took Alex's pulse; his heart was still beating and the flesh was warm. Dr Ferrenby was certainly alive, but what was wrong? Worried, Nick moved on; he would have to return to him later.

Then he found a man bending over a schoolboy.

'He's trapped, Officer,' the man gasped over his shoulder. 'The carriage wall gave way, and crumpled on him . . .'

'Can we lift the woodwork? You and me?'

'Yes, with a spar . . . hang on, there's a bit of a luggage rack over there, I'll use that.'

'You all right, son?' Nick addressed the youth who was lying on his back, his face pale and drawn.

'It's my legs, I can't move them, something's pressing down on them.' He was fighting to hold back the tears.

'Right, we'll soon lift this stuff!' Nick said briskly, and with the help of the other passenger and their makeshift lifting gear, he managed to raise the collapsed fabric and drag out the youth. Sure that the boy had a broken leg, Nick quickly made a splint out of some pieces of the damaged luggage rack. As he carefully eased the suffering boy on to the seat, he tried to reassure him. 'Look, son, you'll be OK. This splint will keep your leg firm until we can get you to hospital.'

Having bound the pieces of luggage rack to the boy's leg, Nick thanked his helper. 'You were great. We need all the help we can get. Can you give me a hand? We'd better get all the able-bodied people together and then evacuate the injured and take them along to the tunnel behind the train. They're safe in this coach for now, but the emergency services can't get to them here – that's if they get through at all in this storm. But British Rail have their own emergency plough and they might come by rail . . . if we can get everybody into that tunnel, they can be picked up – it's a double line there.'

The man nodded willingly. 'Sure, anything to help.'

'Right, now I'm going back to my motorbike to give a situation report and to ask for all British Rail rescue services as well as our own. I'll be back in ten minutes. Can you cope?'

'Sure,' repeated the man.

'What's your name?' asked Nick.

'Stevie,' said the man. 'Stevie Walsh.'

Kate coped surprisingly well with the Landrover.

Driving very steadily, she managed to manoeuvre it through the narrow lanes where its four-wheel drive dealt easily with both the deep, level layer of snow and the many drifts. She arrived at Farm Cottage without any mishap, albeit with the vehicle smothered in thick, clinging snow, and parked outside the cottage. Roy Marshall, hearing her arrival, came to the door carrying an oil lamp.

'I thought it was an ambulance,' he said, looking at the small, snow-encrusted vehicle.

'It can't get through,' she said. 'They're cut off, the road between here and Ashfordly's blocked. Now, where's Ellen?'

'I got her up to the bedroom. The contractions are stronger, she says. Can you cope?'

'With your help, yes,' said Kate as she hurried inside and removed her coat. 'Now, first thing, some boiling water. Can we boil some without electricity? A pan on the open fire? And while you're doing that, I'll have a look at Ellen.'

By the time Roy had placed a pan on the fire, Kate had concluded her examination of Ellen and she was not very happy with what she had found.

'I'm afraid baby's not in a very good position for a quick and easy birth, Ellen. I need more facilities than we have here. I need to get you down to the surgery. I think there's time; I got through without too much hassle. So, can you hang on for another half-hour or so?'

Ellen attempted to smile. 'I'll try,' was all she could say.

Kate went downstairs to where Roy Marshall was busy with the fire, poking it to make it provide more heat. 'It doesn't matter now,' Kate interrupted him. 'We must leave. I've got to get Ellen into the surgery – there's a slight complication. Now, I'll need her overcoat and some thick blankets. Can you fix those?'

Within five minutes, the little party was leaving the cottage in driving snow, with Roy helping Ellen along to the waiting Landrover. Kate opened the front passenger door and they manoeuvred the bulky woman inside, Roy fussing over her like a mother hen while Kate arranged the blankets to provide the greatest warmth.

'It's not far,' Kate reassured her. 'There's a good heater, so you'll not get frozen stiff!'

Roy climbed in beside Ellen, the three of them sitting close together on the front bench seat as Kate started the engine. Very steadily, she guided the Landrover along the narrow lane, its lights picking out the grotesque shadows formed by the drifting snow. She drove with the utmost care, relying on a slow, steady speed instead of a nervous dash.

'Can't you go any faster?' demanded Roy, as Ellen began to moan softly.

'I could, but we'd probably skid off the road on these corners,' Kate snapped. 'And I want to get her there, not get myself stuck in a ditch!'

'Sorry, but she could give birth at any minute . . .'

'Yes, she could. I know that, I'm a doctor, remember?'

'Sorry, it's just that I'm so bloody worried!'

Kate was firm. 'We must keep calm and we must keep going, Roy. We've got to keep our eyes on the road, and our wheels on the road as well. Right?'

'I'll shut up!' he said, his eyes twinkling.

She turned to smile her gratitude, but that tiny movement was fatal. As she took her eyes off the road for the briefest of moments, the Landrover skidded on a bend, and in a fraction of a second, its two nearside wheels were in the ditch. With a sickening crunch, it came to rest. Kate cursed; angrily she pressed the accelerator, but that only made things worse; as the wheels spun, the heavy vehicle sank deeper into the snow and the soft earth beneath.

'Now you've done it!' snapped Roy. Beside him, Ellen was whimpering in fear and apprehension.

'We'll have to push,' said Kate, climbing out. 'Ellen, can you shift into the driving seat and press the accelerator while we push from behind?'

'I'll try,' she replied unhappily.

But it was impossible. Nothing could move the vehicle.

'What now?' Roy was angry and upset. 'This is a right mess, if you don't mind me saying so. Stuck out here in the bloody wilds of Yorkshire with a pregnant woman and no medical help . . .'

Kate didn't need informing of the situation. 'I'll wait with her,' she said with studied patience. 'You'll have to go back to the telephone kiosk and just hope it works. Ring my house, my husband should be in; if he's not, ring Ashfordly Police to see if they can suggest anything; one of the moorland rescue service vehicles, a tractor even. Now, we must keep the engine running to keep Ellen warm.'

Roy Marshall set off through the whirling snowflakes as Kate wrapped her arms around the sobbing Ellen.

'What are we going to do?' wept Ellen. 'I feel so awful, I'm sure the baby's coming, I know it is.'

'Roy won't be long.' Kate tried to sound reassuring.

But when Roy reached the kiosk, the telephone was dead. He banged on the dial but it was no good. It was absolutely silent. He looked around despairingly. At first, all he could see was the wasteland of snow, brightening the landscape around him. Then, in the distance across the moor, there was a glow. It was a farmhouse with an oil lamp in the window.

He set off towards it.

CHAPTER FOUR

When Nick returned to the mayhem, Stevie Walsh told him, 'British Rail called on their internal phone. Their rescue train will be another two hours at least, maybe longer.'

'Oh, bloody hell,' Nick swore. 'These people need warmth and something to drink. How many have we got in the tunnel?'

'A lot – the guard's shepherding the walking injured in there now – but it's dark, there's nowhere to sit and there's one almighty wind blowing right through.'

'I reckoned on half an hour's wait, no more. But two hours . . .'

'You need to get them to the village hall, Constable,' advised Stevie. 'There's chairs and toilets and tea-making facilities.'

'But how? It means a long walk from here, too far for some of these people in this weather. Look at old Ferrenby, he should be here, helping to examine them, but he's incapable. He's in a state of shock. And there's a few more like him, plus that kid whose leg was trapped.'

Then, as if in answer to a prayer, Nick heard voices at the far end of the platform. Turning, he saw a lot of torch lights bobbing and weaving through the darkness. A party of helpers had arrived, led by Claude Jeremiah Greengrass and George from the pub.

'Mr Rowan,' Claude shouted, 'we was going to look for Alfred, but I reckoned you needed us first. I've brought all the regulars from George's pub, and a few besides we've gathered on the way, so is there owt we can do?'

Nick felt relief wash over him. 'Claude, you couldn't have timed it better. Have you got transport?'

'Aye, on the hilltop, we left it all there, tractors, cars, lorries, even Arnold Merryweather's bus. He can't get out of the village tonight, but he can drive up and down the main street.'

'Right, most of the passengers are sheltering in the tunnel. We need to get them out and on to our transport, then take them to the village hall. If you can arrange some way of reaching them by road, it'll save a long walk.'

'I've a stock of food,' George volunteered. 'Nothing to warm it on, mind, but there's bags of crisps and pickled eggs.'

'Anything and everything will be useful, George,' Nick answered gratefully.

Greengrass interrupted, 'There's a cart track down to the tunnel entrance at yon end, Mr Rowan, an old cattle crossing. We can get down there, I should think, with tractors.'

'Good, then if we can alert the WI ladies, I'm sure they'll rustle up some tea and cakes and blankets. And

56

there's the injured, Dr Ferrenby's among them, so don't expect any work from him. We'll need more people to care for them . . . right?'

'I'll see about the arrangements for food, Nick,' offered George.

'And I'll see about getting those people out of the tunnel, Mr Rowan,' said Greengrass. 'I know my way around those parts, you know. First, I'll fetch all the helpers into the waiting room and you can tell 'em what's needed. Now, have you seen Alfred anywhere round here?'

'No, Claude, sorry. Never a sight of him. But if I do . . .'

Claude shrugged his shoulders sadly. 'Aye, well, just asking.'

And so the rescue attempt began. In a very short time, more villagers heard of the drama and joined the volunteers. Soon a way was ploughed through the snow by several tractors and positive plans were being made to transport the bewildered passengers away from the station.

Satisfied that all was going smoothly, Nick went to find the keyholder of the village hall, Joe Brown, who was among those helping at the railway station. Joe welcomed the idea of using the premises, but issued one note of caution.

'The power's off, Mr Rowan,' he said. 'We've no light, no heat and no power to boil kettles and things. They can use the hall for shelter by all means, but I'd better remind you it's not like a hotel, we can't do much for them while they're in there, not till the power's restored.'

'I appreciate that, Joe, but the thing is to get them into a dry shelter as soon as we can. That's our priority right now. It's going to be two hours or more before British Rail's own relief train arrives, so I reckon the village hall's our only answer. The tunnel's only a short-term solution, it's far too uncomfortable and cold, and the station waiting room's far too small for everyone.'

Stevie Walsh stepped forward from the crowd of helpers, his face gleaming from the cold.

'Surely one of the local farmers or smallholders has a portable generator we could borrow?' he suggested. 'They use them for milking during power cuts and I knew a farm which kept the whole house lit up with a generator. If we could find one and connect it to the hall's power supply, we could bring up the lights and get the heating going . . .'

Nick pondered the idea. 'Most of them will be needed for milking, either tonight or in the morning,' he said. 'What we need is somebody with a smallholding who's not using their generator tonight!'

'Like Claude Jeremiah Greengrass?' suggested Stevie.

'Will he have one?' asked Nick.

'He had one before I got put away, Mr Rowan. He used it to power his sawbench. He's cut up many a tree with the power of his little generator.'

Nick nodded enthusiastically. 'Come on, let's ask him.'

They found Claude enquiring of the guard whether Alfred had, by any chance, jumped into the guard's van for a ride. Nick explained Stevie's idea.

'It's illegal, Mr Rowan, tapping into the mains . . .'

58

Claude began, blinking innocently. 'I mean, it's not the sort of thing I'd ever do or even think about doing.'

'But you do have a generator that's not being used? If we went up to your spot, could we fetch it back and use it to produce power for the hall?'

'Aye, well, I suppose so. It'll need a drop of petrol and t'plug might need cleaning, but I reckon it'll start. Mind, I know nowt about connecting such a thing to the mains, me being an honest individual, like.'

'Stevie?' asked Nick.

'I know how to do that, Claude,' he said without hesitation. 'Come on, stop messing about, these people need hot drinks and warmth.'

'Aye, well, if the law says it's all right, it must be all right. I wonder if Alfred's gone home by now? He's mebbe there, eh?'

'He might just be there, Claude, sitting in your favourite chair while you've been gallivanting about looking for him.'

'I'll flay the hide off him if he is!' snarled Claude. 'Come on, Steve, we've got work to do. Damned dogs . . .'

'Have you a trailer, Claude?'

'Aye, and a small tractor. If somebody could run us up to my ranch, I can be back here in less time than it takes to boil a kettle.'

As Walsh and Claude Jeremiah disappeared into the snowstorm to beg a lift, Nick set about supervising the movement of those in the tunnel and still on board the train. A regular relay of tractors did manage to run down the lane which crossed the rails near the tunnel. By clambering on board the tractors in twos and threes, the stranded people were lifted up the lane to the main road, where Arnold's bus was waiting. A mighty cheer arose when the first busload moved away, heading for Aidensfield village hall.

Nick was already at the hall with Joe Brown when they arrived. By the light of their torches, Nick and Joe surveyed the large, cold room. There were plenty of chairs and Joe found some candles and oil lamps, but in these conditions it was not the most pleasant of reception areas. Some of the village ladies were arriving with baskets of food and blankets, and so the relief of Aidensfield began.

Finally Stevie Walsh returned, carried on a rough-sounding tractor driven by Claude Jeremiah. Both were smothered in wet snow but behind them they bore a portable generator on a trailer. The entourage shuddered to a halt.

'Here's t'power generator, Mr Rowan,' Claude called. 'A real beauty, it is. Served me for years, it has. But me, being an honest person, has no idea how to make a connection, you understand. Stevie says he'll fix it.'

As the ex-prisoner set to work, Greengrass stood transfixed, silently admiring the skills of this man.

'The man's a genius, Mr Rowan, a real genius,' he enthused. 'Look at those hands, the hands of a craftsman, they are . . .'

Nick nodded in agreement. 'Thanks, Claude, for helping like this, it really is appreciated.'

Claude shrugged, blinking into the snow. 'Aye, well, one good turn deserves another. You've not seen anything

60

of Alfred, have you? He's not gone home, I checked all my outbuildings and shouted his name. I don't suppose you've had a chance to look around lately!'

Guilt tugged at Nick once more. 'The minute this emergency's over, Claude, we'll resume our search for Alfred,' he promised. 'Now, look, more people are arriving, they need chairs and cups of tea . . .'

'Right, I'd better go and get mine first, then, so I can be free to help George and them others,' and Claude vanished into the depths of the dark hall. He began to shout, 'Alfred, Alfred, are you in here, you daft bugger?'

As Nick went in to check on the progress of the operation, the lights suddenly came on. A massive cheer arose from the rescued passengers and as it died down Claude announced proudly, 'It's my generator that's doing this, you know. Now, where's that tea?'

But Nick's attention was upon Alex Ferrenby. He was sitting on a chair like a wax figure, alone, silent and forlorn. Nick went across to him.

'Alex? It's Nick!'

The old man jumped. 'Nick? Where are we? What's happened?'

'Everything's OK. You're going to be fine. Now, you just sit there, Alex, don't move.'

'Where's Kate? Is she helping?'

'She's attending to another emergency, she'll be here as soon as she can.'

'Oh, well, that's all right,' and he resumed his fixed gaze. Nick patted him on the arm and went to help with handing out cups of tea. Poor old Alex. What had happened to him?

Outside the village hall, as the snow continued to fall, Stevie Walsh's gaze fell on Claude's deserted tractor and trailer. Transport! The keys were in the ignition, and on the spur of the moment, he unhitched the trailer, wiped the snow from the seat and settled in the driving position. In seconds, he was chugging away – towards Farm Cottage near Elsinby.

Roy Marshall was struggling back to the stranded Landrover, his clothing caked with frozen snow and his fingers and toes numb with cold. He found the vehicle with its engine still running.

Ellen was in the driver's seat, sobbing and distraught as the pains continued to grip her, while Kate did her best to ease her discomfort. Roy opened the passenger door.

'It's no good,' was all he said. 'Their phone's off as well, they've no power, there's drifts five feet deep up there. It's terrible, Doctor, it's a nightmare.'

'You'd better hop in for a few minutes to get warm,' suggested Kate. 'We'll have to have another go at freeing the Landrover, that's all we can do. I don't want Ellen to give birth here . . .'

'Can't we go home?' pleaded Ellen.

'You can't walk back in your condition, not in this weather,' said Kate. 'Look, let's sit and think for a minute, there's bound to be an answer . . .'

As if on cue, a pair of lights materialised through the

snowstorm, two high and bright lights, far too close together to be a motorcar's headlamps.

'Somebody's coming on a tractor!' shouted Marshall. 'How about that?' and he leapt out of the Landrover to stand in the lane and wave down the oncoming tractor. The women watched as it eased to a halt in front of them. Kate climbed out too, her heart lifting at the thought that this might be a farmer, perhaps one of her own patients upon whom she could call for help.

A powerful young man leapt from the driving seat; he was smothered in snow but sounded very cheerful nonetheless. Kate did not recognise him.

'Trouble?' he asked.

'We need to be towed out of the ditch,' Kate said. 'Once we're back on the road, we can manage. We're heading for Aidensfield.'

'I've just come from there. Nasty business with the train,' he said.

'Train?' asked Kate.

'Derailment in the station. Nobody's killed, though. They're in the village hall now, drinking tea.'

He provided a brief account of the derailment, highlighting the part played by the villagers in rescuing the injured passengers.

'Oh my God, it all happens at once!' cried Kate, appalled. 'Is there a doctor there attending the injuries? I'm a doctor, you see . . .'

'Dr Ferrenby was on the train, but he's in a state of shock. He's not able to do much. There's help around, though. The whole village has turned out. George from the pub has organised food, and we've got power on at the hall. Anyway, let me tow you out of here, it'll only take a moment with the tractor.'

Stevie busied himself fixing the towing rope and then said, 'You, mister, into the driving seat and put it in third, keep it in a high gear, ease it out gently, don't rev too hard or you'll get the wheels spinning. That'll get you nowhere.'

'Right,' said Roy, still shivering from his previous outing.'

'Gentle on the accelerator,' their rescuer reminded him. 'If we both give power, I'll be able to haul you out, right?'

'Yes, sure, we must be getting on, we've a pregnant woman in here, she's due any minute. We're off to the surgery . . .'

'Pregnant woman, from up the road?'

'Yes, Farm Cottage, at the end of this lane.'

'Well, fancy that! What a coincidence. Anyway, first things first, let's get this crate out of the ditch.'

Ellen moved across to the passenger side as Roy settled behind the wheel. At a signal from Stevie, he engaged a high gear. The rope between the two vehicles tautened and the large rear wheels of the tractor bit into the ground. At the same time, Roy let out the clutch and the Landrover's wheels began to turn very slowly in third gear. It was the work of a minute to get the Landrover back on to the highway. Roy was about to climb out to thank their rescuer but he was already at the passenger door, hauling it open. He peered inside and saw Ellen, huge and groaning.

'Well, well, well, so who have we here?' His voice retained a jovial note but beneath it his tone was steely.

'Hello, Stevie,' she whispered. 'Thanks . . .'

'So, it's baby time, is it, Ellen? And who've you been with then, while I was away? Who's the proud daddy?' He turned to stare at Roy, his eyes suddenly full of menace.

Ellen groaned anew, almost a scream of agony, and Roy shouted, 'Let's go, we must get her to the surgery . . .'

Kate's recognition of their rescuer and her understanding of the threat in his voice made her realise he could wreak havoc with the delicate situation. She had to remain calm and in control; so much depended on her. 'You've been very kind,' she said, hoping her smile didn't betray her alarm. 'We can manage now, thank you.'

'I'm going the opposite way, up to Farm Cottage,' Stevie said. 'A bit of urgent business. So drive carefully, take care of my wife, she needs the best.'

'Why are you going to the house, Stevie?' asked Ellen in a tight, pained voice. 'There's nothing there, nothing at all.'

But he gave no answer, merely tapped the side of his nose with his forefinger, in a gesture which said, 'Keep out of my business.'

As the tractor was disconnected and vanished along the lane, Kate drove carefully towards Aidensfield. The storm had eased a little and the heavy snow was now reduced to a few lighter flakes, although the wind was still whipping it into drifts. She negotiated them with skill and made good use of the road where the plough had pushed through and where other vehicles had formed tracks. Finally, they could see the village hall with its lights blazing.

'We'll take her there, Roy,' she said, her voice tinged with relief. 'We need light and power and it looks the only place with both. There's a room at the back and it's near enough for me to fetch my gear from the surgery.'

And so, struggling through the snow, Kate joined the other orphans from the storm in the warmth of the village hall.

Although aware of Ellen outside in the Landrover, as she made her preparations, Kate found time to chat to several railway victims, asking about their condition and promising to attend to them very soon. She noticed that most had a cup of tea, some food and a chair; whoever had organised this had done well, even to the extent of producing light and power. Before bringing in Ellen, she went to examine the anteroom at the rear; to her delight it contained a camp bed bearing a mattress.

Satisfied she'd done all she could, she went outside to help Ellen walk the short distance from the Landrover. Aided by Roy Marshall, the pregnant woman, oblivious of the stares of the rescued passengers, made her precarious journey across the floor of Aidensfield Village Hall, groaning and panting, sighing and wheezing with the constant pains. A woman stepped forward from the crowd and to Kate's relief she recognised her as Mrs Gillet, a retired midwife who, before her retirement, had regularly assisted Dr Ferrenby.

'I can help, Doctor,' she offered.

'Thanks, Edith.' Kate smiled gratefully. 'The child's

due literally any minute – it's a difficult one. I'm going for my equipment. Can you cope for a few minutes?'

'I've delivered some of the bairns in this village in worse conditions than this!' said the midwife. 'Come along, Ellen, in here, please. You're in safe hands now.'

While Kate and Mrs Gillet attended to Ellen in the privacy of the anteroom, Nick took a well-earned breather over a cup of tea and a ham sandwich. He was sitting at a table with Roy Marshall who was chewing his fingernails and not eating a thing. But Nick was quietly proud at the way in which the village had responded to the rail emergency and, as he looked around, he saw that new friendships were being made. The people of Aidensfield were befriending the stranded passengers and he smiled in satisfaction as the tension began to change into an atmosphere of relief tinged with humour and even happiness.

The boy with the injured leg was cheerfully awaiting Kate's professional expertise when she'd finished with Ellen, but Nick's only real concern was for poor old Alex Ferrenby. He had not moved from his chair, he had not offered to treat any of the casualties and it was clear that he was in need of professional help himself. The minute the power returned, Nick would take him home, but that was pointless at the moment. He was far better sitting here among the others.

Then Claude Jeremiah bustled towards Nick.

'Mr Rowan, I know you're a busy man and I know you want to get out into the snow to find Alfred, but somebody's nicked my tractor.'

'Nicked it? On a night like this?'

'Well, it's gone. I reckon that's nicked if I didn't give permission.'

'And you haven't given permission?'

'Have I heck! I mean, everybody here's off the train, and nobody wants a tractor do they, not now!'

'Stevie was on a tractor,' said Roy. 'When he pulled us out of the ditch.'

'What ditch?' asked Nick, who then persuaded Roy to tell the whole story of the rescue. Nick listened carefully. 'So where was he going?'

'He said he was going to Farm Cottage, our house, on some urgent business. I've no idea why he wants to go there, there's nothing there for him. But I couldn't stop him.'

Light dawned. 'Bloody hell!' cursed Nick. 'I know what that means. Is the Landrover outside now?'

'Yes, here's the keys.'

'If anybody asks for me, tell them I've gone to Farm Cottage!'

At that moment, there came the sound of a lusty cry from the lungs of a newborn baby.

'Roy, congratulations,' said Nick, hurriedly shaking his hand. 'You're a proud father! Now, Claude, you're coming with me.'

'C . . . c . . . coming with you? You're not arresting me, are you?'

'No, we're going to find your tractor. I've a good idea where it will be and you'll have to drive it back. Besides, I might need you to push me out of a ditch.'

Claude shook his head doubtfully. 'I'm not very good at physical things, Mr Rowan. My old heart, you know, my wartime experiences. It was tough in the trenches, fighting in conditions worse than this . . .'

'All right, you drive and I'll push,' said Nick.

'I think our policemen are wonderful,' grinned Claude Jeremiah, following Nick out of the hall. Outside, the snow had ceased to fall and the sky was clearing, but the ground was covered to an even depth, with drifts in exposed places. Aidensfield was as pretty as a picture, with the roofs all white and the lights of candles and oil lamps adding colour to the charming scene.

'By gum, Mr Rowan, it reminds me of a Christmas card,' called Claude as he scuttled along behind Nick.

'Come on, Claude. We've got to move fast.'

'Where are we going?'

'Farm Cottage, Elsinby.'

'There's some nice pheasants up there, Mr Rowan.'

'I'm not interested in pheasants at the moment, Claude.'

'I could allus get you a brace if you need any, just give me the word. I can get 'em fairly quick, you know. And cheap. I can allus get cheap birds for my friends.'

'Not tonight, Claude. Now, you did say you were driving, didn't you?'

'Aye, well, on second thoughts mebbe not, not in these conditions. Not this expensive Landrover anyroad. I might cope with my tractor, if you can find it.'

'I'm sure we will find it, Claude.'

'Do you think Alfred will be there an' all? He might recognise the smell of it, mightn't he, and he might have followed it, thinking it was me.' He paused. 'Poor old Alfred.'

And so the unlikely team of Claude Jeremiah Greengrass and PC Rowan set out for Farm Cottage.

As Nick and Claude were leaving Aidensfield, Sergeant Blaketon, Alf Ventress, Phil Bellamy and several more police officers were arriving aboard a railway rescue train which had battled through the snow from Strensford, calling at Ashfordly *en route*. They were accompanied by British Rail officials and rescue teams, ambulance men, first-aiders, two doctors, five nurses and a host of others, professional and amateur, who had been recruited to deal with the disaster.

Slowly the train eased into the tunnel near Aidensfield Station and disgorged its load of people and equipment. Sergeant Blaketon, first on the scene, was confronted with a snow-covered coach, an engine with steam hissing quietly from its valves and other evidence of a serious derailment, but not a sign of any casualties. He hurried on to the platform and found the porter.

'Where is everybody?' he demanded.

'Up at the village hall,' said the porter. 'They got lights and power going up there.'

'And the seriously injured?'

'Up there as well, taken by tractor and bus and car.'

'Anybody dead?' Blaketon continued.

'Not that I know of, Sergeant; tell you what, young

Constable Rowan and Claude Jeremiah did a good job between them, and George from the pub. You can be proud of your men, Sergeant.'

'Well, in that case, we'd better get up to the hall. Come on, everybody!' he called. 'They're all in the village hall.'

And so, apart from some British Rail engineers who had to remain at the scene to decide how to clear the tracks of the debris, the team of would-be rescuers began to trudge towards Aidensfield Village Hall. Fortunately, the snow had ceased to fall, although the road was ankle-deep in most places and it was cold and wet. The sight of the brightly lit hall and the sound of voices inside was a heartening one.

Sergeant Blaketon spotted Kate bandaging a woman's hand and made his presence known; he introduced his team of helpers and soon they were moving among the casualties, assessing their needs and attending to a whole range of minor cuts, bruises and grazes. Kate went over to see Dr Ferrenby, who had barely moved the whole time he'd been there. He was sitting with his eyes closed but when Kate spoke he opened them and smiled at her, brightening at her presence.

'Does your head ache, Alex?' she began.

'No, it's just that I feel so tired, so very very tired.'

She began to examine him tenderly, instinctively knowing that something was not right.

At the moment, she did not know exactly what the problem was, but she did know that poor Alex would need lots of care in the days ahead.

Meanwhile, Sergeant Blaketon had found George Ward who, assisted by several of the village ladies, was organising hot food and soup.

'Well done, George,' Blaketon was in a congratulatory mood. 'Now, is PC Rowan around?'

'No, he's gone off with Claude Jeremiah,' smiled George. 'He said something about looking for Claude's dog.' He grinned mischievously.

'You mean those two idiots have gone out in this weather to look for a bloody dog when there's a major railway incident to deal with?'

'I can't think why else they'd go, Sergeant,' said George, enjoying the moment. 'I mean, poor old Claude is in a pretty bad state, you know. He's been out all day looking for Alfred.'

'I don't believe it! Here we are, with a major disaster in the village, and Rowan spends time looking for a poacher's dog . . . These city-bred constables have no idea, George, no idea of priorities . . .'

'Cup of tea, Sergeant?' asked George innocently.

'There's your tractor, Claude.' Nick pointed ahead and carefully drew the Landrover to a halt, taking care not to make it skid.

'Will Alfred be with it, Mr Rowan?'

'Who knows?' smiled Nick. 'Now, I don't want Stevie to know I'm here. So we'll park here and I'll walk. I need my torch – and my truncheon.'

'Shall I come, Mr Rowan?'

'No, this might be dangerous, Claude . . .'

'Aye, well, in that case, I'll sit here and guard the vehicle.'

The house was in darkness, save for an oil lamp in the kitchen, but the door was wide open and some snow had blown in. Nick entered without using his light. He began to explore the house; like so many of these moorland cottages, it was quite extensive with lots of small rooms and thick walls. He froze as he heard a chinking sound from the scullery. Treading without a sound, he moved towards the noise. Cautiously entering the scullery, the first sight that greeted him was Stevie Walsh crouched on the floor; he had been chipping away at the masonry behind a chest of drawers and Nick was just in time to see him remove several of the stones to reveal a hollow behind. In that hollow lay a small dusty suitcase. Stevie was so engrossed in his work that he had not heard Nick's approach and Nick waited, watching the man in the light of the oil lamps and candles around him.

Stevie drew out the case and pressed the catches; the lid flew open to reveal scores of high-value banknotes.

'Ours, I think,' said Nick, his voice reverberating in the silence.

'God!' Stevie slammed the lid shut, seized the case and stood defiantly before the policeman.

'It's not yours, Stevie,' Nick said quietly. 'It's stolen property.'

Stevie's hands tightened round two case. 'Ten years I got for this, Mr Rowan. I've served more than seven. I've earned this, this is my reward for doing time.'

'No, it's not. You're going to hand it over, Stevie. I'm going to confiscate the money.'

Stevie drew himself up tall. 'Fancy your chances do you? Against me? One against one.'

'I've help outside, Stevie. An old mate. And if you have a go at me, you'll get even more time for that, won't you? And look at the weather, you'll never get away in this lot.'

'I could try, with all this money.' His voice was almost petulant.

'The money goes nowhere. If you don't hand it over, next time they put you inside they'll keep you there for longer. They might even throw away the key, eh?'

'So you're going to take me in, are you?'

Nick raised his eyebrows. 'I'm going to give you a chance, Stevie, a chance to go straight. You were great tonight, at the station and in the village hall. You've got guts and you could do well outside, if you keep your nose clean. There's no need to begin a life of crime again. You deserve better than that. Give me the money and I'll tell my sergeant you handed it over voluntarily, that you wanted to make a clean start. All right?'

Stevie looked at Nick, his eyes hard and disbelieving.

Nick continued, speaking quietly and slowly, 'I'll not mention finding you like this, that's my part of the bargain. You hand in the money and you go, that's all.'

'You mean I can go free? You'll not have me for touching this stolen money?'

'That's what I'm saying, Stevie. That's the chance you earned yourself tonight.'

'But where can I go on a night like this?'

'I can give you a lift into Elsinby or Aidensfield, then it's down to you.'

Quietly Stevie Walsh handed over the suitcase. Nick locked it, then said, 'Come on, Stevie. I'll give you a lift.'

But as they were heading for the waiting Landrover, Nick heard a commotion in an adjoining barn; the sound of flapping wings and squawking. He hurried inside. There, in the light of his torch, was Alfred chasing the hens. A broad smile on his face, Nick closed the door and went over to Greengrass who now emerged from the waiting Landrover.

'Is this your reinforcements?' asked Stevie in disbelief.

'That's him,' grinned Nick. 'An old soldier of immense bravery and experience! And a police dog, of course. Well, a CID dog, actually. A dog in heavy disguise!'

'A dog, Mr Rowan?' asked Greengrass. 'I didn't see any police dog here!'

'Well, he's in disguise, Claude. I thought I'd disguise him as a lurcher, to merge into the countryside, so to speak.'

'A lurcher? You mean they've got lurchers as police dogs, Mr Rowan? By, Alfred would be proud. Which reminds me, have you seen anything of my Alfred?'

Nick nodded quietly. 'Yes, he's in that shed behind the cottage.'

'You're joking? You mean that – you mean you have found him after all?'

'I have, Claude.'

Claude shook his hand excitedly. 'Well, I mean, is he safe? Is he all right?'

'He's busy worrying somebody's hens, Claude, which is an offence, as you know . . .'

But Claude Jeremiah didn't hear those words. He shambled off to find his dog, shouting, 'Alfred, leave off! If I catch you worrying hens, I'll skin you alive . . .'

'Come on, Stevie,' said Nick. 'How about that lift?'

As Nick walked into Aidensfield Village Hall with the suitcase, Sergeant Blaketon was sitting at a table eating a ham sandwich and drinking a cup of tea. He saw Nick and left the table to stride towards him.

'Rowan, of all the foolhardy things to do, to go hunting for Greengrass's dog when you've got a major incident like this . . .'

'I found him, Sarge,' beamed Nick. 'I found him.'

'I don't care about that. Your duty was here, with these people . . .'

'I found this as well, Sergeant,' and Nick placed the suitcase on a table and flicked open the lid. 'Twenty-five thousand pounds. Stevie Walsh handed it over. He wants the money restored to the owners, he wants to make a new start.'

Blaketon looked at Nick. 'Pull the other one, Rowan, how did you come by this money?'

'Good detective work, Sergeant,' and at that moment,

Claude Jeremiah Greengrass entered the hall with Alfred. The villagers all cheered as Alfred galloped into the room, went straight over to Blaketon's table, stood on his hind legs and natched the sergeant's sandwich then crept craftily under a bench to eat it.

'Greengrass!' bellowed Blaketon.

CHAPTER FIVE

High on the North York Moors above Aidensfield there is a stretch of moorland which lies in the shadows of Fylingdales Ballistic Missile Early Warning Station. It is called Holtby Moor and from time to time, Nick patrolled the bridleway which passes close by. The bridleway forms a very useful short cut between two streams which are very popular with picnickers and ramblers. Sometimes, when lone hikers get lost, they take shelter here; at other times, moor fires begin, having been started by careless tourists. Nick, like all conscientious police officers, believed that people needed to be reminded of their responsibilities when visiting these beautiful areas; he also knew that the occasional sight of a police uniform could persuade people to behave themselves.

Except, of course, Claude Jeremiah Greengrass.

One quiet afternoon, Nick decided to walk along the bridleway. The snows of winter had thawed and there were signs of spring everywhere. New shoots were appearing on the trees; the days were growing longer; and the moors were looking less threatening with patches of new grass growing among the heather. Enjoying a few minutes of calm, he suddenly noticed a man hammering a signpost into a patch of earth at the edge of Holtby Moor.

Nick was too far away to read the words on the sign and although the man was too distant to be clearly identified, Nick recognised the familiar bulk and ambling gait of Claude Jeremiah with Alfred at his heels. His old pick-up truck was parked nearby. Secure in his own patch of moorland and concealed behind a young spruce tree, Nick waited and watched until, eventually, Claude stood back with an indication of satisfaction, admired his handiwork, and left the scene, calling to Alfred to get into the truck. As the battered old pick-up bounced and trundled across the rough moorland, Nick strode across to inspect Claude's sign. It said: 'PRIVATE PROPERTY – KEEP OUT.'

Nick was baffled. He stood and surveyed the surrounding patch of moorland. There was nothing here but a windswept area of heather and bracken, interspersed with partially concealed boulders and inhabited only by red grouse and moorland sheep. In a patch of green a long way below was Aidensfield with its stone cottages, while to the west was a higher bulk of moorland upon which stood Fylingdales Early Warning Station. Nick scratched his head as he pondered the reason for Claude's notice; why place such a warning sign on this deserted place?

Back at his motorcycle, he radioed Ashfordly Police Station. Alf Ventress responded.

'Alpha Four Six Six to Control,' Nick repeated his call

80

sign. 'Have we anything on file about Holtby Moor, near Aidensfield?'

'Negative,' said Alf. 'The only time we hear about it is when somebody finds an unexploded bomb left over from World War II. And it's mighty windy too – for all sorts of reasons, therefore, you're likely to get blown off that moor.' He chuckled at his own joke.

'So why might Claude Greengrass want people to keep off?' Nick pressed his colleague for some clue.

'Search me. Maybe he thinks there's hidden treasure there or something. So far as I know, there's nowt but heather and rocks. I should think he could have the moor for nowt if he really wanted it.'

'It looks as though he has acquired it,' said Nick.

'He's welcome to it,' retorted Alf.

'But it's near Fylingdales,' Nick reminded Alf. 'A top-security establishment if ever there was one.'

'You're not saying Claude's turning his sticky hands to spying, are you?'

Nick frowned. 'No, course not. But, well, it's a bit odd to say the least. He's up to something.'

'My advice is to get off that moor before you're blown off and stop worrying about Claude Jeremiah. If he wants to acquire a useless piece of unproductive land, then it's his problem, not yours. Forget it, Nick.'

Nick shook his head doubtfully. 'If it was anybody else, I would forget it, Alf, but with Claude, well, I know he's up to something devious. He did say something about coming into money so I wonder if he's got some kind of deal going with this land? But thanks for the advice. I'll

keep my eyes on that man! Delta Four Six Six to control –
over and out.'

As Nick resumed his patrol, he was determined to
find out just what his old adversary was plotting. Being
Greengrass, he wouldn't be planting signposts on an
isolated patch of moorland just for the good of his
health – he'd be scheming in some devious way. George
Ward, landlord of the Aidensfield Arms, was the one to
ask . . .

'Morning, George,' Nick greeted the affable landlord.
'How's things?'

'Quiet, Nick, but ticking over nicely. In fact, I've got a
paying guest – bed and breakfast. First one since Christmas! A lady called Miss Smith. Maiden lady, well spoken,
middle-aged and quite well off, if the look of her clothes is
anything to go by.'

'She clearly recognises a classy establishment, George.
She's not a secretary, is she?' Nick asked with a straight
face.

'I don't know what she does for a living, Nick, I never
ask my guests . . .'

'A joke, George! Take a letter, Miss Smith . . . you
know, office jokes and things . . . all secretaries were
called Miss Smith!'

It was clear that George had no idea what the policeman was talking about, so Nick changed the subject.

'George,' he said. 'It's Greengrass. What's he up to?'

'Up to? How do you mean, Nick?'

'I saw him on Holtby Moor this morning, about an hour

ago. He was putting up a "Keep Out" sign, it said it was private land.'

'He's been after that patch of moor for a few weeks now, so I'm told,' George grinned. 'I did hear he's nearly done the deal, which would make him a landowner. Mind, I wouldn't have bought that bit, it's only big enough to keep a couple of sheep on and isn't worth anything. You can't build on it, you couldn't open a moorland café or build a house right up there . . . I reckon he's been conned, Nick.'

'Did he pay a lot for it?' Nick asked.

'A fair bit,' said George. 'A customer of mine was in the Northern and Provincial Bank in Ashfordly when it opened this morning and saw Claude plonk a fistful of notes on the counter in return for a banker's draft. Claude doesn't believe in bank accounts, as you know, so this isn't a cash purchase, Nick. If he's had to get a banker's draft, it sounds like an official deal of some kind.'

'But nobody in their right mind would spend good money on a tiny patch of useless moor, would they?' said Nick.

'Right,' said George. 'So that means the old scoundrel's up to something. He's been saying for a while now that he's coming into some money – he got that old Cadillac on the strength of it. How he's going to make anything worthwhile from that bit of moor is a mystery, but so long as he pays cash for his pints in here, I don't really care.'

Nick resumed his patrol and decided it was time to pay a visit to Ashfordly; the divisional mail would have arrived, there would be internal circulars to collect, summonses for eventual service and other routine matters to conclude. He calculated that he could ride to Ashfordly and back before lunch.

When he entered the police station, Alf Ventress was sitting behind the counter puffing at a cigarette, ash covering his uniform; it was Alf's lunch break and he was about to crack a pair of hard-boiled eggs by knocking them together.

'Watch it, Alf,' grinned Nick. 'They might be raw . . .'

'They won't catch me with that trick again!' smiled Alf, though he was very careful how he tapped the shells together, holding them over a piece of newspaper. But they were hard-boiled and he smiled with relief. 'She's got it right this time,' he said placidly.

'Rowan?' bellowed a voice from the sergeant's office. 'Is that you?'

'Yes, Sarge.'

'In my office, now!'

Nick stepped on to the hallowed ground of Sergeant Blaketon's office and stood before the desk. 'Morning, Sergeant,' he greeted his stern-faced superior.

'Anything to report, Rowan?' demanded Blaketon.

'All quiet, Sergeant.'

'It can't be all quiet with a man like Greengrass at large, Rowan. What's he up to now?'

Nick explained about Greengrass's unusual purchase of the piece of moorland.

Blaketon nodded judiciously. 'I'd better have words with the security people at Fylingdales, just to warn them about Greengrass. They don't want a character like that operating on their doorstep.'

'I think he's been conned, Sarge,' suggested Nick.

'Conned? Nobody cons Greengrass, Rowan, he's up to something and I want you to find out what it is. You know he was in the bank this morning, here in Ashfordly?'

'Yes, Sergeant, he was obtaining a banker's draft so he could conclude the purchase of that bit of moor.'

'I'm pleased you are up to date on important matters, Rowan. Clearly, the criminal intelligence system in Aidensfield is functioning correctly. But the reason I want to talk to you is that there was somebody else in the bank, Rowan. A suspicious character.'

'More suspicious than Greengrass, Sarge?'

Blaketon ignored Nick's retort and continued, 'You know there've been some bank robberies in the North Riding recently – Northallerton, Whitby, Stokesley?'

'Yes, I have read the crime circulars.'

'Well, Rowan, a suspicious character has been seen hanging around the Northern and Provincial Bank in Ashfordly. A woman, Rowan. She's been spotted for the past two or three days, waiting around outside the bank, keeping an eye on the premises. Stanley Hepplewhite, the manager, rang me to express his concern. He thinks she might be casing the joint.'

'There's no offence in just waiting outside a bank, Sergeant,' said Nick.

'I know that, Rowan, but even a southern city type like you must admit it's a bit odd. So get round there and have words with Hepplewhite, find out as much as you can, get a description of the woman and circulate it to all stations.'

'Very good, Sergeant.'

'And see if you can prove better than these people who write detective novels, Rowan! They make us all seem duffers, except for Amanda Young. I finished one of her books last night, Rowan.' He produced a paperback from his desk drawer. 'This lady, Rowan' – Blaketon pointed to a photograph on the rear cover but it was too far away for Nick to see with any clarity – 'this lady makes her detectives come alive. She uses real police officers, Rowan, real places and real crimes as the basis for her fiction.'

'She'd find some right characters round here, Sergeant,' smiled Nick.

Blaketon did not heed that remark, but went on, 'She spends hours doing research, Rowan, to get things just right.'

'I had no idea you were an aficionado of crime fiction, Sergeant.'

'Only the very best, Rowan. People who write this kind of quality novel can teach us all a thing or two about research, careful planning and the detection of crime through intelligent thinking. Now, that's what I want you to do with this case. Research it well, find out everything you can and if we have a potential bank robber, or a scout for potential bank robbers, on our patch, we want to know. Got it?'

'Yes, Sergeant.'

Nick walked around to the Northern and Provincial Bank in Ashfordly and was soon settled down with a cup of coffee before the manager's desk. Hepplewhite was a smart man in his middle forties, dressed in a dark grey suit, white shirt and dark blue tie. He was visibly relieved, when Nick explained why he was there.

'I hope I'm not being silly, Mr Rowan, but after a spate of robberies in the area, we have been warned by our head office to be on the alert.'

'It's not silly spotting suspicious characters and telling us about them!' Nick reassured him. 'If only more people would do this, there'd be fewer crimes and more criminals would be caught. Now, what about this woman?'

Mr Hepplewhite explained that over the past two or three days, his staff had become aware of a woman who appeared to be showing more than the usual degree of interest in the bank. She had spent time hanging around in the street just outside the premises, making notes and watching deliveries of cash. The staff had drawn his attention to her, and in fact, she had entered the bank this morning but had not made any transaction. She had simply watched the queue of people going about their routine business.

'Claude Jeremiah Greengrass was in this morning,' Nick reminded the manager.

'Yes, he was. I saw the woman watching him, Mr Rowan. He had a large amount of cash upon him which he exchanged for a banker's draft. But when I came from behind the counter to go into the public area, she quickly left the premises. I lost her outside, although I did once see her in that café just opposite.'

'Has she been in the café before?'

'Yes, watching from there too. She sits by the window

and pretends to drink tea or coffee, but all the time she's making notes.'

'These deliveries of cash, Mr Hepplewhite, do they come at regular times?'

'Yes, same day each week, and usually around the same time of day.'

'Then you ought to change the delivery time; she could be obtaining timings to pass on to her accomplices, you see. She might be doing all this research so that her armed colleagues can come and raid the delivery vehicles. So that's your first priority – change the times of all your regular cash deliveries.'

Nick managed to get a detailed description of the suspicious woman, promised to circulate it to all local police stations and patrol cars and asked Mr Hepplewhite to ring Ashfordly Police Station if the woman turned up again. As the manager escorted him to the door, he suddenly stopped short and said urgently, 'Mr Rowan, she's there . . . in the café, she's just leaving. She must have been at the back, out of my sight . . . that's her!'

Nick stood and watched as the woman left the café and walked quickly along the street towards the marketplace. Rapidly he said his farewell to the manager and hurried after her, managing to keep her in his sights as he pushed through the lunchtime crowds until she disappeared into the Crown Hotel. Nick hurried in after her and was just in time to see her disappearing up the stairs with one of the maids. He halted at the reception desk.

'That woman who just came in,' he said. 'Is she a guest here?'

'She stayed here yesterday and the day before,' the receptionist said. 'She didn't stay with us last night, though, but has left an umbrella behind. She's come back to see if it's still in the room she used.'

'Who is she? It is important,' he stressed. 'May I see your register?'

'Miss Smith,' said the receptionist. 'She gave a Coventry address.'

The name rang a bell. George also had a Miss Smith staying at the Aidensfield Arms; it was a common name though. Nick examined the entry but it told him little more than the receptionist had: 'Miss A. Smith' with a Coventry address. He thanked the girl behind the desk. 'Did she pay her bill?'

'Yes, cash. She was no trouble, Constable. What's she done . . .?'

'Nothing that we know of, but she has been acting somewhat suspiciously . . . Hello, she's coming back.'

Clutching a red umbrella, Miss Smith descended the stairs towards the foyer, thanking the maid for her help and saying that the umbrella had been in the wardrobe. Then she left the hotel. As she passed Nick, she smiled sweetly at him but did not speak and he decided to see where she went. He followed her to the marketplace where she waited at the bus stop.

Within fifteen minutes, Arnold Merryweather's service bus to Aidensfield arrived. Miss Smith boarded the bus and after Hannah, the collosal conductress, had collected the fares, the old vehicle disappeared upon its circuitous route through the countryside to Aidensfield.

Nick hurried back to the police station and told the expectant Blaketon what had happened.

'Then you'd better get yourself mobile to pursue her, Rowan, especially if she's entering your patch! But be discreet! Don't alert her to our interest!'

Kicking his Francis Barnett motorcycle into life, Nick drove back to Aidensfield, knowing that as long as nothing occurred to divert him, he would reach the village ahead of the lumbering bus. He also knew it was lunch-time and he was hungry, but he had little choice but to wait for the bus to come in. When it arrived Miss Smith alighted near the war memorial, then went into a café and sat down at a table. Nick watched her order a light lunch. There was no bus out of Aidensfield for a couple of hours so Miss Smith couldn't go far. Surely now he could have his own meal break. He must not make his interest in Miss Smith too apparent; if she realised he was watching her, she would leave and the whole operation would fail.

Thankfully, he made his way back to the police house, wondering if this was the Miss Smith who was staying at George's inn? If so, he'd be able to keep her under observation fairly easily. Nick reckoned it must be the same person, but he couldn't work out why a bank robbers' researcher would come to Aidensfield.

Over his sandwich, he told Kate about Greengrass and Miss Smith, while she chatted about her morning in the surgery and upon her rounds.

'How's Alex?' Nick asked.

'A bit quiet,' she said. 'He's not recovered from that attack yet, Nick, and his experience in the train crash has really set him back. He's not really fit to resume work. I'm very concerned about him. I'm trying to persuade him to go away – he should take holidays, visit his relations, go for long walks and so on.'

'He needs another interest, something other than his fishing and shooting,' Nick mused. 'Something light-hearted and totally different from his work.'

'There's going to be a talent contest. I'm thinking of putting his name forward as a judge!' smiled Kate.

'Now that would suit him. But what talent contest? Who's organising it? I knew nothing about this!' It wasn't often Kate could surprise Nick about village news.

'Your friend Phil Bellamy's got something to do with it, and Alf Ventress is going to be the MC; it's not in Aidensfield, though, which is probably why you knew nothing about it. It's going to be at the Oddfellows Hall in Ashfordly, to raise money for the football club.'

'I'm not sure Alex would find that very relaxing!' laughed Nick. 'You'd get all the local people expecting him to declare them winners of whatever section they'd entered! You know what small-town politics is like!'

'They asked me too,' she smiled. 'They must think I'm important!'

'Of course you're important! You're a key personality in Aidensfield – and district – and your fame has reached Ashfordly. You rank alongside the vicar and the squire. Did you say you'd do it?'

'I said I'd think about it. They are short of judges, they said. But I'm not sure I'm the world's finest authority on little girls whose mummies think they can sing, or on men who tell jokes that are as old as the hills!'

'I think you should do it. You need to get involved with events beyond the edge of this village.'

Kate shook her head doubtfully. 'I still think Alex is a better suggestion for a judge. He does need something to occupy him, something that's not connected with his work or the locality.'

'Well, I'm sure you've his best interests at heart, luv,' he said. The telephone rang. 'I'll get it.' Nick left the table and reached for the telephone. 'Aidensfield Police,' he announced.

'Is that PC Rowan?' It was a man's voice with a distinct southern accent.

'Yes, PC Rowan speaking.'

'It's Peter Hughes,' responded the caller. 'I was at university with Kate. Remember – we met at the graduation dance?'

'Oh, yes, vaguely.'

'Look, I can't hang on long, I'm in a kiosk, but I'm in the area on a walking holiday, staying at Elsinby, and thought I might call in to see you both. For old times' sake.'

'Yes, sure,' and the money ran out. The telephone died and Nick replaced his handset.

'Who was that?' asked Kate.

'An old flame of yours.' Nick wasn't smiling. 'That Peter Hughes chap who was at university with you. He never liked me, did he, for stealing you from under his nose?'

'Nick, it wasn't like that! He was just a colleague on the

same course as me, that's all. There was no romance
between us, you know that. Anyway, he's married now. I
think it's nice of him to remember us, good of him to spare
the time to pop in.'

Nick made some noncommittal noise in reply and Kate
smiled.

'You're jealous, aren't you?'

'No, I'm not! I just don't like him. He's smarmy, he gets
too close to you, he can't take his eyes off you . . .'

'I like that!' she grinned mischievously. 'I like it when
you're jealous and all protective!'

'If he starts chatting you up when he's here, I'll lock him
up, so help me!'

'Nick, don't be silly. There's no law against a girl having
an admirer! He's just an old friend from the past, nothing
more.'

'I'm going back on duty,' he said gruffly, plonking his
helmet on his head. 'I've got to patrol Maddleskirk and
Elsinby this afternoon and I've also got to keep my eye on
our suspected bank raiders' accomplice! See you later.'

She kissed him with an overenthusiastic show of affec-
tion. 'I love you, darling,' she said as she waved him off,
'not Peter Hughes.'

Later that afternoon, George Ward was stocking the bar
of the Aidensfield Arms when Miss Smith, dressed in
tweedy clothes and heavy walking shoes, approached him.

'Excuse me, Mr Ward,' she said, 'but do you have a
public telephone in the hotel? I need to make a private
call, a very private one.'

93

'There's a kiosk up the village, but if it's very personal, you could use my phone.'

'Thank you, that would very useful. I will pay, of course; you must put it on my bill.'

George took her into the back room of the hotel and showed her the telephone, closing the door firmly behind him to allow her privacy and returning to his chores. He counted his stock, moved the older bottles to the front of the shelves and made sure there were sufficient supplies of all his most popular lines.

After a couple of minutes, though, he realised he needed a duster to clean the higher shelves and went towards the living quarters. As he approached the back room, he heard Miss Smith's voice; she was shouting down the phone and even though the door was closed, he could hear every word.

'I tell you it's not the robbery that's the problem, it's the getaway! It simply doesn't work. I need more time to work on it. Unless I can get that sorted out, there's no point in going through with it. And if I don't, it means weeks of wasted time, weeks of useless observation.'

There was a further pause and then her voice resumed.

'Look, give me a few more days. I'll check the getaway again, minute by minute. That's all I ask for – a little more time to make sure it's right.'

The handset was replaced on the rest with a resounding crash, and George moved around the corner out of sight as Miss Smith stormed out of the room and out of the hotel. He slipped back into the bar and watched her stalk angrily along the main street of Aidensfield. Then he grabbed a piece of paper and wrote down all her words before he forgot them.

Next he rang the police house.

'I'm sorry, George.' It was Kate who answered his call. 'Nick's out, he had to go over to Maddleskirk and Elsinby.'

'I need to see him,' George sounded anxious. 'As soon as possible.'

'If it's urgent, I can ring Ashfordly and they'll contact him by radio. They'll send him here. He could be with you in quarter of an hour.'

'Well, yes, if that's possible, Kate. It is important.'

Kate did as she had suggested and Alf Ventress said he would call Nick on the radio and divert him to the Aidensfield Arms. Within twenty minutes, Nick was entering the pub to find George sitting with a glass of whisky in his hands. He looked quite pale and shocked.

'What's up, George?' Nick asked. 'Ashfordly said it was urgent.'

'Sit down, Nick, fancy a whisky?'

'Not me, George, not when I'm on duty. I wouldn't say no to a cuppa, though.'

George produced a cup of hot tea for Nick and explained what he'd overheard.

'You could be right, George,' Nick said when he'd finished. 'She could be planning a robbery. We know it's the same woman who's been keeping one of the Ashfordly banks under observation, watching the times of cash deliveries and so on. She called herself Miss Smith when she booked into the Crown in Ashfordly. I followed her to Aidensfield. She left the Crown yesterday.'

'Yes, that's when she came here. Remember I told you I'd got a paying guest! Bloody hell!' sighed George. 'Don't say I'm harbouring a felon!'

'Look,' Nick remained calm, 'we need to keep this woman under observation. Where is she now?'

'She went out, very angry she was after her call, stomping down the street. Somebody's putting pressure on her, that's obvious, I lost sight of her, but her room's still booked and her things are still there, so she'll be back, I reckon.'

'Well, if she's walking, she can't be far. There's no bus for an hour or so. We're interested in who she might be meeting; car numbers of contacts, that sort of thing. I think I'd better call Blaketon out to this.'

From the radio on his motorcycle, Nick called Ashfordly Police Station and explained to Alf what had happened, enlightening him as to the morning's discussion with Sergeant Blaketon.

Suddenly the line crackled as Blaketon interrupted the call. 'Wait there, Rowan!' he barked. 'I'll come straight away. I'll see you in the village street. In the meantime, you have a look around and if you see this woman, keep your eyes on her but don't let her know she's under observation. We don't want to scare her off; we want to nail her and her accomplices.'

'Very good, Sarge, she can't be far away.'

'Keep her under discreet observation, make a note of any contacts, numbers of any vehicles she gets involved with, that sort of thing.'

'Very good, Sergeant,' Nick repeated obediently.

Trying to make his perambulations look as normal as possible, Nick began his patrol of the village street. He quickly spotted Miss Smith, walking from the direction of the railway station and heading for the shops. Nick proceeded at a slow pace in the same direction as Miss Smith, pretending not to be interested. He turned off the main street so that he could stand back and observe from a distance, and was in time to see her enter the village stores-cum-post office. At that moment, Sergeant Blaketon's small black car came into view and Nick waved to indicate his whereabouts. To his relief, Blaketon spotted him and turned off the main street to rendezvous with him. Nick climbed into the little vehicle and Blaketon returned to the main street to park and watch.

'Where is she, Rowan?' Sergeant Blaketon was scrutinising the street.

'She went into the post office, Sarge, about five minutes ago. She's still in there. She came from the railway station.'

'Checking train times for a getaway, I'll bet. Was she armed?'

'Armed?' Nick laughed. 'No, I bet she's gone in for some stamps!'

'Just joking, Rowan, just joking. Ah, here she comes now . . . So this is Miss Smith, eh?'

The two policemen sat in the tiny car and observed the progress of the woman along the street.

She was munching a bar of chocolate and carrying a paper bag.

'I've seen her before, Rowan, I'd know that face

anywhere! She must have been mentioned on our crime circulars, in the *Police Gazette* mebbe, or the West Riding Police Reports.'

'You're very observant, Sergeant!' Nick was impressed.

'It comes with years of training, Rowan, but if her mug shot's been circulated, it means she's wanted all over England. If we can prove who she is and why she's here, it'll mean a feather in our caps, a commendation apiece even. Now, where have I seen that photo? I need to find out all about her, her accomplices, her background, that sort of thing.'

'She's heading back to George's pub, Sarge.'

'We need to keep an eye on this woman, Rowan, a very close eye. Now I know what she looks like, I'm going back to Ashfordly to check our circulars for that photo. I need to know what she's suspected of doing, right? And where she's been operating. We can't arrest her, there's no evidence of any crime at this stage, but she could lead us to the real villains. And that's what we want. Real villains.'

'Big-time crime comes to Ashfordly, eh?' grinned Nick.

'Aye, and if big-time criminals come to Ashfordly, they've got me to contend with, Rowan. We'll set a trap, we'll nail every one of them. Now, I've checked the timing of the next delivery of cash to the Northern and Provincial in Ashfordly. It's next Tuesday.'

'So that's when we'll get our bank raided, eh?'

'There's every chance, Rowan. I'll alert Divisional CID and we'll set up a welcoming committee for her and her henchmen.'

'I've always wanted to catch a bank raider red-handed, Sergeant!'

'Me too, Rowan, me too. So if you keep tabs on her while she's here, I'll look after the Ashfordly end of things.'

'As you say, Sarge.'

And so Constable Nick found himself hanging around Aidensfield village street trying to look invisible while Miss Smith pottered backwards and forwards between the shops. When she returned to the Aidensfield Arms, Nick waited for a few minutes and then slipped in via the rear door to see George.

'She's gone up to her room,' George whispered conspiratorially. 'She said she had some notes to write up and wouldn't be down until dinnertime.'

'Did she say what she intends doing later?' Nick asked hopefully.

'She's booked a table in the dining room for seven thirty.'

'Alone?'

'Yes, a table for one.'

'Right, well I'm not hanging around all that time, George. Can you give me a ring if she leaves for any reason? I'll be in my office at home, writing up my notes about all this.'

'Sure, I'll be around all afternoon.'

As Nick approached his police house, he noticed a distinctive royal blue car parked outside. There was a man at the wheel but the engine was silent. As he walked past, he looked inside. It was Peter Hughes, Kate's admirer.

Nick was tempted to ignore the fellow, but Hughes spotted him and leapt out.

'Nick, hi, good to see you.'

He offered his hand and Nick shook it. After some small talk, Nick said, 'Have you been to the house? Is Kate not in?'

'No, I knocked,' said Hughes. 'Look, I can see you're on duty. I'll come back later. How about a drink tonight, all three of us? For old times' sake?'

'Sure,' agreed Nick. 'I'm off duty this evening. How about the Aidensfield Arms, just down the road?' and he pointed to the pub.

'Fine. Eight o'clock?' suggested Hughes.

'See you there,' said Nick, as he turned towards his front door.

When Kate returned at teatime, Nick told her about Hughes and explained the arrangements for the evening. 'It was good of you, Nick. Yes, it'll be nice to have a drink together.'

But at six o'clock, Sergeant Blaketon rang.

'Stay on duty tonight, Rowan, to keep an eye on that Miss Smith. I can't find her picture anywhere, but I know I've seen it. We're short-handed and Division's taking it seriously.'

'As you say, Sergeant.'

'Be on duty in the street outside the Aidensfield Arms, keep her under constant observation. Got it?'

'Very good, Sergeant,' said Nick stoically, his heart plummeting.

It meant that Kate would be alone with Peter Hughes.

CHAPTER SIX

Nick told George that he would wait outside the inn that evening so that if Miss Smith decided to leave George need take no further action. It would all be down to Nick.

As he waited in the darkness, with the night growing more chilly by the hour, he saw Peter Hughes drive past in his smart blue car and felt a twinge of jealousy. Hughes was heading towards Nick's police house and tonight, Kate would be out and drinking alone with that man . . .

But, Nick told himself, Kate was to be trusted implicitly and he need not worry about how she behaved with Peter, even though he was an old flame from her past. And yet he felt uneasy . . . Hughes was here alone. Hadn't he got married not long ago? Nick felt sure there'd been a note from him, a Christmas card perhaps, or even an invitation to the wedding, but because Hughes was Kate's friend and not his, the memories were rather blurred. As he walked up and down the street, therefore, rubbing his hands to keep warm and lurking in the shadows to avoid being noticed, Nick felt decidedly ill-disposed to this extra evening of duty. He could be doing far better things than standing around in the cold watching for a woman who might be tipping off bank robbers and worrying about his wife who was being entertained by an old boyfriend.

At, Nick noted, three minutes to eight, Miss Smith emerged from the Aidensfield Arms. Warmly dressed against the cold evening and carrying a torch, she turned towards the railway station. Keeping behind her at a safe distance in the darkness, Nick followed in the trail of quick footsteps as she hurried along the road, dropping down the steep slope towards the station and leaving tiny clouds of breath on the cool night air. Then she left the road and climbed to the top of a cutting; Nick could see her silhouetted against the night sky – until she suddenly disappeared down the darkened slope, crashing through the gorse bushes and bracken as she went about her mysterious errand. He began to wonder whether she could be meeting some of her fellow conspirators at a secret location; whatever, he had to follow. But he had no means of immediate contact with Ashfordly Police Station, for his radio was on his motorcycle and he'd left that in the village. Was he being led into a trap?

Knowing the landscape like the back of his hand, he was able to follow without her realising he was there, but by the time he reached the top of the cutting, Miss Smith had disappeared from view. She was somewhere down below, pushing through the undergrowth in the darkness and he could hear her noisy progress. Then she screamed; it sounded like a cry of pain or terror.

He heard the crashing of a body in the darkness, the

sighing and grunting that followed . . . then a faint cry for help. Someone was whimpering and calling. It was a woman's voice. His decision made, Nick set off down the dark slope, his eyes growing accustomed to the gloom as he called out. 'Hello,' he yelled. 'Where are you?'

'Over here,' came the faint response. 'Please, do be careful . . . it's loose, some rocks are loose, oh, my ankle . . . I've lost my torch, it's lying about some-where . . . do be careful.'

Nick was too alert to walk straight into what still might be an ambush and he halted before reaching her, listening in the cool, still air for any indication of other people nearby. There was none. Gingerly he inched forward, calling out to her to indicate her precise whereabouts by answering him. Finally, guided by her voice, he found her lying among the bracken, unable to stand or walk.

'I'm PC Rowan,' he said, kneeling at her side in the faint light from the railway station. 'What's happened?'

'It's my ankle, it was so stupid of me to try and come down here in the dark. I've twisted it, sprained it per-haps . . . I don't think it's broken, but I can't stand up.'

'The station's just down there.' He pointed in the direction of the lights. 'There's a waiting room. If I can help you down there, I'll call a doctor.'

In the dim light, he was able to haul the woman to her feet. He told her to put her left arm around his shoulders while he held her tight about her waist. With that support, he would be able to guide her to the station. As they set off, he kicked something metallic and saw a chrome torch gleaming at his feet; picking it up, he pushed it into his coat pocket. Miss Smith obeyed his careful instructions and was soon limping down the slope guided by his strength.

After what seemed like a tortuous journey he led her into the station complex and settled her on a bench in the waiting room before calling Dr Ferrenby. He hoped Alex was fit enough to cope with her.

'Hello, Alex, it's Nick Rowan,' he said.

'Oh, hello, Nick. Kate's off tonight, she was going out for a drink . . . but shouldn't you be with her?'

Nick grimaced ruefully. 'Yes, I should but I had to work, Alex, an important observation job cropped up. Look, I'm at the railway station, there's a lady with an injured ankle. It might be just a sprain but I reckon she needs your attention.'

'I'll be there in a jiffy, Nick. Keep her warm till I arrive.' Alex sounded cheerful and responsive, so perhaps his earlier trauma had eased. Kate had seemed quite confident about leaving him in charge this evening. Relieved, Nick returned to the woman and, borrowing a blanket from the station's first aid cupboard, wrapped it around the now shivering Miss Smith.

Having made her as comfortable as possible, he organised the bearded porter, whose kettle was always on the boil, to make a cup of hot, sweet tea.

'Can I have your name please?' Nick asked her.

'Young,' she said. 'Amanda Young.'

'Young?' he said, writing it down and wondering why she had not said Smith. She gave an address in Wiltshire;

but the Smith name she'd given at the Ashfordly hotel had been followed by a Coventry address.

Soon Dr Ferrenby arrived with his medical bag, seemingly jovial and happy, much more composed than he had been over the last few days. And, Nick noted, he was charming towards his patient. With expert hands, he examined her ankle as she sipped the cup of hot tea provided by the porter.

'Well,' he said after a while, 'I think it's just a sprain. Can you stand up? See if you can put any weight on it? Not too much . . . there we are . . . no? Well, sit down again . . .'

As the all-embracing blanket slipped from her, revealing her face which until now had been in the shadows, Ferrenby looked shocked.

'Good Lord! It's Amanda Young!'

Nick looked at her and at Alex; did they know one another?

'I'm one of your greatest fans,' oozed Alex Ferrenby. 'I can confidently claim to have read all of your novels. But what are you doing at Aidensfield Railway Station in this condition on a freezing night?'

'I'm researching a new book, Doctor. It all hinges on a false alibi and the villain needs to get away by running across country at night in time to catch a train. I needed to know how long it took, timed to the minute, and so I was coming down that bank but I trod on a loose stone and my ankle went over.'

'It could have been worse,' sympathised Ferrenby. 'You shouldn't have tried that walk in the dark.'

'I had to, it's going to be in my book, you see. Anyway, I was lucky, this young constable arrived almost miraculously.'

'I was following you, Miss Smith!' He deliberately used her false name. 'Do you realise you've had half the North Riding Constabulary checking your movements and keeping you under observation! The bank manager reported a suspicious woman watching his branch and we all thought you were plotting to rob it!'

'Really? Oh, what fun!'

'No, it's not fun, it's serious.' Nick was not amused. 'We've wasted a lot of time on keeping you in our sights.'

'I'm sorry if I've been a nuisance,' she said humbly, clearly recognising the seriousness of his voice. 'But I do like to get my facts right. I spend hours on research.'

'So I understand,' said Nick.

She continued, 'I heard that the police in Ashfordly were getting suspicious about me, that's why I came to Aidensfield, and this railway is just right for my getaway sequence. But, truly, I am sorry I have caused all this trouble.'

'And those false names . . . Miss Smith! And two different addresses . . .'

'Amanda Smith is my real name, Constable; Amanda Young is my pseudonym. And my mother lives in Coventry. I sometimes use her address, you see, and sometimes my own.'

Nick wasn't going to be so easily placated, however. 'You've led us all a real dance. My sergeant won't be too pleased to hear about this.'

'Let me talk to him, please. I'm sure I can explain,' she pleaded.

Decisively, Ferrenby took control of the situation. 'Your ankle will need an X-ray, Miss Young, er, Smith. Now, if Nick can help you to my car, I'll run you to Ashfordly Hospital immediately.'

'Are you staying in the area for a while?' asked Nick, carefully polite.

'Another week or so, all being well,' she said. 'I need to finish my research very soon, my publisher is getting anxious. But I'd like to see more of the North York Moors.'

'You're not going to prosecute Miss Young, Nick, surely?' asked Ferrenby.

'No, but I do think she ought to pay for the trouble she's caused.'

'Pay? What on earth do you mean, Nick?' Ferrenby sounded quite alarmed at the proposal.

'There's to be a talent contest in Ashfordly, Miss Smith, and we need another judge, someone of stature from outside the area. I reckon you are perfect!'

'Oh my word,' laughed Ferrenby. 'Yes, indeed, what a splendid idea. I've already been co-opted. How about it, Miss Young?'

'Call me Amanda, please. But yes, please count me in. I'll be delighted to help, it'll be my way of saying sorry for the trouble I've caused.'

'Good, that's another problem solved!' smiled Nick. 'Now I must tell Sergeant Blaketon that we've found and identified the bank robber. I'll see you when you're back from hospital, Amanda. You'll be returning to the Aidensfield Arms?'

'Yes indeed, and thank you for rescuing me, Constable.'

'It's all in a day's work,' said Nick, helping her towards the open door of Dr Ferrenby's car.

Sergeant Blaketon listened with embarrassment as Nick outlined the drama at the railway station.

'I thought I recognised that face, Rowan. I knew I'd seen her somewhere before.'

'Like the jacket of that book in your drawer, Sergeant?' grinned Nick.

Blaketon pulled open the drawer and lifted out the paperback to see the smiling face of Amanda Young staring at him. 'Fancy me not recognising her, Rowan. She does look younger here, though, you must admit.'

'She wants to say sorry for causing us all this trouble, Sergeant, and has offered to help out at the talent contest.'

'What talent contest, Rowan?'

'In the Oddfellows Hall, it's being run by Phil Bellamy and Alf Ventress.'

'Is it? Not in duty time, I hope! I do not want my station being used as the office for a talent show. When is it to be? Why didn't I know about this?'

'You'll have to ask Phil or Alf that question, Sergeant.'

'I most certainly will, Rowan. Now, how has Amanda Young offered to help?'

'She's volunteered to be a judge.'

'Has she now? Well, I'd love to meet that lady. A very fine writer, Rowan, worth reading. You know, I used to be very good at recitations. I could make a very good job of "The Green Eye of the Little Yellow God". I might just enter the contest myself. It's all in a good cause, I trust.'

'Ashfordly Youth Football Club, Sergeant.'

'Well, I believe in our youngsters being kept off the streets. Now, what's your next task?'

'I'm going home, Sergeant, I've done a lot of overtime today, I want to crash out and have a good night's sleep.'

'You do that, Rowan, and thanks for dealing with Amanda Young. She sounds to be a very fine lady, a very fine lady indeed.'

'Goodnight, Sergeant.'

'Goodnight, Rowan.'

'I'll walk you home,' Peter Hughes offered Kate. 'It's the least I can do.'

'No, there's no need, Peter. I'm only a short walk away from home and the streets of Aidensfield are perfectly safe for a woman out alone at night.'

'I insist,' he said. 'It's been a lovely evening, Kate, just like old times. You and me sitting and chatting over a leisurely drink, then me walking you home and then a goodnight kiss . . .'

'There'll be no goodnight kisses tonight, Peter! I'm happily married you know.'

'You know I'm married?' he said, linking his arm with

hers. They began to walk away from the Aidensfield Arms.

'Yes, but I wasn't going to ask about it unless you told me. Your wife's not come with you?'

He shook his head sadly. 'No, we go our separate ways, I'm afraid. Things aren't good between us, not any more. I can see us getting a divorce before too long. I think you and me ought to get together, like we were before, before you met Nick.'

Kate stiffened. 'No chance, Peter. Honest. I have no intention of ever leaving Nick, and besides, ours was never a romance. You and I were just good friends, colleagues at university, nothing more.'

'That isn't how I saw it, Kate. I wanted you, I still do.'

'That's enough, Peter, now just take me home.'

'How about tomorrow? I want to take you out for a meal at a nice restaurant, just the two of us.'

'I'll come if you allow Nick to join us. He is my husband and I love him.'

'But surely, Kate, you aren't serious about settling down here, in the middle of nowhere, with a village bobby as your husband? The whole world's waiting for doctors with your knowledge and skills, you could go anywhere, be anyone.'

'I just want to be Nick's wife,' she insisted. 'Ah, here we are. Home.'

To her relief, Kate could see that Nick was inside; the lights were on and he was bent over the desk in his office, finishing off his clerical work for the night.

'Thanks, Peter, for a nice evening.'

'How about tomorrow?' he persisted. 'At my expense. With Nick if he wants to come. Or the night after if you're both busy tomorrow.'

'I'm judging a talent contest in Ashfordly the night after tomorrow, Saturday,' she said, 'so tomorrow suits me. You'd better come in and ask Nick yourself.'

Nick cheerfully agreed to the dinner engagement and Peter promised to collect them both the following evening at seven thirty.

'Now I must be off,' Hughes said. 'I've left my car at the pub. See you tomorrow.'

When he'd gone, Nick asked about Kate's evening and she explained how they had just sat and sipped their drinks, talking about old times. Nick joked about Amanda Young's mishap and Blaketon's appreciation of her books, saying the author was delighted to serve as a judge at the talent contest. Then they decided to have an early night.

Kate raced upstairs to be first into the bathroom while Nick remained downstairs to lock up.

'If the phone rings,' he shouted up to her, 'it's your turn, remember!'

But that night, there was no call for them.

Next morning, when Sergeant Blaketon walked in to begin his day, he found the floor of Ashfordly Police Station covered with a miscellany of tinned fruit, bottles of wine, boxes of chocolates, a couple of hams and other assorted items.

'Bellamy and Ventress, what's the meaning of this?' He

stared at the goods. 'It looks like the contents of a delivery van. Has one been involved in an accident, might I ask?'

'No, Sergeant,' said Bellamy. 'It's raffle prizes, for the talent contest.'

'I do not want this police office acting as a depository for unwanted goods, Bellamy. I take it that you have not been organising this event in duty time, have you?'

'No, Sergeant, but generous supporters insist on bringing the stuff here. I'll take it round to my flat, ready for the contest,' promised Bellamy.

'Shift it immediately, both of you. What would the Inspector say if he walked in now?'

'He might buy a raffle ticket, Sergeant,' beamed Alf.

'And he might transfer you to Gunnerside, Ventress! Anyway, what's your role in this affair? You're not a footballer, are you? I'd say you were a bit long in the tooth for that sort of caper.'

'I'm MC, Sergeant. Master of Ceremonies. My job is to call in the various acts and look after the judges.'

'You know the famous crime writer, Amanda Young, is to be one of the judges?'

'I do, Sergeant, and very honoured we are to have her services.'

'I am taking part, you know.' Blaketon puffed out his chest. 'I'm going to do my rendition of "The Green Eye of the Little Yellow God". I think she'll enjoy that.'

'It takes all sorts, Sergeant,' said Ventress. 'So we'll see you at the Oddfellows on Saturday night?'

'I shall be there. Now, clear this floor immediately.'

'Very good, Sergeant.'

As they were obeying his instructions the office telephone rang. Ventress answered it.

'Ashfordly Police,' he said.

Alf's face soon told Sergeant Blaketon and Phil Bellamy that something terrible had happened. 'I don't believe it,' Ventress muttered. 'Right, Jack, I'll send somebody round straight away.'

'What is it, Ventress?' Sergeant Blaketon asked anxiously.

'That was Jack Summers from the Oddfellows Hall. Somebody's broken in during the night and smashed the heating pipes on the radiators. The whole place is flooded, the floor's ruined. It was a new parquet floor, remember, installed for dances. He says it looks like the Rocky Mountains now!'

'But the talent contest?' cried Blaketon. 'I was looking forward to that.'

'We'll have to find a new venue,' said Bellamy. 'I'll get round there straight away, Sergeant. To deal with the break-in, of course!'

'Of course, Bellamy, what else would you be doing in duty time?'

By the time Phil Bellamy arrived, other officials and committee members were present and it was clear, even from a preliminary inspection, that the hall was going to be unavailable for functions for some time. It would take weeks to rectify the damage.

'It was deliberate,' said Jack Summers. 'They broke in through a back window and systematically smashed all the pipes and turned the taps on in the toilets, after blocking the sinks and drains. Sheer vandalism! But why? Why do this?'

'Search me,' said Bellamy taking out his notebook. 'OK, Jack, I need details for my crime report, then I've got to find a new venue for the talent contest – we've only a couple of days to get it sorted out! God, who'd be our team's social secretary!'

'And who'd be caretaker of a hall when this happens!' groaned Summers.

'Where's the nearest place big enough to take the numbers we're catering for?' asked Bellamy.

'Aidensfield,' said Summers. 'They've got the same space as we have and it's not far away. You could switch venues – start half an hour later to allow time for people coming here to drive over there, and you've cracked it.'

'Great idea. Thanks, Jack. I'll get Nick Rowan to have words with their caretaker to see if the place is free.'

And so the great Talent Contest of Ashfordly was suddenly switched to Aidensfield Village Hall. This excited a lot of unexpected interest in the village, especially when it was discovered that both doctors, Rowan and Ferrenby, were to be judges.

George, the landlord of the Aidensfield Arms, said he'd compete, lots of parents of small children decided to enter their offspring for the ballet dancing, singing and playing of musical instrument sections, some of the adults would do conjuring tricks, juggling and balancing acts, while one man said his performing Jack Russell terrier was the wonder of the age.

For Claude Jeremiah Greengrass, the contest presented an opportunity to make a little profit, and with this in mind, he went to see Gina Ward, George's niece, at the Aidensfield Arms. She was busy preparing the bar for the day's custom.

'Pint please, Gina,' beamed Claude, handing over a fiver.

'You're splashing out these days,' Gina smiled. 'Wasn't it last night you were celebrating by buying everybody a drink?'

'I've done a very good deal, Gina.' He leaned closer. 'I've made myself a very handsome bit of cash. All honest and above board, an' all.'

'That bit of land on the moor, was it?'

'Aye,' he said, 'I got wind that the Ministry of Defence was going to extend Fylingdales, you see. Careless talk it was. Anyroad, I bought that land off old Sam Blenkiron and, well, it was right in the middle of the bit they wanted. So I sold it for a lot more than I bought it for. I paid off my debts, squared up with that Yank about the Cadillac and I've got enough to give me an income for life, and some to invest.'

'Invest?'

He looked furtively around the bar but there was no one else in at this early stage of the morning.

'Yes, Gina, invest. With your help. I know you're a discerning sort of lass with an eye to making a bob or two.'

'What's the catch, Claude?'

'Catch?' He sounded hurt. 'Who said owt about a catch? No, this is all above board, a legitimate way of making a bit extra. You know about the talent contest?'

'Yes?' she agreed.

'Well, I was thinking. You know it says open to all comers. Well, I thought you, being from Liverpool, like, might know some good artistes.'

'You mean the Beatles?'

'Well, I wasn't thinking of them in particular, but mebbe you could persuade some other group to come and take part in our contest.'

'You must be joking, Claude. Those pop groups wouldn't come all the way from Liverpool just for the chance of winning a book token or a brace of your pheasants!'

'No, no, I wasn't thinking of that. I was thinking, if you could find the right group, not too good mind, but better than owt that the locals will put on, well, I'd pay 'em a fee.'

'You'd pay them?' she cried.

'Well, as an investment. I'd invest in their future, in a manner of speaking.'

'You've lost me now, Claude.'

Claude Jeremiah explained that he was thinking of becoming a bookmaker for the duration of the talent contest. He would take bets on who was to be the outright winner; he knew, he told Gina, that all the mums and dads, aunts and uncles, grannies and grandads, would be backing their own kids.

'So there's money to be made. All we have to do is to make sure none of the locals win. All the money will be on them, won't it? None'll bet on the unknowns. So I'll . . .

er . . . *we'll* clean up a fortune. What we have to do is bring in a sure-fire winner, you see, somebody nobody bets on.'

Gina began to follow Claude's logic. 'Ah, so you're willing to pay a fee for a pop group to come all the way from Liverpool, just to be sure of winning this competition?'

'That's it.' He grinned wickedly. 'I'd see you all right, of course, that goes without speaking. I'm a very reliable chap, you know, when it comes to deals.'

'My Uncle George is having a go, he's got a very good voice,' Gina said. 'Some say I've inherited his talent. So you'd need somebody better than him.'

'Aye, but not anybody famous, I mean, not anybody who's a professional. We need amateurs, but good 'uns.'

'I know a very good group who used to sing in the Cavern with the Beatles. They'll do it if they're free.'

'Tell 'em the pay's good and they've a reliable backer, a well-known local entrepreneur and businessman, financing them.'

'There's isn't much time to get this organised, Claude,' Ginn warned.

'No, well, strike while the iron's hot, that's what I say. Fortune never strikes twice in the same spot, or summat.'

'I'll try to get hold of them this morning. They're called the Mersey Hounds. Red hot over there, they are, very popular. Look, Uncle George has gone to Ashfordly for his meat and bread, so he won't overhear our plans. Leave it with me.'

'It'll make us both rich, Gina, mark my words!'

She smiled sweetly at him.

Flushed with the initial success of his scheme, Claude Jeremiah went around the village knocking on doors and offering to take bets on the outcome of the talent contest. During his perambulations, with Alfred in tow, he collected the names of the various Aidensfield contestants, quoted the odds for them winning, issued the punters with some old bookmakers' tickets he'd acquired and entered their details in a tatty old notebook. He was delighted to find that, without exception, parents placed bets upon their own children to win, and the money poured in.

'I'll be in the hall on the night,' he told them all. 'That's if you want to add to your stakes.'

But he told nobody about the Mersey Hounds.

He was set to make his recently acquired fortune even bigger. Claude Jeremiah Greengrass was aiming to become the richest man in Aidensfield.

There was one man, however, who did not want the talent contest even to go ahead. Mark Sutton had been left out of Ashfordly's successful football team in favour of Phil Bellamy. Bellamy had even scored with one of Sutton's girlfriends and so Sutton had embarked on a secret campaign to ensure that his enemy's fund-raising efforts for the club were all doomed to failure. His first action had been to break into the Oddfellows Hall to flood the place and so prevent the contest taking place; his second had been to remove each of the posters which advertised the event. Now that the contest had been relocated in

Aidensfield, though, he had to begin all over again. The snag was that in such a small village, his unlawful activities might be observed. PC Rowan seemed to be always around the place and so, as he brooded upon the best way to thwart Bellamy's success, Sutton decided to drive over to Aidensfield at night and take a look at the hall itself. There must be some way of halting the contest and making Bellamy squirm.

When he arrived in the village, he went first to the Aidensfield Arms for a drink. There he met some of his footballing friends from other moorland teams, and before long an enjoyable evening was in full swing. Later, he reckoned, when everyone had gone home, he'd take a look at the village hall. There was plenty of time, all night in fact.

That night Nick and Kate were being taken out for their meal by Peter Hughes. As arranged, he called for them in his distinctive blue car and they drove out to the Hopbind Inn at Elsinby which was renowned for its good food. In spite of Nick's dislike of Peter, the evening was a relaxing one, even though Nick had to ensure that he left the pub before closing time – village policemen should never be seen in the pubs on their patch after hours! After thanking Peter for his hospitality, Kate and Nick turned in for an early night.

And then the telephone rang. It was just eleven o'clock.

'Your turn!' shouted Nick.

Kate smiled and went to answer the noisy instrument.

'Aidensfield Police,' she said.

'Hello?' panted someone. 'Can you come quick?

119

There's been an accident, a hit-and-run, somebody's hurt.'

CHAPTER SEVEN

Nick and Kate lost no time responding to the call; both were clearly required in their professional capacities. In their private car, the man-and-wife team rushed through the night towards the location the caller had given, the road between Aidensfield and Elsinby at the sharp corner near Lowlands Farm. Nick knew the corner well; lots of strangers to the area tended to miss it and frequently drove straight through the hedge into the neighbouring field. After a ten-minute drive Nick eased to a halt to find the owner of Lowlands Farm, Ron Aldham, standing at his gate waving a torch. There was a bicycle lying on the verge and Nick saw that its rear mudguard was twisted and buckled. He made a quick examination, and then tested the bicycle's front and near lamps. Both were working.

'They were on, Mr Rowan,' said Ron Aldham. 'I switched 'em off. Bert Wilkinson rides past here every night, he allus has his proper lights on.'

'Thanks, Ron.' Nick went towards him. 'So what happened?'

'Poor old Bert, some lunatic knocked him off his bike and didn't stop. I heard the crash and came out but the car had gone. Bert's in the house, I took him in and the missus is seeing to him.'

'Is he badly hurt?' asked Kate with concern in her voice.

'Shaken up a lot, I'd say, and he was complaining about his arm.'

'I'd better go and see to him. I wonder if he'll need an ambulance?'

'I wouldn't have thought so, he's a tough old character. Come on, I'll take you in.'

'Can I put his bike in your buildings for tonight, Ron? I'll need to examine it in daylight.'

'Aye, no problem, Mr Rowan. Fetch it in.'

Old Bert, who was in his late seventies, was sitting beside the farmhouse fire nursing his wrist. Mrs Aldham had made him a cup of tea which stood on the table near him; he was sipping from it between bouts of holding his arm.

Kate smiled at him. 'Hello, Mr Wilkinson. What happened?'

'Some lunatic racing down the road, going like a bat out of hell. He nearly didn't get around the corner and clipped my back wheel. Knocked me off, he did, sent me spinning into the ditch. Then just cleared off and left me.'

'And you were on the correct side of the road, back light on?' asked Nick.

'Yes, of course I was. I allus rides well into my own side, and all my lights were working.'

'Where are you hurt?'

'This wrist, I landed on it. I'm all right otherwise, just a bit bruised here and there.'

Kate examined his wrist. 'Well,' she said, 'I don't think there's any bones broken, but I'll bandage it tightly and it might be an idea to keep it in a sling for a day or two, just to rest it. Now, we can run you home – I'm sure your bike will be safe enough here till you're ready to collect it.'

Aldham nodded. 'He can call for it any time,' he said. 'He rides past every night, on his way to and from the pub. Been doing it for years, haven't you, Bert?'

'Aye, and with never an accident till now. Bloody motorists, they think they own the roads.'

'Who was it, Mr Wilkinson?' asked Nick. 'Did you recognise the car?'

'No, it all happened too fast. It was a blue one, though, I remember that.'

'I'll just have another quick look at the bike, if I may,' Nick said to Aldham. While Kate bandaged Mr Wilkinson's wrist, Nick retraced his steps to the shed where he'd left the bike and Aldham switched on the interior light. In the dull glow of a low-powered bulb, Nick inspected the heavy old bike. It was coloured black, with strong metal mudguards. Bending close, Nick could see traces of blue paint on the twisted rear mudguard.

'I'll come back tomorrow and take samples of that paint,' he told Aldham. 'If I can find the car it came from, our forensic wizards can match the vehicle with this sample. Even mass-produced cars have their own individual paint style – due to wear and tear, polish and so on.

Then I'll know for certain who hit this bike. Did you see anything at all, Ron?'

'No, we were inside, just about to call it a day when I heard the bang. I looked out and saw the car lights vanish round the corner, but that's all.'

Nick nodded. 'OK, well, thanks for looking after old Bert. I'll run him home now. He is married, isn't he? He won't have to look after himself with just one arm?'

'No, he's got Jinny, she'll see to him.'

'I'm only glad he's not more seriously hurt,' Nick said, thankful he didn't have to take worse news to Bert's wife.

After recording details for his accident report, Nick took Bert home, where Kate advised his wife on how to care for the injured arm, promising to pop in from time to time to see how he was progressing. During the short drive home, Kate chattered away about irresponsible motorists but Nick was silent and thoughtful.

'You're very quiet.' Kate studied him quizzically.

'I was thinking about the blue car,' he said. 'The one that hit old Bert. If that paint left on his bike is anything to go by, it was a very distinctive blue.'

'That'll make it easier to find, won't it?' she smiled.

'If it's a local car, I should be able to trace it,' he acknowledged. 'It might have some scratches on too, on its nearside.'

'Can you think of any blue cars in the area that might be responsible?' she asked.

'Yes,' he said. 'There's one that left Aidensfield for Elsinby tonight. A very distinctive blue one.'

She looked at him closely. 'You don't mean Peter Hughes?'

'Who else?' he asked. 'So tomorrow, I've got to have words with him, and I'll need paint samples from his car.'

Kate looked appalled. 'Nick, you can't, he'll think you're getting some kind of revenge on him.'

'Can't? Of course I can, it's my job. If he didn't knock old Bert off his bike, he's got nothing to fear, has he?'

'There must be other cars that are the same sort of blue, surely?' she said.

'Then I hope I can find one,' he replied, turning into their drive. 'All he had to do was stop, that's all.'

Despite the fact that it was a Saturday, first thing next morning, Nick drove out to Elsinby to search all the bed-and-breakfast establishments for Peter Hughes's car. He knew them all and it was a matter of half an hour's walk around the village before he discovered the car. It was parked in the drive of Honeysuckle Cottage. Nick made a swift examination for signs of damage and found some faint scratches on the front nearside wing. Then he went to the door and knocked. Mrs Linda Gray answered.

'Hello, Mr Rowan, what brings you here at this early hour?'

'It's a Mr Hughes, he is staying here, isn't he?'

'Yes, sure, come in.'

Peter Hughes was having breakfast and invited Nick to join him for a coffee. Nick obliged, sitting at the table while Mrs Gray found a cup.

'Peter,' started Nick. 'This is difficult for me.' He was quickly interrupted.

'Look, Kate's yours, Nick, I have no intention of stealing her from you. It was nice coming to see her again. You're a lucky man, Nick, but it's time for me to be moving on. I've got my own marriage to sort out . . .'

'It's not that, Peter, it's duty for me. You drove straight back here last night, did you? After leaving us?'

'Yes, of course.'

'And did anything happen on the way?'

'Happen? Like what?'

'An accident. Did you see a cyclist between here and Aidensfield?'

'Yes, I passed an old chap riding a pedal cycle. He seemed fine, he was pedalling along nicely.'

'Did you collide with him, Peter?'

'Me? Good God, no! Why, what's happened?'

Nick explained in full, giving details of the hit-and-run accident, and ending his account with the fact that traces of blue paint had been found on Mr Wilkinson's bike.

Peter seemed shocked. 'Look, Nick, if I'd knocked him off, I'd have stopped, I'm not a hit-and-run merchant.'

'I've got to go through our procedures, Peter, if only to eliminate you. It means taking a paint sample from your car, and one from the bike, then checking to see if the two samples match.'

'You go ahead, I'm innocent, and if your forensic chaps can prove that, then I'm more than willing to help you.'

'You'll not be leaving for a day or two?' Nick asked. 'It'll take a few days to get the results.'

'I'll be here,' Peter said. 'But Nick, you don't honestly think it was me, do you?'

'I don't think anything, Peter, I just collect the evidence and let the facts decide. Now, I need to scrape a tiny bit of paint off your car, just half the size of my little fingernail. And then I'm going to do the same with Mr Wilkinson's bike.'

'You do what you like, Nick. I'm innocent, and I hope you can prove it!'

Watched by Peter, Nick took out a small plastic envelope and, using his penknife, scraped a sliver of blue paint from the scratched area of the car.

'Is that all you need?' asked Hughes.

'That's all,' said Nick. 'Now, I've got to scrape the blue bits off the bike.' He paused. 'Look, Peter, sorry to come to you like this, but duty is duty.'

'You're doing your job, Nick and I respect you for that. But you will come and tell me I'm innocent, won't you?'

'Sure.'

After scraping the blue paint from the old bike, Nick rode down to Ashfordly Police Station to ask Alf Ventress to send the samples off to the forensic laboratory for analysis.

'How're the arrangements for the talent contest coming along?' Nick asked as Ventress filled out the forensics form.

Alf sighed. 'Bellamy's off duty today, he's gone to Aidensfield to get the hall ready, and Sergeant Blaketon's wrapped up in his rehearsal of "The Green Eye of the Little Yellow God". If I've heard it once, I must have heard it fifty times. He wants to impress that lady novelist.' Alf's eyes twinkled. 'He's taken a right shine to her, Nick.'

'What about that trouble? Any more vandalism?'

'Not down here, but I did hear a bit of useful information last night. You know a lad called Sutton, Mark Sutton?'

'No, can't say I do,' admitted Nick.

'He's an Ashfordly lad, not very bright and more than a handful of trouble when he's had a drink or two. He's prone to jealousy. We've had one or two problems with him.'

'What sort of problems, Alf?'

'He once hit a chap in the face with a broken beer glass just because he thought the chap was eyeing his girl. Then, on another occasion, he threw a brick through the window of a house because the man there didn't want Sutton visiting his daughter. He gets violent if things don't go his way.'

'Why are you telling me all this?' asked Nick, puzzled.

'Well, he was in the football team till Phil Bellamy took his place, then he was seeing a lass called Margaret Eddison until Phil started taking her out. So I was thinking about that break-in at the Oddfellows, and then how some posters for the talent contest have been torn down . . . I reckon Sutton might be behind all this. He's got the motive for doing things like that, and it's the sort of reaction I'd expect from him. I thought I'd warn you. Now that the contest's been moved to your village, you might find him paying Aidensfield a visit. He'll start at the pub to get himself tanked up with beer to give him Dutch courage, and then he'll set about his troublemaking.'

'Thanks, Alf. What's he look like?'

Alf described Mark Sutton in some detail and added, 'He gets about in a Ford Anglia, a blue one. Nice car, he can earn good money when he wants – he works at the steel works in Skinningrove, something to do with the electrical side of things. He lives in Ashfordly and travels over the moors to work every day.'

'That's probably why I haven't come across him,' said Nick.

'Right. Actually, he's a hard worker when he sets his mind to it but he can be a nasty piece of work when he's in drink.'

'He's off work on Saturdays?' asked Nick.

'Very likely. Certainly on a Saturday night,' said Alf. 'So you'll be at the hall tonight?'

'I will, I'll be in uniform, but not doing my Laughing Policeman act! I'll be watching out for Sutton.'

'I'll be there doing my MC bit in my dicky bow and black suit,' grinned Alf. 'But me and Phil will always come to your rescue if you needs us.'

'I'll remember that,' smiled Nick.

Nick was patrolling Aidensfield village street when an old van painted in masses of psychedelic colours pulled up outside the post office. Nick strolled across to it just as a tall, long-haired youth in scruffy clothes clambered out.

'This Aidensfield?' he asked Nick.

'It is,' said Nick.

'Where's it all happening then?'

'Where's all what happening?'

'The music, the fun, the talent contest.'

'Over there, in the village hall.' Nick pointed to the building. 'Not till tonight, though, you're a bit early. Who are you? Are you entering?'

'Mersey Hounds, best thing since the Beatles, man. We're entering, we'll win, you'll see.'

'You from Liverpool then?' Nick was examining the tax disc in the windscreen and saw that it had been issued at Liverpool. It was up to date. He also saw there were three other men squashed into the van, along with a load of amplifiers, microphones, electric guitars and other music-making equipment.

'Yeh, all the way from the Mersey to the moors.'

'This is a bit out of your league, lads,' said Nick. 'Why come all this way for a village talent show? You boys'd be better off on *Opportunity Knocks* or something.'

'Got our expenses paid, we did. Your local big shot, a Mr Greengrass. He sounds a real gentleman. Offered us a fat fee and free beer in the pub if we'd come and play here tonight.'

'Greengrass? He's paid for you to come all the way from Liverpool?'

'Yes, so our fame is spreading, see. Now, where's the pub? Gina works there, eh? Gina Ward.'

'Down the road, the Aidensfield Arms. Yes, Gina's there. You know her?'

'Used to sing around the Liverpool clubs, did Gina. Nice lass, good voice. Well, see you later, alligator.'

'In a while, crocodile!' retorted Nick, as the man returned to the driving seat and the old van trundled off towards the pub.

Over lunch with Kate, Nick told her about his interview with Peter Hughes. She was not very pleased. He tried to explain that he was merely doing his duty, part of which was to eliminate Hughes if he was not responsible. Kate didn't seem convinced. Then he added that he had heard about another blue car, the one belonging to Mark Sutton who was expected to make an unwelcome appearance tonight.

'Well, he sounds more likely to do a hit-and-run than Peter Hughes,' she snapped. 'But I just hope he doesn't ruin the show tonight!'

'I'll be there to keep an eye on things,' Nick said calmly. 'I got the tip from Alf, he'll be around too with Phil. The show will go on.'

'I'm getting little bribes from anxious mummies and daddies,' smiled Kate, her good humour gradually returning. 'I've had umpteen singers in my surgery this morning, all having their throats examined, or ballet dancers having their toes tested, and the parents have given me boxes of eggs, chocolates, a bunch of flowers . . .' She shook her head. 'I'm not sure what to do, Nick. It's obvious they all expect me to vote their child the winner. If I give the wrong result, they'll never speak to me again!'

'So long as you don't start taking money from them, you'll be fine,' he said. 'Besides, you're not alone. It's a joint decision, it's not just your opinion that's going to count. Now, talking of the show, what's Greengrass up to?'

'Up to? How do you mean?' she asked.

'He's paid for a scruffy Liverpool pop group to come all this way to enter the contest. They're friends of Gina's, they said Claude had paid their fees. Why would they come all the way from Liverpool for a competition in Aidensfield? And, more important, why would Claude Jeremiah spend his precious money to get them here?'

Kate looked puzzled. 'I've got to go and see George at the pub, I'll ask Gina if she knows what's happening. Anyway,' she smiled, 'everybody else seems to be entering the contest. How about you?'

Nick shook his head ruefully. 'Sutton's expected to come and cause bother, I'll have to work. Besides, I might have an unfair advantage, being the husband of one of the judges!'

'I'll let you know what Gina says,' grinned Kate.

When Kate arrived at the Aidensfield Arms, it was almost closing time and she found Gina clearing empty glasses from the bar.

'Is George in?' Kate asked.

'He's rehearsing,' smiled Gina. 'He's going to do his W.C. Fields act. Can I help?'

'You know I was in the other night, with a friend of mine, Peter Hughes?'

'Yes?'

'Did he come back here last night? Just before closing time? He went out for a meal with Nick and me, to

Elsinby. I just wondered if he'd come here for a quick drink before going home?'

'Not last night, Mrs Rowan. I was serving behind the bar and would have noticed him.'

This seemed to satisfy Kate; she'd been worried that Peter might have come here to have a drink or two to drown his sorrows at her rejection of him. She did wonder if he'd been drunk when driving back to Elsinby, but it seemed not. She was happier now she'd asked.

'Thanks, Gina. Now, there is another thing. Your friends, the Mersey Hounds. They're entering our talent contest, I believe?'

'Yes, that's right.'

'And I believe Claude Jeremiah's sponsoring them.' She leant on the bar. 'Now, Gina, tell me, what's he up to?'

'He's opened a book on the results, Mrs Rowan. He's going round taking bets and he wanted to book somebody who's sure to win, somebody who nobody knows. If everybody bets on all the local entrants, who Claude thinks will be bound to lose, then he'll make a killing when his pop group wins, won't he?'

'The crafty old sod!' Kate swore. 'So these Mersey Hounds, are they professionals?'

Gina grinned triumphantly. 'No, they're amateurs and they're rubbish, Mrs Rowan, they're terrible. They'll never win, mark my words. I got them here to get my own back on them. They once played a nasty trick on me in Liverpool. They put something awful in the beer I was serving and it made loads of folks sick. They blamed me.

So this is part of my revenge. Now, there's no pub in Liverpool will have them. They're tuneless. They try to sing all the Beatles songs and make a terrible hash of them. I thought I'd teach Claude a lesson as well. You'll not tell your husband, will you? About Claude acting as a bookie?'

'I think the best lesson for Claude is to lose a lot of his new-found wealth, don't you, Gina?'

'Just what I thought, Mrs Rowan!'

'Then let's go along with his scheme, shall we?'

'Sure,' smiled Gina.

That night, Nick paid an early visit to the Aidensfield Arms and noticed a blue car in the car park. Before entering the premises, he examined the vehicle and saw that it had some slight damage to the front nearside wing. In the lights of the pub, he also saw some black paint adhering to the wing and quickly he scraped a sample into his plastic envelope. He noted the registration number too, then went inside, ostensibly to check that everything was in order. Routine visits to pubs were normal for any policeman on a Saturday night so his early presence would not seem odd.

When he went into the bar, he saw a man sitting alone in one corner with a pint of beer before him. Judging from the description given by Alf, this was Mark Sutton, but Nick decided not to confront the youth at this point. He wanted to catch him in action at the hall, if that was where he was planning to be later tonight. Some two tables away, he saw the Mersey Hounds.

'Isn't it time you lads were getting down to the hall?' he asked. 'The show's due to start any minute.'

'We're last on, grand finale. We thought we'd keep our heads down till then, like.'

Mark Sutton, sitting gloomily on his own, said nothing and refrained from making eye contact with Nick. Behind the bar there was a relief barmaid, Gloria Green from the village, who often stood in for George or Gina.

'Gina not here tonight?' asked Nick.

'No,' said Gloria. 'She wants to go to the talent show, so I'm holding the fort. Her Uncle George is having a go.'

'There's some top-quality acts on tonight!' smiled Nick, turning to leave. 'I hope they raise a lot of money for the kids' football club.'

Nick strolled up to the village hall. Already, there were lots of cars parked outside with people milling around the entrance. He saw children dressed in tutus, scouts with trumpets and bugles, gymnasts, some handbell ringers, adults in barber-shop outfits, several youngsters dressed as the Beatles or the Rolling Stones; a whole galaxy of artistes.

Phil was buzzing about making sure things were operating to his satisfaction, while Alf, on the stage, was testing the microphones and making sure the curtains worked. Then Nick saw Claude Jeremiah hovering in the entrance. He held a small notebook and was approaching people, asking them to place their bets on a list of names he had produced.

Nick sidled up to him. 'I hope you're not loitering or frequenting a public place for the purposes of bookmaking,

135

betting or agreeing to bet, or paying, receiving or settling, bets, Claude, and I hope you are not acting as a bookmaker without a bookmaker's permit.'

Claude spluttered. 'Me, Mr Rowan? No, well, no, I'm just taking a few names down, listing the runners, er, contestants, for the local paper, getting names like reporters do at funerals, I am. If folks want to give me a bob or two for a good cause, well, I can't refuse, I can't help it if they think I'm raising money for charity, like. Always willing to help a worthwhile cause, Mr Rowan, you know me.'

'If I get proof you're running an illegal betting ring, Claude, I'll confiscate all your money.'

'You wouldn't, Mr Rowan? I mean, I've got none, it's not mine . . .'

Nick left Claude to his thoughts. Soon, the contest was under way, a cacophony of awful sounds emerging from the body of the hall.

Nick couldn't help but feel sorry for the judges who had to tolerate the racket, especially Amanda Young whom he'd bullied into this chore. As the contestants gave of their best, Nick melted into the shadows to watch for the arrival of Mark Sutton. Sure enough, once the show was about an hour old, he saw a blue car coming along the street from the Aidensfield Arms. It parked among the others in the official car park and, from the security of the darkness, Nick saw Sutton walk quickly towards the hall.

Inside, the children's section had concluded with every child taking part in a grand finale of singing and dancing. They had been trained by their school and it was a

stunning climax to that section. The applause was deaf-
ening. Alf then announced the adult section, beginning
with Sergeant Oscar Blaketon who was going to recite a
well-known verse. Nick popped into the rear of the hall
and found Phil Bellamy.

'Phil, Mark Sutton's prowling around outside. I'm going
to see what he's up to. Cover me if anything goes wrong.'

'Sutton? He's a nutter! Alf reckons he broke into the
Oddfellows just to spite me.'

'Yes, well he's here now, outside. I'm going out.'

'If you're not back in five minutes, I'll join you,'
promised Phil.

As the applause for Sergeant Blaketon died away,
George began his turn and Nick found himself creeping
around the exterior of the hall, ensuring he was concealed
by the shadows.

For a long time, nothing disturbed the dark night. Then
Nick saw Sutton emerge from the gloom at the distant end
of the hall, and run across to his car. He was tempted to
follow but realised that if Sutton was going to do something stupid, it would surely be here, at the hall, and not in
the car park. He waited, and within a few minutes, Sutton
returned. This time he was carrying the tool box from his
car.

Sutton disappeared again around the far end of the hall.
This time Nick followed, moving silently and swiftly along
the wall. Inside, he could hear Alf announcing that Gina
Ward would be next. As she launched into a top-ten hit
the air was filled with her voice. This was good, decided
Nick, that girl could sing!

As he sidled around the corner of the hall, he saw that Sutton had prised open the external fusebox; before him was an array of electrical wires and fuses. As Nick watched, Sutton switched off one of the circuit breakers and the hall was plunged into darkness. Gina, like a true professional, continued to sing.

Outside, Nick threw himself at Sutton and, struggling, managed to restore the power – just as Sutton turned upon him bearing a huge spanner. Rooted to the spot with horror, Nick realised he had every intention of using it. Just at that instant, Phil Bellamy appeared and seizing Sutton's upraised arm, brought it down in a powerful lock. The man was immobilised.

'Got you, Sutton,' gasped Bellamy.

'Bring him into the hall,' said Bellamy as Nick clipped the handcuffs around Sutton's wrists.

'There's also the matter of a hit-and-run accident last night, Sutton,' said Nick grimly. 'I've got paint samples from your car and from the bike you hit . . .'

Sutton was beside himself with drunken fury. 'He got in my way, the old buffer got in my way just like everybody else gets in my way . . .' he muttered. 'You, Bellamy, you get in my way, you get my place in the team, get my girl, you got in my way tonight. You're all bastards, the lot of you . . .'

Inside, Alf was announcing the final act.

'And now, ladies and gentlemen, we have a last-minute entry. Some young men have come all the way from Liverpool to entertain us this evening. Ladies and gentlemen, a big round of applause for the Mersey Hounds!'

They started with 'You'll Never Walk Alone' and it was awful, and then they launched into a medley of Beatles favourites, which was even worse. In a matter of minutes, the audience was booing them and calling for them to get off the stage. Alf did his best to cool their tempers as, taking advantage of the uproar, Claude Jeremiah tried to sneak out of the hall.

'Not going anywhere, are you, Claude?' said Nick who was standing at the door with Bellamy and their prisoner.

'Er, no, Mr Rowan, not me.'

'The results haven't been declared yet, have they?'

'Well, no, but I reckon those Mersey lot won't win, eh? Not them. I sponsored them, Mr Rowan, brought 'em all the way from Liverpool to play here, as a special act, you understand.'

'I understand perfectly, Claude, but I reckon the winners will be the children. Every parent bet on their own child, I hear, and every child took part in that grand finale, so if that wins, every child has won, which means you'll have to pay all the parents. So I should wait here if I was you, unless you want to be arrested and taken to Ashfordly Police Station with our friend Mr Sutton here. You'd be charged with welshing on your bets, illegally taking bets, acting as a bookmaker without a permit, loitering in a public place for the purpose of betting, and we might even consider false pretences . . .'

'I'll stay here, Mr Rowan,' Claude said quickly. 'I might have a bob or two for some of these parents, money I was looking after for 'em, you understand.'

Nick was right. In their wisdom, the judges declared

that the group of schoolchildren were the outright winners, deftly defeating any criticisms from jealous parents. They also won the children's class, while Gina, a total outsider, won the adult section.

Sutton was taken to Ashfordly Police Station to answer several charges, including the hit-and-run accident, while Claude Jeremiah went home to count his losses.

In bed that evening, Nick congratulated Kate for the joint wisdom of the judges in declaring the group of children as overall winners.

'Yes,' she agreed, 'It was Alex, you know, who suggested that. He *has* got a lot of wisdom, hasn't he?'

'And he's imparting some of it to you, Kate,' said Nick. 'So listen to him when he advises you, eh? He won't be here for ever.'

'I know,' she sighed. 'And there's somebody else who won't be here for ever, isn't there?'

'Who's that?' he asked.

'Peter Hughes. You owe him an apology, remember? So tomorrow morning, you'd better go and say sorry to him for thinking he was a hit-and-run driver.'

'Do I really have to?' he protested.

'Yes you do!' she told him.

CHAPTER EIGHT

'Every time I see you with a woman, Phil, it's a different one!' said Nick to his friend PC Phil Bellamy in the bar of the Aidensfield Arms. 'You'll have to settle down a bit. Look at all the bother when you took Margaret Ellison from that idiot, Sutton. He nearly ruined the talent show and almost spoilt your football club money-raising; he caused no end of bother.' He gave his friend a long look.

'Now I've heard you're knocking about with a woman who's pally with one of our local villains. That really is asking for trouble and you know it.'

Phil clutched his pint to him protectively. 'Leave off, Nick, my private life's my own, right? There's no law says I can't have which woman I want.'

'There's no law, true, but there is common sense! Why take up with Debbie Chapman of all people? I take it Scarman doesn't know?'

Phil looked at Nick in alarm. 'Who said she was Scarman's woman? I didn't think anybody knew, Nick. How the hell did you find out?'

'I keep my eyes and ears open, Phil, and because you're

my mate, I care what happens to you. Now I don't know this girl, she might be OK, but all I'm saying is keep a low profile and for God's sake don't let Scarman find out. Anyway, how did you get involved with her?'

'Through a domestic in Strensford. I went along to sort it out. Scarman had thrown Debbie out on to the street with nothing and, well, I just came along at the right time. She'd tried to make a break from him, she'd got a flat of her own, but he found her and told her to come back to him. I happened to be there to pick up the pieces.'

'To the rescue like a knight in shining armour?'

'More like a constable in big boots. Anyway, I was a shoulder for her to cry on, and it developed from there. She needed someone, Nick, and it happened to be me. She's a decent woman, she's too good for the likes of Jack Scarman.'

Nick shook his head philosophically. 'Well, you're over twenty-one and should know what you're doing. Now, another pint?'

'No thanks,' said Phil. 'I'm on nights in Ashfordly, I start at ten. It's time I was making tracks.'

Nick looked at his watch. It was nine o'clock. He decided he would go home too. It had been pleasant having an evening off duty and being able to have a drink with a pal. Phil drove away as Nick walked through Aidensfield towards his police house. He savoured the fresh moorland air, the peace of the village, the calm and quiet drama of the surrounding moors. He reckoned Kate would be home by now. She'd been speaking at the WI tonight, about her work as a doctor in a vast moorland practice, and she'd said she hoped to finish around nine. WI meetings didn't continue late into the night!

It was in fact almost ten thirty when Kate arrived home. Nick had had some tea and sandwiches for his supper.

'Sorry I'm late back,' she apologised. 'I called in to see Alex. I was worried, leaving him alone and in charge of the practice while I was out, but he said he wanted to do it.'

'How is he these days?' asked Nick, echoing the concern of the entire village. Everyone could see that Dr Ferrenby was far from well and there was widespread concern for him. In his time at Aidensfield, he had become a much-loved and respected part of the community.

'He tends to get very confused about things,' Kate said. 'Yesterday morning, he came into the surgery in his pyjamas; he'd been in bed and thought there was a call-out.'

'And wasn't there?'

'No, I think he'd dreamt it. Then he gets very distressed when he discovers he's made himself look silly, but I do understand. I try to humour him. The truth is, Nick, I'm not sure what to do with him. He's becoming something of a liability, if I'm honest. It's getting to the point where I'm not sure he can deal properly with the patients.'

'He's had a couple of severe setbacks, luv. That attack by the raiders and then the train crash, that combination was enough to upset anybody, let alone a man who's getting on in years. He needs to get away again. He did go to his brother's, didn't he? Could he go somewhere else for a longer break?'

'Lord Ashfordly says he can have a day's shooting any time he wants. That'd be restful, but I think he needs to go away for several weeks. I might see if there's anywhere like a convalescent home that takes in doctors in need of rest and care.'

'You could always pack him off on a fishing holiday,' Nick suggested. 'They're advertised all over the place. A fortnight in Scotland perhaps?'

Kate shook her head doubtfully. 'He's best not left on his own, Nick, he needs somebody around to look after him, especially when he does these silly things. Anyway, I'll keep my eyes open for something suitable. How was your evening?'

'A quite drink with Phil, that's all. I warned him about his love life. He does seem to pick up women who are likely to cause him trouble.'

Kate grinned. 'So who's his present lady love?'

'He's knocking about with Jack Scarman's ex-girlfriend now. Somebody called Debbie Chapman.'

'Scarman? Who's he?'

'A local businessman operating just inside the law; he's into greyhound racing, property development, amusement arcades, gambling machines, that sort of thing. Always on the edge of respectability, but never quite makes it. A bit cheap and flashy, no substance. But nasty when people disobey him. He's not averse to beating the living daylights out of people who cross him but they're always too frightened to complain officially. We can never touch him, he's clever.'

'So what's Phil Bellamy doing getting tangled up with one of his cast-offs?'

'He thinks he's in love!' laughed Nick. 'Love makes us all go funny in the head! Come on, how about an early night?'

Kate smiled knowingly. 'Whatever you say, my Lord and Master!'

'Maybe I'm in love too,' chuckled Nick, and Kate hit him playfully on the arm.

But even as they were climbing the stairs, the telephone rang. They looked at one another and, as one, said, 'It's your turn!'

'You're nearest,' said Kate, running to the top of the stairs and leaving Nick stranded halfway. He plodded down to the office to take the call.

'Aidensfield Police,' he said.

'It's Alf Ventress,' said the familiar voice from Ashfordly Police Station. 'Sorry to ring you, Nick, but there's been a shop-breaking.'

'Where? Aidensfield?'

'No, Ashfordly. St Nicholas Pawnbrokers. I'm alone in the office, I can't attend. You'll have to go, Nick.'

'Me? But isn't Phil on duty in Ashfordly? It's his responsibility, Alf, not mine. I'm supposed to be off duty.'

'He's not answering our calls, Nick. He missed his last point, I can't raise him.'

'Oh, bloody hell, he's not been knocked on the head, has he?'

'I thought I'd give him a bit of time before I raise any alarm, but the shop-breaking needs immediate attention. The owner's at the shop now, waiting for a policeman. He's a Mr Raymond Smailes and there's a witness called Harris.'

'I'm on my way,' said Nick. 'You'll call the fingerprint department and photographer?'

'Leave it to me. A dark minivan with a loud exhaust was seen leaving the vicinity and might be linked. I'm circulating details to all mobiles and fixed stations. You never know, some bright constable might drop across it before it has the chance to ditch the stolen goods.'

'Thanks, Alf, I'll call in when I've interviewed the shop-owner.' Resigned to his task, Nick went to find a civilian jacket, and his notebook and warrant card.

'What is it?' Kate's voice came from the top of the stairs.

'Call-out, luv, I'm sorry, a shop-breaking at the pawn-broker's in Ashfordly. I've got to go.'

'Isn't Phil on duty?'

'They can't find him,' said Nick, reaching for his keys. 'I'm in civvies, so I can pretend I'm CID. I hope Phil's not got himself into trouble.'

'Be careful,' she said, running down the stairs to kiss him goodbye.

Raymond Smailes ran his pawnbroking business in pre-mises which adjoined his second-hand bookshop; it was named after St Nicholas, the patron saint of pawnbrokers, better known as Santa Claus. Ironically, a lot of the goods in the shop were unwanted Christmas presents.

There were two separate shops which shared a common entrance, and the thief or thieves had smashed the glass of the door leading into the pawnbroker's. They had slid back the bolts on the inside and then viciously kicked the door to smash the Yale lock. Once the door was open, they had entered to quickly remove several silver items and an assortment of other objects. These included some binoculars, a camera, and some small pieces of jewellery and glassware. It was all fairly good quality merchandise. The rubbish had been left behind.

The crime had been discovered by a Mr Alan Harris who had been walking his spaniel in the vicinity; he'd heard the smash of glass and the sound of splintering wood, but initially had been unable to determine the precise source of the noise. As he'd toured the narrow, winding streets to investigate, he'd heard the sound of a departing vehicle, one which was very distinctive because of the excessive noise which seemed to come from the exhaust.

He'd started to run towards the noise and had been in time to see a small minivan hurtle out of an alleyway next door to the pawnbroker's. In the dim light from the streetlamps, it had been impossible to determine its colour, except to say it was dark. It might have been dark blue, dark green or even black, but the noise it made was unforgettable. He had not, however, been able to see the registration number. Mr Harris, who knew Smailes well, had rushed to a telephone kiosk to ring the police, and PC Ventress had immediately circulated the somewhat limited details of the van in the vain hope that some patrolling constable might be able to halt it while it still carried the stolen goods. He'd then called out the owner of the premises, Raymond Smailes; he and Harris were both in the shop when Nick arrived.

'I can't give you a precise list of things that have been stolen,' apologised Smailes. 'It'll mean checking my pledge book against my sales ledger, although I can give a rough idea of what's missing.'

'A rough idea will be good enough to start with,' said Nick. 'If we can catch the van with the stuff in it, we'll be able to convict the thief. Now, I'm going to search the whole premises, just to make sure no one's hiding here.'

The rear door, the one used by Mr Smailes when he locked the shop up, was secure, and none of the other windows or doors had been smashed. Nick searched the stock room, the toilet and the rear portions of the premises, but found nothing.

He went back to speak to Mr Harris, who was still holding his spaniel on a lead. 'This van, Mr Harris, what can you remember about it?'

Alan Harris, a widower in his late sixties, could not add a great deal. He repeated his story about hearing the smashing of glass and the splintering of wood some time before the dark-coloured minivan roared away. But apart from that, he could add little more, except to say that only one person appeared to be in the van's front seats. He could not provide any description of that person. Nick took down the details he required for his crime report, thanked Mr Harris for his public-spiritedness, and asked

Mr Smailes to wait for the arrival of the fingerprint and photographic officers. He must not touch anything in the meantime, although he could begin to compile a list of the stolen goods.

Nick returned to Ashfordly Police Station to provide Alf Ventress with an update and was pleased to learn that Alf had made all the necessary arrangements for circulating the crime.

'Any sign of Phil?' he asked Alf.

'No, not a word. I'm thinking about calling out Sergeant Blaketon, but if Phil's just skiving, I don't want to land him on a disciplinary charge. He should have been at his point, he should have been available to deal with the shop-breaking.'

'When's his next point, Alf?' Policemen made points at telephone kiosks in case the office required them. If they were needed, the phone in the kiosk would ring.

'Five minutes, he's due at the kiosk outside the post office.'

'I'll go and wait there myself,' said Nick. 'If he's there, I'll tell him to report in.'

'Right, and thanks for attending the break-in. The boffins are *en route* now.'

Nick returned to the centre of Ashfordly and walked towards the telephone kiosk outside the small post office. Sure enough, Phil Bellamy appeared, his hair all awry looking harassed, rushed and dishevelled. He failed to spot Nick standing in the shadows and took up his stance near the kiosk.

After a few moments Nick approached him. 'And

where the hell have you been, Phil?'

Phil started at the sudden voice. 'God, you scared me, Nick. What are you doing here?'

'I asked where you'd been, Phil. I might have been Sergeant Blaketon or even the Inspector; fortunately for you, it's me.'

'Look, I had to see to something that cropped up . . .'

Nick's eyebrows rose in disbelief. 'A woman, Phil? Have you been with a woman?'

'Nick, what's all this about?'

'There's been a shop-breaking, and I was called out to it.'

'Oh, bloody hell!'

'CID are there now, photographers and fingerprint department, and somebody, somewhere, sometime, is going to ask where you were. It was on your beat, Phil, I thought you were door-knobbing. You'd better have a bloody good story.'

'Where was it?'

'St Nicholas Pawnbrokers.'

'God! I checked it, not long after half past ten. It was secure then, I tried the door handle, I swear it.'

'But you missed your point, Phil, and when Alf tried to raise you, you weren't there . . . It's not down to me to quiz you about what you were doing, but you'd better have a bloody good reason for your absence ready for when Blaketon starts asking questions. I'd suggest you get round to that shop now, have words with the owner and the CID, tell Alf you're not lying anywhere with your head bashed in and then get back to work. Then I can go home.'

'Look, Nick, I'm sorry. I didn't want you to cover up for me . . .'

'Forget it, but don't expect it to happen every time, right?'

Phil Bellamy strode off looking highly embarrassed and worried. He didn't glance back at Nick.

Early next morning, Claude Jeremiah Greengrass was in his battered old pick-up truck.

Accompanied by Alfred, he had been engaged upon what he would describe as 'personal business which was nowt to do with the law'. As they bowled along, Alfred sat on the passenger seat with his head out of the window, enjoying the scents of the fresh moorland air. Greengrass was in a cheerful mood too, humming a Beatles' tune. As he bumped down the rough lane, he passed a meadow on the outskirts of Aidensfield. To his astonishment, a lithe jet-black greyhound was streaking across the field, moving with the magnificent power of a champion and all the style of a thoroughbred. It was a beautiful sight, a dreamlike moment in the life of Claude Jeremiah Greengrass. Entranced, he eased his old pick-up truck to a halt to watch.

This was the kind of dog that could win races and, reasoned Claude, if it could win races, it would win him lots of money. He struggled out of his van to peer over the hedge and so gain a better view. As the dog tore across the turf, Claude saw that it had a distinctive white flash on its head, but apart from that, it was a beautiful polished jet-black colour and seemed to be in first-class condition.

At the far end of the meadow was a young man, about eighteen years old who seemed to be controlling the greyhound, calling it to him and then making it run across the open field.

Claude watched for a few minutes without the youth or the dog knowing of his presence, and the more he watched, the more his admiration increased.

'Now that's a real greyhound,' he told Alfred, then asked, 'But who's the kid?'

The youth looked like a senior schoolboy, a nice, pleasant and somewhat innocent lad, but Claude decided that it would be inappropriate, at this early stage, to introduce himself. He had plans for that dog, plans to which its owner might not give ready consent. So he watched for a few more minutes, then drove away.

Later that morning, Claude went to the Aidensfield Arms to begin his quest for information about the greyhound and its young master. After buying a drink for Gina, he ordered a pint for himself, then asked, 'Gina, my young friend, you know most of the youngsters round here, don't you? Handsome lads, you know. Heartthrobs. Good-lookers like me.'

'Some of them, but not all, Claude.'

'Well, it's a lad with a greyhound, lives somewhere nearby, I reckon. Nice-looking dog, I thought.'

'That'll be David Parrish. He often comes into the village to get things for his grandad. They live up at Ghyll End, haven't been there long. It's a smallholding, his grandad took it on when he retired. He keeps a few cows and moor sheep.'

Claude blinked and nodded his head. 'Oh, aye, I know it. A bit run-down, not well kept like mine.'

'Mr Parrish isn't very fit, he's got chest problems, so David does most of the work, when he's not at school. He's at Ashfordly Grammar School doing his A levels. He hopes to go to university, he wants to be a vet.'

'He's obviously an animal lover. Him and me could be mates, you know, we're so alike in our choice of animal,' beamed Claude. 'Well, thanks for that Gina, it's nice to know who's living in the spot. Now, I'll have another pint.'

For a moment, Gina wondered why Claude Jeremiah should be interested in young Parrish but it was none of her business. She pulled him his pint, then turned away to serve another customer.

Claude realised that David Parrish would be at school now; the boy had obviously been exercising his dog before catching the school bus. Claude decided he could wait. There was no great rush to put his plans into action. He knew that, not far away near Maddleskirk, there was a training day in progress for some of the local greyhounds which were being prepared for the prestigious Maddleskirk Trophy. After draining his pint, Claude departed from the pub and turned along the Maddleskirk road.

It was here that Wilf Welford ran his boarding kennels, one of his sidelines being the training of the greyhounds of a few local owners. Claude had often halted awhile to observe the dogs in training before visiting the local tracks to wager some cash upon them.

Today he wanted to see Jack Scarman's dog, Northern Flash, in action. Local gossip was that Scarman had paid a lot of money for Northern Flash, an all-black dog, but that the dog had not come up to expectations – hence Claude's visit this afternoon.

There was a group of about twenty men watching the events which comprised several training races. Among the group Claude noticed Jack Scarman. His dark hair was greased back and he smoked a large cigar as he stood among the men with Debbie, his present girlfriend, at his side. Wilf Welford was there too; he looked more than a little worried and carried a stopwatch as he prepared some dogs for a training gallop.

'Put him up against the best you've got,' Scarman shouted. 'I want him to race against the best, I want to win that Maddleskirk Trophy. And you're going to get my dog into peak condition for it, aren't you?'

'I'll do my best, Jack, but if the dog's no good . . .'

'No good,' bellowed Scarman. 'But you recommended it! You said I should buy it, that it would be a good investment. You told me it had all the signs of being a winner, the best dog you'd seen for years, you said. Now, let's see what you've done with it. You're the trainer. Run it now while I'm here.'

And so several dogs were brought to the track and placed in the traps, Northern Flash among them.

Distinctive due to his colouring, the dog waited for the off, as keen as all the others. Wilf started the artificial hare. It rattled around the course and once the dogs had it in their sights, the traps were lifted and the dogs leapt forward to give chase. There was no shouting and cheering as there would have been on a real track, but then Scarman had no cause to cheer. Northern Flash was hopeless; it trailed in behind all the others, a sorry specimen. Scarman was furious; his face showed his massive anger and embarrassment as the dog was brought forward. Debbie bent to pet it, but Scarman snarled, 'Leave it, leave the stupid animal. Just think what money I've put into that useless dog. If I enter that for the Maddleskirk Trophy, I'll be laughed off the track.'

'I did my best with him, Jack,' Wilf said, 'but it's just not there. He hasn't got what it takes. I honestly don't think he could win the Maddleskirk Trophy, certainly not against the opposition I know 'll be there on the day.'

Scarman softened a little, disappointment now taking over from his initial anger. 'Take the bloody thing away, Wilf, till I decide what to do with him.'

As the unhappy Wilf Welford led Northern Flash into the Kennels, Claude Jeremiah came forward.

'It's a pity about your dog, Jack, he looks good. What looks best when you buy, though, can perform least well when you expect it, eh?'

'What are you trying to say, Greengrass?' snapped Scarman.

'Well, I mean, you being set on a winner, like, it's only natural you'd be upset at that performance.'

'Upset? That dog could beat them others if they were racing on three legs!'

'Well, as I said, you don't always get what you see, do

you?' Claude's voice had lowered now and there was a tone of conspiracy in his voice. Scarman did not miss it.

'What are you saying, Claude?'

'I'm saying you want to win the Maddleskirk Trophy and I might be the chap to help you, if you know what I mean. Hush hush and all that.'

Scarman glanced around him. 'Go and sit in the car, Debbie, I want to talk business with Claude.'

And so the two men went off to sit in Scarman's Jaguar while Northern Flash was locked in his kennel.

As a direct result of that discussion, Claude Jeremiah went to Ghyll End to speak with young David Parrish. He arrived at the house just as David was leaving with the beautiful dog; it was teatime and David had returned from school.

'By, that's a nice-looking animal.' Claude patted the dog, taking the opportunity to run his hands expertly over its body. 'Fit an' all, I shouldn't wonder.'

'Yes, he runs well. Jimbo's his name.'

'Aye, well, I was just passing and brought some eggs and a brace of pheasants for your grandad. I heard he wasn't too well, so me, being a nearish neighbour like, felt I wanted to fetch him summat, show him we cared sort of thing. Greengrass is the name.'

'I'm David Parrish,' smiled the youngster. 'I'd take you in to see grandad, but he's in bed, resting. He was up all night, with his chest.'

'He needs seeing to,' proffered Claude.

'Dr Ferrenby's being seeing to him. I rang the surgery to ask him to pop in when he's passing, he might have something that'll make grandad breathe better.'

Claude nodded, blinking ingratiatingly. 'Well, I reckon he's in good hands, with you about to help him. Now, this dog of yours, he's a real sparkler, eh? How do you fancy running him on a proper track, just for a bit of fun?'

'A racetrack? Where?'

'Not a proper race, you understand, just a bit of fun, over at Welford's kennels. Me and some mates run a dog or two there. I reckon your Jimbo would enjoy an outing with 'em.'

'Well, I've never had anything to do with greyhound racing, but I suppose it would be all right.'

'Right, well, how about me calling for you tomorrow, after school. We'll see what Jimbo can do, eh? Just as a bit of fun.'

'Yes, all right,' said David, shrugging his shoulders innocently.

'Tomorrow, then,' beamed Claude. 'My treat, I'll come and pick you up.'

The same morning Nick received a telephone call that excited him tremendously.

When he'd lifted the receiver, a voice had said, 'Get yourself down to Williams's lock-ups in Pasture Lane, Ashfordly, Number 17. You'll find the pawnbroker's stuff in there.'

'Who's that?' Nick had asked the caller, but the telephone had gone dead. Normally suspicious of anonymous calls, Nick nonetheless decided this had to be checked out, so he rang Ashfordly Police Station and spoke to Alf Ventress.

'Alf, I'm coming down to Ashfordly. I got a tip-off just now that the pawnbroker's stuff is in a lock-up in Pasture Lane. Can you tell Sergeant Blaketon?'

'Sure. Keep in touch,' said Alf.

Nick then rang the owner of the garages, Ian Williams, and asked him to be there with a master key.

Half an hour later, Nick rode his motorcycle on to the parking area of the garages and found a young man with a mop of thick ginger hair and a beard awaiting his arrival.

'I'm Ian Williams,' said the man. 'What's all this about?'

Nick explained about the raid on the pawnbroker's shop, something Williams had heard about in Ashfordly gossip, and then referred to his anonymous tip-off.

'The caller said the stuff was here, in Number 17. Would you know who rents it?'

'Sure, I brought the files with me. We rent these places by the month, payable in advance. I keep good records.' He turned to his books. 'Yes, here we are. A chap called Peter Bennett. He paid cash for a week in advance on Number 17.'

'Well, I don't know the name,' admitted Nick. 'He's not one of our local villains. Can I have a look inside?'

'I can't see why not. If he's innocent, he's got nothing to fear, has he?'

Williams inserted his master key in the lock and the doors swung open to reveal a single garage space, but with no motor vehicle in residence. At first, the space looked deserted but then Nick spotted a holdall at the back. He strode in to examine it and, zipping it open, found it was full of silverware, jewellery and other items. He saw a pair of binoculars too, and a camera.

'What's all that?' Williams was standing over him, staring at the haul.

'I think it's the stuff from the pawnbroker's shop,' Nick said quietly. 'I'll have to take it there for identification, but I reckon I need to know Mr Bennett's address now.'

'I knew nothing of this,' spluttered Williams. 'I'm not in the habit of letting my premises out for criminal purposes.'

'I believe you,' Nick said calmly. 'So where's this guy live, Mr Williams?'

Once again, Williams turned to his files and, after flicking through several sheets, indicated an entry. Nick began to write down the address, then stopped in a state of shock.

It was the address of Phil Bellamy's flat.

CHAPTER NINE

Nick's first duty was to take the holdall to the pawn-broker's shop for inspection by Raymond Smailes. Under Nick's guidance, he checked the contents without hand-ling them, merely opening the bag wide enough to obtain a sighting.

'It's not all here, Mr Rowan, but there's a good half of the stuff, I reckon. I can definitely say all the items in this bag came from my shop.'

'That's all I need for now,' Nick said. 'I'll have to take these things away with me for fingerprinting, but you'll get them back in due course.'

'Can I ask where you found them?'

'It's a bit peculiar, Mr Smailes, but I got an anonymous telephone call about it. I found them in a lock-up garage here in Ashfordly, but I hope they'll lead us to the thief.'

Nick's next job was to take the goods to the police station and inform Sergeant Blaketon of the grim news about Bellamy's address having surfaced during enquiries. As he entered with the holdall in his hand Sergeant Blaketon was beaming.

'Well, Rowan, Ventress has told me the good news. You've got the stuff, then?'

'Not all of it, Sarge, but there's about half of it here, Smailes has identified it. Without touching, I might add. Alf can send the stuff away for fingerprint examination.'

'Well, this is a good piece of work, a bit of luck on our part, eh? So who's our anonymous informant?'

'I wish I knew, Sarge, but he did lead us right to this loot. There's more information, though, a name and an address.'

'You're joking?'

'False name I think, but real address, Sarge. The chap who rented the garage said his name was Peter Bennett, and he gave this address.'

Nick showed the address to Sergeant Blaketon and then thrust it under the nose of Phil Bellamy. There was a deathly hush in the room as Bellamy reacted.

'That's my address,' he said. 'Bloody hell . . . hey, you don't think . . .'

'In my office, now. Bellamy and Rowan. Ventress, not a word about this, not a whisper outside this office, not yet. Understand? You get busy packaging those exhibits for CID to check them over for fingerprints.'

'Yes, Sergeant.'

Blaketon led the two young constables along the passage and into his office where he slammed the door.

Bellamy was looking sick with worry and Nick was grim-faced; it really looked as if Phil was in the frame for this crime.

'Is this some kind of joke?' Phil croaked as he faced his inquisitors.

'No, Bellamy, this is not a joke. Rowan, tell us exactly what's happened so far. And I don't need to remind you, Bellamy, that you were absent from your beat at the precise moment of this crime, weren't you? I've still not had a convincing account of what you were doing at the material time, and the duty log does show that Constable Rowan had to visit the scene in your place, because of your absence from duty. So, Rowan, you explain things.'

Nick outlined his enquires so far, concluding with the anonymous telephone call which had led him to the lock-up containing the stolen property.

When Nick had finished his account, Phil looked desperately nervous, not at all his usual cheerful and confident self.

'But Sarge, I'm no criminal, this has nothing to do with me,' he protested feebly.

'That's not how it looks from my point of view, Bellamy.' Sergeant Blaketon's face was ashen. 'A crime has been committed on your beat and you were absent at the material time, and so far, you've not volunteered any satisfactory explanation.'

'I didn't break into the shop, Sergeant, you've got to believe me!'

Blaketon continued as if Bellamy had not spoken. 'Next we have a lock-up premises rented by a man giving a false name – though with your initials, and with your correct address.'

'I didn't rent the place, Sergeant . . .'

163

Blaketon still ignored him as he continued, 'And stolen goods were found in the premises you apparently rented under a false name. What am I to think about all this, Bellamy? Can I ignore what the facts are telling me?'

'It's a set up, Sarge, it's got to be.'

Nick felt the time had come to weigh in on his friend's side. 'Sergeant, in my opinion, this whole thing stinks. If Phil was the villain, he would never have given his real address. And who made that call to me? It could only be the burk who put the stuff there for me to find. It's all been laid on, Sergeant, it's got all the hallmarks of a set-up. It stinks, it really stinks does this one.'

'And it stinks to me, Rowan,' Blaketon replied drily. 'Right, Bellamy, I must now warn you that I intend to search your flat immediately. Come on, Rowan, I need you as a witness.'

'No, Sergeant, this is terrible . . . please, no. I'm not guilty.' Bellamy was distraught now.

'Shut up, Bellamy, the less you say the better. Rowan, bring the car round to the door. I hate this as much as you, Bellamy, but I must do my duty.'

Within fifteen minutes, they were entering Bellamy's tiny bachelor flat; it was untidy with unwashed crockery in the sink and dirty clothing lying all over the bedroom floor. The living room needed dusting and there were dirty cups and plates on the floor in front of the television set.

'Sarge, I'm sorry about the state of the place . . .'

'I am not concerned with the state of the place, Bellamy, even if it is like a pig sty. I am looking for evidence of your involvement in a crime. I am seeking stolen property and if I find it, you will be arrested and escorted to the cells. Do I make myself clear?'

Phil slumped on to his settee in embarrassed silence as Blaketon ferreted among his belongings, turning out drawers and inspecting the wardrobe and kitchen cupboards. Nick, meanwhile, noticed a photograph on the bedside cabinet and examined it; it was of a woman in a glamour pose. He was sure he'd seen her around the town, in the company of Jack Scarman, perhaps in one of the pubs. He made no comment and replaced the photograph.

After half an hour's intense searching, Sergeant Blaketon said, 'PC Bellamy, there is nothing here to further implicate you. I shall place that on record. But you know the procedure now? Due to the weight of evidence already available, I am obliged to suspend you from duty as from this moment. Now, hand me your warrant card.'

Almost in tears, Phil Bellamy opened his wallet and passed his warrant card over to the sergeant.

Once again Nick spoke up for his friend. 'Sergeant, this needs to be investigated at the highest level. I'm sure Phil's been set up, this doesn't add up.'

'I am perfectly aware of the seriousness of the situation and I am equally aware of the likelihood of Bellamy being framed, but the entire affair must be impartially investigated under the procedures laid down by the Discipline Code. Rules must be followed, Rowan. The matter will receive the most stringent scrutiny, I can assure you. Now, one of those rules is that serving officers do not have any contact with officers who are suspended from duty. You will therefore have no further discussion or contact with Mr Bellamy until this matter has been resolved. Is that clear?'

Phil looked at Nick and there was a moment of dreadful silence as the two friends began to appreciate the appalling consequences of Phil's predicament.

'Come on, Rowan, back to the office,' said Sergeant Blaketon. 'We've got work to do.'

Greengrass had taken David Parrish to watch Wilf Welford's greyhounds in training. There was the usual small crowd of bystanders, including Jack Scarman and his girl, Debbie. The track owner, Wilf Welford, was also there.

Greengrass and David Parrish were standing together some distance from the edge of the track, while a series of starts and mock races were held. Alfred, Greengrass's lurcher, was tied to the pick-up tailgate, while Claude was airing his knowledge to the youngster who held Jimbo on a leash. Jimbo, seeing the other dogs in action, was whimpering and quivering, anxious to be among them.

'How about your Jimbo having a run?' Greengrass suggested. 'Just to get the feel of things. It's in his blood, son, you can see that. Look at him, he can't wait to get running.'

'Well, if you think it will be all right, Mr Greengrass.'

Greengrass blinked and twitched. 'All right? Course it'll be all right. These are my friends, business colleagues, men of like interests to me, countrymen, like you and your grandad. Now, what these dogs need is a good pacer,

David, a dog that's not racing, but one that'll set 'em a pace, to make 'em go faster, to train 'em. I reckon your Jimbo's just the chap to do that. Come on, fetch him over and we'll show 'em what a good dog can do.'

Claude shambled over to Jack Scarman and Wilf.

'Now then,' he said. 'I've brought along this dog I was telling you about, Jack. Lovely mover, do you fancy seeing him perform? If you need a pacer for this lot, Jimbo'll fill the bill.'

Scarman nodded to Wilf. 'Give him a run, Wilf, set him up with the best you've got – and put Northern Flash in as well.'

'As you say, Jack,' said Welford, taking Jimbo's leash and leading him towards the track. David watched with some apprehension as Jimbo was bundled into the traps along with several other dogs. Northern Flash was brought from the kennels too.

'He's a dead ringer for your dog is that one,' smiled Claude. 'Good job your Jimbo has a white patch on his head, eh? Otherwise you'd never tell 'em apart.'

'He's not used to racing, Mr Greengrass,' said David.

'No, that's why he'll do well as a pacer for these others, they'll learn from him. Now, shut up everybody, they're ready for off.'

With his right arm held high, Wilf indicated that the mechanical hare was about to be set in motion, then his arm dropped to start the run. With a trundling sound, the hare began its circuit. As it rumbled past the traps, the gates were lifted high and the dogs exploded from their places, streaking after the hare with long, loping strides.

The inexperienced Jimbo was slightly slow in leaving the trap but the excitement of the moment reached him and he burst out, rapidly catching the others with tongue lolling as he flew after the speeding hare.

'Look at that . . .' Claude was almost beside himself with excitement. 'Just look at that dog . . . by, I've never seen owt run like that . . .'

Scarman watched with never a word. He showed no emotion as Jimbo overtook the field and raced home the clear and undoubted winner. Scarman's own dog, Northern Flash, came in a poor last.

'What do you think to that, young David?' beamed Claude Jeremiah, placing his arm around the lad's shoulders. 'How about that for a thrill, eh? That dog of yours is some pacer!'

'You said he'd be good, Mr Greengrass.'

'Well, I know my dogs, you see. I'm a bit of an expert, modest with it, mind, but well respected in these parts by those who know.'

'I never thought of him as a racing dog.'

'Well,' said Greengrass with an avaricious grin on his face, 'I never said he was a racer. He's a pacer, one that sets the standard for other dogs when they're in training. Now, having seen Jimbo run here, I reckon he could help those others train up for the Maddleskirk Trophy. I don't think he's up to winning standard himself, not on a proper track with crowds and noise and distractions, so don't forget that was just a training race. What we need is to have Jimbo down here regular like, to get those racers fit, set 'em against him on a daily basis. Then, in time, he might even be allowed a race or two himself, but not just yet. That comes later. This is his sort of apprenticeship, if you understand. What do you think about that, then, about Jimbo coming down here regular, to be pacer?'

'I'll have to have words with my grandad . . .'

'No, keep him out of it. Let's make it our secret, shall we? A surprise, a sort of get-well surprise, if you understand. It'll do him a world of good to know his dog's helping to train those less capable than himself but he's got enough on just now, with that illness of his. Now, I forgot to say, you'll get paid for fetching him here.'

'Paid? It's funny you should mention that. I was hoping to get a job in the school holidays, before I go to college, just to earn some money of my own. I do help Grandad, but he can't afford to pay me, though he does keep me, buys my food and clothes and things. It would be nice to have a spot of money of my own.'

'Well, that dog's your answer! Say no more. Let's start now,' continued Claude. 'Here's twenty quid.'

'Twenty quid?' echoed David.

'That's just for starters, but not a word to your grandad.'

'But this is a fortune, I'd never earn this in a week!'

'It's the sort of money a good dog can earn his master, son. It's to show what's to come, if you play your cards right and go along with my plans.'

'Well,' said David, 'I suppose it would be a nice surprise, he would proud of Jimbo helping others.'

'Proud, he'd be more than proud. He might even be rich when Jimbo's trained up to be a racer. That's what we're aiming for. So shall I have words with Wilf, to have him booked in here regular like? For training sessions, pacing them other dogs?'

'Does it cost anything?'

'Look, I'll see to any costs, right? As a gesture from me, as a token of my faith in your dog. Consider it done. You go and collect Jimbo now, and I'll talk to Wilf.'

But as the youngster went off to collect his splendid greyhound, Greengrass went over to Jack Scarman and said, 'Well, Jack, how about it then? Was that a dog or wasn't it? Didn't I say I had an eye for a dog.'

'Shut up, Claude, don't go bragging all over the district. This is between you and me and nobody else. Now, as you say, you can hardly tell those dogs apart, except for that white patch . . .'

'Just what I was thinking, Jack. And a white patch is easily covered up, eh? And he did leave your dog standing, didn't he? And all them others. Now, I know how much the Maddleskirk Trophy means to you . . .'

'All right, Claude, you don't have to say any more. It's on. Now you get this Jimbo down here on a regular basis, get him used to running and to the crowds. I want him racing fit, able to take on the best in a packed noisy stadium. Right?'

'It's already been fixed, Jack,' grinned Claude, 'me being summat of an entrepreneur.'

'Right. Make his training as realistic as possible. Then on the night, it'll be Northern Flash who's carrying my money. I think we understand the arrangement? There'll be summat in it for you, naturally.'

'Naturally,' beamed Claude. 'Leave it to me, I've got this lad eating out of my hand.'

'I'll be in the Aidensfield Arms tonight,' nodded Scarman. 'Be there, I'll buy you a drink.'

'As you say, Jack. I wouldn't miss that for anything.'

Claude took David and his dog home in the old pick-up, with the greyhound inside and Alfred in the rear. When they arrived back at Parrish's house, Dr Rowan's yellow Triumph Herald was parked outside. Kate was just leaving.

'Oh, hello, David,' she smiled. 'And Mr Greengrass. Been exercising your dogs, have you?'

'Yes, Mr Greengrass has shown me the greyhound track,' beamed David. 'He let Jimbo have a run . . . he did really well.'

'It was just a bit of fun, you understand, Dr Rowan, lads having fun with their dogs, nowt serious.'

'Of course it was a bit of fun,' smiled Kate. 'Now, David, I've seen your grandfather, he's got respiratory problems as you know. He has terrible trouble getting his breath sometimes. He's really Dr Ferrenby's patient, but Dr Ferrenby's not too good himself these days.'

'Grandad said Dr Ferrenby wasn't very well.'

'No, so I've come instead. I've examined your grandfather, and he tells me he does a bit of animal farming?'

'Yes, we keep a few calves for fattening, and a few sheep on the moor.'

'But he never did farming before he came to Aidensfield?'

'No, he's a townie, Dr Rowan, and when he retired he thought he'd like to have a small farm with some livestock. He's always liked animals, you see. And me, I like them too, so I came here to help him. I've always wanted to live and work in the countryside. I fancy being a vet.'

'Well, I hope you achieve your ambition. Now, so far as your grandfather is concerned, I've got a sample of his blood, which I'm having examined, and I've told him not to work with the animals until I've got the results through. So that means more work for you, I'm afraid, feeding the calves and so on.'

'Oh, well, I was arranging to go to the greyhound track every day, but I'll be able to fit everything in.'

'I'll see to that dog of yours, David,' butted in Claude Jeremiah. 'I'll make sure he gets his regular training in. You leave it to me. You look after your grandad, he's more important than a dog, eh, Dr Rowan.'

'Well,' said the youngster, 'it's very kind of you, Mr Greengrass.'

'All part of my generous and helpful nature. See you, later,' and Claude turned around the pick-up and drove away with Alfred, leaving David and Jimbo with Kate.

'What a lovely dog.' Kate patted the sleek coat of the greyhound who responded with a wag of his slender tail.

'He's very fast,' said David. 'Mr Greengrass is very impressed by him, he says he's a good pacer but I've got to keep his training secret from Grandad. Till he gets better, that is. Well, I'd better get in to see to Grandad.'

'He's going to be all right,' Kate reassured him. 'I'll keep in touch about the tests I'm having done.'

★ ★ ★

When Nick returned for his tea, he told Kate he'd bumped into Bellamy in Ashfordly, and explained the trauma of Phil's suspension from duty. Like Nick, Kate was appalled at Phil's misfortune, neither of them believing for one minute that Phil was a bent copper.

'He can be stupid at times,' Kate agreed. 'But he's never a criminal masquerading in police uniform, not Phil Bellamy.'

'He's stupid over women,' Nick told her. 'He's putty in their hands. I think a woman's behind these troubles.'

'How do you figure that out?'

'Just suppose he was with a woman on the night the pawnbroker's was broken into. If that woman was seeing one of the local villains, she might have tempted Phil into her bed to get him out of the way while her friend committed the crime.'

'Would that sort of thing go on in Ashfordly?'

'Why not? It's been done before, all over the place. Policemen are only human, they can all fall for pretty faces?'

Kate just smiled. 'Would you fall for a pretty face?'

'Haven't I already?' he responded, kissing her. 'But seriously, Kate, I reckon Phil's been set up and I think that woman's behind it.'

'What woman?'

'The woman whose photo I saw in Phil's room when I was there. I'm sure I've seen her around with Jack Scarman, and, like I told you, Phil's been seeing Scarman's woman. Knowing the sort of company Scarman keeps, it wouldn't surprise me if he set up a raid on the shop with her help.'

'You've asked Phil about her?'

'Unofficially. If I was seen talking to him, I'd be disciplined so I had to be careful, but he wouldn't say anything about her. He wouldn't even admit he was with a woman – he'd end up with a disciplinary charge for neglect of duty or being absent from his beat, though that's not half as serious as being charged with a crime. Whatever his reaction, Kate, I'm convinced he was with her that night.'

'So what can you do?'

'Well, I told Phil I was going to ask Scarman where his girlfriend was that night. I've left him to stew over that. I said I'd give him till half past seven tonight to think about telling me!'

'So he might ring you?'

'Yes, in the next half-hour!'

'But Nick, you could both get into deeper bother, you're both breaking the Discipline Code!'

'If it means proving a mate of mine is innocent, then I'm prepared to do that,' he replied. 'Anyway, how was your day?'

'I went to see that Mr Parrish – he lives up at Ghyll End with his nephew.'

Kate shared her worries with Nick, telling him in confidence that she felt Alex Ferrenby had misdiagnosed Mr Parrish's problem. He'd been treating him for bronchitis, but in Kate's opinion, the symptoms for bronchitis were not present. She explained how she'd secured a blood sample and was having it analysed.

'So if it's not bronchitis, what can it be?'

'You remember that doctor in the Dales, Nick? I forget his name, but he discovered that some farmers, who work with livestock, can get a disease which he called Farmer's Lung.'

'No, never heard of it.'

'Well, I have. It was in our medical periodicals. It's caused by the spores from mouldy hay; if a farmer is working among hay which has gone mouldy, he can breathe in the spores and they set up a reaction among the air sacs in the lung, which in turn causes breathlessness. The only cure is not to work where there's any risk of mouldy hay.'

'But the poor chap has come here just to do that, hasn't he? He's rearing calves.'

'Yes, I've had to stop him working with his animals until I get the results through, which means that his grandson will have to feed the existing stock. By the way, I saw him with Claude Jeremiah.'

'Saw who?'

'The grandson, David Parrish.'

'What's Greengrass doing with that lad? He's only a schoolboy!'

'They'd been exercising David's greyhound,' she said.

'Not at Welford's place?' Nick sounded horrified. 'That's where Scarman and his cronies get to. They're a real bunch of hard men. It's not the sort of place a decent lad should hang around.'

'Well, he's got to learn about life sometime,' Kate shrugged.

'But not from Greengrass, Scarman and their like! So, how about a drink tonight?'

Kate looked startled. 'A drink, what's brought this on?'

'Well, if Greengrass is tempting young David into greyhound racing, Scarman might be involved. The Maddleskirk Trophy's coming up, I happen to know, being a good local constable, and the word is that Scarman's set on winning it. Now, Greengrass always hangs out at the Aidensfield Arms; Scarman was at the track today, I saw his car when I passed, which means he could also be in the pub tonight.'

Kate laughed. 'Good reasoning, Sherlock Holmes!'

'Simple logic, Dr Watson! And, if they're there, the chances are that woman might be with them. So I thought I'd drop in.'

'But you're off duty tonight, Nick!'

'Country constables are never off duty, Kate, not when their mate is likely to get done for a crime he never committed. Come on, once we've eaten, we'll have a walk down there.'

'Aren't you going to wait in case Phil rings?'

'He's only got a few minutes left before the deadline,' said Nick.

Phil Bellamy did call Nick. He admitted he had been with Debbie Chapman at the time the pawnbroker's had been entered. And he also added that Debbie was Scarman's current woman friend and warned Nick to keep away from

Scarman – he was known to have roughed up a few people who had crossed him, either in business or in love.

'Debbie's frightened to death of him, Nick,' said Phil. 'She wants to leave him but can't get away. She really is terrified. She never set me up, I'd swear to that. She'll be out with Scarman tonight, he told her to be there and she daren't disobey. He's scum, Nick, he's real scum, and bloody dangerous.'

'And you've taken up with his woman? Doesn't that put you in his firing line for something horrible?'

'What do you mean? He has no idea Debbie's seeing me, she's kept it all very quiet.'

'So you believe! But it's not as secret as you think; I'd heard about it! It sounds to me as if Scarman has set you up. I'm sure he knows you're knocking off his woman. Don't forget he's got ears and eyes all over the town.'

'He's never said owt to Debbie about seeing me.'

'So he'll deal with you first, and then her, won't he? He'll want you out of the way before he sets about her, and where better to get rid of a copper than to have him put away inside Armley Gaol or some such place? Once you're out of the way, he'll deal with his wandering woman, won't he?'

'He wouldn't have me sent down, would he? For summat I've not done?'

'You don't know the sort of villain you're dealing with, Phil. Right, leave this to me. And make a note of all your movements, official and unofficial, over the last few months. There might be other jobs they've got lined up to blame you for! And if you have been skiving from your beat or visiting one or other of your lady friends when you should have been on duty, include that as well. If Debbie is as innocent as you say, then she could be your only hope, Phil, your only alibi for lots of crimes.'

'Oh, bloody hell,' said Phil as he rang off.

Shortly afterwards, Nick and Kate were sitting at a quiet table in a dark corner of the pub. Eventually the door opened and in came Jack Scarman, accompanied by a woman.

'That's her,' Nick muttered to Kate. 'The woman in the photo in Phil's flat.'

'And that evil-looking character with her?'

'Jack Scarman, greyhound fanatic, property developer, small-time crook, woman beater . . . you name it, he's done it, but we can never nail him, never get him to court. He's too crafty for that, he always operates just within the law. He's trouble, Kate.'

'I can't understand Claude Jeremiah wanting to get involved with him. He's in a different league,' said Kate.

'He'll be using Claude, just as Claude's using Parrish's lad. Now, somehow, Kate, I must have words with that woman, without Scarman knowing.'

'Not tonight!' Kate protested.

'No, tomorrow perhaps, when Scarman's thinking about greyhounds or developing some of his property. He's got an office in town, he's always there before ten. That's when she'll be at home. I can easily get her address from the register of electors.'

A few minutes after ten o'clock the next morning, Nick Rowan, in full uniform, knocked at the door of Number 21, Ryecroft Terrace, Ashfordly. The door was opened by the woman whose photograph Nick had seen in Phil's flat.

'Deborah Chapman?' He used her full name.

'Yes?'

'PC Rowan from Aidensfield,' Nick introduced himself. 'I'm making enquiries about a break-in at St Nicholas Pawnbrokers. I think you might be able to help with my enquiries.'

'Me?' She looked shocked. 'What's it got to do with me?'

'It's got a lot to do with Phil Bellamy,' Nick said gently. 'So I think I'd better come in.'

She glanced up and down the street, then said, 'All right.'

She offered him a coffee and as she made it, Nick explained about the break-in, how Phil had been absent from his beat at the time, and how the hiding-place for the stolen goods had been revealed in an anonymous telephone call. He added that Phil had been suspended from duty and that, unless this matter was cleared up, he could face dismissal from the force and even imprisonment for a crime he had not committed.

The woman bit her lip anxiously. 'I never knew about that, Mr Rowan, honest. Jack never used me to get at Phil, he couldn't have, he doesn't know about us. I've always been very careful, I've always seen Phil when Jack was well away from the town.'

'Someone's told Scarman,' said Nick. 'Someone's seen

you and Phil together. Even I'd heard you were seeing him. I believe you didn't set up Phil, but I am convinced Scarman's trying to frame him because he's seeing you. And when he's got Phil out of the way, then he'll deal with you, won't he?'

She shuddered at the thought. 'He's vicious, Mr Rowan, you've no idea . . . I hate him, I can't get away from him . . . but if he is setting Phil up, you'll never prove anything against him. He's too cunning for that, he'd use somebody else to do his dirty work, like he did when he threw me out before. When I said I'd not go back, he had me thrown out of my flat and beaten up. He didn't do it himself, he got somebody else to do it, that's how he operates.'

'And would that somebody have a minivan that makes a lot of noise, as if it's got a duff exhaust?'

'Eddie, you mean?' she replied.

'Who is this Eddie?' asked Nick.

'I don't know his surname. He's the one that beat me up. The bastard, he's evil, Mr Rowan, he'll do anything for Jack. Jack always has him on hand when there's likely to be trouble.' She looked almost on the verge of tears, but then she brightened. 'Like the Maddleskirk Trophy greyhound meeting, Jack's plotting something there. He made sure I was always out of the way when he was setting it up. I'm not sure what it is, but I do know he wants Eddie around at the time.'

'Where's this Eddie chap from?' asked Nick.

'He used to live in Leeds, that's when Jack came across him. Eddie knew his way around the hard men in Leeds.

He was into property repairs then, fixing roofs or drive-ways, doing rotten work and charging poor pensioners the earth, then scaring the living daylights out of them when they objected to his charges.'

'Not a very nice fellow at all,' said Nick.

'He's not.' Debbie agreed. 'He's rotten, Mr Rowan, he thinks he's a hard man who can dominate any woman, and he does most of Jack's dirty work. I don't know where he lives now but he often hangs out at Finkle Street garage. He's good with car engines, likes a bit of stock-car racing, that sort of thing. That mini has a special engine, souped up, he once said. It makes one hell of a racket when he revs it up.'

'Right, thanks for all that. Now, it's important you can confirm Phil was with you that night. It means I know he's clear of the shop-breaking charge. Though even so, we need to find out who actually did it.'

'It might be Eddie,' she said in a whisper.

'That's what I was thinking. So leave this with me, Debbie, and not a word to anybody, least of all Jack Scarman!'

'If this gets me free from that bastard, it'll be worth it!' she said.

CHAPTER TEN

Nick's enquiries around the specialist garages in the district quickly produced the name Eddie Mooney and the registration number of the souped-up minivan. Mooney had tinkered with the engine until he had something that sounded like a high-powered sports car. A check with the vehicle registration department at Northallerton revealed an address in Leeds, but a phone call to Leeds City Police showed that Mooney had left that address several months ago, and was now thought to be living in Ashfordly or perhaps Strensford.

Nick then went along to the Maddleskirk Greyhound Track to confirm the dates and times of the forthcoming race meeting, especially of the Maddleskirk Trophy which was the highlight of the event. Men and dogs from all over the north-east of England were expected to arrive, and already extra police officers had been drafted in to control the crowds and traffic, and to ensure law and order on the course. On the day of the meeting, the place would be buzzing with punters and bookmakers. If there was any place where he could guarantee Jack Scarman's presence, along with his minders, it would be here, and it would be during the race for the Maddleskirk Trophy. From a secure telephone kiosk, Nick rang Phil Bellamy and told him to attend the races, especially while the Maddleskirk Trophy was being run. This could be the time for a showdown with Jack Scarman and Eddie Mooney, he explained, and in his view, a public place was far better than one of Scarman's own premises. Nick advised Phil to remain in the background until his presence was required.

'Thanks, mate,' said Phil, and he meant it.

It was that same morning that Kate got the letter she had been awaiting. Its postmark told her it had come from the laboratories and when she opened it, she gave a little cry of delight – just as Alex Ferrenby entered the surgery. He looked rather tired, but he was dressed as if for work.

'Won the pools, have you, Kate?' he smiled.

'No, it's just some good news,' she said. 'About Geoff Parrish.'

'Oh, yes, I had intended to see him, he's had bronchitis, you know, quite badly. But with me being off, I never got round to visiting him.'

'I went to treat him, Alex, that's what this letter is about.'

'Really?'

'I took a blood test, I wanted to check for any reaction against allergies.'

'Are you saying you disbelieved my diagnosis?'

'I read an article in a medical journal, Alex, about a disease which affects farmers who work among mouldy hay. Some of them are allergic to the spores that are produced; the trouble's been called Farmer's Lung. Well, the blood test shows that Mr Parrish is allergic to those spores. The technical name is extrinsic allergic alveolitis, it affects the air sacs in the lungs, and if it's not treated immediately, it can have long-lasting effects.'

'So I was wrong?' Alex suddenly sounded very unsure of himself.

'I had read the article, Alex, you hadn't,' Kate said gently.

'But I could have gone on treating him wrongly for the rest of his life. He'd have been crippled with that breathing difficulty . . .'

'Well, he'll recover now. I must advise him not to continue with his calves and other livestock, and to keep away from hay and straw. Then he'll soon be better.'

'You must forgive me, Kate, I seem to be losing my touch.'

'It's progress, Alex, I happened to have read the right article at the right time, that's all. You're still a good doctor . . .'

'But I'm past it, is that what you're saying?' And he left, slamming the door behind him.

Kate almost went after him, but decided it was best to leave him alone with his thoughts. This might just prompt him to retire, to end his career while he was at the top of his profession. And Alex Ferrenby *was* at the top; he was one of the finest of rural General Practitioners. Or, she told herself, he had been.

Now she must take the news to Geoff Parrish.

He was sitting on a settee when she arrived, in far better condition than on her previous visit. He told her he had not been in the same place as any hay or straw since then, and already there was a noticeable improvement. Kate then explained the results of the tests and advised him that, provided he kept away from hay and straw, and ended his new career with cattle and sheep, he should be able to eradicate his problem.

'What did you do before you came here?' she asked.

'I bred greyhounds,' he said. 'Racing dogs. I won every trophy in the north of England. Here, I'll show you.'

He led her into the lounge where he indicated a display cabinet full of trophies, rosettes and photographs of him receiving awards or showing off one or other of his prizewinning dogs. He added that he'd never had any trouble with his breathing during that career.

'It's not the animals, it's their food and bedding,' she said. 'So the dog that your grandson is training, that's yours, is it?'

'Yes, I trained him before I was ill. His name's Jimbo. Now, if I'd been fit, I'd have been entering him in some of the local events.'

'Well, there's no reason why you shouldn't soon be able to!'

'It would be nice, although officially I'm retired. Jimbo's a greyhound man's dream, Dr Rowan, he's a natural, the sort of dog you wished you'd found when you were at your peak. I haven't really trained him for racing, you see, because of my breathing troubles. I couldn't cope with the effort, the exercise, so our David's been walking him. I'd have liked to have been training Jimbo for the Maddleskirk Trophy. I won it twice before, with other dogs. One day, David might take up greyhound racing, but he wants to go to university to study to be a vet.'

'David's been taking Jimbo down to Wilf Welford's track with Claude Jeremiah Greengrass,' Kate said. 'The dog's been there regularly, I wondered if he was going to enter it for the Maddleskirk Trophy.'

'I knew nothing of this!' said the old man. 'I know Wilf Welford, he trains for a villain called Scarman. But who is this man Greengrass?'

Kate felt she ought to tell the truth about Aidensfield's resident rogue. Mr Parrish listened carefully and then said, 'Thanks, Doctor. You *have* made my day. I was one of the country's most experienced greyhound trainers, even though I say it myself, and I know every trick in the book. Do you think Greengrass is up to something with Scarman? I know Scarman has a useless dog which is all black; like our Jimbo but without the white patch . . . I'll tell you what, Doctor, I'm not relishing what I'm hearing.'

'Perhaps I shouldn't have told you.'

'On the contrary, I'm pleased you have. From what you've said, it seems your Mr Greengrass is trying to pull the wool over my grandson's eyes. Why would Greengrass want to train our Jimbo like that? I've a feeling I might just have to teach him a lesson!'

'He deserves a hard lesson every so often, Mr Parrish. He's had several since we came to live here, but he never seems to learn from his experiences. I wish you the best of luck with him, and with Jimbo. Now, I must be off. Goodbye.'

'Bye, Doctor. When David comes in, I'll get the whole story from him, he's an honest lad. And I'll get the names of the people he's been associating with. Perhaps I'll see you at the greyhound meeting?'

'Who knows?' smiled Kate, taking her leave. 'I expect my husband will be on duty there.'

On the day of the Maddleskirk Trophy greyhound race, the track was busy with a small but enthusiastic crowd. At one side of the track was the public area with the bookmakers in evidence and ticktack men signalling the odds to their colleagues. There was an atmosphere of excitement, with money changing hands, dogs being examined and form being discussed. Greyhounds were being warmed up with short runs by the sides of their trainers.

Jack Scarman and Debbie were talking to Wilf Welford, who stood near a small pony trailer with Northern Flash on a lead. The dog was wearing a highly distinctive body coat; pale blue emblazoned with a bright red flash of lightning along its length. As one race was being prepared, with the dogs being placed in the traps and the bookies shouting the odds, Claude Jeremiah Greengrass arrived in his pick-up. He parked next to the same pony trailer and Wilf acknowledged his arrival. In the pick-up was David Parrish, nursing Jimbo, while tied in the rear was Alfred, the lurcher. Travelling in the open rear section was a mode of transport not unfamiliar to him.

Claude climbed out of the pick-up and said to David, 'You go and watch over there, among those spectators. You'll learn a lot about racing. You can't go into the members' enclosure, it's for folks like me, men of substance who've paid for the privilege, but I'll take Jimbo. It'll get him used to the atmosphere, you see. He'll be all right because Alfred will be with him. Greyhounds love atmosphere, son, they drink it in as if it's their mother's milk.'

'Yes, all right,' said David. 'I'll see you after the big race, then?'

'Done, and if I've played my cards right, I'll be celebrating. Money on the right dog, if you understand. Them that's in the know will be backing Northern Flash, but you're too young to bet, eh, being under eighteen? I know the law, you see, son.'

Claude Jeremiah Greengrass returned to his pick-up to let Jimbo out of the passenger seat before trudging away to go about his business. To Alfred's disappointment he was left tied in the rear.

Nick had also arrived. His presence was not unusual on such an occasion, for at any similar gathering on his beat he would have been on patrol in uniform. It was his duty to control the inflow and outflow of traffic, and to prevent trouble on the track, in addition to looking out for pickpockets, bookmakers who might welsh with their takings or punters who might turn to violence if they lost heavily. He therefore patrolled the public and private areas of the track, although today he was particularly interested in Jack Scarman and his minder,

Eddie Mooney, in his souped-up minivan.

Sure enough, the distinctive sound of a noisy engine alerted Nick to a new arrival. He watched the dark green minivan roar into the parking area, its driver revving the engine every few seconds to emphasise the nature of this innocuous-looking van. Nick checked the registration number against the one he had noted in his pocketbook. It tallied. Among the crowd, Nick spotted Phil Bellamy in civilian clothes, looking every inch a greyhound racing fan. Nick raised a hand; Phil nodded. The arrival of Eddie Mooney had been noted. From this point, he would be kept under very close observation.

Nick wandered down to the rails, ostensibly to observe the next race. From there he saw Mooney, a powerful man in his late twenties with brown hair, walk over to Scarman, who was standing nearby.

Mooney spoke. 'You left a message for me to be here?'

'You're late, I expected you sooner.'

'I went to Leeds to visit my aunt. So I'm here now.' He grinned at Debbie at Scarman's side. 'Hi, gorgeous. Missed me, have you?'

Debbie did not reply.

'She's not very friendly, is she?' commented Mooney.

'She's like one of these dogs, she's learning how to behave,' said Scarman who then opened his wallet and pushed a fistful of notes into Mooney's hands. 'You know what to do, so do it.'

Nick listened to these exchanges, wondering whether they might be related to Greengrass's recent outings with

Jimbo. Then he moved away to keep Mooney within his sights.

Meanwhile, in the official enclosure, Wilf Welford was standing in a short queue before the manager's clerk with Northern Flash on a leash; the clerk was seated at a table and was registering all the graded dogs which had been nominated to take part in the race for the Maddleskirk Trophy.

'Next,' called the clerk.

'Northern Flash,' responded Wilf.

'Owner?'

'Mr J. Scarman.'

The clerk pulled a card from a filing box and checked its details, studying the dog's colour before saying, 'Right, entered. Next?'

While Welford registered Northern Flash, Claude Jeremiah was walking with Jimbo on his lead, weaving among the array of trailers in which the competing dogs had arrived. Many were small horseboxes, the kind that would carry a pony to a gymkhana, and he paused for the briefest of moments outside the one belonging to Wilf Welford, Scarman's trainer. Then, in a trice, he opened the rear door and vanished inside with Jimbo.

Geoff Parrish and David were watching him.

'Will Jimbo be all right, Grandad?' whispered David.

'He'll be fine. Now just you stay with me and keep your eyes on that trailer. I know what game they're playing, and it'll be interesting to see who plays it best, eh? They're getting ready for the Maddleskirk Trophy now. It'll be run in a few minutes, so things should start to happen.'

David still looked puzzled. 'I don't understand, Grandad.'

'You will. Look, here comes Wilf Welford now with Northern Flash. How's that for a bonny body coat? A fair dazzler, isn't it?'

Mr Parrish and David watched Wilf and the colourfully coated dog make their way to the pony trailer.

Inside, unseen by anyone, Claude Jeremiah Greengrass was quickly but effectively applying some stove blacking to the white marking on Jimbo's head. The finished job looked perfect – Jimbo was now a totally black greyhound with not a glimmer of his former white patch. Meanwhile, outside, the odds on Northern Flash were shortening because of the unexpectedly heavy betting on this dog, initially regarded as a rank outsider. Claude could hear the calls of the bookies and hurried because he wanted to place more bets before the odds were too greatly reduced – although he'd already bet a substantial amount in advance.

Wilf entered the trailer and whispered, 'All right, Claude?'

'Aye, just finished.' He chuckled. 'You can't see the join, as they say. Now, let's have that jacket and I'll put it on Jimbo, then nobody'll tell the difference.'

The switch was quickly made. Without protest, a nervous Northern Flash was put into a kennel hidden beneath a horse blanket at the rear of the trailer. The kennel door was closed behind him, and the concealing blanket was lowered again.

'I've just time to get more bets on,' said Claude. 'You

stay here till I get back, I'll make sure nobody lets Northern Flash out. And keep an eye on my Alfred, will you? He'll try to follow me now, and we don't want him getting mixed up with them dogs on the track!'

'You've only got five minutes before they call me,' said Wilf, nervously.

'Long enough for a fast mover like me,' and Claude lumbered out of the shelter of the trailer. In the pick-up next door Alfred strained his lead to follow but Claude only shouted, 'Shut up you daft dog,' and hurried off.

In a nifty movement Geoff Parrish materialised and released Alfred who galloped off joyfully in pursuit of his master. Then Parrish wrenched open the door of the pony trailer and shouted, 'Is that your dog tied up there? It's off, heading for the track . . .'

'Bloody hell!' said Wilf, rushing out in pursuit of Alfred.

The moment he was out of sight, Geoff Parrish and David, who had now been suitably briefed, entered the trailer. With the speed of one experienced in handling greyhounds, Geoff Parrish released Northern Flash from the Kennel, removed the colourful coat from Jimbo, and replaced it on Northern Flash. Jimbo was then popped into the kennel and the horse blanket returned to its position. Then they left. It took but seconds, and when Wilf returned to fasten Alfred in the rear of the pick-up, the real Northern Flash was waiting in his beautiful sky-blue coat. Now the runners were being called to the start and Wilf seized Northern Flash's lead and hurried to the starting traps.

'Now we'll get Jimbo,' said Geoff Parrish. 'And let this be a lesson to you, young David!'

'Thanks, Grandad. I hope Greengrass loses a lot of money!'

'I feel sure he will, and not just him, I fancy,' smiled his grandfather, still a little short of breath. 'Come along. We'll get Jimbo then. I think we should go and watch the big race.'

Having placed Jimbo in Geoff's car, they headed for a good vantage point on the track in time to see Claude Jeremiah Greengrass emptying his pockets and placing all his cash on Northern Flash. It was less than two minutes to the off.

As the tension mounted in the final moments before the race started, Eddie Mooney appeared at Scarman's side. Greengrass was there too, looking proud and confident, while in the background, their eyes on Mooney, stood PCs Nick Rowan and Phil Bellamy.

The constables were prepared to wait a little longer; Nick had spotted old Mr Parrish and David moving towards the finishing line, being particularly anxious to watch the outcome of this race. But suddenly, the starter was signalling that the dogs were ready. A hush fell on the crowd and all betting was halted. Scarman could be heard congratulating Mooney and several others who had placed money on Northern Flash on his behalf.

If the dog won, the bookies would suffer an enormous loss, while Scarman was set to make a fortune. He couldn't wait to be the proud recipient of the Maddleskirk Trophy.

They heard the distinctive rumbling noise of the mechanical hare as it moved towards the starting traps; the dogs were growing excited and the crowd was shouting, and then, with an almighty crash, the traps flew open and the dogs burst out. The race was over in seconds, and Northern Flash was fourth. A poor fourth.

Scarman stared in disbelief; Claude could not understand, but he was quick enough to hurry away as the crowd surged towards the bookmakers to collect their winnings.

'Greengrass, I want words with you!' screeched the angry Scarman, chasing after Claude, who now began to run through the crowds, hoping against hope to find some kind of refuge before Scarman caught him.

Mooney stood alone.

'Now,' hissed Nick, removing his handcuffs from his pocket. 'Ready?'

'You bet!' grinned Bellamy.

'This is an official arrest for questioning, Phil, not a Wild West show, remember?'

'I just want that man inside,' said Phil grimly.

Nick came upon Mooney from behind and tapped him on the shoulder.

'Eddie Mooney?'

'Yeah, who wants to know?'

'PC Rowan, I'm arresting you on suspicion of breaking and entering St Nicholas Pawnbrokers in Ashfordly . . .'

'You can go and get stuffed!' growled Mooney, quickly

bringing his fist up, but Bellamy was behind him now. In a trice, he had that arm locked in a secure hold and twisted behind Mooney's back.

'As I was saying,' smiled Nick, 'I'm arresting you on suspicion of breaking and entering St Nicholas Pawnbrokers in Ashfordly. You are not obliged to say anything but what you say may be taken down in writing and given in evidence.'

'Bastards!'

'Got that, Phil?' smiled Nick. 'I think the courts will be interested in his reaction. Come along, Mooney, you're going to the cells.'

As they walked towards Nick's bike to radio for a car, they passed Claude Jeremiah who was with Scarman and Wilf Welford. Claude was rubbing Northern Flash's head, and saying, 'But this black won't come off, Jack . . . this is your own bloody dog . . .'

'Well, so who rung the changes, Greengrass?'

'Trouble, Claude?' asked Nick as he passed by.

'No, Mr Rowan, no trouble. Just a bit of confusion about a dog.'

Scarman saw Mooney being led away, but made no comment. He wanted nothing to do with Eddie Mooney now – Eddie was on his own.

He turned to Greengrass. 'You owe me an explanation, Claude, and, I suspect, a good deal of compensation for my losses. Now, I'm a reasonable man until folks don't pay. You know that, don't you?'

'Aye, well, I'm a man of substance myself, Jack, a man of means . . . I mean, I'll see you all right, so I will.'

'Of course you will, Claude. Of course you will. I'll see you tomorrow. In the Aidensfield Arms, with your pockets full of money, all for me. I'll work out what you owe me. Right?'

'Right, Jack.'

'Mr Scarman to you,' said Scarman.

When Eddie Mooney's flat was searched, the remainder of the property stolen from the pawnbroker's shop was found, along with many more items from similar crimes. Faced with this evidence, he confessed to the shop-breaking, but he steadfastly refused to implicate Scarman.

'He'll go down for a year or two,' said Sergeant Blaketon afterwards. 'Well done, Rowan. And Bellamy, here's your warrant card. You're back on duty, a wiser man I hope.'

'Yes, Sergeant,' said Phil Bellamy.

'You know, I still don't understand why Scarman tried to frame you, Bellamy. And I still can't work out where you were when that shop was broken into.'

And he walked into his own office with a knowing smile on his face.

'He knows summat,' said Phil.

'Don't we all?' said Nick. 'Life has no secrets. Well, I'd better get back to Aidensfield. I've a feeling poor old Claude Jeremiah will need some protection very soon. I might just ask him if he's got any good greyhound racing tips.'

It was several weeks later when Claude Jeremiah

Greengrass went out to the old wrecked Ford Popular which he used as a henhouse. Accompanied by the ever-faithful Alfred, he fed his hens, collected some eggs and then lifted the seat of the old car to reveal a space beneath it. It was here that Claude kept the old biscuit tin, bearing a picture of the Queen's coronation on the lid, in which he hid his spare cash.

His secret hiding place was empty.

'Alfred!' he yelled. 'Hey, somebody's pinched all my money!'

He searched the car, scattering hens and causing feathers to fly as he looked for any sign of his roll of banknotes, but there was nothing. Someone had sneaked into his secret place during the night to take his cash. There had been fifty pounds, he knew. Fifty hard-earned pounds. And his precious tin.

'You can't trust anybody these days,' he grumbled to Alfred. 'Come on, this is a job for the police.'

A few minutes later, he was hammering on the door of the police house. Nick answered, dressed in a sweater and slacks.

'Morning, Claude,' he smiled. 'You're out early.'

'Early? I've been up half the night with worry, Mr Rowan. I've come to report a crime.'

'You mean you're going to admit committing one?'

'Gerroff, it's nowt like that. Look, somebody's pinched my money, my life savings.'

Nick shrugged. 'Well, you'll have to go to Ashfordly and tell them, Claude. I'm off duty. It's my day off today.'

'Day off?' Claude snorted 'Policemen don't get days off, do they?'

'Yes, they do.'

'Well, I can't get to Ashfordly, my battery's flat and the pick-up won't start.'

'There's a bus in half an hour . . .'

'Bus? I'm not going all the way to Ashfordly on a bus. I'm a ratepayer, Mr Rowan, I pay your wages, it's blokes like me that keep this country going.'

'OK, I'll make a note now and I'll come around to visit the scene and investigate the crime when I'm back on duty.'

'Right, well, I suppose that'll have to do. I thought I'd get better service than this, me being a pillar of this community and a ratepayer.'

'I've said I'll deal with the matter, Claude!'

'There's one law for the rich and one for the rest of us, I can tell you,' grumbled Claude. 'I bet if I'd been Lord Ashfordly, you'd have got your notebook out sharp.'

'You'd know about laws, Claude, you seem to break most of them. So how much did you say's been taken?'

'Fifty quid! My life savings. And my cash box. Well, an old biscuit box with Her Majesty's coronation on the lid. Very loyal subject, I am. It was a good box, was that. You don't get tin boxes of that quality nowadays.'

'After your deal with Jack Scarman I'm surprised you've got anything left to pinch, even a tin box!'

'Aye, well, he knows nowt about that spare cash, Mr Rowan. You don't tell folks like him everything, do you, so I'd be obliged if you didn't let him know. This was my nest egg, you see.'

'And where did you keep it?'

'In the henhouse. Well, it's an old car I use as a henhouse. My flock of Rhode Island Reds crossed by White Leghorns love the upholstery, you see. They're very content, sleeping there at night.'

'And you kept your money in the mobile henhouse, which isn't locked?'

'It's not mobile, it failed its MOT.'

'I've never come across a henhouse before which failed its MOT, Claude.'

'Well, I could have scrapped it, but the hens love it. Anyway, I shut it against foxes at night, but folks round here don't need to lock up, Mr Rowan, there's no criminals about the place. I mean, I've never had owt pinched before.'

'Well, that doesn't surprise me. Now, who's been prowling around the Greengrass estate, Claude?'

'Trespassers, poachers, ramblers crossing my land, sneak thieves . . .'

'But somebody knew it was there. It's not everybody who keeps his life savings in a motorised henhouse, is it? So you go home and get thinking, then I'll come and visit you and we'll get the fingerprint experts out to examine the scene of the crime.'

'You mean my house will be swarming with coppers?'

'You're a ratepayer, Claude, and you deserve the very best, so I'll call out the Crime Squad, the CID, the police dogs to search the premises, the fingerprint officers to check for prints left by the thief and then I'll come and search the premises to see if you've mislaid the cash and the tin.'

Claude gaped. 'You mean I've got to subject my private premises to this kind of invasive scrutiny just because somebody's pinched my money?'

'If a crime has been committed, Claude, ratepayers like you, pillars of the local community, deserve only the best. Just like Lord Ashfordly.'

'Do you think I'd better go and have another look around the spot first, before you make it official, like?'

'Right, Claude, as you wish. I want only the best service for you, you know.'

'You're being sarcastic now, Mr Rowan.'

'Who, me? Never!'

'Right, well, I'll go and have another look around myself, before your fellers come along and disrupt my way of life. I might have misplaced it, mightn't I? I mean, I'd look a bit daft if they found it when I said it had gone, wouldn't I?'

'Very possibly, Claude,' and Greengrass pottered away from the police house. The last thing he wanted was a load of detectives and police constables searching his house.

Back inside, the telephone rang.

'You get it,' Kate called from the kitchen.

'No, it's your turn,' Nick shouted. 'It's my day off!'

CHAPTER ELEVEN

The call was for Kate. Helen Rawlings, the wife of a gamekeeper on Lord Ashfordly's estate, explained that her daughter, Susan, was ill. Susan was at Ashfordly Grammar School where she was working hard for her forthcoming A levels, and Helen expressed concern that her daughter might be overdoing things or getting into a state about her exams. Kate promised to come around after morning surgery.

When she arrived, Helen Rawlings, an attractive woman in her late thirties, apologised, saying that it was her husband, Matt, who'd insisted on calling the doctor.

'He dotes on Susan. She wasn't very strong when she was little, you see, and he's so concerned whenever she's poorly.'

'He'll be having a busy time, just now?' Kate commented.

'Yes, it's the annual shoot on the estate. He's up to his neck with work. All Lord Ashfordly's business contacts and friends are coming today, so everything's got to be just right.'

Kate nodded understandingly. 'He's invited Dr Ferrenby, that was kind of him.'

'Yes, I heard the doctor hasn't been very well lately.'

'I think he was overdoing it, Mrs Rawlings, and that knock on the head when his surgery was raided didn't help, nor did his involvement in the train crash. But he'll be all right given time, and outings like this shooting day to help him to relax.'

'Please send him our regards.'

'I will,' promised Kate. 'He looked very splendid this morning in his shooting gear, plus fours and tweed suit! Very much the country gentleman. I'm sorry he couldn't come to see Susan.'

'I'm pleased you've come,' smiled Helen Rawlings. 'A woman's touch is sometimes best. Come along, I'll take you up to her room.'

They paused outside the door while Mrs Rawlings knocked, saying, 'Susan? Dr Rowan's here.'

The door opened slowly to reveal Susan in her night-dress; she looked extremely pale and unwell.

'I told you I didn't need a doctor,' she snapped at her mother. 'I told Dad, but he didn't listen either!'

'If you're unwell, Susan, it's only natural your parents are concerned,' retorted Kate. 'Now, let me in and I'll have a look at you.'

'Shall I come in as well?' asked Mrs Rawlings.

'No, Mum, leave me alone. I can manage,' and so while Susan admitted Kate, her mother returned to the kitchen downstairs. Kate looked around the room; it was that of a typical teenager, with a transistor radio, posters of pop stars and pop groups, a CND poster and school books spread across a desk.

'So, Susan, what's wrong?' Kate smiled and sat on the bed, indicating that Susan should join her.

'I'm all right, honest, I'm just tired.' The girl tried to shrug off her sickness, whatever it was.

'Your mother said you'd been sick.' Kate was now rummaging in her bag for a thermometer. 'How many times?'

'Three.'

'When?'

'Just after I came to bed. It's happened to some other girls at school, there's a bug going around.'

'Have you eaten or drunk anything that's different, something you don't normally have?' asked Kate.

'No, nothing, just my ordinary school dinners and the usual things at home.'

'All right, open your mouth, I want to take your temperature.' As Susan obeyed, Kate received a strong whiff of alcohol. She tested the girl's pulse too, then said, 'Susan, you've been drinking!'

'No, I haven't!'

'I can smell it on your breath. Don't lie to me.'

'You won't tell my mother, will you? It made me sick . . .'

'I'm not surprised, it must have been a lot to leave a smell like that. You've been drunk, that's what's wrong. You've had an almighty hangover and it's not left you yet! So, what you need is lots of water to flush you out, and then some exercise and fresh air.'

'Dad said I could help him if I felt up to it.'

'Well, that might not be a bad idea, but you look awful. Get some rest first, and no more drinking, except copious amounts of fresh, clean water!'

'So what will you tell Mum?'

'I'll say it sounds like a tummy bug, something you've picked up at school. But this is the last time I cover up for you – keep off the drink and concentrate on your exams, without overdoing it. And plenty of fresh air and exercise should help you get over this one.'

'Thank you, Doctor,' smiled Susan. But her pale face bore a very worried look which Kate did not miss.

Having enjoyed a leisurely breakfast after Greengrass's departure, Nick decided he might do some work on his old car; he'd managed to buy a vintage MG from Greengrass, a rare vehicle, the true value of which Claude had overlooked. He changed into some overalls, then decided he needed some petrol with which to clean some engine parts, so strolled down to the garage with a can in his hand. As he arrived, Malcolm Mostyn came out to greet him.

'Ah, Nick, glad you've come. I've been ringing your house . . .'

'Sorry, Malcolm, I was in my garage. I didn't hear the phone. What's the matter?'

'We were broken into last night.'

'Not you as well?' groaned Nick. 'Much gone?'

'Cash,' said the garage owner. 'Not a lot, I don't leave a lot lying around at night. Just some loose change in the till. I reckon there was about fifteen shillings in silver.'

'How did they get in?'

'Through a back window. They smashed the glass, reached inside to open the catch and climbed through. There's some muddy footprints on my desk and on the floor.'

Nick followed Malcolm inside where the trail of evidence was easy to distinguish. He studied the marks and the mode of entry and said, 'It looks like someone fairly agile to get in through that window. A youngster, obviously.'

'That's what I thought, somebody after a few bob.'

'I'm off duty today, Malcolm, but I'll ring the office at Ashfordly and get the fingerprint people organised. They'll want to examine the woodwork around the window and so on. It's funny, Claude Jeremiah reckons he had some money taken last night as well, he's doing a double check for me.' He grinned. 'He doesn't want our experts rummaging through his house.'

'I heard somebody had got into the pub too,' said Malcolm. 'George was on about it this morning. I didn't know my own spot had been raided an' all! I've just discovered it.'

'I thought I was going to have a quiet day off!' grumbled Nick. 'What's gone from the pub? Money from the till?'

'George couldn't see that anything was missing, but a back window had been smashed.'

'I'd better get across there and have words with him,' said Nick. 'I'll come back for my can of petrol, I just wanted a gallon to wash my engine parts with.'

'I'll fill it up, Nick. Call back when you're ready.'

Nick found George in the cellar of the Aidensfield Arms preparing for the day's opening. He'd been planning to call at the police house when he went to the shop and had mentioned the break-in to Malcolm when Malcolm had popped in for some cigarettes earlier. Entry had been through a small window in the kitchen at the rear of the premises; George always left the drawer of his till open at night so that would-be thieves could see that it was empty. No cash had been taken, therefore, and George was baffled.

'Cigarettes not taken? Spirits?' asked Nick. Those were the usual objectives of thieves who broke into licensed premises.

'No cigarettes are missing, I just got my order in yesterday and they're stacked up in my back store in boxes of 200. I'd know if one of them had gone. They could have taken a bottle or two of something I suppose. I'd never miss a single bottle. If they'd taken a crate then I would know.'

Nick told George about Claude's missing money and the raid on Mostyn's Garage just across the road, and asked George to keep his ears open in the pub. If it was youngsters doing it for a dare, then their boasting might just surface during the next few days.

Nick returned to Mostyn's, collected his can of petrol and paid Malcolm. He was just walking back to the police house when Bill Francis, the butcher, hailed him.

'Nick,' he called from the forecourt of his shop, 'have

you a minute? Somebody's broken into my van during the night.'

'I don't believe it!' cried Nick.

Someone had smashed the quarterlight of the passenger's window, reached in and opened the door. They had then crept into the rear of the empty van where the till was kept: Bill Francis did a round of the villages every Tuesday and Saturday, selling meat from the van, and so he carried a small till in the vehicle. Something around two or three pounds in small change had been taken.

The time had come to report this mini-crime wave to Sergeant Blaketon, and to the CID. Clearly, someone had done the rounds last night, breaking into anywhere that might contain cash, however small an amount. This was not the work of a travelling criminal, thought Nick; it had all the appearance of somebody local, somebody with knowledge of the habits of local business people so far as their cash was concerned. It seemed that Claude Jeremiah had been right; the thief or thieves had even known of his secret hiding place.

From his office, Nick rang Ashfordly Police Station and Sergeant Blaketon answered. He listened with growing agitation as Nick outlined the series of minor crimes. 'Rowan,' he ordered, 'you'd better book yourself on duty!'

Nick's heart plummeted. 'But it's my weekly rest day, Sarge.'

'Consider it cancelled,' said Blaketon. 'If you've got a crime wave in Aidensfield, you can't swan around all day doing nothing about it.'

'Couldn't one of the Ashfordly men come out and deal with the incidents?'

'Not today, Rowan. You know it's the annual shoot on Lord Ashfordly's estate? The final one of the season?'

Nick was puzzled. 'Yes, but that's no concern of ours, Sergeant. It's all on private property, there's no call for a police presence.'

'But our new Assistant Chief Constable is a guest, Rowan. That means he'll be in the area, and will surely take the opportunity to call at Ashfordly Police Station to inspect us. I'm having to get all my books and records up to date. I'm having to have the whole bloody place cleared of cigarette ash because Ventress spends his days in a cloud of smoke and I want my police station in peak condition in case Mr McLeod happens to call. And call he will, Rowan, either today or tomorrow. So I have no men to spare for your crime wave. Which means you will have to deal with the problem yourself, which in turn means you will have to book yourself on duty, as from this minute. Got it, Rowan?'

'Yes, Sergeant,' capitulated Nick.

'When Mr McLeod arrives, Rowan, I want him to find a highly efficient police unit, a well-oiled machine, a . . .'

'I was going to fix my old MG, Sarge . . .'

'Rowan, I want none of your cheek. This is an important day for Ashfordly Section. Now, he'll be arriving about now, I should say, for a sherry before setting forth, and when the shoot's over, I expect he'll pop in to inspect my station. Which means, Rowan, I don't want any crimes left unsolved. So you'd better set about detecting that crime wave of yours, hadn't you? Every minute counts, Rowan.'

'Yes, Sergeant.'

Tension was mounting on Lord Ashfordly's estate too. Matt Rawlings, anxious to ensure that every detail was correct, had asked his son, Chris, to wash and clean some of the vehicles which would be used by the shooting party. Outside his cottage there was parked a Landrover, a game cart and a tractor and trailer. Chris, a sullen twenty-year-old, was dressed in gamekeeper's clothing because his father had persuaded Lord Ashfordly to provide him with work as his father's apprentice. But the lad's heart was not in his work.

'What a bloody mess, Chris!' Matt snapped at his son. 'I thought I told you to clean these vehicles? Look at them! You've splashed a drop of water here and a drop there and that's it! You've been here since half past seven this morning and they're not a bit different, still covered in muck and grime. Get them clean, you useless lout! You're hopeless, bloody hopeless. You can't do anything, can you?'

'I've cleaned them, Dad, I did my best.'

'Call this your best? God knows what your worst'll be like. Look, I need those vehicles by ten o'clock – the trailer first, it's for the beaters – and I need them clean and shining like new. This is a very important day. All Lord Ashfordly's friends are coming, very important people. So get the hose out again, get a brush and clean off the mud, then wash and polish them all. Right?'

Chris sighed the sigh of one who had been through all this before and went to turn on the water. His father, face flushed with anger, stormed into the house to find the list of guests and double check that he had counted the correct number. His wife Helen was in the kitchen, clearing away the breakfast things. She had heard the exchange outside.

'Go easy on Chris, Matt, he does his best.'

'A small child could do better. He's my own son and he's useless at everything. There's nothing he can do properly!'

'That's because no one can match your expectations. You set yourself such a high standard of work that you assume everyone else will be as good. Well, they're not, they've got to learn . . .'

'Our Susan's bright enough, she can do things well. Anyway, how is she? Has the doctor been?'

'Yes, it was a stomach bug, something that's going round at school. She's told Susan to drink a lot of water and then get some fresh air. She was talking of coming out to help you.'

'God knows I need another pair of hands, somebody who can do things properly. OK, when she's ready, send her out. But I don't want her to overdo things.'

'You mollycoddle that girl, yet you demand so much from Chris,' said Helen. 'You should ease up on the lad. He really does try to please you.'

'Then let's see how he performs today, with all these bigwigs around the place. That'll test him all right! We'll soon see whether he's a man or a mouse!'

'Matt!'

But Matt had gone through to the room he used as his office and begun to hunt for the final list of guests.

Nick, now in uniform and on duty, began his enquiries. His first task was to have a word with Claude Jeremiah Greengrass to see whether he had confirmed the loss of his money. If this was a genuine crime, and not a mere misplacement of Claude's savings, then it would have to be recorded and due enquiries made. There might be a pattern to be detected in this series of crimes which had beset Aidensfield which would suggest the identity of the perpetrator. Or, of course, Nick mused, the guilty party might be Greengrass himself, and he could have invented a raid on his own premises in a vain attempt to put himself in the clear. But, considered Nick, Claude was not the sort of person who would break and enter premises. Besides, he could never have squeezed through the windows in the garage or the pub.

It did however occur to Nick that if Claude had had to refund Jack Scarman after the fiasco with the greyhound, then the scruffy old buffer might be short of cash. Had he pretended to be the victim of a burglary to claim on his household insurance, perhaps? Nick reckoned Claude was not the type to have his house contents insured, however; to meet the payments required for his conglomeration of belongings would surely demand some sacrifices. And Claude did not make sacrifices.

As these thoughts whirled around in Nick's head, he walked towards Claude's untidy establishment on the edge of the moors. Before he got there, however, he came across the familiar sight of a distinctive army greatcoat, its wearer leaning on a drystone wall with a pair of binoculars to his eyes. Alfred the dog was standing nearby.

'Well, well, Claude!' Nick said, creeping up behind him. 'Spying are we? What's so interesting?'

'I'm bird-watching, Mr Rowan. It's my hobby. There's a cirl bunting down there.'

'Cirl buntings are found only in the south of England, Claude, and then only rarely. They're not seen this far north. I reckon you saw a yellowhammer.'

'Aye, well, I'm just learning, you see,' and he pulled a battered bird book from his overcoat pocket. 'It's my new hobby. Everybody needs a hobby, Constable.'

'And I reckon Alfred's a great help in bird-watching. He'll not scare them away, will he?' said Nick. 'So whose land are you looking at? Lord Ashfordly's, if I'm not mistaken. And would your chief interest be pheasants, I wonder?'

'Pheasants? I don't count them as birds. They're live-stock, game.'

'Birds, Claude. Pheasants are birds just like grouse and partridges, which are also game. So what's so interesting over there? Can I have a look?'

Claude grudgingly handed over the binoculars. In the distance Nick could see Lord Ashfordly's shooting party making its way across the far edge of the estate. A tractor was drawing a trailer loaded with beaters and all appeared to be enjoying themselves. Most of the beaters seemed to be young people from the village out to earn some extra pocket money, although some adults were there to supervise them.

'An interesting sight, Claude,' commented Nick. 'There's a flock of Great British Bluebloods over there,' and he handed the binoculars back to Claude who looked through them before realising he was being mocked.

'Gerroff, you daft constibule!'

'Claude, I was really on my way to see you about your missing money. Did you check your premises like you said you would?'

'I did, every inch. And it's gone, Mr Rowan. Vanished. Tin and cash, the lot.'

'There's been other raids overnight,' and Nick outlined the various crimes to Claude, asking whether he had any idea who the perpetrators might be. Claude shook his head, adding that he was not a copper's nark but he still had no idea. He did venture a theory that it might be kids, though.

'I mean, who else would break into a butcher's van to nick a few shillings?'

'Well, your crime has been entered in our log, Claude, so you can expect our fingerprint men to be here sometime today.'

'I'd better be getting back, then, I don't want 'em wandering all over my land.'

'Just like Lord Ashfordly doesn't want you wandering all over his land, either. With or without your bird-watching equipment.'

'They can fingerprint my henhouse and that's all,' said

Claude, stalking off. Nick returned to the village to continue his enquiries.

At the end of that afternoon, with darkness descending, Lord Ashfordly expressed his satisfaction about the shoot. In his view, the day had gone exceedingly well, and his guests had been impressed by his hospitality, his organisation and the bag they had secured. There had been a lot of pheasants, which meant that none of his guests would leave empty-handed.

He asked Matt Rawlings to make sure the shot pheasants were placed in the game larder to hang overnight, ready for distribution the following day. All the guests, except Dr Ferrenby, were staying at Ashfordly Hall, and a fine dinner had been arranged. Ferrenby would be at the dinner though, Lord Ashfordly said, and so Rawlings was asked to have his pheasants ready to collect later in the evening.

Because this was the final shoot of the season, all the beaters and other helpers were invited to the Hall for drinks which would be served at five thirty. After reminding everyone of that invitation, Matt drove to the game larder with some helpers and hung all the pheasants ready for the next day. With a key he carried on his belt, he locked the door, making sure that the entire bag was secure for the night. He could relax; he had earned himself a drink or two.

Up at the Hall, the shooters, known as 'guns', were generous in tipping everyone who had helped, the beaters receiving their fair share. Helen Rawlings carried sandwiches around, while other helpers bore mugs of tea, glasses of beer, soft drinks and cakes. There was a lot of chatter and laughter and a lot of congratulatory noises. Susan, now feeling much better, although not entirely fit, moved away from the crush and leaned against a pillar. As she did so, one of the young beaters – Richard Francis, son of Bill Francis, the butcher – followed her. He was in the same class as Susan at school, and the two often travelled together on the bus. But Richard, now a handsome young man, had begun to regard Susan as more than just a school companion. Now she was a desirable woman.

He moved closer. 'Susan,' he said, 'how about seeing *Goldfinger* with me? After school, say Monday?'

Susan shook her head. 'My dad would never let me, you know he always comes to meet me off the bus.'

At that very moment, Matt came into the Hall, washed and brushed up, closely followed by his son, Chris, also neat and tidy. Matt noticed his daughter talking to young Francis and went across to her.

'Hi, Susan, you all right now?'

Susan nodded. 'Yes thanks, Dad, the fresh air did me a lot of good.'

'How about getting home? I'll run you back if you want. It's back to school tomorrow, the holiday's over, so what about an early night, eh?'

'Thanks, Dad, but I'll walk. It'll do me good, honest.'

She moved away from the pillar as if to begin her walk home, and Richard Francis moved with her. Then Chris, her brother, stepped forward.

'I can run you home,' Chris said.

'No, thanks, Chris,' Susan said firmly. 'I'll walk, like I said.'

Richard, however, was not to be put off.

'I'll walk back with you,' he volunteered in turn.

Chris stood in his way. 'No you won't,' he said belligerently. 'You'll leave her alone, right? We don't want you wasting her time, Richard. Keep away from her. Understand?'

Richard nodded, taken aback, as Susan left Ashfordly Hall for the long walk home.

It was seven thirty in the morning and Kate was trying to awaken Nick.

'Nick, half past seven. Are you awake?'

He grunted under the bedclothes and turned over, so she tried again. 'Nick, I really would like a cup of tea in bed this morning . . .'

Another grunt was the result, and then the telephone began to shrill downstairs.

'It'll be for me,' Kate said. 'Mrs King's baby's due any time.' She climbed out of bed, put on a dressing gown and hurried to take the call. But it wasn't Mrs King.

'Nick?' she shouted. 'It's for you, Matt Rawlings.'

He struggled into wakefulness as he pottered down the cold staircase and lifted the handset.

'Morning, Matt, it's PC Rowan.'

'You'll have to come, Nick, somebody's raided the game larder.'

'On the estate?'

'Yes, broke in during the night. All the bag's gone –

three hundred and fifteen pheasants!'

'Who the hell wants three hundred and fifteen pheasants?' cried Nick. 'And how did they carry them away?'

'You'll come, will you? Immediately? His Lordship's doing his nut. They were for his guests, to take away today after lunch.'

'I'll come,' said Nick. 'And I'll ring my sergeant as well, I think he ought to know about this.'

Sergeant Blaketon leapt out of bed as if all the hounds in hell were on his tail and without even stopping to polish his boots, jumped into his little black Ford Anglia and drove as fast as he could to Ashfordly Hall. Nick got there just before him and was inspecting the smashed door of the game larder, with Lord Ashfordly and Matt Rawlings, when his sergeant arrived.

'This is outrageous!' fumed Lord Ashfordly. 'The entire day's bag gone, Sergeant. And all my guests will be expecting their birds later today . . . Really, this is most embarrassing – and you know your Assistant Chief Constable, Mr McLeod, is with us, Sergeant. He's expecting to receive his share too. What am I going to tell them?'

'We'll begin enquiries immediately,' was all Blaketon could offer.

'Wait,' said Lord Ashfordly. 'I do not want word of this to circulate, understood?'

'My Lord?' asked Blaketon.

'If you start asking questions in the locality, every Tom, Dick and Harry will know about this. Under no circumstances must it reach the ears of my guests, is that understood? I demand the utmost discretion. And Rawlings?'

'Yes, my Lord?'

'You will replace those pheasants immediately. I don't care how you do it or what it costs, that larder will be replenished before any of my guests require their birds. So go to it.'

'Yes, my Lord,' said the bewildered gamekeeper.

'I'll start with Claude Jeremiah,' said Nick. 'I won't say where the pheasants have gone from, I'll just say there's been a lot stolen and we're looking for them.'

'Greengrass?' bellowed Sergeant Blaketon. 'I couldn't think of a more likely suspect.'

'He was seen around the woods yesterday,' said Rawlings. 'Several of the beaters spotted him.'

'And I saw him,' Nick added, 'with binoculars. He said he was bird-watching.'

'And those birds were pheasants, Rowan. What are we waiting for?'

Claude Jeremiah was in bed when they arrived, but their hammering on his door roused Alfred who barked until Claude made his dishevelled appearance. As Nick and Blaketon pushed their way into his untidy living room, they noticed a brace of pheasants on his table.

'So, Greengrass,' said Sergeant Blaketon. 'We've caught you red-handed, haven't we?'

'Red-handed, Mr Blaketon? What have I done now?'

'Pheasants from Lord Ashfordly's game larder. Three hundred and fifteen of 'em!'

'Three hundred and fifteen flipping pheasants? What would I do with all those?'

'There's two here,' said Blaketon, pointing to the birds on his table.

'I bought them, fair and square,' said Claude. 'Look, I'm a man of means now, I don't need to go risking my freedom for three hundred and fifteen flaming pheasants.'

'You were seen in the woods, I saw you watching with binoculars, Claude.'

'But you never saw me taking pheasants, Mr Rowan, and I didn't. Now you're on my property, and I'm innocent, which makes it a false accusation, Sergeant Blaketon, so if you don't get off my land, I'll lodge an official complaint about your conduct.'

'That money's gone to your head, Greengrass,' said Blaketon. 'But we'll be back, when we've got the evidence.'

'You do, and when you come back, you can tell me the name of the thief who nicked my money!'

Blaketon and Nick looked at each other. They knew they had to leave; they had no evidence against Claude and even if the pheasants on his table were from Lord Ashfordly's estate, it would be difficult to prove. One pheasant was like any other. They had no real lead for the pheasant felony, nor indeed for the theft of Claude's money or the other recent crimes.

'I'm going back to Ashfordly office, Rowan,' said Sergeant Blaketon. 'You spend the day here, on enquiries. And I want results before the ACC discovers his pheasants have vanished.'

Nick had no idea where to begin his extra-specially discreet enquiries.

CHAPTER TWELVE

Nick's early start to the day meant that the village was just coming to life as he began his patrol of the main street. The first person he saw was George Ward, putting several empty barrels and some crates of bottles outside in readiness for the arrival of the delivery wagon later in the morning.

'Morning, George.' Nick offered the usual pleasantries, adding, 'Look, if anybody offers you cheap pheasants today, give me a call, will you?'

'Greengrass been at it again, has he?' asked George, his eyebrows raised in wry amusement.

'I think this job was a bit out of his league. There's over three hundred been nicked. Don't ask where from, it's not for public consumption.'

'It wouldn't be hard to guess, would it, with there being a shooting day not a million miles from here yesterday. But right, I'll call. Three hundred gone! Wow, there's a few good dinners among that lot!'

'Exactly what somebody else has in mind.'

George nodded. 'Right, now, while you're here,

Nick, you'd better know that our Gina did a check on the bar stock yesterday, and reckons there's a bottle of gin missing. We usually keep a spare below the counter, ready to slot into the optics. She says it's vanished.'

'One bottle of gin? Is that all?'

'Yes, I can't see anything else has gone missing. Who'd break in to pinch a bottle of gin, Nick?'

'Search me, George. But thanks.'

Nick's next call was at Bill Francis's shop where the butcher had already been at work for several hours; he was now preparing his counter and display for the day. Nick entered to find fourteen fresh pheasants hanging from the rafters.

'Who's your supplier for these pheasants, Bill?'

'A chap in Ashfordly, Harry Penrose. Why?'

'Legitimate, are they?'

'Sure, he breeds them for domestic consumption. Why all the questions?'

'Some have been nicked nearby, I'm not allowed to say where from. More than three hundred, to be honest. We're trying to find out who's getting rid of them.'

'Aye, well, if it's who I think it is who's lost them, I'm not sorry. He's got more money than me. But Penrose is straight, Nick, you can ask him. Besides, you can't tell one pheasant from another, can you?'

'OK, thanks. You'll give me a call if anybody does offer you lots of them cheap?'

'Sure,' said Bill as his son, Richard, emerged into the shop in his school blazer.

He bade farewell to his father and said he might be late home tonight, he was thinking of may be going to see a James Bond film after school.

'Did you enjoy beating yesterday?' Nick asked the lad.

'Yeah, it was good fun, Mr Rowan,' replied Richard quickly and hurried away to catch his bus.

'He's got his eye on Matt Rawlings's lass,' smiled Bill. 'He keeps trying to get her to go out with him, but she's a close one, is that. Her dad's too protective if you ask me. Damn it, Nick, she is seventeen. Big enough and old enough, as they say. But he still treats her like a little kid.'

'So Richard's hoping to get her to go to the pictures with him, eh?'

'And a good thing, I say,' smiled Bill. 'Well, I must be getting on. I've got my sausages to string up now.'

Nick was in time to see the school bus come to a halt outside the post office and the assembled gang of children clamber noisily on board. Among them was Susan Rawlings; Nick saw her kiss her father's cheek before joining the others.

'Have a nice time,' he said, handing her some money as she boarded the coach. She thanked him as the door closed.

Rawlings saw Nick approaching and smiled. 'She's staying late tonight, Nick, going out to a film with a girlfriend, she says. Carol somebody or other. Who'd have a young daughter? I worry myself sick about our Susan. I mean she *is* attractive.'

'I'm sure she can look after herself,' smiled Nick.

'Aye, but I saw the way some of those beaters looked at her yesterday. It worries me sick, the way some lads ogle young lasses.'

'It's all part of growing up, Matt. But I'm pleased you care, some parents don't give a toss about their kids. Now, any more developments about the famous pheasant felony?'

'I've got to find replacements for every one before his Lordship's guests leave,' said Rawlings. 'I've had words with some of the other estates and breeders hereabouts. I can rustle up enough, I'm sure. I'm getting lots delivered when I get back; it'll cost His Lordship a bomb but I reckon the crisis is over. All that matters to him is not to look a twit in front of his guests.'

'Well, I've got no leads yet. I'm convinced Greengrass isn't responsible, Matt, even though he was in your woods for some nefarious purpose yesterday.'

Rawlings nodded. 'Thanks for trying, Nick. If I get any tips, I'll call you.'

When Ashfordly Grammar School's day ended at half past three, Susan Rawlings walked towards the bus stop with her friends. Richard Francis was waiting, seeking an opportunity to have a quick word with Susan about going to the pictures.

He knew she had planned to stay in town this evening because her dad had said something to her before she'd boarded the bus this morning, and had given her some money. Right now, Susan was talking to a group of classmates. When they heard the bus groaning up the slope towards the bus stop she bade farewell to her friends.

'I'll see you tomorrow,' Richard heard her say.

Without a glance at him, she hurried away towards the town centre, almost at a run. Richard was frozen with indecision. Clearly, she'd not seen him or, if she had, she had taken deliberate action to avoid him. Or did she expect him to follow her? But she was moving very quickly away and, as the others boarded the bus home, he decided to follow her. She continued her rapid pace along the street, ducking into a narrow alley between the King's Head Hotel and the Black Lion Inn. He turned in after her to see her hurrying up the slight incline, looking neither left nor right as she made her way through the narrow lane. She emerged at the far end where the lane formed a junction with a busy street. Here she stopped for a moment to decide which direction to take, and then moved away towards a council estate which stood at the far side of the junction.

Richard saw her stop a child who was wheeling a bicycle and ask for directions, whereupon the small boy pointed along an avenue of council houses.

Susan resumed her hurried mission, walking swiftly along the footpath towards one of the houses. Then, outside Number 15, Acacia Avenue, she stopped. There seemed to be a moment of uncertainty as she gazed around. Richard thought she was going to turn and walk away – but, after taking a deep breath, she opened the gate and stepped through. With apparent confidence, she knocked on the front door, which was eventually opened by a smiling middle-aged woman. It was evident to Richard that she had been expecting Susan, because she was admitted straight away and the door closed behind her.

Puzzled, Richard wondered what to do. Perhaps this was a relation of Susan's? An aunt or great-aunt, maybe? Perhaps she'd gone there for tea before going to the pictures? Richard had nothing to do, and as it was a long time before the next bus back to Aidensfield, he decided to wait.

It was dark by the time Susan emerged, and Richard thought she looked sick; the brisk energetic walk had gone and she seemed to be struggling to move. He waited until he felt sure she was heading back towards the lane between the two pubs, then ran ahead to accost her.

'Susan?' He was standing under a streetlamp when she reached him.

'Oh, Richard, hi.' Under the glow of the light, she looked even more pale and tired.

'You all right?'

'I don't feel too good,' she admitted, trying a brave smile. 'I think I must have eaten something.'

'Shall I get us a taxi home?' he said. 'I've got some money, I was saving some of my beater's pay.'

'That would be nice.' Her smile revealed her gratitude. 'It's cold, hanging around for buses.'

'Do you want something to eat?'

'No, I had something not long ago,' she said. 'I just want to go home. Do you mind?'

'No, course not.'

Solicitously Richard took her to Halcombe's Taxi Services where he was able to secure a ride to Aidensfield. During the short run, Susan barely said a word; she huddled into a corner of the rear seat, clutching her hands about herself and clearly not wishing to communicate with Richard. The taxi dropped Richard off outside his father's home which adjoined the butcher's shop, and the driver took Susan on to her parents' cottage on the Ashfordly estate.

At three o'clock the following morning, Nick was lying awake. He was restless and couldn't sleep; the problems of the spate of crimes on his beat just wouldn't allow his brain to relax. He tossed and turned in bed and his wakefulness also prevented Kate from sinking into a deep slumber.

'What's the matter, Nick? For heaven's sake try to relax!'

'Sorry, luv,' he apologised. 'I can't get to sleep, it's all those crimes, the thought that somebody's out there, breaking into property on my patch. It's so bloody annoying.'

'Don't take it personally, Nick,' Kate said gently.

'I can't help it; it's as if somebody's got it in for me, proving I'm powerless to stop them. It's not Claude Jeremiah, I'm convinced of that. So who else would steal his Lordship's pheasants? And nick a single bottle of gin from the pub? Is one person responsible for all these crimes, or is it a gang?' He sighed. 'I want to stop the crimes, Kate, but I can't be everywhere at once. I can't stand around and guard every house and shop in this place, twenty-four hours a day.'

'And you need your sleep, Nick.' She turned and put her arms about him under the covers. 'Try to relax. Try counting pheasants!'

'Kate!'

Suddenly the telephone rang out.

'I don't believe it!' grumbled Nick. 'Whose turn is it this time?'

Kate kicked him under the sheets. 'You're awake, you go.'

'Not another burglary or shop-breaking, I hope!' He put on a dressing gown and struggled downstairs in the chill of the night to answer the call.

'Aidensfield Police.' His tired voice was little more than a croak.

'It's Helen Rawlings.' She sounded tearful and distraught. 'Can Dr Rowan come straight away, it's urgent, it's Susan.'

'Susan?'

'She's bleeding, Mr Rowan, it's terrible . . . please help us.'

'She'll come straight away,' Nick reassured Helen. 'I'll drive her over.'

Kate told Nick she could manage on her own, but he insisted on driving her to the remote keeper's cottage. While she dressed and decided what to take with her, Nick rushed into some old clothes and got the car out of the garage. At the back of his own mind was the thought that he'd be driving through the village and the countryside in the early hours of the morning and so, if there were any villains abroad, he might just come across them. But the journey to the Rawlings's cottage was uneventful.

When they arrived, Matt Rawlings rushed out to meet them. 'Thank God!' he breathed. 'Come in, Doctor, she's in a terrible state, she won't let us near her.'

Leading Kate inside, Matt hurried up the stairs with Helen hard on his heels. Nick remained in the living room where a fire was smouldering in the grate. He picked up a log which lay in the hearth and tossed it on to the embers as Matt's pale-faced son, Chris, appeared in the doorway, looking terrified. As soon as he saw the policeman in the room, however, he turned around and went back upstairs.

Helen Rawlings led Kate into Susan's room. The bed-side light was burning and the girl lay in bed, her hands gripping the top of the sheets which were pulled up to her chin. The expression on Susan's white face was one of abject terror and she was groaning with pain. She looked, thought Kate, like a young girl in fear of her life and it was obvious that a swift physical examination was necessary.

'Could you wait downstairs, please?' she asked the anxious parents. Helen and Matt closed the door. Kate heard them descending the stairs, and Matt's voice saying, 'Chris, you'd better come down, the doctor's here.'

Kate turned her attention to Susan whose dark eyes stared at her from the bed. 'Susan, I must examine you,' she said gently.

'No, I don't want anybody to touch me, go away.'

'Susan, your mother said you were bleeding . . .'

'I went to the loo, it was just a very heavy period . . .'

'I think not. Your mother would know if it was just a heavy period, so come along, let go of those sheets and let me look at you,' and Kate went forward to prise the girl's fingers away.

'No, please, you mustn't . . .' but the voice was weak as Kate gently released the sheets and turned them down. Underneath there was a mass of bloodstained sheets, cloths and clothing. Then Kate found the source of the blood.

Susan was weeping now. 'She said it would be nothing, she said it would be all right, that it wouldn't hurt . . .'

Kate looked at her. 'You've had an abortion, haven't you, Susan?'

The girl nodded, her eyes showing that she was a very, very frightened young woman. Kate remained calm, knowing she must reassure Susan that help was on hand. She returned the bedclothes to their former position and said, 'You need to go to hospital. I'm going to ring for the ambulance.'

As she went downstairs to make the call, the sound of Susan's uncontrollable sobbing followed her.

'Can I use your telephone?' Kate addressed the worried family. 'I need an ambulance, we must get her to hospital without delay. She's haemorrhaging badly.'

Within the hour, Susan was in Ashfordly General Hospital on a blood drip and was being wheeled into a ward for further examination. A doctor and a nurse were in attendance; Kate had a quiet word with them before returning to Susan's parents in the waiting room. Chris had not come with them, there being no room in Nick's car for anyone else.

'She's in good hands now,' she told Matt and Helen. 'She's on her way to the theatre for an operation, an emergency operation, that is. The surgeon is already here, waiting. She'll get prompt attention and she'll be all right, although she has lost a lot of blood.'

'I don't understand,' said Matt. 'What's happened to her? Is it her appendix or something that's burst? That stomach trouble she was having . . .'

'No,' said Kate, knowing they must be told the truth. 'She's had an abortion, Matt. And it's gone wrong. Very badly wrong.'

'Abortion?' he whispered. 'My Susan's had an abortion? Are you sure?'

'Yes, there's no doubt about it. I'm sorry.' Kate looked at Helen. She must have guessed what had caused such a severe flow of blood. Susan's mother sat with her head bowed, weeping silently into her hands.

'But she's never had a boyfriend, Doctor, we were so careful with her, she never stayed out late.'

'Staying out late isn't all that's needed to get pregnant, Matt. Now look, she's going to need all the love, help and sympathy you can muster. She needs you both now, more than ever in her life before, so please don't reject her. The baby's gone, you might want to know that, but it's going to take Susan a long time to get over this.'

Helen looked at Kate through her tears, 'Oh, I can't believe this . . . but thank you, Doctor, we'll take care of her, we love her so much, don't we, Matt?'

'Aye,' was all the bluff gamekeeper could say.

Because unlawful abortion was a serious criminal offence, Nick was obliged to inform his superiors, and so next morning, his first duty was to motor to Ashfordly Police Station. Sergeant Blaketon was in his office when Nick entered.

'Good morning, Rowan, I take it you've come to inform me that you have cleared up the Aidensfield crime wave and arrested all the guilty parties?'

'No, Sergeant, I've come to report another crime, much more serious.'

'I don't believe this! What is it this time?'

'Abortion, Sergeant. Susan Rawlings, Matt Rawlings's daughter, she's only seventeen. She's had an unlawful abortion. She's in hospital.'

'You have got your hands full, haven't you, Rowan? So who carried out the abortion?'

'I don't know yet, the girl's not in a fit state to be interviewed. She was taken into Casualty last night.'

'Right, well, this is serious stuff, Rowan, and don't forget the ACC's got his eyes on this section. He never called while he was staying with His Lordship but I heard, on the grapevine, that he does intend to visit us.'

'I'm sure he will appreciate our efforts, Sergeant.'

'Yes, but I do not want an illegal abortion as well as other unsolved crimes to ruin my statistics. So find the boyfriend, start with him. Then I want you to see that girl and get her to name the abortionist. We'll have to stop the woman, Rowan, before she does it again.'

'Her parents say she never had a boyfriend, Sergeant.'

'Then how did she get pregnant, Rowan? You're not telling me we've got a rape as well, are you? If that lass got herself pregnant, she must have had a boyfriend. So find him and ask him what he knows. And get the girl interviewed the minute she's fit to talk. This is a DPP job, you know, all abortion prosecutions must be reported to the Director of Public Prosecutions, so we need this one tidied up and a proper and thorough investigation made, Rowan. So get to it.'

'Very good, Sergeant.'

'Oh, and Rowan?'

'Yes, Sergeant?'

'There is one crime you can forget. Lord Ashfordly called in late yesterday. We are to ignore the stolen pheasants. He wants us to overlook the crime and says he will not support any prosecution we might bring.'

'He can't do that, Sergeant! What's he playing at?'

'He says all his guests went home with their pheasants. He managed to secure sufficient by various means, and he insists there is nothing more to be done.'

Nick looked shocked. 'But Sergeant, a crime was committed and it's our job to apprehend the person or persons responsible.'

'Not in this case, Rowan. So forget the stolen pheasants. It's one crime less to worry about, and one less for our month-end statistics. So concentrate on this abortion. Right?'

'Yes, Sergeant.'

Nick returned to Aidensfield, and after Kate had

finished her surgery, told her of Blaketon's orders.

Kate looked worried. 'It's not part of my job to ask who did it, Nick. I can't put that sort of pressure on the girl right now.'

'But you'll be going to visit her today?' Nick persisted.

'Yes, of course I will, but as a doctor, not a detective!'

'But can you ask? All I want is a name, Kate, the name and address of the woman who carried out the abortion.'

Kate frowned. 'I'll ask but if she refuses, I will not put pressure on her. She's in no fit state to be questioned, Nick.'

'That woman is a criminal, Kate. She's just as much a criminal as a rapist or a burglar. She's got to be caught and stopped.'

'So what will you be doing while I'm doing your job for you?' There was more than a hint of sarcasm in her voice.

'I'm going to see Matt and Helen Rawlings. I need to know Susan's movements yesterday. Where she went, who she was with, who saw her and so on.'

'It won't be easy, talking to them.'

'No, but it has to be done,' sighed Nick.

When he arrived at the Rawlings's cottage, Helen, red-eyed and weary, offered him a coffee. He accepted and settled down at the kitchen table while she called Matt; he came in carrying a shotgun he'd been cleaning, and was followed by Chris, also with a gun. The two men, silent and morose, sat down at the table as Helen prepared the coffee. Nick explained the purpose of his visit.

'I'm sorry to have to come like this,' he apologised. 'But

whoever did that to Susan has committed a criminal offence. Now, there'll be no action against Susan, but we must find the woman who carried out the abortion. That means I have to find out who she was with yesterday, where she went and so forth.'

'She went to school as normal.' Matt spoke quietly. 'I put her on the bus, like I always do. She said she was staying after school to go to the pictures with a friend. I gave her a few bob to buy some sweets and things. But Nick, I can't understand this . . . we never let her stay out late, we always knew where she was and who she was with . . .'

'The money you gave her, Matt, that wouldn't be enough to pay for an abortion, would it?'

'Good God no, it was just five bob. We give her pocket money for school, nowt more than a few bob.'

'So she went off to school. What time did she get back?'

'Before seven, she wasn't late,' Helen said. 'She said she'd been to the pictures with Carol and they'd seen that James Bond film where a woman is coated with gold paint.'

'*Goldfinger*? It's on at the Lyric in Ashfordly,' Nick confirmed. 'How was she?'

'Tired,' said Helen. 'She looked washed out, actually, but I put it down to some tummy troubles she's been having, something going round at school. I know now it wasn't that, it was morning sickness.' She shook her head sadly. 'I should have realised she was pregnant!'

'I can't believe our Susan got herself pregnant,' Matt expounded. 'She must have been raped, somebody must have forced himself on her and made her too frightened to tell us.'

'She was three months pregnant,' said Helen quietly. 'The hospital told me last night.'

'So last night,' Nick persisted, 'she came in, and then what?'

'She went straight to her room. She said she had some homework to do. Chris took her up a drink, didn't you?'

Chris nodded. 'She was a bit quiet, but I never thought anything was wrong. She never said she was ill.'

Nick turned his attention to the younger man, who was still nursing the gun. 'Did she mention meeting anybody? Who she'd been to the pictures with? Anything like that?'

'No, she just thanked me for the drink and said she wanted to be on her own, so I came out.'

'OK, thanks, Chris. So how did she get home from Ashfordly last night?' Nick asked.

'A taxi,' said Helen. 'It dropped her at the door. It was one of Dan Halcombe's from Ashfordly.'

'Right, thanks, well, I don't want to distress you further, but I must have a look at her room, to see if she's left an address or anything that might lead us to the abortionist.' He looked around at the worried family. 'I stress that we are not going to prosecute Susan, it's the woman who carried out the illegal operation that we're interested in. Can you show me Susan's room, Helen?'

'I'll get back outside,' said Matt. 'Come on, Chris, we've a lot to do.'

With Helen in attendance, Nick searched Susan's

bedroom, checking her school satchel, her notebooks, a diary they found and various other items of paperwork, but there was nothing which suggested an abortionist's address. Then Helen opened the wardrobe and produced an empty gin bottle.

'I found this under her bed,' she told Nick. 'We don't have gin in the house, it's not one of our bottles. I think she must have been trying to abort herself by drinking gin. That's how women used to get rid of babies themselves. But please, don't tell Matt, he's taking this very hard, Nick. Very hard indeed. He worships our Susan.'

Nick accepted the bottle, recalling that a bottle had been stolen from George's pub. Was this the one?

'Has any money been missing from the house lately?' he asked Helen. 'If Susan went to an abortionist, she would have had to pay quite a lot of money, you see.'

'No,' she said, clearly in all sincerity. 'She's never stolen any money, Nick, she knows better than to steal.'

'All right, well, thanks for your help. I do hope she gets well. Now, I must see what the taxi driver can tell me.'

On his way out of the grounds, Nick saw Chris Rawlings in one of the sheds and stopped for a talk.

'Chris,' he said, 'you're pretty close to your sister, I believe?'

'We get on all right,' said the youth, not looking Nick in the eye.

'Did she confide in you?'

'Not really, no.'

'I wondered if she'd ever mentioned her worries, about being pregnant, I mean.'

'No,' he said.

'Did she borrow any money from you?'

'No.'

'Did she mention seeing a lad, had she a boyfriend she wanted to keep from your parents?'

'I can't help, Mr Rowan, I know nowt.'

It was clear that Chris had no intention of helping Nick, and so the policeman drove into Ashfordly to call upon Dan Halcombe.

'Hello, Mr Rowan, not wanting a taxi are you?' Dan greeted him. He was a cheerful character who was popular with all his customers, young and old alike.

'No, but I'm interested in a run you did from Ashfordly to Aidensfield last night. A run on to Lord Ashfordly's estate.'

'That's right, I took a lass to the keeper's cottage, Matt Rawlings's lass.'

'That's the trip. Now, where did you pick her up?'

'She came to my office in Ashfordly, her and a lad.'

'A lad? Who was the lad?'

'Bill Francis's kid, young Richard.'

'Thank you very much,' smiled Nick Rowan.

CHAPTER THIRTEEN

When Nick returned to Aidensfield, he found Bill Francis cleaning out his van. He was swilling the interior with cold water and whistling as he worked. He stopped as Nick approached.

'Hello, Nick, not a bad day for the time of year.'

'Hello, Bill, is your Richard at home?'

'Aye, he's in his room. Summat I can help with?'

'Not at this stage, thanks, I'd better see him in private first.'

'Not been misbehaving, has he?'

'I hope not,' said Nick. 'Shall I go up?'

'I'll show you.' Upstairs, Bill tapped on a door and said, 'Richard, PC Rowan's here, he'd like a word.' Richard opened his door and Bill, clearly interested to know why the constable should wish to interview his son, lingered just a moment.

Nick dismissed the butcher with a quick, 'Thanks, Bill. See you later.'

The room was that of a typical teenager, rather like Susan Rawlings's in many respects. There was a CND poster, some other posters of pop stars, a range of model aircraft, some on shelves and others hanging on cotton from the ceiling.

There were also school books and football shirts, with one of Middlesbrough FC's club scarves hanging over his wardrobe door.

'Hello, Richard, can I come in?'

'Mr Rowan! Good heavens . . . yeah, sure . . . sorry the place is in such a state.'

'I've come about Susan Rawlings,' began Nick, pacing up and down the room.

'Susan? Why, what's happened?' The look of surprise on his face was genuine, Nick felt.

'She's in hospital. I wondered if you knew anything about the reason?'

'Me? No! Why should I know about it? Look, Mr Rowan, what's happened?'

And then Nick caught sight of a large biscuit tin. He lifted it down from its perch on top of the wardrobe. It bore a picture of the Coronation on the lid and when Nick looked inside, it was empty.

'Richard? This tin, where did you get it?'

'Why, what's it to you?'

'Look, this is serious. This looks very like the tin that was stolen from Mr Greengrass, together with fifty pounds.'

'I didn't steal it, I didn't steal any money . . .'

From that point, Richard refused to say anything more about the tin.

Nick told him about the abortion and warned him that

242

he was now under suspicion of stealing the tin of cash from Claude Jeremiah Greengrass, and of helping Susan to get an abortion.

'Me? Mr Rowan, I don't know what you're talking about! I've not stolen that tin, or the money, and I've not done anything to Susan that would make her want an abortion. I never got her pregnant, honest. God, why do you think it's me?'

'You came home with her in a taxi, the night she was taken ill.'

'She was in Ashfordly, I saw her looking poorly and so I got a taxi home. I had some money from when I was beating for Mr Rawlings and Lord Ashfordly.'

'Why were you in Ashfordly, why didn't you come straight home from school?'

'I . . . I . . . well, I thought Susan might go to the pictures with me. It was *Goldfinger*. But she ran away. I followed her.'

'Where to?'

'The council houses, she went into a council house.'

'Which one, Richard?'

'Number fifteen, it was Acacia Avenue. I remember the name on the wall.'

'How long was she there?'

'A long time, more than an hour, and when she came out she was looking poorly, so I got a taxi home.'

'You mean you waited outside all that time?'

The lad blushed and said, 'Yes, I wanted her to go out with me, you see.'

'So you never got to the pictures, and neither did she,

eh? And you expect me to believe you had no idea why she was in that house?'

'No, I thought she must be visiting an aunt or something.'

Nick spent a further half-hour trying to extract from Richard Francis an admission that he had made Susan pregnant and that he had stolen money from Claude Jeremiah Greengrass, and other places including his own father's van, to pay for an abortion. He suggested that Richard had then accompanied Susan to an abortionist, remaining in the background until she had been ready to come home. But throughout his accusations, Richard remained adamant that he was not responsible for any of the matters in question.

Nick sighed and left, taking the tin with him. He told Richard he was taking it to Claude Jeremiah to see if it was the one stolen from his premises. And if it was, Richard would have to be interviewed again, at length, and by more senior police officers. Bill Francis was waiting outside and expressed surprise when Nick left with the old biscuit tin under his arm. Nick felt he owed some explanation to the butcher and told him the reason for his visit.

'But our Richard's no thief, Nick! And as for getting the lass in the family way, he's not capable of that!'

'I suggest he is, Bill. Neither of those two are children any more, they're both healthy teenagers.'

'Aye, but our Richard's never been given the come-on by young Susan. He's followed her about like a lovesick puppy, but he wouldn't know how to go about getting a lass pregnant!'

'Well, somebody got her pregnant and somebody paid for an abortion. And whoever it was probably nicked money from the garage and from your van as well. They might even have nicked all those pheasants!'

The butcher was red-faced with distress. 'I'll have words with our Richard, Nick. I want to get to the bottom of this as much as you. But I'd swear my lad's not a criminal.'

'See you, Bill,' was all Nick could say before he rode away with the biscuit tin in his pannier.

His first call was at the Greengrass establishment where Claude Jeremiah readily identified the tin as his property; he was sure it was his because of some holes he'd punched in the lid when he'd carried some day-old chicks in it. Nick then drove down to Ashfordly for a discussion with Sergeant Blaketon, who listened attentively to his account. When Number 15, Acacia Avenue was mentioned, Alf Ventress piped up eagerly. 'Edith Gillet, retired midwife. She's just moved there from Aidensfield. She's only been there a week or two.'

'Has she?' barked Blaketon. 'Then we ought to be having words with that lady. Is she known as an abortionist, Ventress? Any local gossip along those lines?'

'Not to my knowledge, Sarge,' Alf said. 'She seems to be a very decent woman. Not your normal seedy back-street abortionist.'

'Can you interview her, Rowan? It's your case, you'll know her if she used to live in Aidensfield, and you'll know what to say. Don't forget to ask if she knows that kid of Francis's.'

When Nick knocked on the door of Number 15, Acacia Avenue, Mrs Gillett responded, smiling and welcoming.

'Oh, Mr Rowan, what a surprise. Do come in.'

She invited him inside, saying she had just made a pot of tea and that he would be most welcome to have a cup. He accepted and they chatted about her retirement, her work for Dr Ferrenby and the respect she bore for him. She also praised Kate for her youthful enthusiasm and expressed her present worries about the state of Alex Ferrenby's health. Then Nick had the awful task of referring to the reason for his presence.

'Mrs Gillet, I'm not here for a very pleasant purpose. Do you know Susan Rawlings, the gamekeeper's daughter from Lord Ashfordly's estate?'

'Yes, I do,' smiled his hostess. 'A nice girl.'

'She had an abortion, Mrs Gillet, and she was seen to come to your house shortly beforehand.'

'An abortion? Good grief, I had no idea!'

'It went wrong afterwards, Mrs Gillet, Susan's in hospital now, in a serious condition.'

'Oh my God . . .' Mrs Gillet was genuinely shocked at this news and the cup of tea in her hand began to rattle as her hands shook with nerves. 'The poor girl.'

'You were a midwife, Mrs Gillet, well known and respected in Aidensfield and district. We know that Susan was here the same evening as she had her abortion.'

Mrs Gillet shook her head. 'The poor, poor child . . .'

'I have to ask you this, Mrs Gillet, but did you perform an abortion on Susan Rawlings? You know it is a crime, that abortion is illegal.'

'PC Rowan, I was a midwife for all my working life and my career was dedicated to caring for pregnant women. I am not likely to risk my name and my reputation, especially in retirement, by carrying out an illegal abortion. Of course I did not operate on that girl!'

'But you do admit she came to the house?'

'She came to me for some advice, Mr Rowan, confidential advice on female matters, and I gave her the advice, free of charge. That's all.'

'What sort of advice?'

'You of all people should know that I cannot betray such a confidence, Mr Rowan.'

'Mrs Gillet, she came here directly from school, we have a witness. She took a taxi home and went straight to her room where she was later found haemorrhaging. The only place she could have obtained an abortion was here, in this house.'

Mrs Gillet drew herself up tall in her chair. 'She could have done it herself, Constable. She did not receive an abortion in this house.'

'And do you know a youth called Richard Francis? We have reason to believe he paid for the abortion, with money he stole in Aidensfield.'

'Yes, of course I know him, but he never came here with her. It was between Susan and me, and we had a chat, nothing more.'

'Then you won't object if I search your house?'

'If it's my medical bag you want, Constable, it's over there in the corner,' and she went for it. She laid it on the table and opened it to reveal a whole kit of midwifery

247

equipment: speculums, forceps, scissors and dressings.

'I keep this for old times' sake,' she smiled at Nick.

Nick knew he was beaten. There was no way he could prove that this woman had aborted Susan Rawlings, unless Susan herself provided the necessary evidence.

'I'm really sorry to have bothered you, Mrs Gillet,' Nick said with some difficulty.

'You have your duty to perform, PC Rowan,' were her only words as she showed him to the door.

After his interview with Mrs Gillet, Nick drove around to the police station to acquaint Sergeant Blaketon with recent developments. Before he could let a word out, Blaketon demanded, 'What's going on, Rowan? While you were round at Mrs Gillet's, I've had Claude Jeremiah Greengrass on the phone. He doesn't want to prosecute for the theft of that money.'

'Why not, Sarge? Did he give any indication?'

'He said something about it all being a misunderstanding; he said Bill Francis has brought the money back, so he wants us to forget about it. I don't understand it, Rowan. Does that mean Richard Francis stole it? I thought he denied all knowledge of that crime?'

'He did, Sarge. Maybe his father thinks he really did steal the cash.'

'Or perhaps his father wants to minimise the fuss if the kid goes to court for helping to procure an abortion. That makes two victims of crime not wanting to prosecute – first Lord Ashfordly and then Claude Jeremiah Greengrass. I wouldn't have thought there was any collusion there, Rowan, but stranger things have happened.'

'A conspiracy of silence, Sergeant.'

'A worrying trend, Rowan. How can we perform our duty without the co-operation of the public? It puts us in an impossible situation. Now, what about your interview with that suspected abortionist? Anything positive resulted from that?'

Nick told Sergeant Blaketon how his visit had gone and Blaketon shrugged. It was a recurrence of many a similar report – in lots of cases of abortion, the identity of the abortionist was usually known, but a lack of evidence prevented any prosecution.

'OK, get away home, Rowan, let's see if there's any other way of proving a case against Mrs Gillet. And how is that girl?'

'Still very poorly, Sergeant.'

'You realise that if she dies, we've got a case of homicide on our hands? The abortionist would be charged with murder.'

'Yes, Sergeant.'

'Then let's hope the girl recovers. We don't want an unsolved murder on our patch, do we, Rowan?'

'No, Sergeant.'

Nick drove home in a reflective mood. As he travelled the picturesque route between Ashfordly and Aidensfield, it seemed that a lot of answers had been provided. Richard Francis had got Susan Rawlings pregnant; the kids had been too afraid to tell their parents and had decided on an abortion. Without the necessary funds, they had resorted to theft in order to raise the money, with Susan, or someone on her behalf, stealing a bottle of gin in the hope it would help in bringing on a miscarriage. This seemed to be the situation, and yet Nick realised it was all speculation. There was no proof for any of his theories.

At home, he took off his boots and sat before the fire toasting his toes while Kate made a pot of tea. She'd bought some fruit cake in the shop and they were looking forward to a cosy break together.

'I saw Susan again at the hospital,' Kate said. 'She's far from well but refuses to say anything about her condition. I'm sorry I couldn't help you with questioning her. It's really not my job.'

Nick shook his head. 'It was wrong of me to ask. I shouldn't take advantage of your profession and our relationship. Forgive me.'

'I know you want to find the abortionist, and so do I, Nick, believe me. But you know the Rawlings have decided not to prosecute if anyone is arrested? I saw them at the hospital today too. They just want to forget the whole thing. Matt will be ringing you. All they want is for Susan to recover, and I can understand that desire.'

'But if we stop our enquiries,' Nick protested, 'it means Mrs Gillet will be free to do it again. And next time, the mother could die . . . Susan nearly did, didn't she?'

'If we hadn't found her in time, yes, it could have been far more serious.'

He could not understand modern society, Nick grumbled. The law was there to protect its vulnerable members, but it needed the co-operation of all its members if the system was to function for the benefit of everyone.

'Nick,' said Kate when he'd finished. 'You mentioned Mrs Gillet, the retired midwife?'

'Yes, it was her, but we'll never prove it. The timings of Susan's movements are almost evidence enough, but Mrs Gillet is crafty: she knows we can never prove it was her without Susan's evidence. And now her folks want us to drop our enquiries. So where do we go from here?'

'You have a nice relaxing night off,' Kate smiled, 'and stop trying to rectify all of society's ills!'

Next morning, Kate had a long discussion with Dr Ferrenby before surgery. Ferrenby said he'd known Edith Gillet for years! She'd been a midwife in the district for decades and had always given excellent service with total reliability. The news that Kate imparted, that she had probably aborted Susan Rawlings, was a terrible shock to him.

'Kate, I am going to see that woman, and I want you to come too. If I only do one more thing before I retire . . .'

'You're definitely retiring?' she asked.

'Well, I'm seriously thinking about it!' he said with just a hint of deviousness in his smile. 'But before I do, I want to do my best to stop people aborting babies! It's murder, Kate, it's inhuman. Women talk about having control over their bodies, but it's not their body they are destroying, it's the body and the life of their unborn child . . . They should exercise more self-control, keep sex within the state of marriage, and there'd be no problems.'

'Alex, you are old-fashioned,' Kate smiled. 'Look, girls

have been getting pregnant before marriage right through history and nothing's going to stop them. Abortion will be made legal. You know there are moves already to do that, and it serves no purpose prosecuting somebody like Susan Rawlings just to prove that society objects to what girls and boys do naturally. I'll come with you to see Mrs Gillet, but I won't condemn abortion – although I do condemn the injuries she inflicted on that poor girl.'

Later that day, Kate stood beside Alex Ferrenby as he knocked on the door of Number 15, Acacia Avenue. Mrs Gillet's expression when she saw Ferrenby told Kate everything. Her face showed a mixture of horror and fear, and foreboding too.

'Dr Ferrenby! Is it about Susan Rawlings?'

'It is, Edie.'

Kate, in an attempt to ease the woman's obviously deep concern, said, 'She is improving, Mrs Gillet. She's getting better and there's no longer any concern for her life. I'm her doctor, I'm in regular contact with the hospital.'

'You'd better come in, both of you.'

Over a cup of tea, Ferrenby said, 'Edie, this must stop.'

Mrs Gillet opened her mouth to object, but Ferrenby stemmed her flow of words. 'Don't treat us as fools. I know you did that abortion, but the police can never prove it, and Susan won't reveal your name. Without her evidence, you can't be prosecuted. But I don't understand your actions. After years of helping me, years of delivering babies on these moors, you've turned to abortion. I can't understand that, Edie.'

Edie was silent a moment, gazing into her tea cup. 'I lost my own daughter when a back-street abortion went wrong,' she said eventually. 'I vowed I would never let other girls take that risk. I knew what I was doing, I wanted to help girls in desperate trouble.'

'But it's a crime, Mrs Gillet,' said Kate. 'Taking money for carrying out abortions . . .'

'I could never take their money, I always gave it back. I saw myself doing a service, being able to help. Word gets around. I've done lots of them since I retired, Dr Ferrenby, got a lot of girls out of trouble, saved their lives even.'

'Susan may never be able to have children,' said Kate quietly. 'You've punctured the uterine wall, she may be sterile, and she nearly died through loss of blood.'

'We're talking about my patients and Kate's patients, Edie,' said Alex. 'Now, I'm almost on the point of retiring too, but I want this to stop. It's gone too far. That is why we are here, to tell you to stop. Either you agree, or we inform the police of your activities. I'm sure, from the records in my surgery, that we could provide a dossier for the police. It would be circumstantial evidence, Edie, enough to back the circumstantial evidence of Susan's injuries.'

Mrs Gillet was weeping quietly by this time. 'I'll get my bag of equipment, Dr Ferrenby. You must take it away with you. I'll never do it again, never. I swear.'

Several days later, while Nick was out on his motorcycle working an early patrol and Kate was in the kitchen preparing breakfast, there was a knock on the door. When Kate opened it, Susan Rawlings was standing there. Smartly dressed, she was holding three envelopes, a bottle of gin and a suitcase.

'Oh, hello, Susan. You're up and about early.'

'I'm much better now, Dr Rowan. I want to thank you for all you did.'

'I'm pleased you're better. You're young and you'll make a full recovery. So what brings you here at this hour?'

'I'm going to catch a train to stay with an aunt in Harrogate, but before I go, I want to give your husband these.'

'Well, he's out on an early patrol just now.'

'Maybe you'd do it for me? In this envelope is the money I stole from Mr Greengrass, in this one the money I got from the garage and in this one the money I stole from Mr Francis's van. I want Mr Rowan to return it all, please, and this bottle of gin is to replace the one I took from the pub.'

'You stole all those things? But I thought it was Richard . . .'

'Richard Francis had nothing to do with it, Dr Rowan, nothing to do with anything.'

'But he had the tin, Mr Greengrass's tin which had had his money in.'

'Yes, it was in my satchel. I was going to throw it away but he saw it, he said it would be useful for keeping bits of his model aircraft in, and I hadn't the heart to tell him where I'd got it from. He follows me around, you know, like a little dog. He's a bit of a nuisance, but harmless. He never touched me, Dr Rowan, I swear.'

'But the abortion, I thought the money would have gone on that?'

'The lady never took anything, she said she was doing me a favour, so I want to return it all.'

'All right, I'll pass these to my husband. How long will you be away, Susan?'

'I'm not coming back. Dad doesn't know yet, it would kill him. He just thinks I'm going to my aunt's. Well, I am, but only till I'm really fit. Chris has run me down here to the village, he's waiting to take me to the station. Mum knows I'm leaving for good, she'll tell Dad eventually.'

'But why, Susan? Your parents love you, you've got over the worst and now it's time to rebuild your life, to look to your future. You're a bright girl, good at school I'm told. You go could to university.'

'It's not over, Doctor, it never can be while I'm here.'

'Susan, I don't understand.'

'Doctors keep secrets, don't they? If I told you something, and asked you never to tell anyone, you'd keep that secret, as a doctor?'

'Yes, of course.'

'And not even tell your husband?'

'Not even my policeman husband; he keeps his professional secrets and I keep mine.'

'It was Chris,' she said, lowering her gaze.

'Chris?' puzzled Kate.

'My brother, Chris. He was the father of that child,' and

tears came into Susan's eyes. 'My dad worships me, but never gives Chris the time of day. Yet he's so much better than me, so much more capable.'

'Oh, my God . . .' breathed Kate.

Susan continued, 'If only Dad would give him a chance, he could do really well. So with me out of the way, maybe Dad will appreciate Chris's good points.'

'But Chris . . . and you . . .'

'Yes, I know. Awful, isn't it? He stole those pheasants, you know, to help raise more money. He sold them all . . . Dad must never know, he'd kill Chris, he really would. We've left an envelope for Lord Ashfordly, with the money in it, anonymous.'

'Susan, how awful!'

'So you see, I can't stay, can I? Chris loves me, his own sister . . . I must go, and never come back.'

'Oh, Susan,' and Kate flung her arms around the child and held her tight. 'You are so brave.'

Susan was weeping but, wiping her eyes, she said, 'I must leave now. The train goes soon.'

And then she was gone.

When Nick returned for his breakfast, Kate told him of Susan's visit. He listened carefully.

'So Richard was innocent after all?' he said. 'I must go and apologise to him. He was the father, though?'

'No, I can tell you that, but I'm sworn to professional secrecy about some aspects of this case,' said Kate.

'I've just seen Susan and her brother saying goodbye at the railway station,' said Nick. 'They didn't see me, they were kissing like a pair of lovers, then she rushed down to the platform in tears.'

'Just regard the whole matter as closed, Nick,' advised Kate.

'There's only one man who's come out of this with any profit!' said Nick. 'And that's Claude Jeremiah Greengrass. He was given fifty pounds by Bill Francis who still thinks Richard stole the money, and now he's got back the actual money that Susan took. So he's fifty quid in pocket!'

'That's until Bill Francis discovers the truth too,' smiled Kate. 'If Claude doesn't return the cash to him, I reckon his sausages and bacon will be a bit on the expensive side over the coming months!

'So now that the excitement's over, you can settle down to a quiet day just pottering around Aidensfield?' said Kate. 'Oh, one thing. Alex Ferrenby has invited us for dinner this evening.'

'Well, that's nice. What's on the menu?' asked Nick.

'Pheasant!'

CHAPTER FOURTEEN

Following their excellent dinner, at which the pheasant had been cooked to perfection, Alex Ferrenby took them into his comfortable lounge and offered them each a liqueur. Kate settled for a Cointreau while Nick opted for a brandy, then, with a brandy for himself, Alex threw a log on the fire and settled down with them.

'I did invite you here for a reason.' He spoke softly and with some emotion. 'I'm sure you guessed that anyway, from what I let slip after dealing with Susan Rawlings so I expect you know what I'm going to say. It's something which affects you both, but especially Kate. Kate, you more than anyone know the state of my health, you've seen my behaviour over recent weeks – my forgetfulness, my uncertainties, my unreliability. I know the attack on me didn't help, nor did my experience in that train crash, but you know and I know that I would have reached this state anyway. I am growing too old, it's as simple as that. I know that I've become something of a liability to this practice and so I thought I would call it a day. In other words, I'm going to retire.'

'Alex!' She tried to sound surprised, but in her heart of hearts she had known this was inevitable.

'I could have soldiered on, I know,' he continued. 'You are far too polite to force me into making that decision. I have done my work for the community and now it's your turn.'

'You've given me wonderful guidance in the time I've been with you,' she smiled.

'But you know that I'm old-fashioned, Kate. I find it more and more difficult to keep abreast of new developments, new medicines, new methods of treatment. Things are moving ahead at a very fast rate and I know I cannot keep pace. Quite simply, it's time for me to pack it in and hand over to a younger person of my choice – to you.'

Kate's eyes sparkled. 'Oh, Alex, I'm so pleased for you. You've worked hard for the village and you really deserve a long and happy retirement. And I couldn't be prouder about stepping into your shoes. If I need guidance, I know you'll always be around to help me.'

Alex smiled fondly. 'When you arrived at Aidensfield you looked so young and, well, vulnerable in a way, nothing more than a slip of a girl.' Ferrenby's eyes were moist. 'I felt I could never pass on to you my years of experience on these rather inhospitable moors, and I felt you'd be unable to cope with the farmers and villagers, and the weather, and the terrain itself – but you've adapted so well I'm really proud of you. Your medical knowledge is sound, your attitude towards your patients is ideal, the support you get from Nick is so welcome . . . well, it's everything I could have hoped for. I've no

hesitation in recommending that you assume responsibility for this practice. Whether you take on a partner is a
matter for you to decide, of course; it's not my job to
influence you in any way.'

Nick smiled. He felt a glow of happiness at hearing
those words from Alex Ferrenby. 'Alex, thanks. I know
how much you've meant to Kate over the past months, a
shoulder to lean on, wisdom there for the asking, that sort
of thing. I wish you well too.'

'There is just one problem,' added Ferrenby. 'And that
is the surgery. It's in my private house, as you know, and
when I retire I shall be moving to something smaller, more
manageable, perhaps in Aidensfield but perhaps else-
where, like Strensford. Since my wife died, I do find it
hard coping with such a big home, even with help from my
daily. But when I move away, it means I shall have to sell
the house, which in turn means you will have to find other
premises. I'm sorry about that – unless you and Nick
bought my house, of course!'

Kate shook her head. 'Oh, we couldn't afford it, even
on our joint pay, and besides, Nick is tied to the police
house while he's the village constable. But thanks for the
advance warning. So what timescale are we thinking
about, Alex?'

'Well, I'll have to inform the relevant authorities of my
impending retirement and give due notice to various
statutory bodies. So we're thinking in terms of six months.
When I give my formal notice of retirement, I'll let you
know, but I'd say that I'll be gone before Christmas. I'll
probably finish in the autumn, Kate, October or

November. That gives you time to find a surgery and to make your own plans.'

Kate went over and kissed the old doctor on the cheek. Nick followed, shook his hand and said, 'Oh, Alex, it is such a difficult decision to have to make. I think you have done the right thing, I really do. You deserve a long and happy retirement.'

'I've been offered a cottage beside the River Esk for a few days fishing if I want to make use of it,' he said. 'Before I retire, I mean.'

'I think you should accept,' said Kate. 'I can cope and you're still not really fit. Why not take a nice long holiday to get properly on form before you retire? You don't want to finish work feeling tired and unwell, do you?'

'No, you're right of course. I'll have words with the owners and fix a date. And Kate, I'm so pleased you are to be my successor, it does mean a lot to me. I can end my working life confident in the knowledge that my patients will be receiving the very best of care.'

With tears in her eyes, all Kate could say was, 'Oh, Alex . . . I shall miss you.'

'We shall all miss you,' added Nick.

Shortly after eight o'clock the next morning, Gillian Siddons, a pretty young woman in her early twenties, was cycling along a lane on the outskirts of Aidensfield. She was heading for Badger Cottage, the home of her ex-nanny, Mary Begg, and was carrying some eggs in a basket hanging on the handlebars.

Mary Begg's tiny cottage was built of local stone and

looked picturesque in an old-fashioned sort of way; it needed a coat of paint upon its woodwork, the gate was hanging off its hinges and the garden was overgrown. Gillian did not notice these things – she had been coming to this house several times a week for the past four or five years and the house had always been in the same condition. It looked perfectly normal to Gillian as she parked her cycle against the fence. She went along the path and tapped on the door.

'Mary?' she said. 'Mary, are you there?'

Normally, Mrs Begg responded with a cheery, 'Is that, Gillian? Come in, lass.' But this morning, there was no response.

'Mary?' Gillian entered cautiously, calling her name again as she entered the lounge. Mary was sitting in a chair facing the fire, which was burning. There was a cup of tea, half full, on the table at her side.

'Oh, you are there.' Gillian went forward. 'You've dropped off again . . . Mary?'

There was no response. Normally, if Mary had fallen asleep in her chair she would wake at the sound of Gillian's voice. Gillian went forward to touch the old lady's shoulder. 'Mary?'

She discovered the worst: it seemed as if Mary Begg, her nanny for years, had died quietly in her chair.

Gillian, a sensible girl, did not panic but closed the house, locked the door and rode home to call the doctor. She was in time to catch Kate before morning surgery started. Kate didn't waste any time in driving down to Badger Cottage. When she arrived, Gillian's father,

Jack Siddons, was waiting at the cottage at Mary's side. Kate's quick examination confirmed their worst fears – the old lady was dead and, as she had had a history of heart trouble with regular attention from Kate and Alex Ferrenby, Kate said she was prepared to certify the cause of death. This meant the police would not have to deal with the case as a sudden or unexplained death, and the relatives could go ahead with the funeral straight away.

'The body will need to be taken to the mortuary,' Kate said. 'Is that something you can arrange, Mr Siddons? The undertaker will see to everything. And are there any relations who can come and see to the cottage and make the funeral arrangements?'

'Aye,' said Siddon. 'There's a grandson, Kevin. He used to live with her when he was at school. I think he's down south now, somewhere in the Birmingham area. The cottage is mine, actually. When Mary retired, I bought it so she could live there in peace, on her own. So I can see to the house. Her next-of-kin will have to see to her belongings, but they'll be all right there for a while. I'm not going to ask them to clear the house just yet!'

'Would you have Kevin's address?' Kate asked him.

'No,' he said abruptly. 'No, we were never that close to him. Mebbe it'll be in Mary's house somewhere. But I don't want our Gillian to be bothered looking, she's got a lot on her plate just now.'

'It's her wedding soon, isn't it?' smiled Kate.

'Aye, this coming Saturday.'

'Well, if you've no objection, my husband can search

the house for Kevin's address, he's used to that sort of thing.'

'That's fine by me,' said Jack Siddons. 'Well, I'll get in touch with the undertaker, and you'll keep me informed?'

'I will,' promised Kate.

'Poor old Mary,' said Jack sadly. 'She was good to our Gillian and she was looking forward to the wedding. Mebbe she'll be watching from wherever she is on the day, eh?'

'I'm sure she will,' agreed Kate.

When Kate returned to the police house, Nick had left. There was a note on the table saying, 'Gone to Ashfordly for a conference with Sergeant Blaketon.' Sighing, she decided that a search for the address of Mary's next-of-kin would have to wait. She left the house again and took her little yellow car along the road to the surgery. There was already a small queue of people; Alex was seeing some of them and others were waiting for Kate.

'I'm sorry I'm late,' she apologised. 'But it's bad news. Poor Mary Begg has died.'

And so the village was informed of another death within the community.

It was lunchtime when Nick returned from Ashfordly. He and Kate sat down for a light meal of poached eggs, and Kate told him of Mary's death. Nick agreed to search the house for a possible address for Kevin.

'So what did Sergeant Blaketon want?' she asked. 'What was the urgent conference all about?'

'Highway robbery,' he smiled. 'Over the past few weeks, a succession of lorries have been raided on the A1 in the North Riding. When they've been parked at night, in laybys or outside transport cafés, somebody's been breaking into them and nicking high-value loads: furniture, whisky, kitchen equipment, TVs and so on. But somebody's been nicking seafood as well!'

'Seafood?' asked Kate.

'Shrimps, prawns, crab and lobsters, that sort of thing. We think it's a specialist gang who've got an outlet for seafood, to restaurants, hotels and similar places. Anyway, the most recent was in our area last night: a lorry parked overnight in a layby near Loftus was raided. Its load of prawns was nicked.'

Kate smiled at the absurdity of it. 'I think it's so silly, stealing prawns. I mean, they've got to be used nearly straight away, haven't they? Or they go bad. Unless they're all frozen.'

'Well, all the country constables were called in for a conference this morning. We've got to get around our hotels and pubs and other outlets, to see if anybody's selling them.'

Before embarking upon his enquiries, however, Nick accompanied Kate to Mary's cottage. He obtained the key from Beth Siddons, Jack's wife, and upon arrival at Badger Cottage was pleased to see that Mary's body had been removed by the undertaker. It now lay in the chapel of rest adjoining his premises. Nick, accustomed to making searches of this kind especially in the event of a sudden death, had no qualms about rifling through Mary's meagre belongings, but Kate couldn't help feeling she was intruding. Nick's first point of interest was a small bureau in the corner of the living room. When he lowered the front to form a working surface, he found it contained lots of letters, tied together in small bundles. It was the work of a moment to untie the knots. Soon he found one signed, 'All my love, Kevin', and the address at the head of the paper was in Birmingham.

'I think this will be him,' Nick said, making a note of the address in his pocketbook. 'There's no telephone number on the letterhead, so I'll ring Birmingham City Police and get one of their foot patrols to inform Kevin.'

He and Kate were about to leave when the front door opened and a man's voice called, 'Hello, Mr Rowan?'

When Nick reached the door, he saw Walter Pettigrew standing there.

Walter, a miserable-faced man in his fifties, ran a smallholding near the Siddons estate. He kept a few goats and pigs, and bred pigeons in the hope he'd win a major race. But success of any kind had always eluded him.

'Hello, Walter. What can I do for you?'

'Well, I just heard, in the pub, about Mary. I didn't know whether it was true or not, so I thought I'd pop down to check.'

'Yes,' Kate told him. 'This morning, she died very peacefully in her chair.'

'Them Siddonses should have cared better for her, called more often.' There was a hint of bitterness in Walter's voice. 'She should never have been left on her own like this . . .'

'She had a family, they live away,' Nick volunteered.

'Aye, a grandson, that's all. Siddons wouldn't let him

live here with her, he had to go away to work. That was a
condition of her getting this house. Chasing away her only
family . . .'

'Why would Mr Siddons do that? He cared for her,
Walter,' said Nick. 'He gave her the house.'

'That lad of hers, Kevin. He was courting Siddons's
lass, Gillian, but he wasn't good enough, not for the
high-and-mighty Siddonses. They wanted rid of him, and
that's how they did it. Mary and the lad lived in the big
house till then, you see, in a flat on the west wing, when
he was younger, that was, but, well, when he grew older
he started courting Gillian.'

'She's a pretty girl,' said Nick.

'Aye, that was the trouble. Jack had his heart set on
somebody higher than Kevin Begg for a son-in-law, and
when he found out about Kevin, he sent him packing. He
did it by giving Mary that cottage, and making it a
condition that only she could live in it. Crafty sod! He'll be
coming back, will he, Kevin, for the funeral?'

'Yes, I expect so, I've got to contact him.'

'Aye, well, I'll be able to pay my last respects when
she's buried. A fine woman, she was. But they should
have cared better for her.'

'She was eighty-three, Mr Pettigrew,' Kate told him.
'Gillian came almost every day, but there was nothing
anyone could have done this morning. Nothing at all.'

'Well, I hope they let her have a decent and proper
funeral before they take the church over for that big
wedding!' and Walter Pettigrew turned on his heel and
walked away.

'What's got into him?' asked Kate, taken aback, as the middle-aged man stalked away towards the village.

'Walter? He grumbles about everything and everyone,' smiled Nick. 'Nothing's right for Walter. If it's fine, he wants rain, and when it rains he wants the sun to shine. He's that sort of fellow. If he's not grumbling about something, he turns into a right misery!'

'He doesn't like the Siddonses, does he?' she said.

'Well, they do play a bit high and mighty. There are times you'd think Jack was Lord of the Manor the way he behaves. He thinks himself a cut above the rest of the local farmers but he's only the same as them when all's said and done, even if he happens to have made a few pounds.'

'And while making his money, he's made the Walter Pettigrews of this world very envious.'

'You always get people who are jealous of success, Kate,' said Nick. 'Even in the police force! There's something deep in the English mentality that criticises success. Come along, I've got to start asking about stolen prawns now!'

'And I've got some sick visits to make.'

Nick first rang Birmingham City Police to ask if they would deliver a 'request message' to Kevin Begg, the term used for this kind of emergency service to those who did not have telephones. The duty inspector assured Nick that an officer would call at Kevin's address and ask him to go to Aidensfield immediately. Leaving his motorcycle at home, Nick did a foot patrol around the village, asking about the prawns. Bill Francis the butcher said he'd not been offered any, and neither had George Ward at the Aidensfield Arms. The post office and shop did not sell fish anyway, and a travelling butcher who came to the village from Ashfordly also shook his head. Nonetheless, Nick did ask them to notify him if they received such an offer and warned them that the stuff might well be the proceeds of crime.

As he was walking past the Aidensfield Arms, a short and rather dapper little man hailed him. He climbed out of a clean and very smart Rover car.

'Ah, Constable,' he smiled. He was about fifty, Nick reckoned, perhaps a little older, and he wore an expensive tweed suit with gold cufflinks in his sleeves and well-polished brogues.

'Yes?'

'I'm looking for the home of a Mr C. J. Greengrass,' said the little fellow. 'I believe he lives hereabouts?'

'Yes, he does. A friend of his, are you?'

'Old comrades in arms, we served together in the war and I've always been promising myself that I'd look up Claude if I was in the area. I thought I'd come for the point-to-point at Ashfordly next week. It's in the grounds of Ashfordly Hall, isn't it?'

'Yes,' said Nick. 'This coming Tuesday is the date. We're expecting a big crowd.'

'That's good news. Well, I'm a few days early so I thought it was a chance to visit my old comrade! Bailey's the name,' he said cheerfully.

'Well, Mr Bailey, Claude lives along that road,' Nick pointed, giving the man instructions as to how to reach

Claude's tumbledown house, which looked more like a scrapyard than a home. Nick wondered how this smart gentleman had become acquainted with Claude. It was another minor task for him – to discover what Claude was up to now!

The main talking point in Aidensfield was the big wedding: all the well known and influential people in the area had been invited, as had most of the villagers. There were to be more than two hundred guests who would see the beautiful daughter of the Siddons family marry Richard Talbot, the son of the estate manager at Carnforth. Kate was a guest, being the family doctor, and Nick was invited too, as her husband. A relief constable would be drafted in, most likely Phil Bellamy from Ashfordly to park the cars and act as security man for the wedding gifts: already, lots of expensive presents from wealthy friends and relations had arrived and were on display at the farm. A marquee had been erected in the grounds ready for the reception and car parking facilities had been organised. Already, the floor of the marquee was being laid, even though there were five whole days before the big event. As was the new fashion, the future bride and groom had written out a list of presents and this was being circulated among the guests. Flowers had been arranged through a florist in Ashfordly and Nick had been up to the house several times to discuss details like signs to the farm for strangers, car parking both at the farm and outside the church, and whether or not Jack had considered the problems of putting toilets near the marquee.

From a policing point of view, the wedding was not

likely to cause any problems; George's pub was not being used and so even if any of the guests became too boisterous, the problem of unruliness and unwelcome noise in the village would not arise. Anything of that sort would go on on private property well out of earshot. Where wedding arrangements were concerned, therefore, Nick felt he could relax.

The next day, Kevin Begg arrived from Birmingham. He'd travelled by hitching lifts from friendly lorry drivers and private motorists and arrived at Aidensfield around ten thirty in the morning. He'd left his own flat at six o'clock and had made very good time, thanks to a sports car which brought him all the way from Bromsgrove to Thirsk. A lorry had picked him up near Thirsk and, fortunately, had been heading for Ashfordly. His first call was at his grandmother's cottage; he had a key, he'd cut himself one some time ago in case he was ever faced with a situation such as this, and he was able to let himself in.

Capable and efficient, he spent the morning tidying the cottage and preparing himself a bed, then went to the undertaker to see the body of his grandmother and to discuss the funeral arrangements. At lunchtime, he decided to visit the Aidensfield Arms for a pint and a snack.

As he walked towards the pub, he encountered Gillian riding a horse towards him. She was about to turn into the lane which led to her home, so he waited as she drew closer.

'Hi, Gillian,' he greeted her, reaching out to pat the horse's head.

'Hello, Kevin. You've got here in good time. I was sorry about your grandmother.'

He smiled gently at her. 'She had a good long life, Gillian, she looks at peace now. I've just been to see her. Thanks for looking after her the way you did. She often wrote to me and said how caring you were.'

'Well, she looked after me when I was little . . .'

'I often think about those times, Gillian,' Kevin said suddenly lost in thought. 'And when we were at school, going out like we did. Walking on the moors, going to the pictures together . . .'

Gillian looked down, obviously upset. 'Don't, please, Kevin, it's over, finished.'

'But now I'm here, well, can't we have a night out, when the funeral's over. Or just a drink somewhere on our own? I do miss you, you know,' he pleaded.

'No, Kevin, don't . . .'

At that moment, Sergeant Blaketon's car appeared and turned into the farm entrance.

'Something happening at your place, is there?' Kevin nodded towards the police car.

Thinking quickly, Gillian said, 'There's been a spate of robberies recently, isolated premises are being attacked, they're going round warning us all and giving advice about crime prevention.'

'You'd never get that sort of personal service in Birmingham!' He smiled ruefully. 'But look, maybe before I go back, we'll see each other around the place? I want to see

273

your dad sometime anyway, about the future of the cottage.'

'I'm sure we will see one another, Kevin, and pop in any time to see Dad about Mary's cottage. Well, I must go, lunch will be ready and I promised Mum I'd drive her into Strensford.'

'OK, see you. 'Bye.'

Kevin stood and watched as Gillian guided the horse along the lane breaking into a fast trot as she approached the magnificent farmhouse. She looked splendid, Kevin thought. Very splendid indeed. Then he turned into the Aidensfield Arms. He arrived in the bar in time to hear Claude Jeremiah Greengrass, in the company of a smart-looking little man, boasting to George and the assembled regulars about his past acquaintanceship with the well-dressed gentleman.

'Banger Bailey,' beamed Claude. 'We were squaddies together, mind that's going back twenty years. He was in the Catering Corps.'

'Why are you called Banger?' laughed Gina. 'That's no sort of a name!'

'He made the best sausages in the Northern Union, did this chap. That's why we called him Banger,' breezed Claude.

'So what are you doing here?' George asked Banger.

'I'm in the catering business, I've got a mobile canteen. We cater for gymkhanas, country fairs, events on race-courses, rural shows, that sort of thing. I'll be at the point-to-point in Ashfordly, but had a few days to spare. So I thought I'd look up my old comrade in arms, Claude Jeremiah Greengrass.'

'You'll be here for the wedding, then?' beamed George. 'He didn't use me, he said he was getting some big caterer in.'

'Who? What wedding?' asked Claude.

'You wouldn't know,' beamed George. 'It's for the smart set. All the nobs are invited, a right posh affair it is. You know Jack Siddons, he likes to pretend he's summat he's not. It's that lass of his, Gillian, she's marrying a toff from up in the dales, a fellow who's into estate management.'

Kevin couldn't believe what he was hearing. Gillian had never said a word about a wedding – he'd been talking to her only minutes earlier, and she hadn't mentioned it!

'Did you say Gillian Siddons is getting married?' Kevin asked abruptly.

'Aye,' said George. 'On Saturday.'

Then Claude recognised Kevin.

'You're Mary Begg's grandson, aren't you? Up from Birmingham?'

'That's me, Kevin Begg.'

'Sorry about your grandmother,' said George. 'She was one of the best, Kevin. She was well looked after by Jack Siddons and that lass of his – she called in nearly every day did Gillian, looking after old Mary.'

But Kevin wasn't listening. Gillian getting married? But she had always said she loved him! When they were young they went everywhere together. And now this!

The men in the bar were chattering around him but their words washed over him. Devastated by the revelation, he left the Aidensfield Arms and went back to the cottage.

There were tears in his eyes, but the expression on his face was one of fury.

At a quarter past seven the next morning, the telephone was ringing in the police house at Aidensfield.

'Your turn!' said Nick, kicking Kate into wakefulness. 'I got it last time!'

'No you didn't, I did,' she retorted, snuggling further down. 'I got it last time, I distinctly remember!'

'Well, I'm not getting it this time!'

'And nor am I!'

They lay for a few minutes as the shrill bell filled the entire house with its urgency. Nick grumbled and groaned, and then said, 'All right, all right. I'll get it this time!'

He struggled down the cold staircase and into his office, snatching at the persistent instrument.

'Aidensfield Police,' he said.

'It's Jack Siddons, Nick,' came a panting voice at the other end of the line. 'You'll have to come, somebody's broken into our house overnight and stolen our Gillian's presents. All her silverware and china, all the best bits – including a family heirloom!'

CHAPTER FIFTEEN

When Nick arrived at Clough Farm, he found the family
waiting, Jack looking angry, Beth tearful and Gillian
surprisingly unconcerned. Jack escorted Nick into the
lounge where one of the large windows was wide open.
The glass had been smashed and the window catch
released from the outside. Jack explained that lots of
presents had arrived in advance of Saturday and Beth had
arranged them in this room so that they formed an
attractive display. They ranged from canteens of cutlery to
glassware such as decanters and wine glasses, along with
bedding, pillows, towels, some silverware and expensive
china. There was one very valuable item, an antique silver
punchbowl given to them by the groom's grandfather; a
family heirloom. That had gone along, with some of the
more portable items, although the bulky stuff like bedding
and sheets had not been stolen. Jack could not give a very
comprehensive list of what was missing without writing to
all the guests to ask what they'd sent, although he had a
fairly good idea of what had gone.

'And you were asleep upstairs all the time?'

'Yes,' said Jack. 'And we never heard a thing. Not a whisper. I mean, not even the dog barked and he always barks at strangers. Whoever it was knew their way round the place, that's pretty obvious.'

'I'll have to call in the CID,' Nick said. 'They'll want to test the window and this room for fingerprints, so it mustn't be touched until they've gone. Now, if I can use your telephone, I'll ring our office at Ashfordly and start an immediate search of the area. I'll visit antique shops, second-hand dealers and so forth, just to see if there is any early attempt to sell any of the stuff.'

Nick went away to make his call, leaving Jack with his wife and daughter.

'I didn't want a big wedding, Dad,' Gillian said, rue-fully, 'I didn't want all this fuss . . .'

'I'm going to give you the very best, Gillian, I'm going to give Aidensfield a wedding they'll remember for years to come. So just shut up. And you might show more concern about the missing presents!'

'I don't care about them, I just wanted to get married in a quiet way without all this palaver and disruption . . . And look at it now, the thieves have come and taken the lot! It means more disruption, the police here and more people about the place . . .' and she ran off, crying. Beth heard her clatter upstairs, then the door of her room slammed shut.

'You could be more gentle with her,' Beth said to her husband.

'She doesn't appreciate what I've done for her,' he grunted. 'All the money and effort I'm putting into this wedding, and it's all for our Gillian!'

'And not for your ego, Jack? You're not putting on a big show just to impress your so-called friends, are you?'

'Don't be stupid, woman!' he snapped.

PC Rowan returned. 'My colleagues are coming out to help make a detailed search of the grounds, Jack. We do this in burglary cases – sometimes the thieves hide the stuff and come back to collect it when the fuss has died away. So if you don't mind, we'll carry out a very detailed search around the premises, indoors and out.'

'Fine, yes. Anything.'

'Now, have you had any unexpected visitors lately? People you don't know?'

'Only those who've been delivering presents, Nick. I can get a list of those if it'll help.'

'We might have to question them all about their where-abouts last night, so yes, that will be useful. Well, I think I'd better start looking around the outside, Jack. Perhaps while I'm doing that, someone could begin to make a list of all the things that have gone, as complete a list as you can.'

'I'll do that,' Beth said.

Sergeant Blaketon and Phil Bellamy arrived within twenty minutes and were greeted by Nick. He showed them the break-in point, explained how there had been no footprints on the lawn outside the window, and how the presents had been carried off, probably via the same means of entry.

Blaketon listened and then said the CID had been

informed and were *en route*, their estimated time of arrival within the hour.

'So, Bellamy and Rowan, it's time to begin a thorough search of the outbuildings and grounds.'

While that search was beginning, Claude Jeremiah Greengrass and Banger Bailey arrived at the farm in Banger's smart Rover. They looked puzzled at the sight of Nick's police motorcycle in the yard, parked beside Sergeant Blaketon's car.

'This place is swarming with coppers, Claude,' breathed Banger.

'Ignore them, mate. The coppers around here are a useless lot. There's only two vehicles, for God's sake. They'll be here for the same reason as us – about this big posh wedding.'

Banger still looked worried. 'But the mere sight of 'em makes me nervous, Claude. Very nervous, in fact.'

'Don't be daft, come along in. Jack's a fine fellow – besides, he's got plenty of money and he's allus in the market for a bargain.'

Claude pressed the doorbell which was eventually answered by Beth, carrying a sheaf of papers.

'Oh, it's you, Claude.'

'Yes, good morning, Beth. I just wondered if your Jack was in.'

'Well, he's a bit busy right now . . .' she began.

At that moment, Jack appeared behind her.

'Claude, what brings you here this time of day?'

'Well, like, this is a pal of mine, Banger Bailey, best

cook the army ever had. He's into catering now, you see, runs a very fine establishment with the very best food, and well, seeing you're having a big wedding we wondered if you might be interested in his services.'

'Well, Claude, it's kind of you to consider us, but we've already booked the caterers. Plumptons from Ashfordly, they're doing the whole range of catering for the big day. I want the very best for my daughter, Claude,' he said proudly.

'Aye, well, that's what I thought. But well, we thought it was worth a try.'

'I do a very good line of fish courses,' chipped in Banger. 'Very popular now among the nobs are fish courses. You start with soup, then you have a fish course, then the main course and the sweet after that.'

'We're not having a fish course, are we, Beth?' Jack asked his wife.

'No, it added a lot more to the cost of the meal, you see, with over two hundred guests.'

'I could offer you a very select selection of prime North Sea fish for a fraction of what you'd pay anywhere else,' smiled Banger.

'Really?' Jack smelled a bargain here.

Banger did not miss the cue. 'And you could use your existing caterers to serve the fish, I won't hog the day.'

'It would be nice to have a full meal,' said Jack thoughtfully. 'I mean, we do have some very influential people coming here on Saturday. We ought to do things properly.'

'And I'm used to the big occasion,' said Banger. 'Race

meetings, country fairs, agricultural shows, you name it, I've catered for it. I know what the best people are eating these days.'

'Well, it's difficult making a decision right now, I can't really concentrate. I am very busy, we've just been burgled . . .'

'Burgled?' gasped Claude. 'You?'

'All the presents have been stolen. The police are here now . . .'

'I thought I could smell 'em!' laughed Claude. 'So, Jack, to cheer you up, how about a nice fish course with the wedding breakfast?'

'You'd better come in,' said Jack 'Busy as I am, I don't believe in missing a bargain, and I *do* believe in striking while the iron is hot. Come in. Beth, can we find a drink for these gentlemen?'

While Beth was deciding where to seat Claude Jeremiah in his filthy old greatcoat, Sergeant Blaketon, Nick and Phil were combing the undergrowth outside the splendid farmhouse. Phil was probing the vegetation with a broom handle. Suddenly he struck something. Slashing down the nettles and briars, he found a pillowcase, stuffed with silverware.

'Sarge,' he shouted in his excitement. 'Here, I think I've found the stuff!'

As Blaketon and Nick ran towards Phil, they could see five or six white pillowcases not very well concealed among the shrubs. Blaketon went forward and opened the top of one – inside were two canteens of cutlery and some silverware. He also spotted some candlesticks and spoons, egg cups and photograph frames.

'Well done, Bellamy. Right, don't touch it any more, leave it for CID. And we'll have to keep guard on it in case the villains return to pick it up.'

'They won't come here, will they, Sarge?' Nick said. 'Not in broad daylight anyway, it's too close to the house. They'd be seen long before they even got here.'

'Just leave the stuff till CID come. Now we'll pass the glad tidings to Jack and Beth.'

As they returned to the house, Claude was just leaving. With a suspicious glance at his old adversary, Blaketon informed Jack of the recovery of at least some of the presents. Blinking ingratiatingly, Claude Jeremiah suggested that maybe the stuff had been removed as a joke, not as a serious attempt at stealing it.

'And why would a man of enormous criminal expertise such as yourself, Greengrass, come to such a conclusion?' asked Blaketon, his voice laden with sarcasm.

'It stands to reason, Sergeant, if you think about it. First, who'd steal that kind of stuff, wedding presents? There's no money to be made reselling that, is there?'

'How would I know, Greengrass?' demanded Blaketon.

Claude drew his lumpen body up tall. 'Because it's your job to know, Sergeant, and I'm a ratepayer who pays your wages to know that. I'll have you know that me and Banger here fought in the war, together, shoulder to shoulder, to make the country safe for the likes of you!'

'Then you'll know which campaign medal this is!' snapped Blaketon, tapping the ribbons on his uniform breast. 'I fought an' all, remember. Now then, why do you think this is all a set-up, Greengrass?'

'Well, they abandoned the stuff too close to the house, didn't they? If they'd wanted to steal it, I mean really get away with it, they'd have hidden it miles away, behind a hedge, so they could pick it up when the heat had died down.'

'Go on, Greengrass!' smiled Blaketon.

'Well, Mr Blaketon, they wouldn't dump it in the grounds of the bloody house they took it from, would they? They'd be seen coming back for it.'

'Maybe they were scared off?' suggested Bellamy.

'Who by? I was talking to Jack in there and they said everybody was asleep, even the dog never barked. Scared off? No, Mr Blaketon, this was done as a piece of mischief.'

'That's right!' said Jack. 'The dog never barked, not a whimper.'

'I'm inclined to believe you, Greengrass,' said Sergeant Blaketon, finally. 'But in my view, it's not in your normal scheme of things to help the police like this. I smell a rat!'

'Aye, well, you'd never trust your own granny, you wouldn't. Look, the only reason I'm telling you this is that I don't want Jack's big day to be ruined.'

'All right, a noble thought. So who would cause mischief of that kind?'

'You've only a few fields between here and him,' smiled Claude. 'Walter Pettigrew, didn't he have a bit of a barney with you, Jack, years ago? Summat about a parcel of land? He took you to court, if I remember, and he lost. He's never been the same since.'

'Aye, I remember something about that,' breathed Blaketon. 'You won the case, Jack, and went from strength to strength, while poor old Pettigrew failed.'

'We were in the right, Mr Blaketon, it was our land and had been for centuries. He tried to claim it, the old sod . . .'

'He did, 'an all. I remember that carry-on,' beamed Claude. 'So there you are, Jack, don't say I never help you. If it is old Pettigew, he's not after spoiling your lass's day, he's after making you suffer, that's what. That's my opinion for what it's worth.'

Jack nodded. 'Thanks, Claude. I do appreciate your help in all this.'

'And I hope you'll show your appreciation in a positive sort of way, Jack. Now, I don't normally grass on folks like this, but, well you're a customer of mine now, having just done the best deal you'll ever do, so this information is my present to your Gillian. Mind, if Pettigrew is behind all this, he might try summat else. He's daft enough to keep doing all sorts of things, just to spoil your day.'

'We'll certainly keep a special eye open for signs of trouble, me and these officers,' smiled Jack Siddons. 'Now, Claude, you ought to come to the wedding, you and your friend.'

'Well,' said Claude, 'I am a man of some stature now, quite well respected in these parts, and I know I'd fit in and I'd be pleased to come under normal circumstances, but I've other commitments. Me and Banger here. Business ventures to see to, like.'

'I do appreciate this, Claude. Well, gentlemen?' and

Jack turned to the policeman. 'It looks as if all you have to do is tidy up the loose ends, eh? And get that daft bat Pettigrew locked up before he does any more harm.'

'Rowan?' shouted Sergeant Blaketon.

'Yes, Sergeant?'

'This is one for you. Go and see Pettigrew and get him to cough this crime. And when he does, lock him up for burglary.'

'Yes, Sergeant.'

'I want this matter cleared up before the wedding day. We don't want to spoil the big occasion, do we?'

'Very good, Sergeant.'

'Thank you, Sergeant.' Jack Siddons was looking more relaxed now. 'This hasn't turned out so bad after all. What with Mary Begg dying and then this, I really did think my luck had left me. Now it seems to be on the turn again.'

'I'll see you on Saturday, then?' smiled Blaketon. 'I'm looking forward to the wedding.'

'You're a guest, are you, Sergeant?' asked Nick.

'Yes, I am!'

'I knew all the toffs were coming!' chuckled Greengrass. 'It's mebbe best I'm not seen hobnobbing with such company.'

'And because I am a guest, I fully intend that Gillian will have the loveliest day of her life, and so I want everything to go as smoothly as possible. I mean that for your sake too, Jack and Beth,' smiled Blaketon.

'We have worked so hard for her,' said Jack.

'Now,' smiled Blaketon, 'where is the bride-to-be? I think she should know we've found her presents.'

'She went out on her bike while you were talking to Mr Greengrass. Just came downstairs and rushed outside. I saw her ride off,' said Beth.

'Where did she go?' demanded Jack. 'I don't know what's the matter with that lass. Here's us doing our best and her heart's not in the job at all.'

Beth shrugged. 'I've no idea where she went, she never said.'

'Oh, she'll be back,' Jack said. 'It's nerves, the excitement's getting to her. I'll tell her when she gets in.'

'Right, well we'll be off,' said Blaketon. 'See you soon.'

'And us, Jack,' smiled Claude. 'It's nice to do business with you. You'll never regret this.'

As Nick rode his motorcycle away from the farm, he wondered what kind of business a man like Siddons would be doing with a rogue like Claude Jeremiah Greengrass. And, in Nick's opinion, that friend of Claude's didn't look too trustworthy either. But Nick had more important things to deal with than to worry about Claude Jeremiah's business dealings.

His first task was to interview Walter Pettigrew.

Nick rode through the village and turned down a rough track to Spinney Farm, the home of Walter Pettigrew. Although it adjoined the Siddons farm, the two spreads could not have been more different. The Siddons had a beautiful farmhouse surrounded by acres of productive land which was all kept in pristine condition, while Walter's house was in desperate need of modernisation and his land looked neglected and poor. In addition to his goats, pigs and pigeons he had a few blackfaced moorland sheep on the heights and a small herd of dairy cattle. Nick knocked on the door but as there was no reply, he wandered round the buildings. He found Walter in the feed shed, measuring out some cattle cake.

'Now, Mr Pettigrew, how's things?'

'Same as usual, bloody awful. Milk yield's going down and prices are going up. Anyroad, what can I do for you?'

'Siddons was burgled last night, Mr Pettigrew.'

'Serve him right, he can afford it.'

'They lost some wedding presents.'

'I've nowt against the lass, but that father of hers is a bastard, Mr Rowan, a snob and a bastard. I've no sorrow for him.'

'Were you out and about last night, Mr Pettigrew?'

'Me? No, I was in bed by eleven and slept till six.'

'So you never saw anything? Heard noises? Noticed vehicles on Siddons's property?'

'Nope, nowt. He deserves everything he gets, that one. He took my land off me. And look at me now, struggling to make a living, existing a year on the money he spends in a month.'

'Would you object if we took your fingerprints, Mr Pettigrew?'

Pettigraw glared at him. 'Are you accusing me, Mr Rowan?'

'No, it's for elimination purposes.'

'Well, I've nowt to be afraid of, I never burgled his bloody house. All right, you can have my prints.'

'Thanks,' said Nick. 'I'll have our CID come down later.'

Friday was the day of Mary Begg's funeral and almost the entire village attended the service. During her long life, Mary had been well known and respected by the community, and the vicar delivered a touching tribute.

Following the interment, there were light refreshments in her cottage, comprising ham sandwiches, home-made cakes and copious quantities of tea. These had been organised by Kevin Begg and supplied by George of the Aidensfield Arms. Some of the village ladies, friends of the deceased, had rallied around to help Kevin and now they all arrived to pay their respects. Among them was Gillian Siddons, pretty in her black coat with matching shoes and gloves. Although she came to the cottage, she did not make small talk with the elder members of the community.

She wandered around the familiar place, touching the rocking horse on which she'd played as a child, opening the dolls' house that Mary had kept, looking at photographs on the mantelpiece and thinking of all the good times she and Mary had had. Mary had been more like a mother to her, more like a member of the family than her own parents. As a lonely only child, Gillian had spent hours in Mary's company, playing games, learning to draw and sew, finding out about the wildlife around her. And then Kevin had come along. When his parents had died in the car crash, Mary had taken him in and the two children had become inseparable. Kevin and Mary, going everywhere, playing together, going to school, growing up . . .

'Penny for them,' said a voice behind her. She turned to find Kevin standing there with two cups of tea in his hands. 'I brought you some tea. You've not eaten anything?'

'No,' she said, 'I couldn't. Poor Mary . . . she was so good to me.'

'To us,' he reminded her. 'I often think of our days together. We had a great time, didn't we?'

Gillian took the cup and sipped from it.

'What are you going to do when this is all over, Kevin?'

'I'd like to stay here, in the cottage, and find work in the area, but your dad would never let me rent it, would he? Especially now you're getting married!'

She stared at him! So he knew!

'I overheard people talking in the pub,' he said quietly.

'I didn't want you to know,' she began.

'You don't really want to marry that man, do you?' Kevin came close and spoke softly. 'Your heart's not in it, surely Gillian!'

'Please, Kevin, don't. I'm upset enough as things are, losing Mary.'

'But I love you, Gillian, you know that. We've loved each other all these years and now we can get together . . . You could persuade your dad to let you have the cottage, we could be together here, you and me, like it used to be . . .'

'No, Kevin, don't. It won't work. I'm marrying Richard, he loves me and there is a house available for us on the estate he manages. I wanted a quiet wedding, not a big fussy event like Dad's organised, but I am marrying Richard tomorrow. You'll be there?'

'Me? I didn't get an invitation, and you know it! I can't just turn up! Your dad's always done his best to keep us apart, I wasn't good enough for you, Gillian, not in his view anyway. It's my grandmother who's brought us together again, it's an omen, surely? Imagine those happy times all over again, just the two of us . . . I do love you, Gillian, and you know it . . .'

'Kevin, don't. I'm going. I must go now.'

'No, stay,' he pleaded.

'No, I just get upset by it all . . . please leave me alone.'

And placing her cup on the sink as she had always done, Gillian hurried out of the house and started to walk home.

As she hurried back to the farm, Claude Jeremiah hailed her.

'Is your dad in, Gillian?' he asked.

'Yes, he went straight home after the funeral,' she told him.

'Well, I'm just off to see Kevin to pay my respects, then I've a delivery for your dad.'

'He'll be there.' Gillian tried to produce a happy smile for Claude Jeremiah, but she knew it looked rather false. She hurried on.

When she arrived home, her parents were outside and the place was a hive of industry. There were poles and canvas sheets everywhere, tables and chairs waiting in furniture vans, people milling around, catering vehicles with portable ovens and refrigerators. At the sight, Gillian burst into tears and galloped upstairs to her room. Her mother, witnessing this, went to try and comfort Gillian but the girl was lying on her bed, sobbing and refusing to talk.

'What is it, Gillian? Look, shall I get the doctor? Is it nerves, is everything getting too much?'

But Gillian merely sobbed and sobbed.

Claude Jeremiah Greengrass and Banger Bailey arrived at the farm within half an hour, Banger with several containers in the boot of his car. Claude sought out Jack Siddons who was busy at the marquee and said, 'Jack, I've brought the stuff. Where do you want it?'

'Oh, right, aye, well. The caterers are over there, at that end, Claude. Where the portable fridges and things are. Take it over there and we'll put it in a fridge, then I'll tell the caterers. How much is there?'

'Enough for two hundred,' said Banger. 'And a bit extra for yourself, Mr Siddons. A bonus. A taster.'

And Banger produced a small bag of prawns which he handed to Jack. Jack smiled. 'I'll try them with my tea tonight, lads. Now, Claude, here's the money,' and Jack Siddons pressed some notes into Claude's greasy fist. 'And a tip for you both!'

As Claude Jeremiah and his friend disappeared along the lane back to the village, Jack Siddons placed his bag of prawns in the fridge and decided it was time to position the direction signs around the entrances to Aidensfield.

The flowers would be arriving too; he'd decorated the church for Mary's funeral, and now some of those flowers, with lots of additions, would be arranged for the wedding.

He'd wanted the very best and so the entire parish church would be adorned with the most beautiful floral display ever seen in Aidensfield. The team of flower-arrangers were scheduled to arrive at a decent interval after the funeral to transform the old church into a place of dreams. Jack's plans for the decor of the church would take hours to complete so it had to be started today. He was assured the flowers would remain fresh for tomorrow's ceremony.

'I'm going down the village,' Jack shouted to his wife. 'I'll put the signs up and make sure those flower-arrangers have arrived. You keep an eye on those folks at the marquee. I don't want it blowing down at the slightest puff of wind!'

'Right you are,' called Beth from the kitchen.

By the end of that Friday, Nick was no further forward in his investigation of the burglary at Clough Farm. Examination of Walter Pettigrew's fingerprints revealed that he was not responsible and Nick went to thank him for his co-operation. Upon his return from Walter's farm, he found Jack Siddons hammering wooden signs into the grass along the verges, pointing variously to the parish church and especially to his own farm which lay off the beaten track.

'I'm sorry, Jack, but I've not arrested anybody for that burglary yet. It wasn't Walter, we've eliminated him through his fingerprints.'

'Well, I can't think of anybody else who's got it in for me, Nick. Maybe it was an ordinary burglar who got disturbed. Well, so long as nowt else happens. I'm not too bothered, to be honest, now we've got the presents back. I've fixed the window and put locks on. What do you think to my signs?'

'A good idea, your farm being hard to find!'

'Even for burglars, eh?' grunted the burly farmer. 'Right, well, it's time I got along to the church now. You've got to keep these folks on their toes, Nick, they allus try to cut corners if you let 'em. And nowt's going to spoil our Gillian's big day!'

During his patrols, Nick passed Mary's cottage and saw Kevin clearing out her things. He had borrowed an old van and was filling it with her clothes and other belongings, some of which would be dumped on the tip and others which he would sell or even take to Birmingham. As Aidensfield prepared for a happy event to follow Mary's sad and lonely death, Nick went home for his tea. He was looking forward to the big event tomorrow. For Jack's sake, he hoped everything went smoothly.

For Jack, it had been a tiring day, and it was not over yet. He had a short rest before his evening meal, at which he asked Beth to serve the prawns; she declined to have any because she did not like them, while Gillian wasn't eating anything. Their daughter was still in her room, uncommunicative and sullen. Jack had not lost his appetite, though; he tucked into the prawns with considerable relish before turning to his pork chops and apple sauce. Beth watched him; he was enjoying this, she realised. He really was putting his heart and soul into the arrangements for Gillian's wedding, but Gillian seemed unable or unwilling to respond in a similar way.

Beth went to her daughter's room and sat on the bed; Gillian lay beneath the covers, pale and unhappy.

'Gillian, you do want to marry Richard, don't you?'

'Yes, I do, Mum. I really do. I just get upset at all this fuss. It's my day, not Dad's. He's running around as if the Queen was coming . . .'

'It is important to him, you know. You are our only daughter and he just wants the best for you.'

'I don't want to spoil things, Mum, but I do wish he'd asked me what I wanted instead of rushing into things like he has.'

'Try to make it a happy day for us all, darling.' Beth leaned forward and kissed Gillian. 'And don't spoil your father's fun . . .'

'Fun?' she cried. 'Is that what it is? Fun?' And she buried her head in the bedclothes. 'I just want everything to be all right!'

'It will be, it will be,' sighed Beth, leaving the room. 'Tomorrow, everything will be fine.'

But at eight o'clock that evening, Nick's telephone rang. Kate was busy ironing his best white shirt in readiness for the next day, and he was in his office, writing up his pocketbook.

'I'll get it,' he said. 'Hello, this is Aidensfield Police.'

'Mr Rowan, it's Mrs Surtees at Curlew Cottage. I look after the flowers at the church, you know.'

'Yes, of course.' He knew the little grey-haired lady who was one of the stalwarts of the parish. 'So what can I do for you?'

'Well, I've just been to lock up the church for the night and, well, somebody's been in. They've smashed all those lovely flowers that were put in for the wedding. They're ruined, trampled on, crushed . . . every one of them. It's terrible, it really is . . . I wasn't sure what I should do.'

'I'll come straight away,' said Nick.

CHAPTER SIXTEEN

It looked as if a hoard of vandals had rampaged around the church. Flowers were strewn everywhere; they had been thrown on to the floor and trampled over, cast across the pews and scattered along the aisle. Some had had their heads pulled off and others had their leaves stripped from the stems to be thrown around like confetti. As Nick surveyed the damage with Mrs Surtees standing mute with shock behind him, he asked, 'Has anything belonging to the church been damaged, Mrs Surtees? Books, altar cloths, candlesticks?'

'No, it's just the flowers, Mr Rowan. It's the sort of thing children would do, isn't it? So silly and pointless . . . who'd want to do this just before a wedding?'

'I wish I knew,' sighed Nick. 'Well, I'll go and tell Jack and then I'll make an official report of the damage. Jack'll probably want to come back with me to see what's happened. Will you still be here?'

'Yes, somebody will have to clear up the mess,' she said. 'We can't leave it like this, can we?'

It was just as easy for Nick to ride up to the farm as it

was to return to his own house and ring Jack Siddons. When he got there, Beth said, 'He's not at all well, Nick, he's been violently sick; he's upstairs lying on the bed.'

Nick explained what had happened and she shook her head in disbelief. 'Oh, this is terrible! Who's doing all these things, Nick? Wait there, I'll tell him. He'll want to know.'

Pale as a ghost, Jack Siddons appeared a few minutes later, still fully dressed but looking like death warmed up. His face was pinched with pain and he was almost doubled up as he walked.

'My bloody stomach, Nick, God, the pain's terrible . . .'

'Have you eaten something that disagrees with you?'

'No, nowt that I know of. Anyway, Beth says somebody's been in the church messing about with the flowers.'

'Look, I think you should see a doctor. I'll ring Kate.'

'No need, it's just stomach-ache. Nerves, perhaps. Mebbe I've been doing too much, all this rushing around. Anyroad, who's done this to my flowers? Kids, was it?'

'I don't know, but they're ruined. You'll need some more before tomorrow. I'll make enquiries, but I'm wondering who's got it in for you if it's not Walter Pettigrew.'

'All that can wait, Nick. My priority is to get that church in a proper state for Gillian's big day tomorrow. I'll come down straight away . . .'

'Dad, what's happened now?' Gillian had appeared dressed in a casual sweater and jeans. 'Why is Mr Rowan here?'

The state of her hair told Nick she had been asleep, or at least lying down in her room.

She looked ill too, but nothing like as fragile as her father. Nick explained the latest incident, but her reaction was strange.

'It's only flowers, Dad,' she said almost dismissively. 'They don't matter!'

'Don't matter?' he almost exploded. 'Course they matter! Everything matters . . .'

'Dad, I just want to get married, that's all. The trimmings aren't all that important.'

'Do you want to see them, Jack?' Nick asked quietly. 'Mrs Surtees is waiting to lock up.'

'Aye, I'd better come,' he said.

'I'll take you down there, Dad,' offered Gillian. 'You're in no fit state to drive, not like that.'

'And Beth?' Nick smiled. 'Ring Kate, will you? Ask her to pop down to the church as well? I want her to have a look at Jack and he'll be fairly handy when he's in the village!'

'Thanks, Nick, he wouldn't let me get her out to see him; he said it would wear off.'

And so Nick on his motorcycle led the Siddons's car along the track and eventually to the church. Only Jack's sickness prevented him from hitting the roof at the sight of the devastation as Gillian tried to calm him down. When Kate arrived, Nick had a quick word with her before she approached Jack. He was sitting in one of the pews, miserable but not defeated, his anger spent. Gillian, Nick and Mrs Surtees were clearing up the mess.

Nick saw Kate speak to Jack at length, quizzing him about anything he might have eaten, then she carried out a swift but skilful examination.

'I'm sure it's food poisoning, Jack,' she said. 'You've got rid of the worst, judging by what you've told me. So if you don't eat anything else, you should be fit enough to give your Gillian away tomorrow. I've got something at the surgery that will help, call before you go home. I'll go there now.'

'Food poisoning?' he gasped, his stomach still aching as if he'd been kicked by a mule.

'What have you been eating today that you don't normally touch?' she asked him.

'Well, I had a nibble here and there, some vol-au-vents and things, bits of stuff the caterers are bringing in. I sampled some of it, then I had some prawns.'

'Prawns?' Nick heard the word and in the back of his mind, he recalled a recent meeting with Sergeant Blaketon. 'Where did you get the prawns, Jack?'

'Well, it was a deal I had, a bulk supply offered very cheap, cheap enough for me to order enough for all my guests.'

'And the supplier? Jack, you're not going to tell me it was Claude Jeremiah Greengrass, are you? No wonder he was so helpful over your burglary, offering his expert advice . . . He was after off-loading a load of rotten prawns!'

'They tasted all right to me,' Jack said.

'And I had none, neither did Mum,' said Gillian, who was now sitting in a pew close to her father.

'But I had some of the other grub too, samples, little fancy bits of this and that,' said Jack.

'Look, Mr Siddons,' said Kate. 'If any of that food is suspect, you must not give it to your guests. Food poisoning can kill people with weak dispositions – old people for example. So, I'm sorry but you can't use any of it.'

'But it's all here, Dr Rowan, in containers and freezers, all ready for tomorrow . . . There's more to come in the morning, fresh stuff, salads and things.'

'Sorry, Jack, but you can't risk giving poisoned food to a large group of people. The result could be devastating.'

'It'll be those prawns, luv,' said Nick to Kate. 'I'll bet Claude has got them on the cheap . . .'

'There isn't time to have all the items of food analysed, Nick, not before the wedding. We can't risk it, even if it was those prawns.'

'I'll have Greengrass's guts for garters!' snarled Siddons. 'But he wouldn't try to poison me, would he?'

Nick shook his head. 'No, that's not his game, Jack.'

'But, I mean, with all these other things, the burglary, the flowers and now this, it does look as if somebody's out to get me, doesn't it? I mean, somebody could have poisoned those prawns, or that other food, and got Claude or the caterers to give it to me . . .'

'Oh, Dad,' Gillian said, 'I am sorry, I know you've tried

to make it a lovely day tomorrow, but so much is going
wrong . . .'

At the sound of her voice, he perked up and said, 'And
it's going to be a lovely day tomorrow, Gillian. You do
want to marry Richard, don't you? Here, in this church,
before your friends and family?'

'Yes, I do, but I'm so worried something else might go
wrong, there's been so much trouble.'

'Is that what's been bothering you, lass?' he asked her.
She nodded.

Nick recognised the signs. 'Gillian, do you know who's
behind all this? Has somebody been pestering you?'

'No,' she said. 'Not pestering me . . . but . . .'

'I know!' snarled Jack. 'It'll be that Kevin Begg, he
always did follow you round, and he's back, isn't he? He
was rotten right through, that lad, I saw through him even
if the others didn't. Right sweet on our Gillian, he was, till
he went away. And now he's back for his granny's
funeral . . .'

'Kevin? You mean he might have been doing all these
things, Gillian?' said Nick.

'He wanted to stop the wedding,' she said quietly. 'I
told him it was no good, that I love Richard and that I was
marrying him. But Kevin wanted me to call it off, he kept
on about the old days, when we were children.'

'I never did trust him, it was his eyes,' said Jack.

'We were real good friends,' said Gillian. 'But that was
a long time ago. It's over now, I don't love him and there's
no question of me wanting him, not now. I wondered if it
might be him when the dog didn't bark during the

burglary. He never ever barked at Kevin when we were little. He's an old dog and they used to go everywhere together.'

'Thanks, Gillian,' said Nick. 'I'll go and have words with him. There's no time like the present, as they say. I'll bet he's in the pub.'

'And when we get this floor cleaned up,' said Kate, 'you come to the surgery, Jack, and I'll give you one of my magic potions, and tomorrow you'll be as right as rain!'

'Thanks,' said Jack, turning a curious shade of green.

Nick was right. Kevin Begg was in the Aidensfield Arms and although he was not drunk, he had had sufficient to make him tottery on his feet.

'Come on, Kevin,' Nick said gently, 'you're going home.'

'You're not arresting me, are you, Constable?' The young man put on a show of bravado for the benefit of the regulars. 'Arresting me for breaking into Jack Siddons's house?'

'I want to talk to you about that, outside,' said Nick. 'Come along, sunshine, no trouble.'

Outside, away from the glances of the regulars and with the benefit of the fresh air, Kevin Begg sobered up slightly. Nick took his elbow and began to steer him along the street towards the lane which led to Badger Cottage.

'So what are your plans now, Kevin?'

'Finish off here, tidy up the cottage, then go back to Birmingham. There's nothing here for me, not now.'

'You thought of staying, did you?'

'For a time, yes. I used to live here, you know, at Clough Farm with my granny. When I was a lad . . .'

'That was when you fell in love with Gillian, was it?' Nick said.

'I've always loved that girl, Mr Rowan. I thought she loved me, I though she might have waited for me.'

'But she's marrying someone else, eh?'

He nodded morosely.

'And how did you feel about that? Upset enough to try and poison her father?'

'Poison him? Jack Siddons? I never tried to poison him, Mr Rowan, believe me!'

Having terrified him with the story of the poisoned food, Nick said, 'All right, so what about the other troubles? The break-in, the flowers in church . . .'

'I know nothing about them, Mr Rowan. I wouldn't do that, I wouldn't harm Gillian!'

'But you might hope to have the wedding postponed, just a little, just enough for you to try and win her back, eh?'

'Mr Rowan, I didn't come here for that, I came for my grandmother's funeral!'

'And when you got here, there was another shock, eh? Gillian was getting married. Look, I can arrest you on suspicion of that burglary right now, and that means I can take your fingerprints. Suppose your fingerprints match some we found on the wedding presents that were dumped in the grounds of the farm, eh? I reckon they might tell us a lot, don't you? And those vases in church? Somebody lifted them up and tipped out the flowers,

Kevin, and left very useful sets of fingerprints behind. So, if it was you, perhaps you might like to tell me about it?'

They were outside Mary's cottage now and Begg spoke quietly. 'You'd better come in, Constable. I've been a real fool, a real idiot. I didn't want to spoil Gillian's day, honest, I just wanted her to consider me, after all this time.'

So Kevin Begg admitted to Nick that he had broken into the house to remove the wedding presents, and had entered the church to destroy the flower arrangements, merely in the vain hope of delaying the wedding. He said he'd never had any intention of stealing the presents and in fact, had left them so that they would quickly be recovered. The farm dog, old Ben, hadn't barked at him because Kevin had taken it a toffee, a treat he used to give it years ago.

'I'll pay for any damage,' he offered. 'I'll pay for the flowers to be replaced, it's the least I can do.'

'I'll have to report this to my superiors,' said Nick. 'Strictly, I ought to arrest you and charge you with burglary, but I accept you had no intention of stealing the presents.'

'I'm not leaving yet, I want to see Gillian get married, Mr Rowan. I'm going to apologise to her parents, and to her; I know there's no place for me in her life, and when the wedding's over, I'll go. The cottage can be used by somebody else. I've been a bloody fool, I don't know what came over me.'

Nick decided that an arrest would be somewhat heavy-handed, and besides, even if he did arrest Begg, he'd be released on bail pending further enquiries. So Nick would delay his official response until after the wedding. Rightly or wrongly, that was his decision.

As he walked away from the cottage, he encountered Claude Jeremiah Greengrass stumbling home from the Aidensfield Arms.

'I didn't see you when I was in there a few minutes ago, Claude.' Nick said, watching the old rogue sober up with astonishing speed.

'Aye, well, I saw you, Constable Rowan. You need keen eyes to do my job, you know. Alertness, the ability to merge into the background.'

'So where's your mate, then? The little chap with the fancy Rover?'

'Just gone, Constable Rowan, he's got Ashfordly Point-to-Point to cater for and he's set off early, to get himself parked in a good position, you see.'

'I hear he supplied some prawns for Gillian's wedding?'

'Aye, a bargain, they were. Straight from the North Sea, fresh as shrimps and tasty as crabs they were.'

'They were rotten, they'd gone off. They made Jack ill and he's had to throw out all the food he'd got organised for the wedding. He's after your guts, Claude, and the authorities will be investigating a case of food poisoning. So we'll want to have words with your pal, at the point-to-point or wherever he's gone. And we might ask him a few questions about some stolen seafood, we might just learn that he and his catering emporium happened to be in the vicinity when certain lorryloads of perishables were nicked, eh, Claude? And that means we might come back to you to have you arrested for receiving stolen property, doesn't it?'

Claude blinked in consternation. 'Well, I hardly know the chap, really, Mr Rowan. I mean, it was twenty years ago . . .'

'I thought you'd been comrades in arms, I thought you and him had made the world a safer place for the likes of me, Claude, by your bravery and selfless sacrifice. I thought you were mates of old . . . so you said.'

'You're not serious, about Jack being poisoned, are you, Mr Rowan?'

'Very serious, Claude. In fact, you can ask him yourself, he's just coming out of the church on his way to Kate's surgery . . .'

'No, well, I might just get away home for a quiet night!'

Kevin Begg did remain for the wedding and in fact was instrumental in preventing Walter Pettigrew from dumping a load of manure in the place the official cars would occupy outside the church. Whether or not Walter's intention was malicious or whether he really was bringing a load of manure for the vicar was never determined, but it was Kevin who intervened as he passed the church on his way to the pub. His parting words were: 'Walter, this is Gillian's day, forget your feud with her father. This is nothing to do with Jack Siddons, this is Gillian's wedding.'

Soon news of the incident spread though the village and was put to Sergeant Blaketon by Nick. Nonetheless, Kevin would have to be brought to the police station and

bailed to appear at a later date in Ashfordly Magistrates'
Court on two charges, one of burglary and one of malicious damage. However, Blaketon felt sure that, once the
full circumstances had been explained to the magistrates,
Kevin would escape with perhaps a conditional discharge.
To date, he had no criminal record. Kevin agreed to this
course of action, and, after the wedding, he was taken to
Ashfordly Police Station and bailed to appear at Ashfordly Magistrates' Court on a date to be determined.

After all his trials, Jack Siddons did see his daughter
married in a splendid manner. She looked radiant, as only
a happy bride can, and he looked every inch the proud
father. Afterwards, the reception was superb, even if the
food had been prepared in an almighty rush.

'Next time you want me to cater for a wedding,' said
George Ward of the Aidensfield Arms, 'I'd appreciate a
bit more warning!'

'Next time there's a wedding in this family, George,
you'll get it!' smiled Jack Siddons.

'I'll tell you summat, Jack,' said George as they drank a
brandy to the health of the bride. 'That was a wedding
Aidensfield will remember for a long, long time.'

'Me an' all!' smiled Jack ruefully. 'Another brandy?'

'Aye, why not, you're paying!' chuckled George.

In the following months, the life of Aidensfield settled
down to a period of tranquillity. Nick was able to
consolidate his position as the village constable and
found that the people trusted him and respected him.
Even Sergeant Blaketon spent less time supervising him

than hitherto and the bluff sergeant allowed him to administer his rural beat in the way Nick felt best. Although he was expected to enforce the law when required, he was also regarded by the public as a humane policeman, willing to help those less fortunate than himself if the occasion demanded. Old people asked him for advice on the completion of official forms, and householders came to him for guidance on crime prevention around the home. Even some youngsters approached him for tips on how to pass their driving test or for an explanation on the law on drinking in public houses and hotels. And Nick would always be happy to help to them, whoever they were.

Kate was also finding herself welcomed into more homes – the ailing Dr Ferrenby was passing more work to her and asking her to visit those of his patients with whom he found it difficult to deal due to their condition. In many cases, Kate was able to prescribe up-to-the-minute medicines or treatment and her success rate meant that her stature was rising too. To her satisfaction she found that by working this vast moorland practice she was expanding her experience while winning the trust of many of the old doctor's patients.

One of Kate's innovations was to organise fitness classes in the village hall. These were intended for retired people, men and women, who would normally have little contact with others beyond the confines of their own homes. At first, Kate had found them very shy about attending such a class, but when she explained that they did not have to strip to their underwear or dress up in leotards, some decided to come along 'just to see what's going on'.

Gradually, her class expanded, with husbands and wives, friends and relations, all walking to the village hall to partake in very gentle, but very stimulating exercise with pleasant music in the background. In no time, new friendships were formed, old feuds were forgotton and a spirit of comradeship was created at the keep fit sessions. There were regular rest periods during the programme which ran from 10.30 until 11.30 every Wednesday morning, with coffee and biscuits to follow. The sessions became more of a social gathering than a gymnastic display, but Kate realised that their value lay in the fact that so many of these people, all in their late sixties or seventies, actually walked to the village hall and then remained to chat and laugh over coffee. That alone was of enormous benefit to them; the exercises were something of a bonus.

In time, Kate grew to know those who were regular attenders – there was dear old Mrs Paxton with her corns, Mr Wright who performed his exercises with a pipe in his mouth, Miss Houlston who blushed if she had to exercise while standing next to Mr Field, and Mr Clark who clearly had a crush on old Mrs Cook. But one lady seemed to sparkle more than the others. In her mid seventies, a neat but rather small figure with beautifully kept grey hair, spectacles and somewhat old-fashioned clothes, she was always cheerful and full of fun, rather like a cheeky sparrow in many respects, and during the coffee breaks she had her group in fits of laughter.

She was the life and soul of the gathering, and when she walked across the floor, her tiny feet almost twinkled like those of a fairy dancer. Surprisingly fit and agile, the range of exercises were never a hardship for her.

Kate discovered that her name was Jane Thompson, and that she lived in Moorview Cottage, high above the village. The beautifully positioned house overlooked the railway line and enjoyed stunning views across Aidensfield and district. From there, Jane walked miles during the week, coming into the village for her shopping or venturing down to Aidensfield to catch a bus to Ashfordly for a hair-do or to buy her clothes. Jane had been widowed about a year earlier but kept herself busy at home with her greenhouse and gardening.

One morning, Jane's daughter, a Mrs Jennifer Bradshaw, came into the hall with her mother. They were late and the old folks were just having a breather.

Jennifer apologised to Kate. 'Sorry, Dr Rowan, are we very late?'

'No, we've only been going a while, we're just having a rest. Come in.'

Jennifer helped her mother off with her heavy overcoat, but the old lady snapped, 'I can manage, our Jennifer. I'm not senile, you know!' Jane scurried off to the cloakroom to dispose of her coat and tidy her hair.

'I brought her this morning because I wanted a word with you, Doctor.'

'Yes, of course, any time.'

'I thought if I came at the end of this morning's session, when they're having their coffee and biscuits, we might have a chat? I don't want Mother to overhear us.'

'All right,' agreed Kate. 'That will be a good time. Your mum will be in the thick of them, telling them jokes and being the life and soul of the party as usual!'

And so the arrangement was made. Jennifer Bradshaw, a confident woman in her forties, arrived shortly before the end of that morning's class, to see her mother sitting among the others, telling them stories and making them laugh, as lively and full of fun as ever. Kate obtained a coffee and some biscuits for Jennifer and they adjourned to a quiet corner of the hall.

'So,' smiled Kate, 'what is it, Jennifer?'

'It's Mother,' she said. 'I'm worried about her health, she's not the same as she was.'

'She is getting older, and the loss of your father must have had some effect, Jennifer. I think she's a remarkable lady, very fit for her age both mentally and physically.'

'It's the mental aspect that I'm concerned about.' Jennifer fiddled with the cup instead of drinking her coffee. 'You see, once or twice, I've heard her talking to Dad; when she's alone in her greenhouse, for example, she'll be chatting away to him as if he's still alive, telling him about her day, about the plants she's growing, and passing on local gossip.'

Kate smiled reassuringly, 'That's quite normal,' she said. 'It's a way of coping; after a lifetime together, the loss of a partner is a tremendous shock.'

'I know she suffered when Dad died. They were very close and that cottage is very remote; they sometimes went days without seeing another person.'

'But your mum does get into the village, and she does enjoy the company of other people.' Kate glanced across to where Jane was telling some bawdy story. 'I think she copes remarkably well, and if I were you, I shouldn't worry too much about her chats with your father. Lots of widows and widowers do that.'

'There's more, Doctor,' said Jennifer, still fiddling with her coffee cup. 'I think she's getting confused. She says she's getting funny telephone calls late at night.'

'Funny? You mean obscene?'

'No, nothing like that. The phone just rings and then goes dead.'

'No messages?'

'No, nothing,' said Jennifer. 'I've been up to the cottage to sit with her, but there's never been any of those calls while I've been there. You see, with this business about Dad, I'm not sure whether she's imagining those calls as well, or whether they're actually happening.'

'She seems quite rational to me,' Kate said. 'I'd say she was very much in possession of all her faculties. Have you reported the calls to anyone? The police or the post office? They can investigate nuisance calls, you know.'

'I know, but I'd feel such a fool if she was imagining the whole thing. I wish she'd come to live with us. My husband and I are more than willing to look after her, and she wouldn't be such a worry to us.'

'So how can I help?' asked Kate.

'Well, you're a doctor and you are seeing quite a lot of her now that she's coming to your classes. I don't want to make an official fuss about all this, nor do I want Mother to know I've spoken to you about it, but, well, I wondered if you would keep an eye on her when she's here? Just to see if there is any sign of mental deterioration or confusion.'

'Yes, of course I'll do that,' smiled Kate. 'It will be a pleasure. Now, what about these phone calls? Shall I mention them to my husband?'

'Yes, but not officially because they might not be real.'

'But if they are being made, they might be happening to other old folks who are on their own, some kind of juvenile joke perhaps, done by village children. I'll ask him to bear it in mind and I know that when he's out on patrol, he'll keep an eye on your mother's cottage.'

'Thank you, Doctor.' Jennifer Bradshaw smiled gratefully.

That same morning, just as Nick was leaving to begin his day's patrol, the garden gate opened and in stormed Claude Jeremiah Greengrass accompanied by the faithful Alfred.

'Now don't you run away, Constable, I've got a complaint to make,' he shouted.

'A complaint, Claude?' smiled Nick, wondering what was agitating the scruffy fellow. 'Somebody been stealing eggs from your hens, have they?'

'No they haven't, and I wouldn't bother you with that sort of thing anyroad. Now listen, I've been shot at.'

'Shot at? You?'

'Aye, me. Well, Alfred really. Both of us.'

'Did they hit either of you?'

314

'You're not taking this seriously, are you?' Claude growled. 'Look, I was heading for Arncliffe Woods this morning, walking through the fields and minding my own business, when somebody took a pot shot at me. With a twelve-bore. I'm telling you straight. Alfred ran for his life and I got myself hidden behind a tree, I can tell you.'

'Trespassing, were you? Trespassing in pursuit of game? Poaching, in other words?'

'I wasn't, we were on a public right of way, Mr Rowan, it's a public footpath through them woods and we were doing nowt wrong. Now it can't be right to let guns off when folks are walking on public footpaths, can it?'

'True, Claude. Who was this gunman? Did you see him?'

'I did, it was that chap Walker. Raymond Walker.'

'Isn't he chairman of the local branch of the National Farmers' Union?' Nick asked. 'That Walker?'

'That's him, Mr Rowan. Thinks he's God Almighty at times, but he has no right to shoot at us, and no right to stop me and Alfred from using a public footpath.'

'Is that what he was trying to do? Stop you using that path?'

'Yes, that's what he yelled at me. It's through his land, I know that, but it's been a public footpath for years, Mr Rowan, and always will be. So I want you to have words with him and warn him off.'

CHAPTER SEVENTEEN

Nick drove through the beautiful moorland countryside to Raymond Walker's imposing home. A successful farmer and businessman, he had renovated the old farmhouse which overlooked the village from the edge of the moor above the railway station. It was not too high on the bleak moorland but stood below the rim of the surrounding hills, almost in a valley of its own. Below it were spread the meadows and arable acres of Walker's farmland. There were woods too, and some moorland streams which flowed from the deserted heatherclad heights. It was, in fact, an idyllic location.

As Nick drove into the premises on his Francis Barnett motorcycle, he noticed Raymond Walker sawing some logs with a noisy power saw. Nick eased to a halt and hoisted his bike on to its stand, then walked across to the powerfully built man. Walker was in his mid forties, Nick estimated, a hard-working and ambitious person.

'Morning.' Walker switched off the saw and laid it on a bench.

'Morning.' Nick removed his helmet and wiped his brow. 'Mr Walker?'

'That's me.'

'I'm PC Rowan, Aidensfield Police.'

'I know who you are, Constable.' His manner was abrupt and almost curt.

It was clear to Nick that this was not going to be an affable conversation, and equally clear that Walker was not going to invite Nick into the house for a coffee, as most farmers would have done. His attitude was that of a tough businessman rather than a moorland farmer. Dispensing with the usual pleasantries, Nick went straight to the business of his visit.

'I've had a complaint about you, Mr Walker.'

'Have you?'

'I understand you shot at a man and his dog this morning.'

'Greengrass and his dog, you mean? Are you saying that old rogue's had the audacity to complain to the police?'

'He did make a formal complaint to me about your behaviour and I am obliged to investigate the matter.'

'If I had intended to shoot that dog, it wouldn't be alive now, Constable. He'd have been burying it instead of making such a fuss. That man was trespassing on my land with that lurcher of his, and I warned him off. It was a shot in the air, not aimed at either Claude or that confounded dog of his. That was no more than any other farmer would have done, whether it was Greengrass or a townie wandering about with his poodle.'

318

'I understand he was on a public right of way, Mr Walker. There is a right of way across your land, I believe, a footpath through the woods?'

'There is, though a right of way doesn't mean poachers can come and take my game. They're still trespassing if they're there for the purpose of taking game, as I'm sure you realise, Constable.'

'I do know that, Mr Walker, but Claude Jeremiah was . . .'

'You're not protecting that old villain, are you?' Walker interrupted.

'I'm not protecting anyone, Mr Walker, but everyone has the right to pass and repass along a public right of way without being harassed, even Claude Jeremiah Greengrass and his dog.'

'The dog wasn't on a lead, Constable. It was roaming over my land.'

'There is no law about keeping dogs on a lead, Mr Walker, except at lambing time, and then it's only a local by-law.'

'And did Greengrass tell you about those sheep of mine that have been worried?' the farmer went on. 'Eight dead and another five or six injured in the last two months?'

'Are you saying Claude's dog was responsible?'

'No, I wouldn't go as far as that, but I've a right to protect my livestock.'

'You can't shoot a dog if it's not worrying them,' Nick said. 'Nor can you go around discharging guns at people who are simply walking along a public right of way.'

'I can shoot vermin on my own land . . .'

Nick interrupted, 'If your sheep have been subjected to attacks lately, why haven't you reported it to the police?'

'There's no point, is there? It's too late then. Dogs should be banned from fields and moors where there's sheep and lambs. I've oft said that in print and I'll keep on saying it until somebody takes some notice.'

'But if you had reported the sheep-worrying incidents, we could take action against the dog-owners who are responsible. Besides, there might be other reports which lead us to the culprits.'

'The damage is done by then, Mr Rowan. Those dogs want stopping before they start. And that's what'll happen if I catch any chasing my sheep. Now, you're not a country-born chap, are you?'

'No, I'm from London.'

'Then you'll not understand country ways, Constable. When it comes to protecting my own livestock, I take whatever action is right at the time, and if that means shooting a dog, then I shall shoot a dog and you'll never know a thing about it.'

'It's a different matter when you threaten people with guns when they are on a public right of way, Mr Walker, and that is what I'm interested in at this moment. I have received no reports of sheep-worrying in recent weeks, either from you or from anyone else, and so that does not concern me.'

'So you believe the word of that old rogue Greengrass rather than me, a respected farmer and businessman, and chairman of the local branch of the National Farmers' Union?'

'I have received a formal complaint about a member of the public being threatened with a firearm while walking in a public place, Mr Walker, and you know as well as I do that such behaviour cannot be tolerated. If I receive any further complaints about your behaviour in that respect, I shall submit a report to recommend you are not a fit person to be in possession of any firearm.'

'You wouldn't do that!'

'Try me,' smiled Nick, returning to his motorcycle. As he drove away, he fumed at this man's attitude. He was inclined to believe the word of Greengrass on this occasion, but proof of Walker's threats was difficult to obtain.

Half an hour after leaving the farm, Nick's radio crackled into life. It was Sergeant Blaketon and his message was curt.

'Alpha Four Six Six, I want to see you in my office immediately.'

'Ten four,' acknowledged Nick, wondering what was so urgent.

Alf Ventress, wallowing under a cloud of smoke, indicated to Nick that Blaketon was in his office and not in a very good mood. Alf managed to convey this message by some curious hand signals because Blaketon's office door was open. Nick understood Alf's coded waves and signals. Wondering what lay ahead, he tapped on the office door.

Blaketon shouted, 'Come in,' and when he saw it was Nick, said curtly, 'Shut that door, Rowan, and sit down.'

Nick pulled up a chair and sat before the sergeant's desk. Sergeant Blaketon, on the other hand, got up from his armchair and began to pace up and down the office.

'Rowan,' he said, 'I thought you were settling in very well at Aidensfield. In fact, I was telling the Superintendent just the other day that you were doing a good job, that you had developed an affinity with the local people and that you had quickly grasped the essentials of dealing with country folk in a diplomatic manner.'

'Thank you, Sergeant.'

'Don't thank me, Rowan. Listen. Now all those high hopes of mine were dashed this morning when you went to visit Raymond Walker. You do know who he is, don't you?'

'A farmer, Sergeant, a farmer like a lot of other people around here.'

'A wealthy man, Rowan, a businessman, a benefactor to many local charities, a member of umpteen local committees, chairman of the NFU and a close friend of the Superintendent.'

'Is he?' Nick sounded surprised.

'And you have been accusing him of threatening behaviour with a shotgun and have also had the audacity to warn him that he could be forbidden to possess firearms!'

'If he behaves stupidly . . .'

'Him? A farmer, a man of distinction in these parts?'

'He threatened Greengrass and his dog with his shotgun, Sergeant.'

'Greengrass? That paragon of virtue? That well known law-abiding citizen of Aidensfield? That dog-lover . . .'

'Sergeant, Greengrass has just as much entitlement to walk through Walker's land on a public right of way as any other person, with a dog if necessary, and he should not be subjected to threats, especially from a man armed with a shotgun.'

'Rowan, when it comes to an account of the truth of that incident, who do you think will be believed? Greengrass or Raymond Walker?'

'It's not a question of who's going to be believed, Sergeant,' Nick said stubbornly, 'it's a case of what is the truth, and for once, I believe Claude.'

'So it's one man's word against another. Well, Rowan, I don't want any repetition of this, so I expect you to warn Greengrass to keep off Walker's land. Right?'

'But he's entitled to be there, Sergeant, so long as he sticks to the footpath.'

'Just warn him off, Rowan, that's an order!'

As he drove back to Aidensfield, Nick felt himself grow increasingly angry at the attempt by Walker to use his influence and power to stop people using a public right of way. He could appreciate the man's concern if Claude and Alfred had been wandering about his land away from the footpath, but in Nick's view, this smacked of something deeper. In spite of Blaketon's strong defence of Walker, Nick knew there was no way he could ban Claude from using that public right of way. He could advise him to keep away, but he could never compel him.

Turning all this over in his mind, he made his way to Claude's ramshackle home.

'I've had words with Walker, Claude, and I've warned him about his conduct.'

'I should think so!'

'But he's made a complaint about me! I got it in the

neck from Blaketon because I threatened Walker with confiscation of his right to possess firearms if he didn't restrain his activities.'

'Aye, well, good for you, Constable. I'm not one for complaining to the police, but, by gum, he deserved it. I think he's up to summat, Mr Rowan.'

'Like what, Claude?'

'Dunno, but I'm going to find out!'

'You keep off that land of his, Claude,' Nick warned. 'He might not miss next time – he might shoot Alfred!'

Claude looked crafty. 'He might not see me, Mr Rowan. I know a bit about camouflage, you know. Us old soldiers learned how to get around unseen in the jungles of Burma and similar spots, dodging bullets from the Japs and coping with snakes and scorpions.'

'Blaketon wants you to stop going on to Walker's land.' Nick tried to reason with Claude.

'It's a public footpath, Mr Rowan. I know it's not been used for ages and it's overgrown with briars and weeds, but it's still a public right of way, it's on all the maps. I've checked.'

'Blaketon thinks it would be wise not to risk walking there, especially with Alfred.'

'Aye, well, the more Walker wants me to stop, and the more he uses his influence to have me stopped, the more interested I am in finding out why, Mr Rowan. Why stop an innocent chap like me taking a stroll with my dog? He's up to summat and if he's frightened of somebody finding out what it is, then it must be illegal, eh? I'll find out and I'll let you know!'

'Claude . . .'

'I know, keep my eyes and ears open for men with guns, and don't let Alfred chase the sheep.'

'I don't want to know about all this, Claude,' and Nick drove back home. It was almost lunchtime.

Over their usual sandwich lunch, Nick and Kate discussed their respective mornings' activities, including Kate's discussion with Jennifer Bradshaw. She told Nick of Jennifer's worries over her mother's mental health and of Jane's conversations with her dead husband. She also mentioned the nuisance telephone calls and asked Nick whether he knew of any other similar pieces of mischief.

'I've not come across any,' he said. 'If it's local kids being stupid, I would have been told. They'd probably use the telephone kiosk rather than their parents' phones, but I've not heard of any other cases.'

Kate frowned. 'Jennifer's not sure whether her mother is imagining things or whether this is real, that's why she hasn't mentioned it before. Jane's state of mind is a bit suspect. It must be if she's talking to her dead husband as if he's still around. But, as I said to the daughter, a lot of widows and widowers do that. It's not uncommon and it's by no means a sign of mental disorder. I mean, people talk to themselves, to their dogs and cats, and even to cows and horses!'

'But this woman's daughter is clearly concerned about her. Do you treat the old lady?' he asked. 'Is she one of your patients?'

'She's on our list, yes. Alex once treated her; just after

her husband died she had a breakdown and he arranged
specialist counselling for her. She recovered fully, according to our records. I've never had to attend to her,' Kate
added. 'She's a very spritely old thing, she never seems to
ail at all.'

'So what will you do now?'

'There's not a lot I can do,' she admitted. 'But I thought
I would make a point of popping in to visit the mother if
ever I'm in the vicinity.'

'Good idea,' he said. 'And I'll pop in when I'm passing.'

'She has a greenhouse, you know,' Kate added. 'She
spends hours in there and that's when she talks to her
dead husband.'

'You might get some plants for the garden,' he said. 'It
certainly needs some! Offer to buy a few from her.'

Kate smiled. 'That's a lovely reason for popping in to
visit her.'

Next morning, Kate had to call on an expectant mother
not far from Jane's cottage and she decided, on impulse,
to pay the widow a visit. She parked in the drive of the
cottage; built of local stone, it was a picturesque house in
a beautiful location and the sun was bathing the entire
area in its crisp and clean glow. As Kate walked towards
the door she looked at the greenhouse but there was no
sign of Jane; it was rather early to be working there. She
rattled the door knocker and waited.

Jane's voice called out, 'Who is it?'

'It's me, Dr Rowan,' Kate responded.

'Oh, all right, wait a minute.'

Kate heard the distinctive noises of heavy objects being moved inside the house, and then came the sound of bolts being withdrawn and keys turned. Eventually, the door opened to reveal the tiny figure of Mrs Thompson.

'It's like Fort Knox here!' smiled Kate. 'Is there any need to barricade yourself in like this, Jane?'

'I'm frightened at night, Dr Rowan, I'm terrified, honest I am. I push a chest of drawers against the door. I've told our Jennifer all about it but she thinks I'm making it all up.'

'Making what up?'

'Those telephone calls, and prowlers outside, banging on my doors and windows, making noises, frightening noises.'

'How long has this been happening?' Kate was horrified.

'Over the past few weeks. It started well after Charlie, that's my husband, passed on.'

'Can we talk about it inside?' Kate asked.

'Yes, thanks, come in, I'll put the kettle on.'

Over a cup of tea in Jane's neat and tidy kitchen, with pot plants upon every surface, the old lady poured out her heart to Kate. It seemed that over the last six or eight weeks, someone had been conducting a campaign of terror against her. Late at night, the telephone would ring and when she answered it, there would be no voice at the other end, just the sound of deep breathing and terrifying groans. The usual time for the calls was between eleven o'clock and midnight. And earlier in the evening, when she was sitting by her fire, she would hear noises outside, knocking on her door, but when she opened it, there would be no one there.

Another trick was to scrape something down the glass of her kitchen window so that it made a screeching noise. Sometimes there would the sound of tins being rattled and bells ringing. It all took place outside the house and at night, under the cover of darkness.

'Why didn't you tell my husband?' Kate asked.

'I couldn't see the point. I told our Jennifer and her husband, but they thought I was imagining things. Eric, that's my son-in-law, well, he said it was the wind rattling things and howling around the house.'

'And could that be the case?' Kate asked.

'Yes, I suppose it could. I mean, it is an exposed site up here and I must admit the wind makes some funny noises at times. Then when I mentioned the phone calls, he said it would be kids messing about or somebody getting the wrong number. But it isn't, Dr Rowan. I'm not senile and I know which is wind noises and which isn't, and I know a nuisance phone call when I get one.'

'I think it would be sensible if my husband came to talk to you about the phone calls and things. I believe you, Jane, and I'm sure Jennifer does. She's very worried about you, she told me what was happening.'

'They want me to go and live with them,' said Jane. 'They're a nice couple, they've been good to me in the past but they don't want me living with them. Their way of life's not like mine, and I'd be in the way.'

'I'm sure you wouldn't be in the way! They wouldn't ask if they didn't mean it!' Kate said.

'I'd prefer to keep living here, in spite of all those noises and phone calls. Jennifer comes to see me every day. Her house is just along the lane so it's not as if she lives miles away.'

'Right,' said Kate. 'I'll explain all this to my husband and he'll come to see you. You tell him everything. He might be able to get the telephone exchange to intercept your calls.'

'I don't want to be a nuisance to anybody. Will it cost anything, to get them to intercept my calls?'

Kate shook her head reassuringly. 'No, not a penny, and it's not being a nuisance, Jane. The exchange will want to stop those calls just as much as you do. And Nick will keep a watch outside, just in case somebody *is* prowling about. Look, in future whenever you think somebody's is roaming about outside, just ring us. You've got the number?'

'Yes, Jennifer wrote it down for me, but I didn't like to be a nuisance. Thank you so much, Dr Rowan. It has made me feel happier. Now, more tea?'

'No thanks, I've lots more calls to make.'

'But you've time for a quick look in my greenhouse? I have some nice border plants just coming on, and some lettuces. I can let you have some seedlings, you'll both be too busy to attend to the garden, I expect.'

'We don't get a lot of time for that sort of thing,' Kate admitted. 'Thanks. Come along, show me your famous greenhouse.'

While Kate was inspecting the beautiful array of young

plants in Jane's greenhouse and admiring the stunning views across Raymond Walker's land, Claude Jeremiah Greengrass was trudging through the countryside not very far away. As always, he was accompanied by the faithful Alfred.

The pair of them were heading for the point where yesterday morning Claude had been confronted by Raymond Walker. This time, however, Claude was not using the public footpath. He was moving quickly along under the cover of shrubs and trees, dodging between the drystone walls and high hawthorn hedgerows as he made his way towards Walker's land. The reason for his urgent errand was that he had seen a builder's lorry head this way not many minutes earlier. In the back there had been some fencing posts and barbed-wire netting, and it was making for Walker's land, but not by a conventional route. It had slipped along the bridleway which led past Jane Thompson's cottage before disappearing into the woodland below.

But the noise it had made during its progress through the wood had enabled Claude to identify its location and so he was now heading that way, dodging between the trees like a wraith, with Alfred on his heels. It didn't take him long to find the lorry. It was parked at the edge of the wood, just off the beaten track, and two men had unloaded the contents of the lorry and were working on the path.

Claude watched in silence. Very soon, he realised that they were erecting a barbed-wire fence which completely blocked the right of way. The high posts were hammered into the ground and made secure, then strands of barbed wire were linked to them, some of it being supported by the surrounding trees. Claude looked about him – there was no way through except by this route. Eventually, when the men had finished, they took a signboard from the lorry and erected it beside the fence. Its message read, 'PRIVATE LAND. KEEP OUT.'

'You bugger, Walker!' cursed Greengrass. 'I'll fettle you, so I will!'

With no further ado, he loped back into Aidensfield, closely attended by Alfred. He found Nick just mounting his motorcycle outside Mostyn's Garage after filling his tank with two-stroke mixture.

'Mr Rowan,' he said, 'you'd better come with me and be sharp about it. I've summat to show you!'

'Important, is it?'

'Aye, very. Very important to this community, it is. Come along, the walk'll do you good.'

Nick left his motorbike and accompanied Claude Jeremiah Greengrass into the woodland, avoiding the public footpath and wondering if he was to be confronted by a gun-wielding farmer. They soon arrived at the site of the new fence, which Claude pointed out with a grand gesture.

'That's why he didn't want me using that path, Mr Rowan, he wants to block it off. He put that fence up not an hour ago.'

'But nobody except you uses this path, do they?' Nick asked. 'It's overgrown, it's impassable anyway! There's no point in keeping footpaths open if folks aren't going to use them.'

'But it's on all the maps, Constable. It's been there for centuries, you can't just block off a footpath, it's against the law.'

'Not against the criminal law, Claude, and my job is to enforce the criminal law, not the civil law.'

'Does that mean you aren't going to tell him to take that fence down?'

'I can't, Claude, it's not within my power. It's a civil matter, a job for the civil courts. Somebody like the Ramblers' Association or the Ashfordly Hikers' Club could make representations. Or even take a civil court action.'

'Can anybody do that, then? Take a civil court action?'

'Yes, the law's there for everybody to use.'

'So how would I go about starting off a civil action against this chap?'

'You would have to see a solicitor first,' said Nick. 'And it would cost you money, legal charges and so on.'

'You forget I'm a man of means now, Constable, I have money in the bank and I'm very capable of fighting for my rights. And this is one of them, the right for me and Alfred to walk along that path whenever we want, without restriction or hindrance. That applies to anybody else that happens to want to use it in the years to come.'

'Well, if it's going to make you happy, Claude, and do a public service, I wish you the best of luck.'

'You'll have to be my witness,' beamed Claude.

'Me?' cried Nick.

'Aye, you, I've shown you that fence, which means I can summons you to attend court, as my witness, against that blackguard Walker.'

'Is it that important, Claude?'

'If it teaches somebody not to fire shotguns at me and Alfred, then yes, it's very important.'

'Right, well, Claude. Count me in. Between us, we'll show that man what the great British public can do!'

As Nick left the wood, he spotted Kate's car leaving Jane's cottage; she pulled up at his side and smiled.

'I've bought some lovely little plants for you to put in the garden, when you've mowed the lawn and cleared the weeds,' she said slyly.

'Me, a gardener?' he laughed. 'That's your job!'

Kate ignored him, adding, 'And while you're here, will you pop in and see Jane Thompson? She has a lot to tell you.'

'More telephone calls?' he asked.

'And a prowler!' she said, driving off.

'Your work never stops, does it, Constable,' smiled Claude Jeremiah. 'It's nice to be wanted!'

'You've not been prowling around Jane's cottage, have you, Claude?' Nick asked more out of humour than seriousness.

'Would I do that?' he said. 'No, lad, I'm not one for upsetting widows who live in cottages others might want.'

'What do you mean, Claude? Cottages others might want?'

'Well, it stands to reason, doesn't it? That bit of land Jane's cottage is on is right next to Walker's farm isn't it?

He had a go at getting it years ago, but Charlie, that's her dead husband, refused. But Walker won't have given up. If he could buy this land, he could expand his own farm and get access to more land the other side of Jane's, over the road. There's some good building sites over there. Jane's little house is worth a mint, Mr Rowan. Bear that in mind when you're making your enquires.'

'I will, thanks, Claude.'

'One good turn deserves another, even if it means helping the constabulary,' grumbled Greengrass as he turned away towards the village.

'You are being public-spirited today!' smiled Nick.

'And,' Claude added, 'I'm out and about at night myself. I'll keep an eye on the spot! I might just drop across somebody prowling about.'

'I think you might know who's behind all this, Claude.'

But Claude Jeremiah Greengrass just chuckled and went on his way.

Nick found Jane in her greenhouse where she was listening to some pop music on her transistor radio. At his arrival, she turned off the set.

'You're a fan of The Who, are you?' he smiled.

'And Herman's Hermits, and my plants like the music, too.' She smiled wickedly. 'It makes them grow better! You did get here quickly. I was only just talking to your wife.'

'We met down the lane,' he said. 'Can you tell me about all these bits of bother you've been having?'

And so, for the second time that day, Jane Thompson explained the occurrences, detailing them with a clarity that suggested to Nick that they were not part of her imagination; he was convinced these things had actually happened. He listened carefully, making notes where necessary.

'Mrs Thompson,' he said eventually, 'you appreciate that your house stands on some very attractive land? Local landowners would pay handsomely for it.'

'Yes, I know, but Charlie would never part with it, he said it was mine for life and I must never leave it. And I have no intention of leaving. Jennifer and Eric keep asking me to live with them, but I don't want to. This is my home, Mr Rowan, and nobody is going to force me to leave.'

'So you've no idea who's causing these nuisances?'

'No, and neither has Charlie.'

'Charlie?'

'Charlie, my husband. He keeps me informed.'

'But I thought he had died?' said Nick.

'Yes, he did, a year or so ago,' she said quite calmly.

'Look,' he said, trying to dismiss the last remarks, 'I'll have words with the telephone exchange and they'll monitor your incoming calls until we tell them to stop. We can soon find out who's behind all this. And if you hear prowlers outside again, ring me straight away, or ring Ashfordly Police if I'm not in; they'll send somebody out to check the area.'

'Yes, all right, Mr Rowan. And thank you for your attention.'

'I mean it, Jane, you must call me.'

'Yes, of course I will. Now I'd better be off. Jennifer

will have my lunch ready. I mustn't be late, must I?'

'I'd give you a lift, but I walked here,' said Nick.

'Then you can escort me to my daughter's,' she beamed. 'That'll be something to talk about at the old folks' fitness club!' And she chuckled away to herself at the thought.

That night, Nick and Kate had their supper in front of the blazing fire while watching television. It was a cosy evening and they had been discussing Jane Thompson.

'I'm not sure about her mental condition, Kate,' Nick said. 'I mean, she talks about Charlie as if he's still alive, but she knows he's dead. She told me Charlie had no idea who was plaguing her with telephone calls.'

'She's not batty, Nick, I know she's not.'

'But she did have a breakdown, didn't she? After Charlie died?'

'Yes, that's often a way of purging grief.'

'So she's not entirely sane?'

'She's as sane as you and me, Nick Rowan!'

He laughed, then changed tack. 'Claude told me that Walker's been interested in that cottage for years; he made several attempts to buy it when Charlie was alive. I wonder if he's trying to force her out? I mean, she is getting on, and she's been invited to live with Jennifer and Eric, so if Walker could persuade her to do that, he could offer to buy the cottage, thereby expanding his empire. If he's ruthless enough to block a right of way, then he's certainly capable of using dirty tricks to buy a property he's set his heart on.'

'I've never thought of Raymond Walker as being that type of person,' said Kate.

'He's a hard-headed businessman, Kate and he strikes me as being the sort of guy who always gets what he wants, whatever the cost to others. He'll be blocking that footpath in the hope that people will stop using it and then forget about it – though he hasn't bargained for Claude! I don't think he'd think twice about terrifying Jane to get her out of her house.'

'Thanks for calling in to talk to her,' Kate said. 'It must be awful for her, all this harassment.'

'I'm having her telephone monitored,' he said. 'I made the arrangements this afternoon and I've told Jennifer. So if chummy tries his tricks tonight, we'll nail him.'

'Does that mean sitting up until midnight to see if we get a call for help?'

'I'm afraid so, but it's very cosy in front of this fire.' He reached out and put his arm around her shoulder.

'Mmm,' she murmured. 'Let's hope there are no calls tonight.'

But there were.

Just after a quarter to midnight, Nick's telephone began to shrill.

'I think this will be for me,' he said.

337

CHAPTER EIGHTEEN

It was Claude Jeremiah Greengrass on the telephone.

'Get yourself up to Jane Thompson's quickly,' said the familiar voice. 'Somebody's smashed her greenhouse to smithereens.'

'Claude, when?'

'Now, just now. Get yourself up there, Mr Rowan!'

And the telephone went dead. Nick told Kate what had happened and said he would go in the car; Kate offered to accompany him because Jane might need help. When they arrived, they found Claude and Jane, with Alfred lurking in the background, examining the shattered remains of her greenhouse. The light from their torches told a sorry story. Glass lay everywhere; every pane had been broken, while inside, many of her trays and pots of plants had been overturned and kicked all over the floor. It was a cruel scene of utter devastation.

'Took your time getting here, didn't you?' Claude shouted angrily as Nick approached.

'Calm down, Claude.' Nick spoke quietly. 'Jane, what happened? Did you see anybody? Hear anything?'

'I was reading, Mr Rowan, I'd locked up and was having a quiet read in bed when I heard a crashing outside, then there was the glass breaking, lots of it. I knew it must be the greenhouse, it just went on and on . . .'

'You should have telephoned me straight away!' Nick said.

'I tried, but the telephone's been cut off.' She was weeping silently now. 'I couldn't get help, I had to let them do it. I was too frightened to go out and stop them.'

'Kate, see to her,' said Nick as he went around the side of the house to examine the incoming telephone wires. Sure enough, the entry cable had been severed with one clean cut. Claude had come up behind him and was staring at the cable.

'There's no prizes for guessing who did that, Mr Rowan,' said Greengrass.

'What were you doing here?'

'Minding my own business,' said Claude. 'Doing a bit of walking by the light of the stars in them woods over there, contemplating on how peaceful it is in Aidensfield. Then I heard the crashing of all that glass and I guessed what was going on. I ran over here as fast as I could – fleet of foot I am when I get steam up – and found this. Her phone wasn't working, so I ran down the lane, I used Owen Brown's phone at Heather Cottage.'

'Did you see anyone, Claude? You must have been pretty close to the villains.'

'That's what puzzles me, Mr Rowan. I mean, you'd think I'd have heard somebody running away or even seen

'em on one or other of these paths. But I never saw a soul.
Maybe he heard me coming, eh? And got himself hidden
somewhere pretty quick. I'm not exactly a little chap.'

'You barging through those trees and bushes would be a
bit like a bull elephant lumbering after its mate, Claude.'

'Aye, well, I might have frightened him off, whoever it
was. But I got here first, eh?'

'You did, and maybe you stopped him from doing
something worse, so thanks, Claude.'

'Aye, well, us law enforcement officers have to stand
together, Mr Rowan. See you in court, eh?'

'Court?'

'As chief witness in my blocked footpath case, remember! I've arranged to see my solicitor tomorrow, to
start my action against Walker. I'd best be off now. Come
on, Alfred, this is no place for you. You might get glass in
your paws.' He lumbered away, followed by Alfred.

Nick went inside the house, where Kate had taken Jane
and was making a cup of warm, sweet tea – always a good
means of combating the initial effects of shock.

'Jane,' Kate was saying, 'you can't stay here now.'

'They're not going to drive me out, Dr Rowan, they're
not!'

'Do you think it is Raymond Walker?' Nick had to ask
the question. 'He could be very interested in acquiring this
cottage and land.'

'I just don't know' Jane spoke through her tears. 'I can't
think of anyone who would be so horrible to me. My
greenhouse, years of work gone. Mr Walker would surely
never do that. Charlie built that for me, you know, by

himself. So I'd have something to do, some interest in my old age . . .'

'I'm going see Walker now,' said Nick.

'Now?' cried Kate. 'But it's midnight!'

'Strike while the iron's hot,' said Nick. 'Look, you stay here with Jane and I'll collect you on the way back. Jane, do you think we should ask Jennifer to take you in for tonight?'

'No,' she said with determination. 'They're trying to get me to go and live with them, and I don't want to. I want to keep my independence.'

'But after what happened tonight, it could get worse . . . Whoever is trying to get you out of this cottage might do something worse next time . . .'

'Oh, Doctor, I don't know what to do,' and the old lady dissolved into tears as Kate put an arm around her to offer a little comfort.

'Give me half an hour,' said Nick.

In spite of the late hour, the lights were still blazing at Walker's farmhouse when Nick drove on to the forecourt. He rang the bell and Walker came to the door within seconds, clad in smart evening dress and a bow tie. Quickly, Nick examined his shoes and trouser bottoms – they were clean, with no sign of mud.

'Constable Rowan? To what do I owe the pleasure at this time of night?'

'You've been out?' asked Nick, who was not invited in.

'I have. My wife and I, and some guests who are staying with us, have been to the annual dinner of the National Farmers' Union at Ashfordly. We've only just returned and we are having a nightcap before retiring. Why this late visit? Greengrass been shot at again, has he?'

'No, there has just been a case of malicious damage,' and Nick explained what had occurred at Jane's cottage, including an account of the cut telephone wires and the past incidents. 'I was wondering if you'd heard or seen anything, especially as you were just on your way home.'

'No, never saw a thing, never saw anyone on the road back there.'

'Am I right in thinking you have made an offer to buy her cottage?' Nick pressed home his questions.

'I have, and that's no secret. When Charlie was alive I made him a good offer but he rejected it, and when he died, I had words with the Bradshaws, but they refused and that was that. The cottage is in my way, I'll admit that. I could expand my land and even think of utilising some of it as a building site if I could get my hands on Jane's house.'

'Worth getting her out, is it?' said Nick.

'Constable Rowan, I think you are going too far!' snapped Walker. 'Are you suggesting I am stooping to harassment to get an old lady out of her home?'

'I am not suggesting anything, Mr Walker. I am just trying to establish what's going on and why someone is apparently doing everything possible to persuade Jane to leave.'

'You've got a bloody nerve, coming here at this time of night and making such insinuations! I have not done anything intended to drive her out!' And he slammed the door in Nick's face.

When Nick returned to the cottage, Kate was still with Jane, who had calmed down and was sitting beside her dying fire.

'No luck?' said Kate.

'I don't think it was Raymond Walker. He's been out all night and besides, he still had his shoes on, and they were clean. They'd have been muddy if he'd come here. Are you going to spend the night at Jennifer's?' Nick asked Jane.

'No, I am not! They want me to go there and I want to stay here . . .' the old lady insisted. 'And stay here I will!'

So Kate and Nick had to leave Jane in her remote and vulnerable cottage. As they drove home, Nick said, 'I'll pop up there regularly.'

'And so will I,' smiled Kate. 'She can become our joint social conscience!'

Next morning, Nick received another irate phone call from Sergeant Blaketon, who, ignoring his protests, instructed him to attend his office at ten fifteen on the dot.

As Nick rode through Ashfordly, he spotted a most unlikely sight walking along the street – Claude Jeremiah Greengrass dressed in a smart suit. His hair had been cut, he had had a shave and he was carrying a briefcase. The surprise was so great that Nick braked and eased his bike to a halt to continue his observations. Claude strode on, nodding his good mornings to passers-by, and then turned towards an office block. He mounted a flight of steps and entered through a large, ornate doorway. Nick chugged forward and saw that it was a solicitor's office. So Claude had meant every word about his threat to sue Raymond Walker!

Nick then drove around to the police station and parked in the yard before entering the lion's den of Sergeant Blaketon's office. The signs from Alf Ventress suggested that Blaketon's mood was far from cheerful.

'Rowan? Is that you?' came the call.

'Yes, Sergeant.'

'In here, Rowan, now!'

Yet again, Nick found himself sitting, while an angry Sergeant Oscar Blaketon marched up and down his office with his hands behind his back.

'This has gone far enough, Rowan,' he was saying. 'This is almost victimisation, harassment by the police, and I am not having it in my section. It is criminal, Rowan!'

'What is, Sergeant?'

'This continuing persecution of an upstanding member of the community, Raymond Walker no less. He has made another complaint, Rowan; he says you called at his house at midnight last night and got him out of bed to accuse him of harassing an old lady out of her home. He says you claimed he had vandalised her greenhouse, cut off her telephone and performed other acts calculated to cause her to abandon her house.'

'He was not in bed, Sergeant, when I called,' and Nick went on to explain his version of last night's events, stressing that at no time had he accused Walker of any unlawful acts. He had merely been making enquiries to ascertain whether Walker had seen or heard anything suspicious.

'Look, Rowan, Raymond Walker is not the sort of person who would attempt to frighten an old lady out of her home purely for his own financial gain. Now listen. Go home, get out a map of your beat and put a big ring around Raymond Walker's farm – and then consider it a no-go area!'

'Greengrass is going to make it very much an all-go area, Sergeant.'

'Greengrass? What's he got to do with all this?'

Nick explained the legal action that Claude was intending, adding that he had just seen the very fellow, in a smart suit, visiting a local solicitor.

'I don't believe this, Rowan! His sudden wealth has affected his sanity! You mean to tell me that Greengrass is volunteering to go to court?'

'Yes, Sergeant, and he's calling me as a witness!'

'This I cannot believe. Things are going from bad to worse. Aidensfield has never been the same since you arrived, Rowan, and now, with you and Greengrass working together, I don't know where the police service is heading, I really don't'

'We're working together to stop villainy, Sergeant. Is that all?'

'Yes, Rowan, that is all,' sighed a heavy-hearted Sergeant Blaketon.

That same morning, Jane Thompson stood and surveyed the wreckage of her greenhouse. She had not slept at all during that awful night and now, in the cold light of this new morning, all her hopes and aspirations had gone. Her life lay before her in a jumble of broken glass and ruined plants, precious plants that she had nurtured from seed. With them gone, there was no hope left. They had won, whoever they were; they had forced her out of her home and she could fight them no longer.

'You always said I should never leave, Charlie,' she whispered, 'it would be like pulling up my own roots, you said. You were right; look at these roots, scattered around and dying. Like me. I shall die soon, like my plants. But not here. I wanted to die here, Charlie, and have you near me when I drew my last breath. That was my hope. I never thought it would come to this. Forgive me, Charlie, but I can't stay here. Not now.'

And she went inside to begin packing.

It was several days later when Kate decided to pay another visit to Jane; she'd not come to the fitness class on Wednesday and no one had seen her around the village. She'd not been for her shopping either. Worried that some harm might have come to the old lady, Kate drove to her picturesque home and was startled to see a builder's lorry parked near the entrance and some men busy within the grounds.

Raymond Walker was there, apparently giving orders to the builders. Kate strode in; the house looked deserted. There were no curtains at the windows, and none of the sills bore the pots of plants which had been so much a part of Jane's life and happiness.

'Mr Walker, hello. I'm looking for Jane Thompson.'

'She's gone, Dr Rowan. She's left here, and taken all her things.'

'Gone? But where?' Kate demanded.

He spread his hands in a gesture which said he didn't care. 'I've no idea, have you asked at her daughter's?'

'No, I'll try there next. She's not been in the village today, I was worried.'

'I've not heard she's died, if that's what you mean, Doctor, but she has got a new home somewhere. This is my place now, I've bought it.'

'Really?' Kate said, and after a quick look at the devastation still apparent in the garden, she left. She went straight down to Jennifer's house, only a short distance away, and knocked. Jennifer's husband, Eric, answered the door.

'Is Jane here?' Kate asked him. 'I've just been to see her at the cottage, but I understand she's left.'

'Yes, she didn't want to stay there any longer.' He kept her at the door. 'Me and Jennifer tried to get her to come and stay here, with us, but you know how stubborn she is. She refused point-blank.'

'So where is she now? I need to know, Mr Bradshaw, she is a patient of mine.'

'She's in an old folks' home. High Lawns in Ashfordly. It's very nice, she's got her own room and we'll help to pay for her keep. She seems to have settled in. Jennifer's over there now, in fact, she had some shopping to do in Ashfordly and said she'd pop in to see her mum.'

'I'm surprised, to be honest, Mr Bradshaw. She was always so determined to stay in her home.'

'Maybe you didn't see her like we did, Dr Rowan. But it's all for the best. She refused outright to come and live with us and she really was getting beyond the stage of looking after herself. And you know she always talked to old Charlie, she believed he was looking after her, just like he did in life.'

'You'll tell Jennifer I called?' Kate said, turning to leave.

'Sure,' said Eric Bradshaw, closing the door.

Kate decided to drive immediately to Ashfordly to visit Jane. There was something in the tone of Eric Bradshaw's voice and in the manner of his dealings with Kate which she found unacceptable. She could not say what her uncertainties were, for, on the face of things, the arrangement did seem entirely reasonable and practical. Kate knew how Jane had loved her home, and Aidensfield and the people in it, and yet, throughout her trials, she had stubbornly refused the hospitality of her own daughter and son-in-law. In Kate's view, that seemed odd.

High Lawns occupied a beautiful position on the western edge of Ashfordly. The former home of a shipping magnate, it had once been a hotel and was now a very pleasant home for old people. Privately run, it was clean and modern, and it enjoyed a superb aspect across the North York Moors.

Kate was shown to Jane's room where the old lady, her sparkle gone and her face pale and drawn, was sitting in a wicker chair on a balcony. The open window looked out over the grounds and there was a beautiful bunch of flowers in a vase on her dressing table. But Jane was far from happy.

'I didn't expect to find you here,' Kate said.

'I never expected to be here,' she said quietly. 'It's good of you to call, Doctor, I do miss Aidensfield and those classes. And my plants.'

'I see you've been given a lovely bunch of flowers,' Kate indicated her dressing table.

'Mr Greengrass brought them,' she said.

'Claude? Good heavens!'

'He's a lot better than some,' said Jane. 'He was really good to me the night my greenhouse was wrecked.'

'Was it that that really forced you to leave?' Kate asked, recognising an opening for her to air her own concerns.

Jane did not respond but the expression in her eyes was enough for Kate.

'I'll call again, may I? Just to keep an eye on you?'

'It's a free country,' said Jane. 'I can't get to see you or my friends at the classes. I've no car, no transport from here.'

'I'm sure you'll get lots of visitors,' said Kate, deciding it was time to leave. Jane clearly did not want to talk about the reasons for her departure from her beloved home.

The following day, Kate received a telephone call from the old folks' home. Jane Thompson had walked out that morning in pouring rain without even an overcoat, and the only thing she had taken was the bunch of flowers from her dressing table. She'd not been seen for about an hour and a half, so she could have been absent all that time.

'I'll tell the police to look out for her. Maybe she's heading back home,' Kate said. 'You'll ring us if she returns?'

And so a search began for the missing woman. Kate informed Nick, who alerted Ashfordly Police with a description of Jane and then drove immediately to Jennifer and Eric's house. Jane was not there. Jennifer had not seen her mother since yesterday, when she had seemed quite settled in the old folks' home, but said she would ring round Jane's friends in Aidensfield to see if she'd caught a bus back to the village.

Nick then went to the churchyard; he wondered if she had returned to her husband's grave in her moments of anguish. He had no idea where Charlie was buried and so had to tour the entire graveyard in his search.

When he found it, Jane was not there, but there was a large and beautiful bunch of fresh flowers lying by the headstone. Nick stooped to read the card: it said, 'From Claude Jeremiah Greengrass.'

As he puzzled over why Claude would put flowers on Charlie's grave, one of the church cleaning ladies appeared at the door carrying a mop which she shook in the fresh air.

'Mrs Thompson was here not long ago,' she said, seeing his interest in the grave and the flowers. 'She put those flowers on the grave.'

'Which way did she go?' Nick asked. 'We're worried about her.'

'Back up to her house,' said the lady. 'She looked a bit

bedraggled, if you ask me. Certainly not fit to be out on a day like this with no topcoat.'

'Thanks,' said Nick, realising that her old cottage was the obvious place to begin such a search. He arrived within a few minutes and was greeted by Raymond Walker, who looked furious.

'This time,' he snarled at Nick, 'you might prove to be useful. The silly old bat's come back into the house and is staging a sit-in! We want to start demolishing it and we can't while she's there. So can you get her out?'

'But it's her house, isn't it?' said Nick.

'No, it's mine. I bought it off her son-in-law, Eric Bradshaw. It belonged to him, Mr Rowan, and I've bought it, quite legitimately I might add, without harassing the old lady and without smashing down greenhouses or cutting telephone lines. Look, I just want her out, she's trespassing. I'm asking you to arrest her and take her away.'

'Trespass isn't a criminal offence, Mr Walker, and I can't arrest anyone for it. It's a civil matter, as I'm sure you know, being chairman of the NFU.'

'Well, look, she's holding up my work, I've got expensive machinery standing idle while she's sitting in there. Can you have words with her?'

'Sure,' smiled Nick. 'I'll have words with her. I want to find out what's behind all this.'

Nick entered the now empty hall. The floorboards were bare, there was no furniture and all the plants had gone. The place was covered in the dust of some preliminary demolition to an outbuilding. As he walked further inside, he saw Jane sitting on the stairs. Oblivious to anyone else, she was talking to Charlie.

'You were right, Charlie. You saw through him. She didn't, though. That's the trouble with our Jennifer, too trusting. I'm pleased you liked the flowers, it was kind of Mr Greengrass to bring them . . . I said Jennifer had made a mistake marrying that Bradshaw but would she listen? She would not . . .'

'Jane?' Nick spoke softly as he moved closer to her.

She looked up and smiled. 'I'll come quietly, Mr Rowan, I just wanted a last look at the old spot before they knock it down.'

'I wanted a chat with you first,' said Nick, sitting on the step at her side. 'I was surprised you sold it, I thought you'd never do that.'

'It wasn't mine, not really,' she said softly.

'How do you mean? I thought it belonged to you and Charlie?'

'It did, it took Charlie a lifetime's work to buy it, but after he died, well, I got a bit low and I think I went a bit funny in the head, and when Eric suggested I should sign it over to him and Jennifer, I did.'

'You mean it's theirs?'

'They said I could stay here as long as I wanted, they'd never ask me to leave, they said, not ever. But then that man Walker began to make new offers. He'd asked Charlie to sell the house years ago and Charlie said no. Anyway, when Charlie died he started again with more offers, first to me, but when I said it wasn't mine, he went to see Eric a few times with bigger offers. You see, I began to realise that Eric wanted me to go and live with him and Jennifer so he could sell the house to Walker.'

'So Eric's been trying to force you to leave?'

'Yes, that's what Charlie just told me, when I went to put the flowers on his grave.'

Realisation dawned on Nick. 'Jennifer must have told him I was having your telephone calls monitored, so he cut the wires . . . and when he came back from the pub at night, he had time to come here and do his dirty work without anyone suspecting him. Once he got you to leave, he could sell the place and pocket a nice sum of money – your money!'

'I know, I can't see what our Jennifer sees in him, Mr Rowan, but it's too late now.'

'It might not be too late,' said Nick quietly. 'Look, when you signed the house over to him and Jennifer, you were not fully fit, were you?'

'No, I was getting treatment for my depression or whatever they called it. Mental stress or something.'

'And you asked for the house to be signed back over to you when you were fit again?'

'Well, I did have a word with Eric, but he said it wasn't worth the trouble. The house would come to him and Jennifer one day anyway, he said, so why bother to have it signed back to me? He said I could live there as long as I wanted. Well, it seemed sensible then, but now they've got me out they're selling it over my head. I don't want to live with them, so I booked myself into the old folks' home.'

'Jane, how awful.'

'I've nothing left, Mr Rowan, nowhere to live that I can call my own except a tiny room among a lot of poor old folks that I can't communicate with. And no plants to keep . . .'

'It's not too late,' Nick told her. 'I've come across double-dealings like this before.'

'You have?'

'Yes, and if you were not mentally fit when you first signed the cottage over, then that signing-over has no validity before the law. I know the records in Kate's surgery would support any sickness claim from you. In other words, I believe the house is still yours. You could take court action if necessary to recover it.'

'Court action? Oh, I couldn't, not to our Jennifer.'

'But it's not her that's the trouble, is it? It's that son-in-law of yours, he's behind all this, and he's sold it to Walker. But the deal has no basis in law, I'm sure. Quite simply, the house isn't Eric's to sell!'

'Oh, Mr Rowan, if only you are right!'

'Let's go out now and have words with Mr Walker, shall we? You come with me.'

Jane Thompson followed Nick outside, but remained in the background as Walker came over to the policeman. He was smiling, a smile of triumph.

'Well done, Constable. I see you've done the trick, persuaded her to leave.'

'No I haven't,' said Nick. 'I'm about to persuade you to leave, Mr Walker. You're trespassing. This property belongs to Jane Thompson, not to Eric Bradshaw.'

'But I've seen the deed – it was passed to Eric Bradshaw,

it's his property, Mrs Thompson had transferred it to him. The sale's going ahead, I'm buying the premises and in the meantime I've got written permission to enter and begin demolition.'

'Well, the Contract appears to be defective, Mr Walker, unlawful even, so if you want my advice you'll get yourself off this land before we sue you for damage to the house. If you persist in staying here, I shall consider a fraud investigation against Eric Bradshaw; just think of the publicity that would create if you were seen to be dealing with a convicted con man. Not a very good image for the chairman of the local NFU, eh? And I'll ensure that Jane gets the very best of legal advice. Think of it this way; I have saved you a lot of money today. I hope you'll bear that in mind when you and I have future dealings.'

'Future dealings? Like what?'

'Blocking up a public footpath for starters,' said Nick pointedly.

Walker looked at Jane, who never flinched before his gaze, then shouted to his workmen, 'Back off, lads. Take the gear away. There's been a mistake. And get down to that wood and shift that fence you put up. It's blocking a footpath.'

'Thanks, Mr Walker,' smiled Nick.

'Wait till I get my hands on that Bradshaw!' snarled Walker. 'I'll sue him for everything it's cost me – and more!'

As the workmen were packing their gear and removing their equipment, Nick went over to Jane. 'We'll have to get you fixed up with some furniture, won't we?'

'I'll go back to the old folks' home for tonight; that'll give Jennifer time to recover my old furniture. She took it to the salerooms in Ashfordly. I hope it's still there.'

Nick's next job was to inform Jennifer of what had happened. She wept when she realised the deception and cruelty that her husband had practised.

'I suspected him myself, Mr Rowan, especially when Mum's phone was cut off. The poor soul . . . she trusted me, and look what we've done for her . . . how could we?'

'She still trusts *you*,' Nick said.

'I can't live with Eric now, not after what he's done. And all for money . . . The house would have come to us anyway, in the normal course of time! Why couldn't he wait?'

'Greed, I suspect. So what will you do?'

'I don't know. I'll move out, this is only a rented house anyway, it goes with Eric's job. But I've no idea where I shall go.'

'You could always go and live with your mum at her cottage,' smiled Nick. 'She does need some furniture, and some comfort.'

'If I do, I wonder if she'll stop talking to Dad?' smiled Jennifer through her tears.

'There's only one way to find out,' said Nick. 'But look after her, make sure she's got a greenhouse, and from time to time fetch her down to Kate's classes.'

'I will,' said Jennifer.

CHAPTER NINETEEN

'Nick,' said Kate over breakfast one morning, 'we'll have to start looking for somewhere suitable for a surgery. With Alex soon to retire, we'll not be able to continue using his house, you know.'

Nick shifted in his chair. 'Funny you should mention that. It's been on my mind too. I thought I'd found a place that might suit you but it's just been sold as tearooms. It was along the village, on the corner opposite the war memorial. I've been keeping my ears and eyes open while I've been out and about, hoping I might come across something. Does it have to be in Aidensfield?'

'Well, yes, if possible. This is where Alex has practised all these years and it is very central for the surrounding villages, where most of my patients are. It's accessible by bus and train, and ideal in lots of ways.'

'OK. But there's no rush, is there? There's plenty of time before Alex packs his bags, isn't there?'

Kate tried not to sound impatient. 'Time passes so quickly, Nick, the months fly past without us realising and I do need somewhere of my own once he leaves us. He's given us plenty of warning. Once he's retired, he'll sell his house and that means I'll lose the surgery. I don't mind renting somewhere to begin with, but I'd like to buy my own place eventually.'

Nick raised his eyebrows in surprise. 'Can we afford to buy somewhere?'

'Maybe not now, but I hope so, in time.'

'Is this urgent, Kate? I'm sure Alex wouldn't kick you out of the present surgery!'

'That's not the point, Nick. Once he's retired and sold the house, I'll have no choice. I can't expect the new owners to let me keep a surgery there. No one's going to want all that equipment and drugs in their house, are they?'

'All right. Point taken. I'm off out on patrol in about an hour and there's some office work I want to catch up with first, but then I'll definitely have a look around,' Nick promised, standing up from the table.

'Thank you, and I'm searching as well, you know. I have my own contacts, but two heads are better than one!' Kate reminded him.

'I suppose we could always build one. You know, a custom-built place with a proper waiting room, consulting rooms, modern equipment, a secure drugs store and so on.'

'That takes time, Nick, and we don't have all that much time. It could take months to find land, get planning permission and erect a new building. We need to find somewhere very quickly, somewhere that's already built but that we can easily adapt.'

'OK. As I said, I'll keep my eyes and ears open. What's Alex doing now? I haven't seen him lately?'

'He's winding down. He's looking after some of his long-term patients, uncomplicated cases who've been with him for years and who are happy with repeat prescriptions. I'm taking on more work, some of it from him, and from now on, I'm also taking on all the new patients.'

'I thought he was going on a fishing trip? Didn't he say something about being offered a cottage at Kelby?'

'Yes, he's going later today. The cottage sounds lovely It's beside the River Esk, not far from Kelby's stepping stones. Remember, we went there for a picnic once? It's a beautiful river, and is renowned for its trout and salmon. I know he's been looking forward to it.'

'What's his state of health now?'

'Poor enough to keep me worrying about him,' she said. 'He's certainly not himself, Nick, he does keep having those spells of dizziness and forgetfulness. He needs to retire, but fortunately he knows it.'

'Good, well if I don't see him before he goes on his fishing holiday, wish him all the best from me. I hope the weather's good to him and tell him I'm looking forward to a nice supper of fresh trout or salmon when he gets back!'

And Nick went into his office before setting out upon a motorcycle patrol of Aidensfield and district.

After morning surgery, Alex came to see Kate.

'Well,' he said, looking smart in his plus fours and tweed jacket. 'That's it. My last surgery for a week. You can cope with my rounds today, can you?'

'Yes, of course, Alex. You take your time getting ready!'

'I've made a list of the patients I was due to see this week, with their treatments and my recommendations. Now, old Mrs Sanderson at Briar House, she needs . . .'

'Alex, it's all in the records. I can cope, honestly!'

'Yes, of course you can. Silly of me . . . I keep thinking you're as forgetful as me! But you're not. Now, I'd better leave my address, just in case.'

He wrote on a piece of paper the words, 'Mallard Cottage, Kelby', and a telephone number.

'I'll try not to disturb you when you're on holiday, Alex, but it's nice to know you're on hand if I need advice. You're not far away, anyway, so I could always drive over to see you!'

'I'm having my meals in the Horseshoe Inn,' he said. 'I'll have breakfast in the cottage, lunch will be a pint and a sandwich in the pub if I can drag myself away from the riverbank, and my dinner each evening will be in the restaurant of the pub – after a nice warm bath to relax in, there'll be wine and good food to complete every day. I consider that real bliss, a real touch of heaven!'

'It sounds like it! I'm envious,' smiled Kate. 'So what time are you leaving?'

'Well, actually,' and he looked rather coy, 'I can go now. A lady patient of mine, along the road between here and Kelby, has offered me lunch and so, well, I thought I might as well accept and then keep going.'

'Do I detect a hint of romance?' smiled Kate.

'Oh, good heavens no!' He shook his head. 'My good-
ness, she's older than me.'

'A spot of good old-fashioned romance would do you a
world of good, Alex,' Kate laughed. 'And age is no
barrier! But, yes, you go. You are all packed?'

'Yes, last night. I've just a few bits and pieces to tidy up,
then I can put my suitcase in the car, along with my tackle
and waders, and I'm ready for the off!'

'Well, an early start will be nice. So it's goodbye, then?'

'Yes, for a few days. Goodbye, Kate, and thanks for
being so understanding during these recent weeks. I must
have been a bit of a trial, falling over my own feet, mixing
up my appointments and coming down to surgery in my
pyjamas and so on!'

'Think nothing of it.' She went over to him and gave
him a fierce hug. 'Just you concentrate on making some
fine catches and we'll see you in a week's time.'

'Yes, and then you'll soon be on your own, eh? Doctor
in charge, the General Practitioner of Aidensfield practice . . . you, not me, Kate. I'm proud to hand it all over
to you!'

'We'll talk about that when you get back,' she said.
'Now, it's time to concentrate on your romantic invitation
to lunch, and then there's a relaxed week of fishing to set
you on the road to blissful retirement!'

He kissed her on the cheek and she responded with
another hug. 'Nick sends his best wishes for a successful
holiday,' she called after him as he left, but he merely
waved in acknowledgement.

Less than an hour later, she watched his beautiful old

car leave Aidensfield with the contented doctor at the wheel. Now it was time for her to go out and see some patients.

Mallard Cottage, which was owned by the landlord of the Horseshoe Inn, was ideal for Alex Ferrenby. It was regularly let to fisherman, being handy for both the river and the inn, while the village shop was a mere hundred yards away. All Alex's holiday needs were here. He reserved a table in the restaurant of the inn for each evening at 7.30 p.m. and told Andrew Bridgeton, the landlord, that he'd pop in for a bar snack every lunchtime.

Each day fell into a routine. Alex would rise and listen to the radio while he had his breakfast, then would potter down to the riverbank for two or three hours' fishing. He liked a break for lunch even if it meant dragging himself away from the riverside, although he did leave his tackle on the bank with the rod primed. One never knew, one might just catch something even in one's absence!

Then followed a further session from the end of lunch until around six in the evening; he had a flask of coffee and bought cakes and biscuits at the shop for snacks during the day. The evening meals at the Horseshoe were excellent and, fortified by a glass or two of wine and one of brandy, Alex would sleep soundly until next morning. It was a happy routine, rich with contentment.

On the Wednesday afternoon of his holiday, he decided to wade into the river so that he could fish a deep pool where the Esk curved in a wide bend. Here the cold water from the distant moors flowed at a much slower rate, whirling ever so gently like a whirlpool in slow motion. Over the years, it had sculpted the earth from the far bank to create this wide open corner where the swift waters appeared to gather for a rest before continuing their run to the North Sea. Where the water had eaten into the sandy earth of the far bank, there flourished lots of overhanging bushes and alder trees. These cast deep shadows over the languid water, and Alex knew that the deep pool below them was a haven for trout. There the fresh, pure water was smooth and dark. The wide bend bore the relics of past floods too – there were tree trunks and branches which had been carried from higher up the dale to lodge against the side of that bank and, here and there, he noticed patches of wool, all that remained of sheep which had died in the higher reaches. On his side of the river, opposite the pool, the water was much shallower; through its green depths he could see the stony bed of the river with water weeds and moss quivering in the strong flow. This was an ideal place for trout.

Alex Ferrenby pulled on his long waders, a single garment comprising thigh-length rubber boots with heavy studded soles topped with waterproof trousers which came up to above the waist. He equipped himself with his rod, net, bag, gaff and bait, and began to wade across the bed of the river. He could feel the water pressing against his legs while the pebbles below his feet moved and rolled with the power of the current. Once or twice, he slipped a little, but the water was only knee-deep at this point. There were some shallower parts, he noted, where moss-covered rocks protruded. He aimed to stand in this

365

shallow part and cast across into the pool, placing his bait beneath the overhanging trees. It was a worthwhile exercise, he told himself, for if there were any fine trout in this part of the river today, that was where they would be.

For the best part of an hour, Dr Ferrenby stood and waited, with never a trout to celebrate. The fish were not biting . . . perhaps he should change his bait? Should he try fly fishing?

He moved his pitch slightly, seeking signs of fish jumping to take insects which hovered over the surface. Then something caught his eye. To his left, a few yards upstream, he noticed a sack caught on the branches of an old tree which had been swept away by floods higher upriver. The remains of the tree had come to rest against the far bank and the sack had floated downstream to come to rest against it. Alex wondered if he was seeing things, for the sack seemed to be moving. After all, he'd not been well recently. This, however, looked real enough. Confusion appeared on the doctor's face and the rod in his hand dropped lower until the tip was touching the water, while he stared for a long time at the sack. And now he was sure it was making a noise . . . there was something in it! It wasn't his imagination! Alex moved slightly; he felt dizzy for a moment, but it passed. Whatever was in that sack was crying for help . . . it sounded like a kitten!

Alex decided to wade across to investigate. After all, the water was shallower at that point; it was some distance upstream from the deep pool. He began to cross the river, treading warily on the loose rocks which lay unseen upon the river bed. As he approached the sack, he called out and the noise stopped. He called again, shouting, 'Puss, puss!' This time, the creature responded. Alex reached out with his rod, hoping to touch the sack with the tip, but he could not reach. The sack moved wildly and wobbled in its precarious resting place against the log. Alex knew he must release whatever was in it. He moved faster now, his determination overcoming his sense of caution as the water grew deeper around his waders, now reaching waist-level but not yet above the top of his waders. And then he slipped.

He stepped on a loose rock somewhere in the depths and lost his footing, then his balance; the relentless flow of water pushed him over as he cried out in alarm. In seconds, he was floundering in the river, the water running into his waders to weigh him down. He fought for his life, dropping his rod and net and struggling to keep his head above the surface, but his feet were treading on nothing; there was no river bed here, only a deep hole in the river bed. He slithered down the slippery slope, the water bubbling and gurgling about his head as he fought for air. But the weight of water in his waders, his own unfitness and the pressure of the water defeated his efforts.

Alex Ferrenby sank to his death in that deep, dark and quiet place, a corner long known locally as Dead Man's Pool.

It was just after ten o'clock when the telephone rang. 'Your turn!' Kate said.

'Is it? I thought it was yours?'

'No, it's definitely yours!' she insisted, and so Nick answered the call.

'Aidensfield Police,' he said.

'I'm sorry to bother you,' said the man's voice at the other end of the line, 'but I'm trying to contact a Dr Rowan.'

'Hang on,' said Nick. 'She's here. I'll put her on.'

Nick handed the telephone to Kate. The caller was Andrew Bridgeton, landlord of the Horseshoe Inn at Kelby.

'I'm sorry to bother you, Doctor, but we're worried about Dr Ferrenby. You know he's been in the village on a fishing holiday?'

'Yes, we're in practice together, here at Aidensfield. What's the problem?'

'Well, he hasn't turned up for his dinner, Doctor. We've been to the cottage, but he's not there. He did come in for his lunch, like he's been doing the last few days, but I'm surprised he hasn't come for his dinner. He booked a table in advance for each evening, so I thought I'd better call you. He did leave your number in case of emergency.'

'Have you checked inside the cottage?' she asked.

'Yes, I went round there. It was unlocked, but that's not unusual. All his clothes are there, his suitcase and toilet things, so he hasn't left.'

'What about his fishing tackle? Is that there?'

'No, it's not, nor are his waders.'

'Perhaps he's forgotton what time it is!' smiled Kate. 'You know what fishermen are!'

'Yes, but there's more . . .'

'Has anyone seen him this evening?' Kate interrupted.

'No, that's odd too. He sometimes popped into the shop for an evening paper, usually around half past six. He didn't go there either today, we've asked. And a friend of mine, another fisherman, has just come in from the river, and he says there's some tackle on the bank not far from the stepping stones, with no one in attendance. It might mean nothing, he might be upstream, but, well, it all sounds a bit ominous.'

'Oh God,' said Kate. 'Oh my God . . . yes it does. Look, I'll have a word with my husband, he's a policeman. We'd better come and look for him.'

'Thanks,' said the caller. 'I'll be here if you need me. Kelby 222.'

'I think something terrible's happened to Alex,' said Kate, explaining the call to Nick. 'Suppose he had one of those funny turns while he was fishing, he could have fallen in . . . Oh, Nick, what shall we do?'

'We'll organise a search for him,' said Nick without hesitation. 'I'll ring Blaketon.'

Sergeant Blaketon pointed out that Kelby was not part of Ashfordly Section, but because it was part of the same division, he would allow his officers to take part in the search.

Blaketon rang Sergeant Molloy, his colleague in charge of the section in which Kelby lay, and Molloy said he could produce two constables in addition to himself. Blaketon said he would do likewise, his officers being PC Ventress and PC Rowan. Blaketon also suggested the Underwater Search Unit be directed to the scene. The sergeants agreed to rendezvous at the Horseshoe Inn, Kelby, at 11.15 p.m. to determine their next action. Due to the darkness, powerful searchlights would be required and field telephones would be needed for personal contact along the riverside.

Nick said he would proceed directly to the Horseshoe Inn, and because Kate wished to be present, he would use his private car.

When they arrived, the car park of the Horseshoe Inn, a beautiful riverside hostelry, was already busy. Sergeant Molloy's team had arrived and several of the inn's regulars, who had befriended the amiable doctor, had volunteered to join the search. They knew the river well and could guide the officers along the banks, advising on the more dangerous stretches of water. One man, Stanley Harland, came forward to say he'd found the abandoned tackle and could guide the officers to it. The Underwater Search Unit arrived within half an hour to complete the search party.

Sergeant Molloy took charge, asking Nick to provide a physical description of Dr Ferrenby. And so the search began. Kate was asked to remain at the inn, to be available if medical aid was required. Molloy's officers would proceed upstream from the stepping stones, one on either side of the river, while Blaketon's men would proceed downstream, one on either bank. Each constable would be accompanied by a local man with knowledge of the river and its footpaths. Ventress found himself having to walk the bank on the left facing downstream while Nick was to search the other. Molloy joined the search upstream while Blaketon went in the opposite direction, and the two Underwater Search Unit frogmen stood by to search the water if that became necessary.

Nick was shown the tackle which remained on the riverside and identified it as belonging to Dr Ferrenby. Among it was a whisky flask bearing his name and the date he had qualified as a doctor; it had been given to him by his parents in 1931. There was also a sandwich box containing some uneaten cakes and biscuits, and a full flask of coffee. Nick informed the rest of the team of this fact; clearly, Ferrenby had been at this point, but his fishing rod, net, gaff and waders were all missing. Nick experienced a sense of doom.

With his companion from the village, Stan Harland, he began to walk downstream along the river bank, noting the shallows in which, by the light of his torch, he could see the rounded pebbles of the river bed.

Then there was a shout.

'Sarge!' It was Alf Ventress. 'Sarge, here, I've found something!'

His voice carried across the water and everyone halted. Blaketon, trudging through the undergrowth nearby, called, 'What is it, Ventress?'

'A sack with something inside. Hold on, it's alive . . .'

By the light of his torch, Alf had noticed the sack wedged among the logs on the riverbank. As he approached, it began to move and the mewing of a kitten sounded from inside. Alf tried to reach the sack but it meant hanging on to the branch of an overhanging tree with one hand while he reached forwards to seize the neck of the bundle. As he lifted it to safety, Blaketon arrived.

'What's in there, Ventress?' he demanded.

'I don't know, Sergeant, until I open it. Now, where's my knife?'

He produced a pocket knife and cut the string around the neck, then popped his hand inside.

'Ow, you little sod!' he cursed, withdrawing a badly scratched hand. The bright eyes of a jet black kitten peered up at him. The creature tried to struggle out, but Ventress quickly closed the sack again.

'What have you got there, Alf?' called Nick from across the river.

'A lucky black cat!' he said. 'It's the lucky one, it's still alive even if it has scratched me . . .'

'Leave it, Ventress,' said Blaketon. 'We've more important things to do.'

Alf laid his trophy on the ground, having first tied a knot in the neck of the sack. He'd collect it on the way back from the search. He'd often fancied a kitten . . .

While all this was going on, Nick was shining his powerful torch across the river towards Ventress, Blaketon and their helpers, highlighting their antics. As the beam swept along the far bank, beneath the overhanging trees, he saw a something bobbing up and down just below the surface in the gentle swell. It looked to begin with like a bundle of clothes; then his torch picked out a patch of white skin.

'Sarge!' he shouted. 'To your left . . . further down . . . under those trees, near the bank. You'll have to lean forward . . .'

Blaketon moved carefully forwards as directed by the light of Nick's torch.

'It's him,' said Sergeant Blaketon. 'God, it really is.'

The body of Dr Ferrenby was suspended in the water where it had been swept a few yards downstream to lodge against a submerged tree branch. It was floating upright with arms outstretched, held in position by the weight of the water in its waders.

'I'll call the frogmen,' said Blaketon with sadness in his voice. 'They'll have to get him out. And we'll need Dr Rowan to examine him.'

The funeral of Alex Ferrenby took place at Aidensfield Parish Church before a packed congregation, followed by burial in the village graveyard.

Hundreds of his former patients arrived and it was impossible for everyone to get into the church; the road outside and the wide grass verge were packed with friends who had travelled miles to say their farewells. Kate was devastated; Ferrenby had been her friend and inspiration even when she was a tiny girl, long before she had left the district to study medicine.

As she knelt in prayer in the church, she realised that an awesome responsibility now awaited her. She was no longer the junior partner in a very successful and long-established rural practice; she was now the only doctor, with all the trials, tribulations and joys that would bring. She thought of all those patients, all those country people who would be depending upon her in the months and years to come. But what a fine start she had been given, thanks to Alex. His family had been most kind to her; they had said they would not put the house on the market for some three or four months in order to give her time to find premises for a new surgery.

Long after everyone else had gone, she stood alone by his grave. 'Thank you, Alex,' she said, 'for your past and for my future.'

The following morning, Nick had to drive to Ashfordly Police Station to collect the doctor's belongings. The inquest into his death was to be held later, and these items would be required.

His fishing tackle, his rod which had been found by the police frogmen a little higher upstream than the body, his net and the gaff which had been hooked on to his belt, the bag of personal belongings he'd left on the river bank all told a story. Kate would have to give evidence too, about his medical condition, and this would be supported by pathological opinions as a result of the post-mortem. It was agreed that he could have died at any time due to his condition; he'd been suffering from a sub-dural haematoma.

It was painful for Nick, having to deal with the sudden death of a dear friend, but it was also his job. He knew he'd have to perform his duties without fear or favour, and he knew too that he'd have to give Kate all the support she needed. In Aidensfield, life, with all its pains and pleasures, would continue.

'Alf,' said Nick before leaving, 'what happened to that kitten you found?'

'I brought it back here, but Sergeant Blaketon took it to the vet's,' said Alf. 'He really upset me . . . I've always wanted a kitten but my missus can't stand cats. So I kept it here. Well, it made a bit of a mess at first, but it could have been trained. I think a station cat would have been a good idea.'

'A sort of puss in policeman's boots?' smiled Nick.

'Rowan!' called the voice of Sergeant Blaketon. 'Is that you wasting Ventress's time in there?'

'Just leaving, Sergeant,' he shouted back.

'A word before you go, Rowan.'

Nick went through to the office where Sergeant Blaketon was sitting at his desk. He had a thick file in his hand and a newspaper on his knee.

'Dr Alexander Ferrenby,' he said, handing the file to Nick. 'This is the file on the sudden death. It contains the pathologist's report and statements from witnesses. The coroner will hold the inquest a week on Friday in the Court House in Ashfordly, at 2.30 p.m. Get round to the witnesses, Rowan, and warn them to present themselves, then notify the caretaker of the courthouse that we shall be using the premises.'

'Very good, Sergeant.'

'Now, Rowan, you knew Dr Ferrenby very well. It seems odd to me that a man of his experience would wander into that deep water. I know his health wasn't all that good, but the coroner will seek our views on the supposed behaviour of the doctor immediately before he died. So, Rowan, any ideas?'

'Yes, Sergeant,' said Nick. 'That kitten that PC Ventress found. It had been marooned there a few days, judging by its hungry condition. And Dr Ferrenby's rod

375

was found in the river at that point, as if he'd dropped it there. I think he didn't realise how deep the water was and fell into a hole as he tried to rescue the kitten.'

'Go on, Rowan.'

'Well, Sergeant, he didn't die of a heart attack, although there were obstructions in his arteries. The pathologist confirmed that. It was death by drowning. There was water in his lungs, which wouldn't have been there if he'd died before going under. And trying to rescue that kitten was the sort of thing Alex Ferrenby would do – he would always attempt to save life, Sergeant, even if it was just a cat.'

'My sentiments exactly, Rowan,' said Sergeant Blaketon. At that moment, the newspaper on his lap moved suddenly, then fell to the floor, and a small black kitten jumped on to Sergeant Blaketon's desk. The result was a very coy expression on Blaketon's face; he looked almost embarrassed.

'Sergeant? I thought you'd taken it to the vet's?'

'For treatment, Rowan, for treatment, not disposal. I thought it was time the station had a cat . . .'

Ventress walked in, beaming, having overheard everything.

'Sergeant, how touching!'

'It doesn't like cigarette smoke, Ventress, but it does like warm coal fires and sardines out of a tin.'

'The official cat,' beamed Alf. 'What are we going to call it?'

'How about Alexander?' smiled Nick.